D0176561

"Robert Morgan secures his place alongside some of the South's finest writers with his new work, *This Rock*. . . . An excellent example of what Southern and American fiction should be."
—Rick Tamble, *The Tennessean*

"You'll buy almost anything off his two full-throated narrators . . . whose voices ring with dread and longing."
—Scott Brown, *Entertainment Weekly*

"Homespun pleasure."
—Nelson Taylor, *Providence Journal*

"A testimony to the power of faith and integrity in the face of life's severest hardship."
—*Publishers Weekly*

"Enriched with a generous serving of details and simple prose . . . absorbing."
—Tracy V. Wilson, *The Winston-Salem Journal*

"Morgan writes very simply about hard times and deep faith, and it is a tribute to his skillful writing that this story will resound with modern readers."
—*Booklist*

"Thank God for poets. And thank God for this one, Robert Morgan. . . . He has something to say to us about life and death. Or maybe his ancestors are saying it through him."
—Emilie Griffin, *America*

"Robert Morgan is so gifted that his books make us better readers."
—Cynthia Adams, *Our State*

"An elegantly crafted, beautifully simple work."
—Britta Waller, *News & Record* (Greensboro)

THIS ROCK

a novel by

ROBERT MORGAN

SCRIBNER PAPERBACK FICTION
Published by Simon & Schuster
New York London Toronto Sydney Singapore

SCRIBNER PAPERBACK FICTION
Simon & Schuster, Inc.
Rockefeller Center
1230 Avenue of the Americas
New York, NY 10020

This book is a work of fiction. Names, characters, places, and incidents either are products of the author's imagination or are used fictitiously. Any resemblance to actual events or locales or persons, living or dead, is entirely coincidental.

Copyright © 2001 by Robert Morgan

All rights reserved, including the right of reproduction in whole or in part in any form.

First Scribner Paperback Fiction edition 2002
Published by arrangement with Algonquin Books of Chapel Hill

SCRIBNER PAPERBACK FICTION and design are trademarks of Macmillan Library Reference USA, Inc., used under license by Simon & Schuster, the publisher of this work.

For information regarding special discounts for bulk purchases, please contact Simon & Schuster Special Sales at 1-800-456-6798 or *business@simonandschuster.com*

Designed by Anne Winslow
Manufactured in the United States of America

10 9 8 7 6 5 4 3 2

Library of Congress Cataloging-in-Publication Data

ISBN 0-7432-2579-1

To the memory of my father,
Clyde R. Morgan, 1905–1991

I would like to thank Shannon Ravenel, Elisabeth Scharlatt, and the staff at Algonquin Books of Chapel Hill for their unfailing help in bringing this book to completion and publication, and especially Duncan Murrell, whose work from the first has been inspiring, exemplary, invaluable.

PROLOGUE
Ginny

MUIR WAS THE buildingest boy you ever saw, from the time he was little. He was different from Moody from the beginning. Moody was always running and playing and chasing chickens or the cat, the way any boy does. But from the time he was five or six Muir was always studying on making something. It seemed to be born in his blood to make things. He cut roads in the dirt of the backyard, and in the sandpile my husband, Tom, hauled up from the river in the wagon. He made bridges over ditches and he hacked out boats with a saw and his pocketknife. He drawed pictures in the dirt, and lines like train tracks. He tied blocks of wood together in trains. He used old tools Pa had left in the shed, and mashed his fingers and cut hisself from time to time.

But Muir's worst enemy from the time he was a youngun was his own lack of patience. The backyard was littered with things he had started and abandoned, wagons with wheels sawed out of a pole, a sled whittled out of sourwood.

"Mama, I'm going to build a house," he said when he was about ten.

"What kind of house, sugar?" I said.

"A log cabin, like Daniel Boone made," Muir said. He took the crosscut saw and axe up to the pine woods above the pasture, and I could hear him chopping there for hours. He was already big for his age. On the way to the mailbox I seen where he had chopped down several yellow pines and made a mess with the brush piled above the road.

"Be careful with that axe," I hollered. I could smell fresh pine rosin and crushed pine needles. It was a good smell.

That night Muir's hands was stained with rosin and his fingers was blistered. A limb had scratched his cheek, just missing his eye. "I've got one layer of logs in place," he announced.

"Are you going to put windows in?" I said.

"I'll put greased paper windows in like old-timers done," Muir said.

"Bugs will stick to the grease," I said.

"Looks to me like you're building a hogpen," Moody said.

"Wherever you live is a hogpen," Muir said to Moody. There was a kick under the table.

"Muir can call it his hunting lodge," I said.

"Be lucky to build a doghouse," Moody said.

Two days later I stopped by the place in the pines to see what Muir had done. He was hacking like a Trojan at a pine pole to notch the end so it would fit in place. His black hair had fell in his eyes and stuck to his forehead. What he had made was a pen two or three feet high. It was hard to believe a ten-year-old had done so much work. He'd sawed down the trees and cut them into lengths and notched them to fit over each other. There was wide cracks between the poles.

"You'll need to chink between the logs," I said.

"Won't do that till winter," Muir said, out of breath from chopping.

"The thing to use is branch clay and straw," I said. "Put it on wet and let it harden."

It give me a satisfaction to see what Muir had done. I'd never knowed a youngun with such an inclination to shape things. He had done the work of a man there in the pines. He had the instinct to build the way my brother Locke had the instinct to be a nurse and wait on the sick. And I was proud because it was almost like I was doing it; the work was part of me. And yet Muir was hisself and thought of things to do I never would have. He had his daddy's blue eyes and ruddy complexion. I felt the pleasure of seeing my flesh and blood go forward on his own with such a will and such an idea of shaping and fitting things in place. I had always believed he would do something special.

It wasn't more than three days later that Muir come running into the house, his face white and his hair roughed up by wind. "Where is Moody?" he hollered.

"Ain't seen him," I said.

Muir stomped on the kitchen floor and turned to run out.

"What is wrong?" I said.

"Moody done it," Muir hollered.

"What has he done?" I said. I had a sick feeling in my joints, because Moody was always getting into trouble.

But Muir was already out the door. I dried my hands and followed him. I seen Moody on the trail from the barn, and I seen Muir pick up a rock under the hemlock tree and run toward his brother. Moody was three years older, and he was wiry and tough, but Muir was catching up with him in size.

"Stop that!" I yelled.

"I seen what you done," Muir shouted.

"Ain't done nothing," Moody said.

I run to Muir and took the rock from his hand. "What has Moody done?" I said.

Muir stomped the ground and his face turned from white to red. "He ruined it," he yelled.

"Who says?" Moody said.

Muir started running up the hill and I followed, and Moody followed me. I had an ugly feeling about what I was going to see in the pine woods. Muir slung open the pasture gate, and I latched it behind us after Moody had gone through. That's when I smelled the smoke. It was the sticky smoke of pine rosin burning.

"What is that?" I said. "Is the pine woods on fire?"

I started running, and Muir started running. When I got to the clearing Muir had made I seen a pile of brush burning inside the pen. The log walls had been tore apart and the poles piled like for a bonfire.

"Grab a limb," I shouted. I took a pine bough and started hitting the blaze. It was a good thing the wood was green and there had been a rain the day before. The pine needles on the ground had not caught fire. There was no way to keep the brush from burning, but we beat out the flames on the logs and kept the blaze from spreading to nearby trees. The fire crackled and hissed as clots of sap busted. I beat the flames with the limb and kicked needles out of the way to make a space of bare ground around the burning brush.

"Who started this?" I said.

"He done it," Muir said and pointed to Moody.

"Must have been lightning," Moody said. Moody had high cheekbones from our Cherokee blood way back, and he always looked a little older than he was.

"I ain't seen no lightning," Muir said.

"Did you do this?" I said to Moody.

"Maybe it was outlaws," Moody said and turned his face away from me.

I grabbed Moody's arm and pulled him out into the clearing. Just then I seen the matches in his shirt pocket. There must have been twenty matches stuffed into the pocket. "Where did these come from?" I said.

"Toothpicks," Moody said.

I felt sick in my bones to think that Moody had done it and would try to lie his way out of it.

"Worse than setting the fire is to lie about it," I said.

"Ain't lying," Moody said.

"Look me in the eye," I said. Moody glanced at me, then looked away.

"He done it," Muir said. Muir had a smear of soot on his cheek. Moody shoved him.

"We will pray about this," I said. I put my left arm around Moody's neck and pulled him toward me. And I put my right arm on Muir's shoulder. Bitter smoke drifted from the ashes of the burned brush and charred logs. It was a good thing there was no wind or the whole pine woods would have caught fire the way they did before Tom died. I bowed my head and closed my eyes.

"Lord, teach us to love one another," I said. "For your commandment, your last commandment, was to love one another. In our pride, and in our anger, it's hard to love and hard to forgive, and hard for us to remember your words.

"Teach us to be humble. Teach us even in our moments of anger to look to you for guidance, and not to vanity and resentment. Teach brother not to fight brother and sister not to fight against sister. Teach mothers to love sons, and teach us to live every day so that any hour we will be prepared to face your judgment, and to live in your will."

When I opened my eyes and raised my head I seen Muir staring at the ruins of his cabin. Logs was scattered at rough angles and partly burned. The whole clearing was a mess. There was tears in his eyes, and I felt tears swelling in my eyes too.

When I looked at Moody he turned away from me. But I thought I seen a tear in his eye too. He wouldn't look at me, and he wouldn't say nothing.

"You will help Muir rebuild his cabin," I said to Moody.

"I can help him cut new logs," Moody said, looking at the ground.

"Don't want no new logs," Muir snapped.

"Moody will help you with the cabin," I said.

"Don't want no cabin," Muir said, staring at the smoldering brush.

FIRST READING

―――

1921

―――

One
Muir

PREACHER LINER SAID he would let me preach the Sunday after Homecoming. He was a big heavy feller with droopy jowls, and he said it as a favor to Mama more than anything else, because no preacher likes to share his pulpit, not any that I ever heard of. But Mama was a pillar of the church, and her pa had give the land for the church and built the first church in the valley back when the county was founded. And for some reason Preacher Liner was afraid of Mama, maybe because she'd read more than him and knowed more Scripture. So when I told Preacher Liner I felt I had the call, that I'd been studying up to preach a sermon, he said he'd let me fill the pulpit, soon as there was an opportunity.

I was only sixteen, but I felt the call, and I waited weeks and months for a chance to preach. I studied the Bible every day and prayed for a sign that I was ready. When I went out to the barn to milk I thought about preaching as I pulled down on the cow's tits. And while I hoed corn in the hot June sun I studied on what I'd say when I was give the pulpit.

Mama said I could go to a revival meeting in one of the little valleys near the head of the river and preach, or might be I could preach in one of the ridge churches like Mount Olivet. But I said I wanted to start in my home church, and then I'd light out to preach in other places, if I was going to preach, if the Lord had really anointed me to preach.

"You don't want to feel too much pride about preaching," Mama said. She had been a Holiness when she was young, but now she was a steadfast Baptist. If they made women deacons she'd have been a deacon. Mama was tall with long black hair she wore in a knot on top of her head. As her hair got threads of gray in it she looked dignified enough to be a deacon.

"Got to have some pride to want to try preaching," I said. "Otherwise I couldn't even think of standing up in front of a crowd."

"I can't see you preaching," said Fay, my younger sister. "You talk too slow and thoughtful. You're my brother, not a preacher." Fay was only thirteen, and bony like Moody was.

"I'd rather listen to hound dogs howling after a fox," my brother, Moody, said. "That's the best kind of preaching I know." Moody almost never went to church anyway, so it didn't matter what he said.

"If Muir has the call, he will preach," Mama said. "The Lord will put the words in his mouth and the Spirit in his heart."

"Only call Muir feels is the call of nature," Moody said.

"I never thought there'd be a preacher in this family," Fay said. She was wearing the blue dress Mama had smocked for her.

"I always prayed there would be a preacher in our family, in this generation," Mama said.

SINCE I LEFT school when I was twelve I'd hunted ginseng in the late summer on the ridges over near South Carolina. And I'd helped Mama in the fields and in the orchards on the hill. I had helped make molasses in the old furnace Grandpa had built in the pasture, and I'd cut tops and pulled fodder. I'd chopped wood and done a little carpentry and masonry for my cousin U. G. that kept the store down at the highway, and I'd laid a rock wall behind the house to hold Mama's flower beds. I'd also built a rock wall for my aunt Florrie, and I'd painted the house for Mama. I'd tried my hand at a lot of things, from digging herbs to hewing and selling crossties to the railroad. But the thing I'd been best at was trapping muskrats and mink and foxes on the creeks and high branches near the head of the river. I liked to walk the trapline, and I knowed every inch of the headwaters and the Flat Woods beyond. I'd learned how to set traps in the water to drown a mink before it could gnaw its foot off, and I'd learned to put a trap on a trail where a fox couldn't see it or smell it. Every winter I made more than a hundred dollars from selling fur.

I'd heard a hundred times that Mama laid in bed without moving for several weeks before I was born. She had anemia and she had kidney poisoning. And she didn't eat nothing but some biscuits and a little milk. She was afraid she'd lose the baby if she moved. "I laid in the dark, for I was afraid even to read," Mama said.

And when I was born she was in labor for seventeen hours; the midwife thought I would be dead. After I was born they saw I was early and poor as a whippoorwill. You could see my ribs I was so starved. And I was too weak to eat anything except to suck on a rag soaked in sugar water, and to nurse a few minutes at a time.

"Muir was so blue he looked like he'd froze to death," Mama said.

But the story Mama liked to tell best was about how my tongue had been tied down by a thread of flesh. "He was so tongue-tied he couldn't even cry," Mama said. "His tongue just kind of wallowed in his mouth, so I took him to a doctor in town and had it snipped free. Everybody said he'd never be able to talk, that he wasn't meant to talk. But I knowed he would talk. He was meant to talk, and after that he howled up a storm."

"He just never learned to talk sense," Moody said.

"I know he was put here for some purpose," Mama said. "He was a marked baby."

Mama said so many times I was marked for something special that I believed it was true. But I didn't know what it was for, until after I'd been saved and after I'd been baptized. I seen that I was supposed to be a witness and a minister. I'd heard about people getting the call, and I started to feel I was one that heard the call. Mama was proud. But it made Moody mad when she talked about how I was marked for a purpose. He acted like she said it to belittle him. He acted like he was mad at everybody most of the time. He snorted and cleared the spit in his throat.

When I read a passage in the Bible I thought of myself saying it from a pulpit. " 'In my Father's house are many mansions: if it were not so I would have told you. I go and prepare a place for you . . . ' " I imagined how I'd swing my arm in the air and slam my fist down on the pulpit. " 'And God shall wipe away all tears from their eyes,' " I said aloud to myself. " 'Neither shall there be any more pain.' "

As I walked along my trapline I said verses to myself. " 'Blessed art thou Simon Barjonah . . . Upon this rock I will build my church; and the gates of hell shall not prevail against it . . . Whatsoever thou shalt bind on earth shall be bound in heaven, and whatsoever thou shalt loose on earth shall be loosed in heaven . . .' "

I got so drunk saying the verses to myself that I would stumble off the trail or bump into a tree. I felt light enough to fly as I quoted, " 'A city that is set on a hill cannot be hid.' "

I stood on top of a ridge above Grassy Creek in Transylvania County and faced the wind and said, " 'I am the root and the off-spring of David, and the bright and morning star.' " I imagined preaching to crowds in tents and brush arbors and in open fields. But mostly I imagined talking to the congregation in Green River Church. I was afraid I'd be tongue-tied when I had to talk.

As I walked through the woods with my squirrel rifle, I was eloquent in one soaring sentence after another. I stood before the crowd and shouted about the glories of heaven. I didn't talk about hellfire and I didn't talk about punishment and damnation. In my mind I talked about the glories beyond the grave, beyond the clouds above the hill. I talked about the sunlit uplands beyond the far shore.

NOW THE OTHER thing I studied on was Annie Richards that lived on the creek road just beyond the church. She was only thirteen then, but she was the prettiest girl in the whole valley. Her blond hair and her pale skin was like something out of a picture. She was slender and she was perfect and she had big gray eyes. She was too young to walk home with boys from church, but she was already a little bit of a flirt. She was quick as a fawn with her gray eyes and red lips. I had my eye on her. I was going to be a preacher, and I was going to marry her. That's what I told myself. The two things was tied together in my mind. All women was in love with preachers.

"WHAT ARE YOU going to preach about?" Preacher Liner said to me the Sunday before Homecoming. When he talked to you he kind of leaned over you. The look in his eyes never seemed to match what he was saying.

"I will preach about the Transfiguration," I said.

"That's always a good topic," Preacher Liner said. "People like to hear about the Transfiguration."

Preacher Liner said he'd be going down to South Carolina the Sunday after Homecoming, and I could fill the pulpit in his place. Panic jolted through me so hard it hurt. In two weeks I'd be standing in front of the congregation. In two weeks I'd be facing all those people that I'd knowed since I was in diapers.

"Glory be," Mama said when I told her I would be preaching in two weeks. "This is the answer to my prayers."

NOW THE THING about worry is it can't do you much good. For worry just wears you down and don't help the least bit. But you can't just turn off worry like it was a spigot. Worry ain't something you can do much to control. Worry creeps up on you at night while you're laying in bed and crawls right into your head. And worry soaks its way into whatever you're thinking about in the daytime.

I figured if I studied out my sermon beforehand it might help. They said preachers in town actually wrote down sermons and read them on Sunday. But no Baptist preacher ever wrote out a sermon on Green River. That would prove you didn't have the call of the Spirit in your heart. Anybody that would write out a sermon and read it to the congregation would be laughed out of the pulpit and never invited to preach again. Only Scripture was worth reading out in the pulpit.

I took my Bible and climbed up into the pines on the pasture hill. Thought if I got on top of the ridge I could think better. The air would be clearer and I'd be closer to God. And the Transfiguration took place on a mountaintop where Peter and James and John went with Jesus. I read in Matthew: " 'While he yet spake, behold, a bright cloud overshadowed them: and behold a voice out of the cloud, which said: This is my beloved son, in whom I am well pleased; hear ye him.' "

That seemed to me the finest passage in the Bible. I said the words over again and made my voice deep in my throat, and I made my tongue curl around the words.

I turned to the book of Luke where it also described the Transfiguration.

" 'And as he prayed the fashion of his countenance was altered, and his raiment was white and glistering.' "

I walked up and down under the pine trees and said the verse. I swung my arm to show the power of the words. I knowed if I could get started in the pulpit I could keep going. It was getting started that was hard. I'd took part in the debates at school when I was eleven and twelve. It was standing and saying the first thing that scared me. The first time I stood before the class I was so dazed I couldn't think of nothing. My throat locked closed like spit had stuck there and glued my windpipe. Next time I debated I determined I'd say one word if it killed me. And I did stand up and say one word, and after that I could say more. But I remembered that feeling of having my tongue and throat froze, like they'd turned to rock.

Last, I turned to the Second Epistle of Peter, where he talked about the Transfiguration.

" 'And this voice which came from heaven we heard, when we were with him in the holy mount.' "

It was the holy mount I wanted to mention in my sermon. For I wanted to say any mountain could be a holy mountain. And that the ground where we stood could be holy ground. I wanted to preach mountainism, for I'd read somewhere that mountainism meant a vision of paradise on earth. But I didn't know if I could say it right.

In his excitement and confusion Peter had talked about building three tabernacles on the mountaintop, one to Moses, one to Elias, and one to Jesus. He'd talked foolish, out of his head. I hoped I didn't talk foolish. I hoped I didn't speak beside myself, once I was in the pulpit. But I understood the desire to build something sacred. I had studied about building almost as much as about trapping and preaching. A life's work should be to build something that inspired people.

I stood under the pines facing the wind and read more verses, making my voice strong and far-reaching as I could. I read in a low voice and I read in a loud voice. I read the verses in a proper voice, and I read them the way a mountain preacher would that hadn't hardly been to school. I couldn't decide which way was best. But I thought, The place for a church is on a mountaintop. The perfect place to say the words of the Bible was on the highest ground in sight.

WHEN MAMA NOTICED how worried I was she said, "Nobody can preach without the help of the Lord. If the Lord wants you to preach, then he'll give you the words to say."

"But I have to prepare the vessel," I said.

"If the Lord don't give you the words they won't be worth listening to," Mama said.

"All the words has already been said," my sister Fay said. Fay had growed gangly and awkward but hadn't begun to show her womanly shape in the dresses Mama made her.

"Don't make no difference," I said. "They need to be said again."

"Why do they?" Fay said.

"That's like saying all the dinners have been eat," I said. "People will still be hungry come dinnertime."

"People need to hear the Word again and again," Mama said. "As long as you go by the Scripture you can't go wrong."

"Are you going to take up a collection?" Moody said. "That's the test of a preacher, how much people throw in the collection plate."

"The collection is took up before the sermon," I said.

"That may be to your advantage," Moody said. Moody had got hurt in a fight in Chestnut Springs earlier that year, and he had a scar on his cheek below the left eye.

"A first-time preacher don't get no money," I said.

But like he did so many times, Moody could change his tune in an instant. He would talk mean and bitter, and he'd mock you and belittle you. And then all of a sudden he'd be a good-natured brother. His name fit him perfect. I knowed he was named after the great preacher Dwight L. Moody, but the name was right for him.

It was the Friday before I was supposed to preach on Sunday morning, and I went out to milk the cows after supper and water the horse and feed the chickens. It was still full daylight, and while I was mixing the crushing and cottonseed meal for the cows Moody come up behind me and said, "You know I want you to do good on Sunday."

"Sure you do," I said.

"No, I mean it," Moody said. "I want you to make that church house ring. And I want you to save so many people they'll demand that you preach again."

"Didn't think you cared," I said.

"I care about my little brother," Moody said. "I want you to scare them so much and thrill them so much they pee in their britches."

ON THE SUNDAY after Homecoming I got to the church a little early. I put on the new herringbone suit I had bought special, and a tie that Daddy had owned. The suit fit so well over my shoulders and hips it give me confidence, and the woven cloth glistened in the sun. The song leader, Mack Ennis, got there almost as soon as I did. The church felt cool inside in the early morning.

"Now, what songs do you want to sing today?" Mack said.

That was the one thing I hadn't thought about. I'd worried about the text I was going to read, and who I was going to call on to lead in prayer, and how long I was going to preach. But I hadn't even considered what hymns I wanted sung.

"Ain't you picked out the hymns?" I said to Mack.

"The preacher usually has some suggestions, depending on the text of his sermon," Mack said.

"What would you normally sing?" I said.

"There is over five hundred hymns in the book," Mack said. "We can sing whatever ones you prefer."

"Why don't we sing 'How Beautiful Heaven Must Be'?" I said. "And then 'Nearer My God to Thee.'"

"This is not a funeral," Mack said.

"And maybe 'On Jordan's Stormy Banks,'" I said.

When Charlotte McKee, the organist, arrived Mack told her what songs we was going to sing. She nodded and smiled at me.

I'd heard of preachers that didn't even appear until it was time for the sermon. They'd stay out in the dark, or in the woods, or even in the outhouse, till it was time for them to appear. And then they'd enter like a prophet come down from the mountain, or like John the Baptist come from the wilderness. But that wasn't the custom on Green River. It would look silly if I stayed outside till it was time to preach.

There was a chair to the side and behind the pulpit where the preacher set. And that's where I waited while people come into the church. I didn't want to look at people as they shuffled in and set down, so I looked at the Bible in my hands, and I even opened it and tried to read. I'd seen Preacher Liner do that. But I couldn't see the Bible verses in front of me because of my nerves. I'd marked the places and I'd memorized the passages so I could recite them if I had to.

When Charlotte started playing the organ I stood up and everybody else stood up. "How Beautiful Heaven Must Be," I called out. But my voice sounded trembly and weak in the empty air over the congregation.

"Page 302," Mack called out.

While they was singing I tried to join in but couldn't even think of the song. I hoped the song would go on forever. I looked out over the faces and tried not to look at any one face. I knowed everybody in the church, but I tried not to recognize them. The light was glaring from the white-painted windowpanes. I kept my eyes on the last window on the left side.

When the song was over it was time to lead in prayer. I knowed the custom was for the preacher to lead the first prayer. I was about to bow my head and start praying when I seen the door open and somebody slip into the back of the church. It was Moody, and he didn't take his hat off when he come in. Moody never did hardly go to church. He was the last person I expected to see there, and he was the last person I wanted to see there. He had said he wouldn't come. He slid into the back row with the other boys and backsliders. He never did take his hat off. It was time for me to start praying, but all I could think of was Moody setting there with his hat on.

I bowed my head, but instead of praying I said, "Will Moody Powell please take his hat off in church." The words was out before I could stop myself.

Everybody in the church turned around and looked back. There was snickers here and there. With a grin Moody lifted his hat and held it a few inches above his head, then dropped it to the floor. There was more snickering and titters from the boys in the back row.

I prayed but don't remember what I said. I had thought for days about what I'd say in a prayer, but I couldn't remember a single word of what I'd planned. Moody had throwed me off. I swallowed twice and said something about thanking the Lord for bringing us all together on such a fine day. My face was hot and the sweat was breaking out under my arms and in my hands.

When I finished praying and opened my eyes I seen Mama looking at me. She smiled and nodded, like she meant to say, You go ahead and do a good job now. There was circles of sweat under her arms. But I couldn't look at her. And I couldn't remember what hymn we was supposed to sing next. It was the offertory hymn and the two deacons, Silas Bane and my cousin U. G. Latham, come forward and took the collection plates from the table in front of the pulpit. Charlotte was looking at me and Mack was looking at me. And I remembered I'd told him "Nearer My God to Thee." But it was too late. Mack frowned and flipped through the songbook and called out, "Number 326."

While they begun to sing, and I pretended to join in, all I could think of was what a gom I'd already made of things. I looked at the collection plates passing among the congregation and wondered why I'd even thought I could preach. How did I know what was the call and what was just vanity? Nobody but Mama had thought I had the gift. What was I going to say when the song ended? For then it would be time to begin my sermon.

When the song was over the deacons brought the collection plates to the front, and Silas Bane poured the contents of one plate into the other and put the empty plate over the money like a lid. Both Mack and Charlotte took their seats on the benches, and I was alone in front of the church. As I stood up I felt the stares of the people like a furnace blasting my face. I wanted to step back out of the heat. I wanted to run out into the fresh air and sunlight.

Stepping to the pulpit, I realized I'd left my Bible on the floor beside the chair. I'd already opened my mouth to speak, but I stopped to pick up the Bible. I spun around and kicked the chair so hard it banged the wall and clattered over on the floor.

When I stood up again behind the pulpit and opened the Bible, the air in the church was absolutely still. You could have heard a spider scratching itself, or a moth belch. The air was so hot and tight it was in pain. The skin on my forehead felt stretched. The skin around my mouth was so tight I thought it was going to break. And my lips was stuck together.

I tried to find the verse in Matthew about the Transfiguration, but I kept turning pages and couldn't spot it nowhere. My hands was so sweaty they stuck to the paper. I thought I seen the chapter, and then it disappeared. I was looking in the Old Testament. It seemed like minutes and hours was passing while I flipped through the pages.

"I want to read you a Bible verse," I tried to say. But the words stuck in my throat. I swallowed and tried again.

There was snickers in the church. The air was dead still, and I could hear the blood pounding in my ears. Sweat gathered on my forehead and dripped down on the pages of the Bible.

Finally I found Matthew 17 and started reading, but I couldn't recall what I'd planned to say about the text. What was the point I'd wanted to make about the Transfiguration? Peter said we should build three tabernacles on the mountaintop, but he'd been talking crazy with excitement. There didn't seem to be much point in speaking about that.

Because I couldn't remember what it was I wanted to say, I kept reading. I read beyond the place where Matthew talked about the Transfiguration. I couldn't think of anything to say.

I seen Annie setting in the third row beside her mama. Annie looked at me and she looked at her lap. Why had I thought I'd impress her with my preaching? Why had I ever thought she cared anything about me? She looked so young she seemed just a child. She didn't care what I said in the pulpit. I'd wanted to say something about going to the mountaintop, but what was it?

"This is what can happen when we go up on the mountaintop," I said. "This is what happens when we get up close to the Lord." But I couldn't recall what else I was going to say. It had all seemed so clear when I'd planned the sermon. But I couldn't remember what the connection was.

"Now let me read to you what Mark says," I said. I crumpled pages of the Bible trying to find the passage in the Second Gospel, but I finally located the right chapter. "Listen to this," I said. But as I read the verses I heard my voice in the still air of the church, and it sounded more like a boy reciting in school than any preacher. I couldn't think of what words to say next, so I just kept reading again. And when I got to the end of the chapter I said, "There is blessings for us on the mountaintop if we'll just go there. We can see the shining face of Jesus, and we can see his raiment white as snow." I could feel the voice coming to me a little bit. It was not the talk I'd planned, but at least I was talking.

"We can stand with our faces in the wind and feel the Spirit moving," I said.

Just then there was a whine in the back of the church. It was like the whine a wet log makes when it burns. The whine thickened to a blowing sound, and I knowed it was a poot, the loudest and longest fart you ever heard. It was like a trumpet and trombone together blowing a fanfare.

I forgot what I was saying and couldn't go on. My tongue was tied and flopped around helpless as a fish in mud. I tried to recall what I'd been saying, but nothing come out. I was froze, and then I seen Moody stand up and walk to the back window. He raised the back window with a groan and a bang and stuck his head outside. Laughter started at the back of the church and swept forward until it filled the whole sanctuary like a mighty song.

T w o

Ginny

I HAD ALWAYS wanted there to be a preacher in the family. From the time I was a girl and started going to Holiness meetings I thought a preacher was the most wonderful man there was. What could compare with a man of God, a man of the Book, a man of the faith? If I had been a man I would have been a preacher myself.

"All preachers have an eye for the girls and a mouth full of easy words," my sister, Florrie, said. She always did like to say the worst thing that come to mind. She would say the most irreverent things, but she married David that wanted to be a preacher, and I married Tom Powell that didn't hardly like to talk at all. Who could have foretold the choices of the heart? But even then I wouldn't let Florrie smart-mouth me.

"Next you'll tell me preachers love fried chicken," I said to Florrie.

"Preachers do like fried chicken," Florrie said.

But Florrie knowed as well as I did a true preacher is the vessel of the Lord. A true preacher is a lamp that lights our feet and burns away the darkness of this world. A true preacher can charge the air in a church and in a congregation, and in a whole community. A great preacher can make the trees and rocks seem witnesses to the power of the Bible. A great sermon can make time itself seem a testimony to the grace meant for us.

The best preacher I ever heard was Preacher McKinney who held the revival where I first received the baptism of fire and spoke in tongues. I had been saved before when I was twelve and been baptized in water and joined the church. I'd heard talk of sanctification and the baptism of fire but never thought much about them until I went to Preacher McKinney's meeting. I'd gone to church all my years without loving it. I'd gone out of duty and habit. My pa had built the church when he come back from the Confederate War. I liked singing and good preaching, but I'd never seen the beauty of fellowship together.

Preacher McKinney's best sermon was not the one where I first spoke in tongues and done the holy dance and received the baptism of fire. I was so stirred by that first service I wasn't hardly aware of the sermon anyway. I looked into his eyes and the Spirit swept me away, as it had to. What happened to me then was meant from the beginning of time. That night Preacher McKinney was the true vessel of the Word, and I was there to receive it.

Preacher McKinney's best sermon that I remember, the one that showed me what a sermon could be, was preached a few weeks later in daylight. It was preached in the afternoon in the little church up on Mount Olivet. It was the funeral service for one of the Tankersleys who had gone to Preacher McKinney's revival and lost her letter in the Green River Church. That's why the service was held up on Mount Olivet instead of Green River. All of us Holiness people had lost their letter in the Green River Baptist Church.

It was the brightest summer day you ever saw. The trees was green and the mountainsides was green, and the weeds along the road was green. Pa and me and Joe and Lily had took the wagon up the mountain. All kinds of birdsong sweetened the air. The world was lush and sharp. It didn't seem like no day for a funeral. The light was so bright it stung your eyes. June bugs circled and buzzed over the grass. The cemetery on the hill above the church was fresh mowed and looked like a garden of stones and shrubbery.

Preacher McKinney stood calm and cool in the pulpit after everybody was seated. His manner was different from what I had seen at the revival. There was a great peacefulness and poise in him. "Let us pray," he said. I bowed my head and listened, for I felt the strength in his quietness.

"Lord, we are here to celebrate life and salvation," Preacher McKinney prayed. "We do not need to mourn the passing of Sister Tankersley, for we know she has gone to a better world, to a long-sought rest. If we mourned we would only mourn for ourselves, for we miss her presence and her inspiration. We will miss her example and her kindness."

When the prayer was over we sung "Work, for the Night Is Coming." It was a slow, simple, sad song that had a strange firmness and comfort. The notes seemed to give voice to the day itself, to the cool little church, to the weeds and woods outside in the sunlight. Out the window I could see a white cloud hanging over the mountain.

Work, for the night is coming. Work through the morning hours.
Work while the dew is sparkling. Work 'mid springing flowers.
Work while the day grows brighter, under the glowing sun.
Work, for the night is coming, when man's work is done.

As soon as the song was over I heard a cardinal in the woods outside. And when Preacher McKinney started talking he didn't holler like he did at revival services. He stood perfectly still and spoke in a voice so quiet I had to listen close at first.

"We are here to celebrate the goodness of our sister," he said. "We are here to take comfort in her strength and example. We are here to strengthen each other with our fellowship and with our song."

Preacher McKinney said our lives in this world didn't have to be lived in misery and aloneness. He said our lives might be hard, but they was not too hard as long as they had meaning, as long as we could see far enough ahead, toward the plan of salvation. Preacher McKinney was so calm and slow he seemed like a different preacher entirely. He said it was our labor that was our wisdom. It was our struggle that was our satisfaction in this world.

Preacher McKinney talked about how we should forgive seven times seventy and help our neighbors. It was the simplest message there was, and yet it was the one hardest to follow. He said in all the New Testament there is only one new commandment: Love each other even as I have loved you.

"Can you feel the hand of Sister Tankersley leading us into the sunlight and into the day and across the threshold to the rest of your life?" Preacher McKinney said. "In the heart of a Christian it is always eternal morning. I am not here to mourn and I am not here to accuse and threaten. You are all the children of the Savior, and you are all my brothers and sisters."

When Preacher McKinney stopped I had to remember where I was. I was not swept away, but set firm and alert on the bench. The air in the church was cool and rare as on a mountaintop. There was sniffles and crying in the church. But they was tears of joy.

MUCH AS I admired preachers it scared me when Muir said he was going to preach the Sunday after Homecoming. It scared me and it thrilled me too, for there was nothing I wanted a son of mine to be more than a minister of the gospel. I was afraid I had put it in his head to preach, and that he was doing it to please me more than answering a call of his own. He was tall as a man, and he was strong as a man, but he was still just a boy too. A mama has power over her children she may not always be aware of.

Before Muir was born I starved myself and I laid in bed for weeks to keep him alive. The doctor had said he would die inside me if I moved. I laid still and lived on milk and biscuits. I knowed he was a marked baby, he was a chosen baby. I knowed he was a baby with a destiny. He was born with a mission, and being born with his tongue tied down was not going to stop him. In some way I did not understand he was a vessel of the Word.

It was hard to know how much to encourage Muir and how much to caution him. For I knowed a preacher has to go where he hears the call, and he has to follow his conscience. But I was his mama also. His daddy was dead, and it was my job to try to guide him.

Muir always was the serious one of my children. He took it after Tom and me both, for Tom was dedicated to his work in a solemn and sober way, and I was dedicated to worship, to living in the Spirit.

I worried about Muir and I loved him. I wanted him not to make my mistakes. He was the age I was when I first went to Holiness meetings.

"You've got to follow the voice you hear in your heart," I said to Muir. I could see how he was studying and troubled. He was one to anguish hisself.

"I feel the call in my blood," Muir said.

I worried when Preacher Liner told Muir he could fill the pulpit the Sunday after Homecoming. The preacher had asked me if I wanted him to invite Muir to preach. I wondered if he thought inviting Muir to preach was a favor to me.

"You must follow the guidance of the Spirit," I said to Preacher Liner. But I didn't know what the right thing was. If Muir tried preaching when he wasn't ready, it could turn him away from the calling later. If he waited till he was older it could be too late.

"I will preach on the Transfiguration," Muir said. I could tell how he was pondering and worrying about the sermon he'd agreed to preach. His cheeks was flushed and he swung his arms when he talked. I couldn't think of a thing to do to help him. If he was going to be a minister the Lord would have to lead him.

When the Sunday finally come that Muir was supposed to preach, I was more nervous than he was. But I couldn't let it show. I tried to be cheerful and confident, like it was all the most natural thing for my younger son to preach his first sermon. But I was twisted in knots and my lips was dry as I set down in church. My dress got wet under my armpits. I tried to smile and it felt like my lips was crawling sideways.

"Lord, let your will be done," I prayed silent. "Be with Muir in this hour of trial. If it is your will for him to preach, show him the way."

But it was like Muir never had a chance that day. When he was flustered, when he got mad, it was like he couldn't decide what to do with hisself. He never could remember nothing when he got excited. He'd rush on ahead of hisself and then forget where he was, forget what he was saying. I thought my heart was going to stop or tear out of my chest as I watched him fumble in the pulpit.

AFTER THE TERRIBLE day when Muir tried to preach, he wouldn't say nothing about it. He stayed out of the house most of the time. He stayed in the woods and in the fields. He stayed in the attic on rainy days looking through Pa's old books and magazines. And even when he was setting at the dinner table or by the fire he wouldn't say much. Me and Fay tried to talk to him. And even Moody tried to be cheerful to him. Moody could be as friendly and considerate as you please if he wanted to.

But Muir lived in his own head, in his own disappointment. He had always lived in his own head with his daydreams. You never did know exactly what he was thinking.

We was setting by the fireplace a few days after that awful Sunday. It was beginning to turn cool, with fall coming on, and the fire felt good.

"Every preacher learns by practice," I said to Muir.

He was scratching on a piece of paper, making pictures of buildings, the way he liked to do. He didn't answer at all, just kept doodling with the pencil.

"You can't be a preacher until you're twenty-one," Fay said, "until you get a license."

"How do you know?" Muir said without looking up.

"It takes a lot of practice to learn to do anything right," I said.

"You can practice on us," Moody said to Muir. "You can try out your sermons on us and if we laugh you'll know they ain't working."

Muir looked at Moody and then back at the sheet of paper without answering. Muir's shoulders was so wide they looked like they was busting out of his shirt.

"What Muir does is up to him," I said.

"I never seen a preacher that was younger than twenty," Fay said.

"A preacher has to make you want to listen to him," Moody said.

"You tell us all about it," Muir said to Moody.

Moody had the stub of an old cigar between his fingers. He lit it with a stick from the fire and blowed smoke toward Muir. "I'm just telling you what I think," he said.

Ever since his daddy died Moody had been mad. But sometimes he would be sorry after he'd done something wrong and would feel ashamed of hisself and try to make up for what he'd done. I know he was embarrassed about what he had done at the church.

But it seemed like either Moody or Muir had to be mad, one or the other. They couldn't both be happy at the same time.

"We know what you think," Muir said to Moody.

"If you want to preach, then go ahead and preach," Moody said. "Don't let a little teasing stop you. I'll even help you."

"How will you help?" Muir said.

"I'll buy you a new Bible," Moody said.

"Don't need a new Bible," Muir said. He looked down at the drawing he had made. It was a building with a steeple on it.

"Moody is just trying to be friendly," I said.

"You need a better suit of clothes," Moody said. "I'll help you buy another suit of clothes."

"I could make you a suit," I said, "if you was to get some good cloth."

Muir gripped the arms of the chair he set in. He looked at his drawing and he looked at me. I seen how anguished he was and troubled in his mind. I seen how hurt he was by people laughing at him.

"Muir will preach again when he is ready," I said in the calmest way I could. "Muir will know what he is meant to do."

"Everybody can stand a little help," Moody said and blowed smoke toward the fireplace.

Muir jumped to his feet, and the book and paper in his lap fell to the floor. He picked up the drawing and throwed it into the fire. His face was white as cotton. "You don't know nothing!" he hollered at Moody.

Moody was took by surprise. "I know enough to stay away from pulpits," he said.

"Don't none of you know nothing," Muir said and stomped the floor. His face was crumbling every which way and there was a tear in his eye as he headed to the door.

Three

Muir

I WAS SO embarrassed by the mess I'd made of preaching that I didn't go back to church for almost a year. I couldn't stand to see the people that had watched me make such a fool of myself. I stayed out in the woods most of the time and trapped and fished and hunted for ginseng. I didn't even want to work around the house, where Moody would tease me about my efforts at preaching.

"GINNY SAYS YOU'RE planning on building something?" my aunt Florrie said. It was the next summer and she had come over early that morning to help Mama make strawberry preserves. She was washing pint jars at the counter and Mama was drying them.

"Muir's thinking of building a castle," my sister Fay said. The strawberries cooking on the stove filled the kitchen with their smells.

Fay always wanted to tease me because she was my little sister and thought I didn't pay enough attention to her. She was skinny as a cornstalk, and she liked to mock me for looking at pictures of castles in magazines and books. She would find pages where I had drawed house plans and make fun of them.

"Muir has ambition," Aunt Florrie said. U. G. was her son, but she'd always treated me and Fay and Moody and our dead sister, Jewel, like we was her younguns. Florrie had a quick wit and a quick temper. She was wiry and dark and nervous as a sparrow.

"I have ambition to get away from here," I said. It was hard to explain how I wanted to build something and to get away from Green River at the same time. I wanted to build a great house out of timber and stone, and I wanted to escape to Canada or the North Woods too.

"I like a man with big plans," Aunt Florrie said.

"Did you ever meet a man you didn't like?" Mama said. Mama and Aunt Florrie liked to tease each other when they worked together. I reckon it was something they'd done since they was girls.

Moody had come in late the night before, long after I'd gone to sleep. He had been down to Chestnut Springs, where he went to drink liquor, and that morning when he got up he looked trembly and hungover. When he was hungover he couldn't stand for people to talk around him, and Mama and Aunt Florrie as usual was talking up a storm. Moody set down at the kitchen table, and then he jumped up and grabbed the milk bucket off the counter and banged it on his way out. He almost never would do the milking, but I reckon he seen it was an excuse to get out of the house.

"He'll feel better after he has some hair of the dog," Aunt Florrie said. Aunt Florrie liked to drink herself and you often smelled liquor on her breath. But I'd never seen her hungover.

"What does that mean, 'hair of the dog'?" Fay said.

"Hair of the dog that bit you," Aunt Florrie said. The jars rumbled in the dishpan as she worked a bottle brush around the mouth of a soapy jar like she was brushing teeth.

"Muir, go out and help your brother at the barn," Mama said. Mama was worried about Moody because he had seemed angrier and more hungover than usual.

"And then you can come back and tell us about your plans to go to Alaska," Aunt Florrie said.

I got up from the table and started for the door. "I'll make sure Moody ain't trying to milk the horse instead of the cow," I said.

"Or milk the chickens," Aunt Florrie said.

"Do they build castles in Alaska?" Fay said as I reached for the screen door.

"Only in the air," Aunt Florrie said.

I could smell the strawberries cooking all the way out to the shed. The scent was right for the late May morning. Dew was so heavy it made the grass white.

I HEARD MOODY'S voice soon as I got beyond the shed. It was about a hundred yards to the old log barn, but I could hear him cussing and fussing. Something banged on the barn wall so loud I knowed it must be the milking stool flung against the boards. I slowed down. Been a long time since Moody had done the milking, though when we was boys after Daddy died he'd done most of the milking, until I got big enough.

"Goddamn bitch!" Moody hollered. I come around the corner of the barn in time to see him hurl the milk bucket against the barn wall. A flame of milk leaped out of the bucket and hit the wall, busting into drops.

"Hey," I said. Moody was tall as me, but lanky and bony.

"Old bitch kicked me," Moody said.

I picked up the milk bucket and brushed the dirt off the sides. Straw had stuck to the wetness around the rim.

"You wasted the milk," I said.

"I'll waste her," Moody said. He had that yellow look in the eye like a dog that don't bark but means to bite you. Once Moody started getting mad it was hard for him to stop.

"I'll do the rest of the milking," I said. I looked around for the stool and found it in the weeds where it had bounced from the barn wall.

"This she-devil kicked me," Moody said. He looked down the hallway of the barn like he was searching for something. I could see what had happened. The cow had sensed he was hungover and mad and hadn't let down her milk. Maybe she was scared, or maybe she just wasn't used to his touch. And because she hadn't let down her milk Moody had got madder and pulled too hard at her tits. If the one milking is nervous, the cow gets nervous. A cow has to be calm to let down her milk.

"Let her quiet down," I said. "I'll finish the milking."

"Nobody kicks me and gets away with it," Moody said.

"A cow don't know what she's doing," I said.

"She kicked me," Moody said. "She knowed what she was doing." He looked in a stall and he looked in the harness room. Morning-sun-lit cobwebs hung from the beams in the hallway.

I touched the flank of the cow and felt her skin quiver under the tips of my fingers. She was tense and nervous from all the hollering. I patted her warm hide. It would take a while to calm her down before I could finish the milking. I would talk to her and give her more crushing and cottonseed meal. The sun made the red hairs on her back sparkle.

I put the stool down beside the cow and was about to set the bucket down when Moody come out of the feed room carrying a short piece of two-by-four that I used to prop open the loft door when we throwed hay or corn into the loft from the wagon.

"What are you doing with that?" I said.

"That cow kicked me," Moody said.

"Put that thing down," I said.

"Out of my way," Moody growled. He held the wood like it was a two-handed sword.

"Are you crazy?" I said.

"Don't call me crazy," Moody said and swung the two-by-four at me. I jumped back out of his reach.

"I'll do the milking," I said. A thousand times I'd seen how much easier it was to do a job myself than to get Moody to do it.

"Ain't no cow going to tell me what I can or can't do," Moody said. When Moody started getting mad it was like something in his blood turned to poison. He got madder because he was already mad. His blood got so crazy he couldn't control hisself.

"Go on to the house," I said. "I'll milk the cow."

"Are you telling me what to do?" Moody said. He shook the two-by-four like he wanted to swing it at my head. He was only three years older than me, but he'd always acted like he was my boss.

"I'm telling you what you don't have to do," I said. I didn't want to set him off even worse.

"Nobody tells me what to do," Moody said. "Certainly not my chickenshit little brother."

Rather than stepping back further I stepped sideways. Moody turned to face me. His eyes looked yellow as somebody's with jaunders.

"Ain't no use for you to get riled up," I said.

I kept my eyes level with his but didn't say nothing else. I figured he might calm down if I didn't argue anymore. Moody couldn't take any kind of criticism. He couldn't stand for anybody to disagree with him or suggest anything. When he was feeling good he could be nice as anybody in the world. When he was feeling in charge he could be as accommodating as you would want. We would work together for days and even weeks as long as nothing set him off, long as he stayed sober. But in recent months he'd been going off to Gap Creek and Chestnut Springs more and more and getting drunk almost every week.

Moody knowed Mama disapproved of him getting drunk, and that made him afraid. And when he was afraid he was in the wrong, that set him off even worse.

Moody kept his eyes level with mine and didn't say nothing else, and I didn't say nothing either. I thought maybe things was going to be all right. His eyes started fluttering the way they did sometimes when he was confused, when he was bad hungover and couldn't remember what he was going to say. Suddenly he spun around and hit the cow on the flank with the two-by-four.

The cow had gone back to eating from her box and jerked with surprise and shook her head.

"Stop!" I hollered.

"I'm going to teach this cow some religion," Moody said. He swung the wood again and hit her near the base of the tail. The cow jumped forward but was restrained by the rope tied to her collar from a post of the barn.

"Stop it!" I hollered.

"You just try," Moody said. He raised the piece and hit the cow on the shoulder. She swung around and bawled and slammed her flank against the barn wall. Her eye was wide with surprise and fear as she twisted to see what was happening. As the cow banged her rump against the wall again, her tail went up and she begun to empty her bowels. A scared cow will always relieve her bowels quicker than you can think.

Moody raised the board again and hit her on the back of the neck.

"You coward!" I hollered. He turned and swung the two-by-four at me and I jerked back. The end of the wood glanced off my forearm. The bone above my wrist felt like it had been touched by hot iron. Anger flashed through me in a bolt of electric current. I'd tried to keep calm before.

I stepped back toward the feed room. There was a lot of dusty harness on the wall, and some shovels and hoes and pitchforks leaned against the wall. I grabbed the first handle I could reach. It was a pitchfork with four big prongs. Moody was lunging toward me, but when he seen the fork he stopped. I held the tines out toward him.

"You're stupid as a cow," he said.

I was out of breath and I didn't answer. I was so mad the air rasped in my throat. Moody swung at the pitchfork like he was sword-fighting. I jabbed at him and stepped back. He swung the two-by-four against the tines and I jerked away.

"You're stupider than you look," he said.

"You are the brains of the family," I said.

Long as I was holding the pitchfork he couldn't reach me. All he could do was try to knock the fork out of my hands with the two-by-four. He swung hard, and I seen the thing to do was drive the pitchfork at him before he completed the swing. I sidestepped and lunged forward. He seen the tines coming at his neck before he finished the swing, and he jumped back. But the stool was behind him and he tripped.

As Moody fell backward into the straw and dirt, I rushed over to him and raised the pitchfork, aiming right at his face. How easy it would be to drive the tines into his nose and cheeks. But I paused for a second. I didn't want to hurt Moody that bad. I didn't want to kill him. I wanted to knock him out so he'd cool off before he come to again.

But I didn't see how I could knock him out with the points of the pitchfork. I'd have to turn the fork around and hit him with the handle. It was the only thing I could do.

"Moody!" somebody shouted. It was Mama. Her and Aunt Florrie and Fay had come running to see what the commotion was about. I guess they'd heard Moody and me hollering or the cow bawling. All of them stood there watching me holding the pitchfork aimed at Moody's head.

I was going to say Moody started it. And I was going to turn the pitchfork around and hit him with the handle. But in that moment Moody had time to recover and jab me in the knee with the two-by-four. He didn't have time to swing, only to shove the end against my leg bone. My knee went out from under me like a knife folding. I tried to stop my fall, but it was too late.

"Stop that!" Mama hollered as I fell. The pain from the knee washed through me to the tips of my toes and fingers, and I went down on the hard ground. As I fell Moody rolled to the side. Bracing hisself on the ground, he kicked out and hit me in the belly. He kicked me in the crotch and in the belly. He kicked me in the shoulder and in the face.

Mama was hollering for him to stop. Her and Aunt Florrie took hold of me, and Moody kicked me again. I was weak from pain as I tried to wrench free.

Moody had got to his feet still holding the two-by-four. He was sweating and out of breath. He still had the yellow look in his eye. I expected him to swing at me again with the two-by-four. Instead he shifted the board to his left hand and reached into his pocket with his right. Out come his switchblade knife, and the blade flashed open. It was the knife he carried down to Gap Creek and Chestnut Springs. Moody was knowed as a knife fighter.

"Put that thing down," Mama said.

Moody waved the knife like it was the end of a whip. "Now let's see who's giving orders," he said, and thrust the blade forward. Because they was holding me, I couldn't get away. The tip of the blade hit my chest but didn't go in deep. I twisted and flung Mama's and Aunt Florrie's hands off my shoulders. They fell back and I jumped sideways, still holding the pitchfork, and I turned it so I gripped it by the collar just above the tines.

Moody held the two-by-four in his left hand and parried with the knife in his right. I jabbed at him with the end of the fork handle. Moody swung at the handle with the two-by-four. Before he could recover from the swing, I slammed him on the side of the head with the handle.

Moody was not quite knocked out, but he was addled. He took a step back with his knees bent, and he dropped the two-by-four and brought his left hand to his forehead. Then he staggered back another step and shook his head.

"I'll kill . . ." he said, but stopped like somebody that couldn't remember what he wanted to say. He was so dazed all the anger went out of him. I thought his knees was going to buckle, but they didn't. He rolled his eyes and acted like he couldn't hardly see. He walked a few steps one way, and then he walked in another direction. I kept my eyes on the knife, but he didn't raise it again.

Moody stumbled over a clump of weeds and had to catch hisself. "Chickenshit," he said. He took a few steps toward the barn and then stopped. Putting his left hand to his forehead like he was trying to think, he started walking toward the pines at the edge of the pasture. He tripped and staggered a few times on brush and stubble but kept going.

Mama and Aunt Florrie watched Moody until he disappeared into the pine thicket.

"You're bleeding," Fay said to me. I looked at my chest and seen a spot of blood on my shirt.

Aunt Florrie unbuttoned my shirt. There was a cut about half an inch long where Moody's knife had touched me.

"Moody has his ways," Aunt Florrie said. "He ain't finished growing up yet."

My right knee was sore as a rising and I had to limp a little as I followed them to the house. The morning looked different after what had happened. It tasted different, and smelled different too. The sunlight was bright, but dimmed by what Moody had done.

My knee was so sore I set down on the bank above the path and pulled up my britches leg. There was a knot swelled up on the side of my knee, already turning blue. The two-by-four had hit me beside the kneecap. If it had hit the kneecap I'd have been crippled. The bone must have been bruised, for it felt sick and weak. But the skin wasn't broke.

I looked out across the pasture toward the pines but didn't see any sign of Moody. He'd probably gone to sleep on the pine needles inside the thicket. After he slept off his hangover he'd show up and act like nothing had ever happened. It was what he always done after we fought, once the devil worked out of him.

I looked at the pine thicket and the pasture and the plowed bottomland and wondered how I was ever going to get away to some better place, where I could do something important.

It was about a month after the fight and my knee was still a little sore. It was going to be the hottest day in July, probably the hottest day of the year. Even before the sun was up I could feel the heat in the closeness, in the weight of the air. There wasn't much dew along the path to the log barn when I went out to milk. The smell of the barn, and the smell of the cow, was sharper than usual. But the milk didn't foam up in the bucket as much as it did in cooler weather.

"Get it strained and in the springhouse," Mama said when I brought the bucket to the house.

"I was planning to," I said.

"Milk will go blinky in the dog days," Mama said.

"Or any other time if it's left out," I said. Mama and me tended to irritate each other in hot weather. And she'd been sharp with me lately anyway. When Mama got mad it would come out slow. You might not know for days how angry she was. It would come out when she give you orders, when she criticized whatever you'd done.

As I strained the milk, I watched the stiff straining cloth melt as warm milk poured through it into the stoneware pitcher. It was like watching starch melt as the fabric lost the shape it had dried in. The wet cloth sunk into the mouth of the pitcher and made a nest of milk.

"I'm going to pick some beans to can," Mama said. It was her way of suggesting I help. It took forever to pick a bushel of cornfield beans because they was so short and slim. Mama expected me to help her and Fay pick the beans and break them up for canning. She didn't expect Moody to help, but she counted on me.

"I'm going to mow below the hogpen and down by the branch," I said.

"No use to mow this late in summer," Mama said. "Most weeds has already gone to seed."

"It's a jungle for snakes and yellow jackets," I said.

"Mowing weeds won't put a thing on the table come January," Mama said.

"Do you want the place to go wild?" I said. It was an old argument between Mama and me. I loved to mow with the scythe to keep the place neat. Mama thought it was a waste of time.

"Nobody pays you to mow weeds around the hogpen," Mama said.

"Nobody pays me to milk the cow either," I said and carried the pitcher out the door.

Long as I could remember I'd liked to cut weeds. People said it was another thing I took after Daddy. Since I was a boy I'd liked to take the scythe and trim along the edges of the fields. I wanted to make everything look like a park. I liked to make the place look groomed. The odd thing was I liked weeds too. I liked the fresh smell of weeds on a hot day steaming their scent through leaves and wilting a little in the sun. I liked the way big weeds growed one behind the other on a bank, reaching up into the sun, crowding every inch of space, with the joe-pye weed and hogweed reaching highest.

I placed the pitcher of warm milk in the cooling box of the springhouse. The water come almost to the bulge of the vessel. The cloth I'd tied over the top would keep the flies out. There was three other pitchers there. Mama or Fay would take one in the evening to leave by the hearth overnight to clabber. Mama would churn the clabber for butter on Thursday. The crocks of butter and pitchers of milk set in the cooling box like people in church with cold air running over their feet. It was dark as a church in the springhouse, and it sounded like a quiet service was going on. I closed the door and left the butter and eggs and milk and raspberries picked the day before chilling in the gloom.

Taking the scythe from the shed, I slipped the long whetrock into my hip pocket. Swinging the scythe over my shoulder like it was a curved rifle, I marched off to do battle with the big weeds. I would take the big lush stalks down a dozen at a time until the ground was flat as a lawn on a Flat Rock estate.

But where to start? I stopped by the hogpen and took the whet-rock from my pocket. Resting the end of the handle on the ground, I begun rubbing the blade with the stone. I liked the feel of whet grains cutting into steel. I worked along the edge of the blade, wearing it dusty and then brilliant, and turned the scythe to sharpen the other side. The blade lit up with my brushing. The whetstone on the steel sounded like an auctioneer: Give me a one and a one and a one. Who'll give me a two and a two and a two? Sold to the gentleman right over there with the flower in his hat!

I blowed the gray grime off the whetrock and slipped it back into my pocket.

"Oof," the pig said, snuffling up against the planks of the pen. "*Oof oof.*" The pig was always lively early in the morning. As the day got hotter it would find a spot in the corner and take a long nap. But now it turned quick as a cat, slamming the side of the pen, hop-ing I'd come with a bucket of slop to pour down the chute.

The pigpen smelled sour. Not just the sour of manure, but of fes-tering summer mud. It was the sour of cobs rotting in the muck, of milk spilled from slop gone rancid. It was the sour of cabbage rotting and old dishwater. It was the sour of old juices standing in hoof pools and turning to ferment. The mud of the pen was deep and black. It was a grease of shit and bone jelly, of silt and fetid creams. Cobs stunk, and stalks of weeds pickled in the slime. Every day I throwed in armloads of fresh weeds for the hog, and the weeds soaked in the ooze. The trembling batter of the pen seeped out through cracks and glittered in the sun. The mud was deeper than the thick-est pillow. Great curds and turds of mud got churned up by the hog's hooves. Flies hung in a glistening veil over the grumbling hog. The air around the pen was a rainbow of stinks and fetors, poots and belches of rotten breath.

The dirt at the lower end of the pen was where I dug for fishing worms in the spring. In the black mealy compost there was twenty worms in every shovelful, orange worms and purple worms threaded like screws. There was wigglers whipping in frenzy like raw nerves and long night crawlers that glistened like snakes, worms with swole bands and blister rings, worms that flattened at the edges. You could dig a canful of worms there in a minute. Tangled together, the worms moistened theirselves with foam and suds and spit of slime.

The muck and musk of the hogpen growed the biggest weeds around the place. Stalks of corn volunteered from seeds in the manure. And sometimes pumpkins and tomatoes growed there too. But it was just plain weeds, ragweed and hogweed, plantains and ironweed, for the most part. Biggest of all was the pokeweed that by late summer reached its purple stalks eight or ten or even twelve feet high. But pokeweed didn't like the richest ground. It thrived along the edges of the spill from the hogpen, in the red clay and leached-out dirt of the old strawberry bed.

I swung the scythe by the path and sliced canes of johnsongrass that dropped like little wheat to the ground. All grass grows jointed canes if left to mature and go to seed. I swept the blade over the ground, cutting everything off at about two inches. The cut stalks and leaves fell where they had growed. This is the way to put the earth in order, I thought. The blade hissed as it swung into the biggest weeds.

Weeds grow on stalks like little towers. Weeds have tubes and wires and shafts in their spines. Weeds have suction lines and veins going up and down inside, pulling juice from roots up to leaf tips. I swung the blade like I was pulling a big crooked oar. There was a rhythm I got into mowing, but it took a while to find it in the morning. Some days I never found the rhythm at all and kept speeding up and slowing down, swinging the blade farther out and closer in.

Ragweed has limbs that grow out of the main stalks like shelves. The limbs was braced and held by brackets. The limbs was kept stiff by the juice inside until the stems hardened. Weeds growed and filled out theirselves in the hot sun. But later in the day everything would wilt a little and go limp at the tips. Leaves that was crisp as new dollar bills in the morning dew would go rubbery and curl at the edges and crumble like spilled dried ink.

The big weeds reached out their limbs like they was resisting me. The weeds growed closer together than an army, their leaves overlapping like shields. The arms waved me back but I advanced a step and a swing at a time, and the weeds fell backward like they was pulled from beneath. This is the way to make weed fodder, I thought.

I didn't think about how broke I was, and I didn't think about what I was going to do in the fall. I didn't think about how I'd made a fool of myself trying to preach. I didn't think how silly I looked, and how all my plans had fell through. I didn't think how Annie ignored me sometimes and flirted with other boys, and made me so mad I felt crazy.

Already I could smell my sweat and the scent of chemicals raising from the cut weeds. The bleeding stalks smelled like perfumes and spices. Fumes rose from the wet leaves like somebody had spilled varnish or paint thinner. It was intoxicating to smell the vapors rising from the felled ragweed and nettles. There was a bunch of chemical smells, of oils and saps and nectars. The scents made me a little dizzy. The air was lit with clear smoke and herbal fogs. There was a dozen different vapors in the air.

Along with the smells there was grasshoppers and beetles boiling up where I swept the blade. There was dust and bits of thistle, seeds and ripped leaves flying where the weed stalks leaned backward and fell. The air was filled with moths that had been sleeping under the leaves, little white and lavender butterflies stirred up by the mowing. Spiderwebs between stalks got tore and spiders jumped out of my way or scurried along the ground between cut stalks. There was spiders along every inch of ground under the weeds, big spiders and little, black spiders and yellow spiders, garden spiders and furry spiders. There was spiders that looked like black pearls. Some resembled boats running on their oars.

Hoppers and leaf mites shook loose from the disturbed weeds and boiled up like dust. Every stalk seemed to have a meal of white and yellow lice on it if you looked close. I swept the blade close to the ground, moving ahead in half circles with every sweep. I wanted the ground to look like it had been mowed with a razor.

The handles jolted almost out of my hands and the blade rung like a sword. I'd hit a rock the size of a grapefruit and seen the white cut the blade made on the weathered rock. Weeds had mashed green stains on the rock. It was a rock I'd mowed into before. I leaned over and picked up the rock and throwed it against the side of the hogpen. The pig snorted and lunged from one side of the pen to the other.

I will not be stopped, I said to myself. I will not be stopped from building something grand. I will not be stopped from serving the Lord in my own way. Where there is not a way I will make a way. I will not be trapped on Green River. A life without a mission has no meaning. I was drunk with sweat, and I was inspired by my labor.

I raised the blade and inspected the edge in the sunlight. The metal was stained green, and leaves and pieces of stalks stuck to the wet steel. All the brightness was covered with weed juice. There was a nick in the edge where the rock had bit a gap in the sharpness. I took the whetrock and begun to sharpen the blade all over again. I couldn't whet out the nick, but I could sharpen around it. The rock had damaged a perfect blade. A few more nicks like that and the blade would be useless. The rock had stood in my way like Moody stood in my way and like my own foolishness stood in my way. The lack of money stood in the way of my going away from Green River. I sharpened the blade like I was punishing steel. The steel felt soft and fat under the grained stone. I rasped the sides until the blade sparkled. I sharpened the nick until it was thin as a razor.

My fury made the sunlight brighter and the weeds more vivid. I could see every weed stalk; every leaf and stick of trash stood out. I seen every separate fly over the hogpen and the silvery grain of the weathered boards. I seen the chalky white butterflies whispering away and grasshoppers clicking and flinging theirselves from weed to weed like giant fleas. My anger made the air shine, and I felt the heat coming up from the weeds and moist ground. The steams and vapors from the ground rose into my face. The weeds had molten gold in their veins that burned my skin.

The big weeds was like everything else that stood in my way. I launched into the stalks, swinging harder and faster. I meant to quell the whole bank of weeds. I meant to quell the whole field. The weeds rose up at me and mocked me and resisted me. The weeds was stampeding into their lushness. The weeds rose in waves higher and higher, about to wash over and bury me in a great flood that would drown every path and clearing, every field and road. Weeds tossed out arms and vines of morning glories caught on bushes and trees. Briars raked everything that passed, catching rabbit fur and fox fur. Big canes of blackberry briars shot up like fountains, crawling with chiggers, and swirled around in bins, washing away in currents over the other weeds.

I'll churn things up and make them alive, I thought.

A foam and a froth of flowers, a swirl of petals and pollen, honeydew and honeybees, tangles and locked arms, tied the vegetation in knots and caught the blade in wads and clots of fiber. I swung the blade harder and harder, cutting weed stalks big as sticks and juicy saplings. I cut skunk cabbage and catbriars and little thorn trees that had volunteered. I cut pine seedlings and mowed rank on rank of hogweed and queen of the meadow. The weeds was taller than I was. I was mowing in their shadow. I felt like a swordsman fighting a whole army. I slashed and slashed with my blade wider than a cavalry saber. I swung farther and deeper into the advancing line.

Something hit me on the cheek hard as a bullet. I turned and seen it was a hornet. Another come at me and I ducked. And then I seen the nest stuck like a loaf of gray paper between two big weed stalks. The paper was crumpled and looked like a brain ripped open. I swung the blade and cut the nest in two. And then I raised the scythe and slammed the end down, crushing the nest like a paper melon. Another hornet drove a spike into my forehead. I seen the nest was filled with hornets and grubs, like a pod full of seeds. I turned and jumped away, pulling the mowing blade after me.

When I turned to look back, hornets was boiling up around the broke nest. They rose in a black fizz, and the pig squealed like it had been stung, and lunged against the side of the pen. The nest was hard to see because it was right at the edge of the wall of weeds where I had stopped mowing. I hurried to the shed beside the corncrib and got a tin can of coal oil from a jug of lamp fuel. Then I checked my pocket to make sure I had matches. The scent of kerosene was like smelling salts in the hot air. Go careful, I said to myself. Go slow because you are stung and riled up. A hornet shot past my cheek as I tossed the kerosene on the paper of the nest.

Standing far back as I could, I struck a match and tossed it. But soon as the match hit the weeds it went out. I lit another one and pitched it slower. This time the flame flickered and started to spread across the stubble. With a whoosh the fire climbed up into the biggest piece of the nest.

The flame leapt higher into the uncut weeds, but in the bright sunlight I couldn't hardly see it. Smoke filled the pulsing air. And along with the hum and roar of the hornets I heard a crackling. At first I thought it was the weed stalks popping, or the joints of the stalks. But there was a crack, and I seen a hornet circle in the flame and fall away. There was a snap, and a hiss like a drop of grease hitting a hot pan. The hornets raged faster and more frantic. They was so angry they wouldn't leave the ruins of the nest. They flung at the fire and attacked the flames. As they touched the fire they busted like popcorn. *Splat!* And *ssss!* I wished I had another can of fuel to throw and burn them up.

But I was quick ashamed of myself. That is what anger will get you into, I said. Anger will destroy, or make you destroy. Anger will make you roar and crack open like the nest of hornets. Anger will turn you into a fool.

The fire smoldered out in the green weeds as soon as the kerosene was burned up.

I backed away and took up the mowing blade and whetrock that was so hot in the sun they almost burned my hands. It was late morning and I had maybe half an acre to mow before dinnertime. Below the hogpen there was big weeds crowding along the edge of the cornfield all the way to the river. Most of the weeds appeared to be in flower, reaching out to show their blossoms to the sun. I put the whetrock in my pocket and turned backward, facing the hogpen. I mowed backward like somebody rowing.

I felt I was swimming in sweat. The sweat flowed over me, trickling and licking. The sweat was carrying all the poisons and anger out of me. The sweat was washing me from the inside. Sweat was a baptism from within, bleeding out the fester of rage. The sweat was cleansing me of the resentment for all that stood in my way.

I was soaked in sweat by the time I reached the end of the field and quit for dinner. I felt wrapped in sweat as I walked to the house. I was so wet, I thought I might go swimming. But I knowed that was a bad idea, to plunge into the river when you was red-hot. Instead, I stopped by the springhouse and dashed water on my face and arms and on the back of my neck. That cooled me off some, and I listened to water from the pipe murmur like it was quoting Scripture.

Four

Ginny

THE FIRST TIME I knowed Moody was in the liquor business was when he was about sixteen. Tom had never had nothing to do with liquor, and Papa had only took a drink from time to time when he felt peaked. I liked to take a dram myself to settle my nerves but never had done no drinking in front of the younguns.

Moody kept going down to U. G.'s store in the afternoon instead of working on the place, and he come back later and later. Sometimes he come back after the rest of us was in bed. And in the morning he'd look washed out, like he had worked all night instead of sleeping.

"Moody, why do you lay out so late?" I said to him.

"Coon hunting with Wheeler," he said.

Back then, it was true that him and his friends Drayton and Wheeler used to hunt coons on moonlit nights. Wheeler had some old coonhounds that roamed around the mountains half the night while the boys set by a fire and listened. And they sometimes cooked a chicken they had stole from somebody's henhouse.

"You can't be coon hunting every night," I said. Moody looked so wore out and acted so irritable I was afraid he was sick. He was always skinny but had fell off a few pounds too.

"Ain't nothing wrong with hunting," he said.

"How can you help Muir in the fields if you're always wore out?" I said.

Over the past few months Moody had worked less and less and Muir had done more and more. It was Muir that pulled the fodder and chopped the wood and made the molasses to sell at the cotton mill. Me and Muir done the milking and boiled the sorghum, so I let Muir, who was only thirteen, keep half the money he got from selling syrup. That made Moody mad.

"Why don't I get no molasses money?" Moody snapped.

The next time I went out to the smokehouse where we kept the jugs of molasses, I seen one had fell off the shelf and broke. The sorghum had spilled out over the dirt in a tongue of glistening brown. I didn't think it fell off the shelf by itself, but I didn't say nothing.

THE NEXT TIME U. G. come by to bring a bag of shorts I'd ordered for the hog, I said, trying to make it sound like a joke, "You're getting more work out of Moody these days than I am."

"He ain't working for me," U. G. said. I knowed that; I just wanted him to talk about Moody.

"I wish I knowed where he went at night," I said. "He's only sixteen."

"I wish I didn't know," U. G. said. U. G. was about seven years older than Moody, and he had always been like a son to me. He was short and strong, built like a pony. He wore silver-rimmed glasses that flashed in the sun.

"What do you mean?" I said.

"Don't want to be no tattletale," U. G. said.

"I'm his mama," I said. "I have a right to know what's happening to my boy."

U. G. looked at the ground and shook his head. He drug his toe across the dirt of the yard like he was drawing a line. "Ain't none of my business," he said.

"What kind of meanness has Moody got into?" I said. My stomach felt so sour I thought I was going to throw up.

"I think he's working for Peg Early," U. G. said.

"What is he doing for Peg Early?" I said. But in my heart I already knowed. Peg Early was the biggest bootlegger down in Chestnut Springs. Her husband had been in the liquor business for years and years, and when he died Peg took over herself and made it even bigger. There was all kinds of rumors about Peg Early, that she paid off the police, including the federal revenuers, that she run houses of ill repute in Chestnut Springs, as well as cockfights and gambling joints. Rumor was that anybody that crossed her would disappear. A shudder passed through me down to my toes. It was also said that Peg Early went regular to church and give a lot of money to the North Fork Baptist.

"What would Peg Early want with a boy like Moody?" I said.

U. G. said Peg used boys to carry liquor across the state line at night. She would pay them two dollars for every five gallons they lugged from Possum Holler across the gap into North Carolina. All they had to do was leave it in a thicket before daylight, and Peg would be there in her roadster to pay them. I asked why she wouldn't carry the liquor up the mountain in a truck.

"No reason to take the risk," U. G. said. "She's covered on every front. She has at least two dozen men working for her."

I was so alarmed I couldn't sleep after U. G. told me that. I had lost my husband, and I had lost my pa, and I had lost my older girl, Jewel, to the 1918 flu, and here my oldest son was getting hisself into trouble, bad trouble. My family had never lived outside the law. I felt like something had slipped loose down in my guts. I had to think what to do. If I throwed it up to him, what U. G. had said, Moody would just deny everything. That's the way he was. Moody would never own up to his doings. I'd have to try another way.

"I want you to stay home tonight," I said to Moody the next day.

"Ain't no little youngun," Moody said.

"You need more sleep," I said. "You'll get sick at this rate."

"You want me to get down on my knees and say my prayers?" Moody said and laughed.

"You will stunt your growth," I said. Moody was poor as a whippoorwill. He had never put on no weight.

That evening Moody was gone same as usual. He didn't pay a bit of attention to me. He was too big to whip, and I was afraid he was too big and too angry to control. What is a mama to do with a big boy that don't mind her? My pa had never had such trouble with his boys.

Nothing I had done before seemed to be of any help. Everything I had learned from raising younguns appeared to be useless. It was my job to look after Moody and to keep him out of trouble. Everything I done or said seemed to make it worse.

One morning when Moody got up I seen he had a black eye and a cut on his cheek. He looked so tired he was bent over. He wouldn't look at me straight. "You have been hurt," I said.

"Run into a tree," Moody said.

"You have been in a fight," Muir said.

"Shut up," Moody said, and shoved Muir back against the kitchen wall.

"Stop that," I said. "Let me put some camphor on that," I said to Moody.

But Moody wouldn't let me touch the black eye or the cut. He jerked away from me and slipped out the back door.

One night soon after that Moody didn't come home at all. He didn't appear at the breakfast table, and when I asked Muir where Moody was, Muir said he hadn't seen him. I can still remember the raw pain that sliced through me. I couldn't go ahead with my work that day, and I didn't know where to look for him. I got my bonnet from the nail by the door. "I'm going to the store," I said.

"Can I go?" Fay said. Fay looked more like Moody than anybody else in the family.

"You stay here," I said.

It always made me a little nervous to go to U. G.'s store by myself. Maybe it was because Hicks Summey and Charlie and Blaine and others was always setting around the store and playing checkers. The store was a man's place. I always felt they was staring at me when I went in there. Some women knowed how to joke with the men and carry on at the store, but I never did. Florrie could talk to the men there by the stove as easy as in her own kitchen.

When I got to the store U.G. was weighing ginseng for old Broadus Carter. It was as pretty an October day as you'll ever see, but dark in the store, and smelling of coffee and leather from the harnesses U. G. sold. U. G. put the roots that looked like a man's private parts in a pan on the scale, and he moved the weight down the markings on the arm. He slid the weight a little, then pushed it back a little. "Can't give you but nine dollars," he said to Broadus.

"That is prime sang," Broadus said. "You know that is prime."

"It's garden growed," U. G. said.

"I dug it myself backside of Pinnacle," Broadus said.

"It's garden growed," U. G. said and held up a root that was wrinkled and withered.

"Maybe some of it is garden growed," Broadus said.

U. G. counted out a five and four ones into Broadus's hand.

"I'm looking for Moody," I said soon as Broadus left.

U. G. looked at Hicks Summey and then back at me. "He was here yesterday evening," Hicks said. Hicks was always hanging around U. G.'s store, and he looked like he had had a drink.

"He never come home last night," I said. I felt an awful chill in my bones, even though it was a mild fall day. I shivered and my voice shook.

U. G. said Moody had left the store before dark with Wheeler and Drayton.

"Where did he go?" I said.

U. G. looked at the ginseng he had bought, and he looked at the men setting by the stove. It was ten o'clock in the morning and I knowed he had a lot of work to do. U. G. was one of the hardest-working men I knowed. He worked as hard as my husband Tom had.

"I'm worried sick," I said.

U. G. took a key out of his pocket and opened a tin box. There was shelves and compartments in the box and he placed the ginseng Broadus had brought him in one of the trays. "I might know where Moody is," U. G. said.

U. G. asked Hicks and Charlie and Blaine to leave, and then he locked up the store. He was so dedicated to business I knowed it pained him to do that. It pained me to ask him to help, but I didn't have no choice.

We got into U. G.'s pickup truck and drove south on the highway. We crossed the river and drove up into the flats of the Lewis place. The highway turned sharp downward at the state line, dropping down into the gloom of Possum Holler and the sickening curves of the Winding Stairs. I had a shudder of dread when I thought of Dark Corner and Chestnut Springs. Ever since Pa had took me to the Indian doctor down there when I was seventeen, I thought it was a place of fearful goings-on.

The deep hollers in Dark Corner was full of stills and hideouts for them running from the law. The dives and taverns along the road in Chestnut Springs was full of gambling and bad women. There was people killed all the time in Dark Corner, killed in knife fights, shot in ambush on the trails. Rumor was the law was afraid to come into Chestnut Springs except in the daytime. The sheriff in Greenville didn't interfere with what went on there. I reckon all the deputies was in the pay of Peg Early.

Even though it was a bright day, I felt we was descending into the depths of some hell. The dark of the hollers looked evil. You felt you was being watched. The rocks on Corbin Mountain above looked ugly as gargoyles. The trees appeared stunted and deformed. The red clay in ditches looked tainted and sour.

"Are we going to Peg Early's?" I said, and my teeth chattered I was so nervous.

"We'll have to," U. G. said.

Peg Early's house was the biggest place in Chestnut Springs. It was two stories with long porches set back high above the highway. The house was painted blue. Water from one of the springs on the mountain was piped into a trough in the yard. I'd heard that when somebody got cut in a knife fight they would wash them off in the trough.

I looked around at the little valley across the road. Without all the houses and taverns along the highway it would be a peaceful valley. There was sycamores along the creek, and a grassy meadow running back to the woods. If it wasn't for the people it would have been a beautiful place.

Peg Early's house had a tavern on the first floor. A motorcycle with purple saddlebags on it, and strings hanging from the grips of the

handlebars, was parked near the door. The motorcycle leaned like it
was about to fall over. Some kind of music come from inside. I couldn't
tell if it was a Victrola, or somebody picking a banjo.

"You stay here," U. G. said. "I'll go in and ask about Moody."

After U. G. disappeared inside the tavern I looked up at the porch
on the second story. A girl in a silky robe was leaning on the bannis-
ter smoking a cigarette. She didn't look more than fifteen, and her
robe was unbuttoned, showing her bosoms. Her hair was curly but
uncombed, like she had just woke up. I nodded to her and said
howdy, but she just knocked the ash off her cigarette so it fell onto
the ground beside the pickup.

A truck passed on the highway and left its smell of oil and exhaust. I heard a woman laughing but couldn't tell if it come from the
first or second story. I looked down the road at the other houses,
hoping to catch sight of Moody. I wondered if Wheeler and Drayton
had come down here with him.

I waited for a few minutes, but it seemed like an hour. I fidgeted
around in the truck seat. I was Moody's mama and it was my job to
find him. If he was in trouble it was my fault. I turned on the seat and
looked across the road. Two men was helping a third into a car over
there. I couldn't tell if the man was sick or drunk or had been hurt.

I wished U. G. would come back and say what had happened. I
rubbed my hands together and gripped the edges of the seat. I looked
at the sycamore trees by the branch across the road, and I watched
the tongue of water from the pipe tickling the water in the trough
and making it shiver. A yellow jacket buzzed by the window of the
truck.

"Where is Moody?" I said between clenched teeth. "Where is that
boy that is my most troubled youngun?" I tried to see into the door
of the tavern, but it was dark in there. The bright sunlight made it
impossible to see inside.

I scooted myself around in the seat, but I couldn't wait any longer.
I had to go in and find out about Moody. I opened the door and
stepped out onto the ground. I tightened my fists and made up my
mind to get to the bottom of this. I had gone too far to stop now.

As I stepped through the door into the dark, I couldn't see nothing at first. The place smelled of sawdust and pepper and the sweet fruity fumes of liquor.

"Howdy, ma'am," a man said.

In the gloom I seen a man standing behind a linoleum-covered counter. There was tables around the room, and a billiard table at the far end.

"I'm looking for Moody Powell," I said.

"Ain't no Moody here," the man behind the counter said. He wore an apron like U. G. wore in his store.

"Where did U. G. go?" I said.

There was other men setting around some of the tables, but in the dark I couldn't hardly see them. Somebody was talking in the room behind the counter.

"U. G.!" I hollered.

U. G. come out from a door at the end of the counter and I run to him. "Where is Moody?" I said.

U. G. shook his head, and a woman appeared in the doorway behind him. I couldn't see her well at first. I don't know how I expected Peg Early to look. I reckon I thought she'd be a heavy woman wearing a man's hat and man's clothes. As she stepped closer I seen she was wearing some kind of shiny slacks, and she was slim as a rail. She had short gray hair and there was a pistol strapped around her waist, and she was holding a cigarette between her fingers.

"Honey, I wish I could help you," she said. "Moody was here last night, but he left."

"When?" I said.

Some of the men around the table behind me had stood up. I felt like everybody was looking at me.

"Sugar, Moody had a little too much and got handy with his knife. I had to ask him to leave," Peg said. She blowed smoke out the side of her mouth. Her face was wrinkled as an old corn shuck, and her lips was painted red.

"Did he get hurt?" I said. "I'm his mama."

"Not while he was here," Peg said. Her smile was easy as a sneer.

"When did Moody leave?" U. G. said.

"How should I know?" Peg said. "It was a busy night." She

drawed on her cigarette. "I'd like to help, but I can't keep track of every Dick and Harry that comes in here."

The man at the counter said, "Can I get you all something?" and the way he said it meant it was time for us to leave.

It smelled like chicken was being cooked in one of the back rooms, chicken with some kind of pepper sauce, and the smell nigh made me sick. U. G. took my arm and we started toward the door. I didn't want to leave until I found out something about my boy.

"You all come back and see us," Peg said. Her voice was hoarse as a growl.

I seen I wasn't going to find out nothing from her. Whatever had happened to Moody she wasn't going to tell us. I let U. G. lead me out into the sunlight. I felt bleached and wrung out, like I hadn't slept in a week. I climbed back into the truck sad and slow.

U. G. started the pickup and was about to back into the highway when I looked up at the second-story porch and seen a girl gesturing to us. It was not the same girl I'd seen there before. This girl had short black hair and was wearing a pink blouse. She waved her hand quick and then pointed up the highway.

"What does she want?" I said.

U. G. opened his door and started to say something, but the girl shook her head and put her finger to her lips. She shook her head like she was scared, then she pointed up the highway again.

"What does she mean?" U. G. said.

I watched her point, and the only thing I could think of was that she wanted us to go on up the highway. Did she just want us to leave? She pointed up the road, and then she pointed at her chest.

"She wants us to meet her up the road," I said.

U. G. put the truck in gear and backed around. The girl on the balcony had disappeared.

"Where?" U. G. said.

"Somewhere out of sight," I said.

Two men stood in the door of the tavern and watched us drive away. On the pavement U. G. went slow, looking for either the girl or a place to pull off. Just around the bend there was another spring, smaller than the one at Peg Early's. It was almost hid by hemlock trees, and U. G. turned in beside it. A trail come down the side of the mountain to the spring.

We set in the truck for about a minute, and then I seen the girl in the pink blouse beckoning to us from the shadows of the hemlocks. We got out and followed her into the brush farther up the ridge. The girl was out of breath from running all the way from Peg Early's.

"Peg would kill me if she knowed," the girl gasped. "But look for Moody at the spring halfway up the mountain."

"What happened?" I said.

"What spring?" U. G. said.

"Him and Josie got caught," the girl said in a rush.

"What spring are you talking about?" U. G. said.

"What did they get caught doing?" I said.

"That's all I can tell you," the girl said, and started running back up the trail. I wanted to holler after her, but we was too close to Peg Early's for me to holler, and I knowed she wouldn't come back. She disappeared into the woods.

"What spring is she talking about?" I said.

Me and U. G. got back in the truck and he put the key in its slot. U. G. looked puzzled and worried.

"Who is Josie?" I said.

U. G. shook his head and started the motor. "Only spring I can think of is the one in Possum Holler," he said.

All my life I'd heard about Possum Holler, but I never had stopped there. We drove by it going to Greenville and going to see the Indian doctor when I was seventeen. It was a deep dark cove at the edge of Dark Corner, which is what they called the wildest section of upper South Carolina. U. G. drove out of the flats of Chestnut Springs and started winding up the curves to the steep part of the mountain. Trees hung over the road and smothered it with shade. In the bend of a curve there was a little haul road I hadn't noticed coming down. It was almost covered with limbs and brush and vines, and when U. G. turned into the track, branches scratched on the windshield and sides of the truck. I blinked as limbs slapped on the glass in front of me. The truck rocked and bounced on the ruts so bad my head hit the ceiling. The road wound around the side of the holler.

U. G. stopped when he seen a girl setting on a rock ahead. Her long blond hair was all tangled up and there was blood on her dress. The cloth was tore around her chest. Her face was puffed with bruises. She set beside a rippling spring, and there was cans and bottles scattered around her.

When we got out of the truck and hurried to her, I seen her face was swole up worse than it looked at first. Her lip was swole sideways. Her eye was puffed out big as a blue Easter egg.

"Are you Josie?" I said.

"What if I am?" she said.

"We're looking for Moody," I said.

"Who are you all?" Josie said.

"I'm his mama," I said, "and this is his cousin."

"Have you got a cigarette?" the girl said.

U. G. patted his pockets and then said all he had was a pipe.

"Figures," the girl said. She talked out of the side of her mouth. There was cuts and whelks on her arm.

"Where is Moody?" I said.

"Peg Early beat us up," the girl said, and her voice caught in her throat.

I heard a groan and looked up the side of the mountain. A man's boot stuck out from under a laurel bush. I started climbing up there, and when I reached the bush I parted the limbs and seen Moody laying in the leaves, pushed up against a rock.

"Leave me alone," Moody said. His shirt was ripped and there was blood on his side. His cheek was swole so it punched out in a rotten bruise.

"What happened?" I said.

"Let me be," Moody said.

U. G. had followed me up the hill, and Josie stumbled along behind him.

"Peg found out Moody was cutting the liquor," Josie said. "He brought it up here to mix with springwater. People complained because Peg was already cutting it herself."

Moody rolled over so he wouldn't have to look at us. He was like a dog that has been hurt and just wants to hide in a thicket.

"Peg found out I was helping Moody and she whipped us both," the girl said. "She had Glover tie us to a tree and she whipped us with a razor strop until Moody shit all over hisself."

"Go away!" Moody cried, like he couldn't stand for us to see him. He rolled over again, and that's when I seen the stain in the straddle of his overalls, and it made me shudder. It was a brown-and-red stain, like it was mixed with blood.

"Just go away!" Moody screamed. I bent over and put my hand on his shoulder. I wanted to hug him to my chest.

"Peg caught me and Moody in bed," Josie said. "I had been letting Moody have it cause I liked him. And I helped him carry liquor too."

I tried to brush the hair off Moody's brow, but he flung my hand away. "Are you hurt bad?" I said. Moody laid there like he was too ashamed to speak. And he closed his eyes, like he couldn't stand to see nobody.

"Who done it?" U. G. said.

"Peg done it," Josie said. "She had that big Glover hold us and tie us down." She busted out crying.

I wished I had a clean washrag to wipe the blood off Moody's face and neck. I was heartbroke just to look at him. "We ought to call the law," I said.

"No!" Moody hollered and rolled to his other side.

I told him Peg Early had to be arrested for beating up two young people that way, that she ought to be put in jail for nine hundred years.

"No cop in Greenville County will arrest Peg Early," Josie said. "She pays them off."

U. G. said that was so. If Peg could get away with bootlegging and whores and gambling it wasn't likely they would arrest her for whipping two young people caught stealing from her.

"Then I'll go to the North Carolina police," I said.

But U. G. told me they would say they had no jurisdiction over what happened in South Carolina. North Carolina and South Carolina sheriffs didn't interfere with each other's counties.

"Then I will call the federal police," I said.

"No," Moody said.

"The feds would arrest Moody for carrying blockade across the state line," U. G. said.

I was so mad I turned around like I was going to stomp off down the mountain. I stomped the ground and tightened my fists. But I seen that getting mad was just selfish. Getting mad wouldn't help Moody or punish Peg Early. The thing to do was take care of Moody. Getting mad was just vanity when my boy needed help so bad.

I tore off a piece of my skirt and wet it in the spring. I found an empty fruit jar, dipped water, and carried it up to Moody. "What you need is a doctor," I said.

"Leave me alone," Moody said.

When I tried to wash his face he pushed my hand away. I seen his hands was swole where they had been hit with a stick or crushed between boards. "This is what the devil has brought you to," I said.

I told U. G. we had to get Moody to the truck and take him home.

"Don't want to go home," Moody said.

"You can't lay out here in the woods for the bears and painters to eat," I said.

I noticed Josie had stepped away to the other side of the spring. I had forgot about her. She was bad hurt too. I asked if she wanted me to wash off her face and bruised arms. She shook her head and wiped the snot off her upper lip. I never saw anybody that looked more pitiful. Her dress was near tore off her.

"Can we drive you home?" I said.

"No," she said and shook her head.

"You got to go someplace," I said.

I would take her to the house if there was no other place to take her.

"Reckon I'll go back to Peg's," Josie said.

"You can't do that," I said. I couldn't believe she meant what she said.

"I better go back," she said.

"You can go home with us," I said. But she started walking into the woods. Her blond hair was tangled and hanging in all directions. As she walked she tried to smooth it out. She limped and stumbled as she tried to pick her way through the leaves and undergrowth down the mountainside.

"Stop her," I said to U. G. I was going to run after the girl, but he put a hand on my shoulder.

"She don't know what else to do," U. G. said.

"You don't have to go back there!" I hollered, but Josie kept on walking until she was hid by the laurel bushes.

MOODY TRIED TO push us away, but I took him under one shoulder and U. G. took him by the other, and we lifted him up. He groaned and cried in spite of hisself, and he was too stiff and sore to walk except in little steps.

"Lean your weight on us," I said. The steps he took was little jerks. It was hard going down the side of the mountain. I expected us all to lose our balance. U. G. and me had to walk sideways to hold Moody up on the steep ground.

"You'll feel better when you get home," I said.

"Don't want to go home," Moody said.

His shirt looked like it had been tore by a saw. He looked like he had been clawed all over.

Five
Muir

I NEVER COULD understand why sometimes me and Mama got on each other's nerves so bad. Some said it was because we was so much alike. I was her boy and I was raised in her house and she was the only mama I'd ever had. But my brother, Moody, was raised in the same house, and he was as different from me as midday from midnight. Other people said the problem between Mama and me was that we was so different. Mama liked meetings and singings and getting together with other people, while I just liked to be off working by myself in the orchard or tramping the woods with a gun, walking my trapline.

"Trappers are as no-count as fiddlers," my aunt Florrie liked to say. But she said it in fun, while other people said it to be mean.

I liked to get up early and leave the house before Moody and Fay and Mama was awake. It was a good feeling to be up while the house was quiet. I could make coffee and grits for myself while it was still dark outside. It was so good not to see my family, I sometimes skipped the grits and coffee just to get my mackinaw coat and gun and slip out into the dark. That way I could be halfway to the head of the river before dawn made the sky look like a stained-glass window.

That's what I wanted to do one day in January, the year after I preached. I knowed I'd have fur in my traps all through the Flat Woods and over on Grassy Creek and beyond the Sal Raeburn Gap. It'd rained for almost a week and I hadn't gone to the traps. Moody and me had fixed the roof of the barn, and I'd split a pile of wood to stack on the porch. Now the rain had stopped and it'd blowed off cold. I knowed there would be mink and muskrats, even foxes and coons in the traps all along the line. Fur was the true gold and treasure of the mountains, and I believed I had a packsack full of it waiting.

I had long practice at getting dressed in the dark. I tried not to wake Moody, who was snoring on the other side of the double bed. I liked Moody best when he was asleep. I slipped on my shirt and overalls by going slow. If you hurry in the dark you'll lose your balance and knock into something. The secret is to go slow and remember where everything is. I found my boots and a pair of socks and tiptoed out of the bedroom on the cold floor.

Soon as I stepped into the hall I seen a light in the kitchen. Somebody was up, because I could smell coffee. I tiptoed down the hall and seen Mama setting at the kitchen table reading her Bible. When she couldn't sleep she liked to get up early and sip coffee while she read Revelation or Acts.

"Morning," I said, like I expected to see her there.

"Morning," she said, not looking up from the table. Mama loved to read more than anybody I ever seen, and she hated to be bothered. I set down at the table and started to lace my boots. They was almost new boots I'd ordered from the W. C. Russell Moccasin Company in Berlin, Wisconsin, with some of my molasses money. Mama had not approved of me buying such expensive boots.

She looked up from the Bible. I noticed the wrinkles around her eyes and the lines around her mouth. "We old folks can just barely cover our feet," she said. "But the young wear leather to the knees." It was something she liked to say. It was something Daddy used to say. Mama had learned to be thrifty after Daddy died. People said she had learned it from him. I was going to say something about needing boots to walk through briars and brush but didn't. I didn't want to argue that early in the morning. I just wanted to get out to my traps.

"You remind me of your daddy," Mama said. She looked up from her Bible again. "He would rather die than ask anybody for help. He was stubborn as an old jackass."

"He worked harder than I do," I said. It was a conversation we'd had many times.

"But he worked at what he wanted to do, and nobody could tell him nothing," Mama said. "Didn't do no good to try."

"I just barely remember him," I said, which wasn't really true, for I was seven when Daddy died, and I could remember him pretty well. But it made Mama talk more if I couldn't remember much.

"He got sick after fighting fire," Mama said. "But he done everything like he was fighting fire. He didn't waste his time hunting and trapping." Mama looked at the Bible like she was remembering things. Sometimes when Mama got to thinking about Daddy's death she would stop talking and not act like herself.

"Can I fix you some grits?" Mama said.

Truth was I was hungry for hot grits, but if I set down and eat, Mama would start telling me all the things that needed to be done on the place. She couldn't help herself even if she wanted to. Though I done most of the work and Moody didn't do hardly any, she still couldn't stand to see me heading off into the mountains, no matter what the weather was.

"I'll just have a biscuit and coffee," I said. Soon as I laced up my boots and tied them I took a cup from the shelf and poured some coffee. Mama made strong coffee in the morning. I needed about two cups before I started out.

"Who's going to do the milking?" Mama said. She turned a page of her Bible, then rubbed her hands together like she was scrubbing them with air. Her hair had gray in it and was held in place by combs. "You'll never make anything out of trapping," Mama said. "Your daddy never wasted his time tramping the woods."

I drunk the coffee so fast it near scalded my throat.

"The road needs fixing up above the spring," Mama said. "Every time you drive on it just makes it worse."

"Moody is not helpless," I said. I grabbed a biscuit and chewed it up and washed it down with coffee. The hot coffee smarted the tip of my tongue and burned a little as I swallowed. I had to get out in the open air and be on my way.

"The gate up by the road needs to be fixed," Mama said. "Tom always kept it tight and greased."

I was going to say why couldn't Moody fix the gate. But it wouldn't do no good to argue any more. Mama would just say Moody was not as handy with tools as me. She would say Moody had to take the Model T and drive her to town or deliver eggs to the store. There was no use to argue. Nobody ever won an argument with Mama.

"I pray about you," Mama said.

I took my shotgun from the corner and slipped out the door fast as I could. When Mama talked about praying for me it was time to go. For next I'd say I would pray for her, and then I'd be ashamed I'd said it. Better not to mix up praying with our quarrels. Mama and Daddy had fought over religion, and she was ashamed of that. It was what pained her the most when she remembered Daddy, how they had fussed and argued about her going to the Holiness revivals. But it was the memory of what a fool I'd made of myself trying to preach that pained me the most.

I drove my feet onto the ground like I was driving nails with each step. As I passed the corner of the chicken house the tip of my shotgun hit the slabs, and the hens fluttered and squawked inside. Calm down, I said to myself, at least till you get out of the yard. You're as bad as Moody to fly off. You'll need all your strength for the day ahead. The miles of trail and the steep mountain slopes can use up all the anger you've got to give.

As I come out along the pasture fence I could see the valley under the stars, the wide bottomland running down to the river, the stars sharp and bright over the pines on the ridge above. The breeze was colder there in the open. I shivered and felt my way along the path. My feet would find the path if I walked without trying to look at the dark ground. I hurried along the fence down to the bank of the river.

In the dark, water whispered and slurped and sparkled under starlight. Around rocks you could hear the spill and splash. I breathed in deep the mud smell, the scent of soaked and rotting leaves. The trail run under the pines along the bank for maybe half a mile to the mouth of Cabin Creek.

When I got to the other side I climbed the sandy bank into my cousin Willie's field. There was a light on in the house above the road and I could smell fresh coffee and bacon frying. The smell made me wish I'd brought something to eat for dinner. Arguing with Mama had made me forget I'd be hungry by the middle of the day.

There was cornstalks in Willie's field, and I hit them with my elbows and the tip of the gun barrel. A rabbit skipped away in the dry weeds. I stepped careful on the sandy soil but still rattled the dry stalks and nettle vines. A real woodsman goes without making any noise. Only clumsy people crash into things.

It was maybe five miles up the valley to the head of the river. There was lights in most of the houses I passed. Beyond Willie's field I walked the road which run alongside the river. A dog barked at me from the Bane place and then run out to the road and followed me. At the Ward place I seen a lantern in the barn where somebody was milking. A lantern hanging in a stable with the yellow light on straw always makes me think of the manger scene in a Christmas pageant.

The farther you went up the river the farther it was between houses. The fields and pastures in the valley got narrower and finally the river itself was just a little creek between steep ridges, splitting off into branches and running back to spring hollers. I followed the biggest branch about to its head and started climbing the ridge to the lip of the watershed. By the time I got halfway I was in stride. When I found my stride I could walk all day without getting tired. I could walk without thinking. As I climbed it got lighter and I could see more and more the trees and rocks along the trail. And by the time I got to the comb of the ridge the woods looked orange in the sun, just showing itself over the rim of the Saluda mountains.

My first trap was a fox set on a trail at the edge of the Flat Woods. I approached it hoping to see a tail or red fur in the early light and streaks of shadow. My breath come short as it always did when I approached a trap. You never know what you're liable to find. Might be a ten-dollar pelt or a groundhog, or a missing trap. Far back in the woods there's nothing to stop somebody from stealing your steel traps if they find your line.

As I got close I seen stirred-up leaves where I'd buried and covered the trap. And I seen the chain of the trap stretched into the brush. My heart kicked with excitement. But then I seen there was nothing in the trap. I run forward and found not even a foot in the clamped jaws. Whatever had sprung the trap had jerked it out of the leaves. That was a fox all right. Must have smelled something on the leaves, or on the chain, and just for devilment had sprung the trap and tore it out of the ground.

I laid my shotgun on the ground. I'd hoped to be killing a fox with it. Instead, the fox was laughing at me somewhere in the woods. That fox stood grinning with satisfaction at what he'd done. I'd walked ten miles to find my trap sprung, and likely he'd peed on the ground just to spite me or done his business nearby to mock me. I thought of ripping the trap off its stake and flinging it into the brush, but I stopped myself. Nobody ever did beat a fox by getting mad.

I took out my gloves from the mackinaw pocket, the gloves I'd boiled to kill any scent. Sweeping the leaves and trash out of the way, I put the trap back into the low place in the trail. Spreading the jaws wide I set the trigger and sprinkled leaves over it. And from a bottle I carried in my pocket I sprinkled drops of scent around the spot. A fox sniffing the scent would not be looking for the trap. Last, I smoothed leaves and twigs over the place. I'll get your hide yet, I thought, and stretch it on a board to hang with the muskrats and mink and coons.

MOST OF MY mink and muskrat traps was along the banks of Grassy Creek. I had a number two trap at the bottom of nearly every muskrat slide and I had traps under overhanging rocks where mink liked to hide and watch for trout. The thing about a trap in water is it has to be in deep enough to drown a mink or muskrat. Otherwise they'll just gnaw off their foot and run, leaving you nothing but a bloody foot clamped in the jaws. But if the trap is too deep, especially in fast water, the rat or mink will swim right over it. So the trap has to be at just the right depth.

Because of the rains the creek had been high, so I might have mostly empty traps. Soon as I got to the creek I seen my first set was empty. I couldn't see the trap itself, but the chain stretched from the bush it was wired to right into the flush creek and there was no ripple or bump on the water to show anything was caught. I had to get closer to see if the trap had been sprung. It's hard to look through rippling water, especially if the sun glimmers on it. I had to get to the edge of the water and hunker down for a closer look. A shadow that must have been a trout flashed away in the pool. But the jaws of the trap was still open.

Had I walked all that way just to find empty traps? A crow mocked me from further up the ridge. I kicked the leaves under a dogwood. The shotgun shells in the pocket of my mackinaw weighed against my side. I could remember what I was thinking when I passed that way a week before: You couldn't know what would be in the next trap.

I rounded the bend in the creek and come to a lip of shoals where I'd put a trap between two rocks. I thought muskrats come down to the creek and entered the water between those two rocks. First thing I seen was that the chain was stretched out in the wrong direction. At the end of the chain was a lump in the water that looked like a big bubble. My breath caught in my throat. It was either a mink or a muskrat.

Problem was, the trap had swung out into deeper water. I stepped into the edge of the creek and seen it was a muskrat in the trap. I pulled the chain in and picked up the rat like a great dripping gob of fur, then turned to step on a rock back to the bank. But the rock turned under my foot like a greased ball bearing.

Something popped and went numb in my foot, and as I stepped out on the bank the foot went wrong and I stumbled. "Now you've done it," I said. I limped up into the bushes, and just then the pain hit me. You wouldn't think a foot could hurt so bad if it wasn't cut or stabbed. The foot in my boot was untouched, except it had twisted was all. It'd turned a little and something inside stretched or broke. The pain was sick heat coming up my leg. The pain turned my stomach and I thought I was going to throw up.

What have you done? I said to myself, and dropped the muskrat at the edge of the water. I had to walk my trapline that day. After a week of rain it had to be done. There was a cold wind coming down the slope, but the pain flashed through me so hard I couldn't hardly feel the wind.

After I set on the leaves, the pain didn't go away. Whether I put weight on my foot or not didn't seem to make any difference. I started unlacing my boot to see how the ankle looked, and got it unlaced almost all the way down when I thought better of it. If the foot started swelling I'd never get the boot back on. And I couldn't walk all the way home without a boot on. Best to keep the boot laced up like a bandage, like a cast, until I got back to the house. I'd heard of doing that with a broke bone, walking on it with a boot laced tight. Should work just as well with a sprain.

I thought I would continue on the trapline like nothing had happened. I couldn't let a sprained ankle get in my way. Mama would nod her head and say she'd told me so when I got back. Might as well have some pelts to show for my pain. I crawled over to the wet muskrat and put my knee on the spring of the trap. Wasn't hard to open the trap far enough to pull the cold foot out. But when I tried to open the jaws again to reset the trap, I seen how much the pain had weakened me. My knee trembled and my whole body trembled when I bent the hurt ankle a little. I got the jaws about half open and then had to let them snap shut again.

It was worse than I'd thought. Not only would I not be able to finish walking the trapline, I wasn't certain I could walk across the mountain and down the river home. Just taking a step was hard enough, much less walking a hundred yards, or half a mile, or ten miles.

The shotgun wouldn't serve as a crutch or even a walking stick. I seen an oak sapling further up the slope. About five feet above the ground it come to a fork. I didn't have nothing bigger than a hunting knife to cut with, but I limped and staggered up the slope, pulling myself from tree to tree. Took me several minutes to hack through the oak with my hunting knife. But when it was done I had a stick about five feet long with a fork at the end. It was just long enough for me to lean on, stooping over a little.

I reached over and got the muskrat and stuffed it in the pocket of my mackinaw coat. I wasn't going to lose my one muskrat after all the trouble. My teeth chattered and my bones jerked with pain.

I'D WALKED TO the edge of the Flat Woods by sunup. But I seen it would take me all day to hobble back home. The wind was icy and hard along the ridge when I finally made it to the top. But I was soaked with sweat under my mackinaw coat, and my armpit against the crutch was getting sore. When I stopped, my foot hurt even worser than it did when I was moving. It was a black, sick pain coming up the side of my leg, a tearing pain like a bone was being scraped with a hacksaw.

"Ha-ha," somebody hollered at me. I looked around to see who could be laughing at my clumsy efforts to walk. But if there was anybody, they was hiding behind a tree. And wind made it hard to hear anybody moving.

"Ha-ha," they called again. I looked around the woods, and I twisted and looked back up the ridge. Was somebody following me and hiding from tree to tree? The pain was so harsh it made the air seem full of shadows.

"Who is there?" I hollered, and sweat dripped into my eyes. "Who is following me?"

Wind tickled through the leaves on the mountainside and rattled the laurel bushes. "Ha-ha," the voice called again. I looked up to see a crow flap out of an oak tree behind me. The bird was black as the devil hisself. "Ha-ha," it called when it lit in another oak further up the ridge, like it was the woods theirselves that was mocking me.

"Please, Lord," I said, "let me get back to the house." I hadn't prayed in a long time. I hadn't prayed since I'd tried to preach at church and made a fool of myself. Thought I had give up praying, but the words just come without me thinking. I was in such pain I wasn't able to think anyway. It was like the prayer was on my tongue without me knowing it.

"Ha-ha," something called again. I looked around for the teasing crow but seen instead a horse's head come through the laurel bushes.

"Ha-ha," a voice called. The horse pulled to the left and I seen Hank Richards setting up on a wagon. "Ha-ha," he called.

I pushed myself back away from the trail and raised the crutch so he could see me. "Whoa!" he called. "Whoa there."

I tried to stand up but was too weak and trembly to make it. Hank jumped down off the wagon and spit out his tobacco. He was wearing a red wool mackinaw coat. "What are you doing here?" he said.

"Turned my ankle," I said, "back on Grassy Creek."

"What was you doing on Grassy Creek?"

"Going to my traps," I said.

"That's a right smart distance," Hank said. He helped me to climb up on the wagon seat. I ignored the pain, now there was somebody watching. Hank put the shotgun and crutch in the back of the wagon, where there was four dead turkeys. He had been hunting beyond Long Rock.

"Giddyup," Hank hollered. The trail was so narrow we had to lean under the limbs of laurels and birch trees. The turkey heads was ugly as the pain in my ankle.

"You don't know how glad I am to see you," I said.

"It's just a chance I come this way," Hank said.

"It's a piece of luck you did," I said.

"Usually go by Pinnacle or Poplar Springs," Hank said. "But something whispered to me I ought to go down by the trail to the river."

"Whispered to you?" I said.

"The Lord must have hinted to me," Hank said.

Hank was not only Annie's daddy, he was a deacon of the Green River Church, and sometimes he held prayer meetings and even led in singing at revivals hisself. He was a carpenter who worked away a lot on jobs, so you didn't see too much of him. In winter he liked to hunt deer and turkeys. I almost laughed at his notion that something whispered to him. But I was mighty grateful to be riding in the wagon. I remembered I'd prayed without quite intending to, and here a few minutes later Hank Richards come by with his wagon. I was beholden to him.

"Awful glad you come this way," I said.

"The Lord works in mysterious ways," Hank said.

The pain in my foot throbbed worse once I was setting down. The wagon jolted on rocks and banged on holes in the trail. Every jolt sent waves of hurt through my foot and leg.

"Are you still planning to preach?" Hank said.

Hank had been there when I tried to preach at the Green River Church last year and people had laughed. He was the first deacon to mention it to me.

"Ain't preached no more," I said. The pain give me courage to admit the truth. "I'm afraid I ain't got the call."

"The call might still come," Hank said. "The Lord's timing may be different from ours."

"My timing was way off," I said. My face felt hot in the cold air. I was embarrassed to be talking with Annie's daddy about my humiliation. Hank was the first person that had mentioned it to me. I couldn't decide if he was being rude or friendly.

"The Lord will lead you," Hank said. "The Lord looks after his own."

It was getting up in the evening. It had took me much of the day to walk myself to the top of the ridge and then back down to the head of the river. My lips felt dry and my throat was dry. In the cold wind my lips felt like they was going to crack. The pain had dried me out and parched me inside.

When we passed the spring below the Evans place Hank stopped the wagon. "Bet you could use a drink," he said. It was like he could read my thoughts. He jumped off the wagon and scrambled down the bank and come back with a coffee can full of water.

I was so thirsty I held the water in my mouth before swallowing it. And then it hurt as it went down my throat. My belly wanted the water so bad it hurt when the cool trickle went down.

"You have saved my life," I said to Hank when we started again.

"We don't get nowhere without we help each other," Hank said.

I'd heard talk like that all my life, but for the first time it meant something. I'd heard Mama talk that way, but it hadn't seemed important. But now I seen how true it was. People could only get along by helping each other. There wasn't no other way. I didn't even resent that Hank had asked about my preaching, I was so grateful to him. I seen he wasn't trying to hurt my feelings.

"We don't have to do nothing fancy to serve the Lord," Hank said as the wagon rattled over the rough road.

It was already dark when we got to the house. Hank drove the wagon right up to the edge of the yard and Mama come to the door to see who was there. Then she run out into the yard holding her elbows in the cold wind.

S i x
Muir

"Honey, you look half dead," Mama said.

I dropped the crutch on the porch and she helped me into the living room. Fay and Moody come in from the kitchen, where they'd been eating supper. "Did you cut your leg?" Fay said. She wiped her mouth with the end of her apron.

"Bet a muskrat bit his toe," Moody said.

Mama helped me into a chair by the fireplace.

"Is your leg broke?" Fay said.

"It's just a sprain," I said.

I started unlacing my boot and felt the tightness under the leather. It hurt just to touch it, and it hurt when you didn't touch it.

"That boot'll have to be cut off," Moody said.

"No!" I said.

Moody took out his knife, which he always kept whetted like a razor.

"You can't cut leather with a knife," Mama said.

"Leave the boot alone," I said. "I can get it off."

"Don't want his fancy boots cut," Moody said. He lit the stub of a cigar he'd left on the mantel. "How much did them boots cost?" he said. "A winter's worth of skins?"

Mama took the scissors from Fay. She pulled out the laces of the boot and looked for a place to start cutting. There was no easy place to start. The golden oiled leather was sewed tight.

"Just cut the tongue," I said. "If you cut the tongue the boot will come off."

Mama started snipping the leather of the tongue. It hurt whenever the scissors touched my skin.

"Now help me pull," Mama said to Moody. Moody grabbed my boot and jerked it with a twist. It hurt so bad I thought I was going to black out. We all looked at the boot in Moody's hands like we expected it to be full of blood or holding a piece of my foot. But there wasn't any blood on the boot, and there wasn't any blood on my sock either. The sock was stained by wet leather was all.

Mama started pulling off the sock, and that hurt like she was peeling off the skin. My ankle was swole so bad it looked a little crooked.

"Wiggle your toes," Mama said. I wiggled my toes through the stiff pain. "Nothing's broke as far as I can tell," Mama said.

"Ain't that a pretty leg," Moody said.

While Moody stood by the fire and smoked his cigar, Mama washed the foot and ankle. They kept swelling up and you would have thought the washing made them bigger. The boot had kept down the swelling. And the pain was getting worser, the more it swole up. I would not have thought a foot could give you so much pain when there wasn't any bones broke and the skin wasn't even cut. Only the warm water seemed to give any comfort, and the heat from the fireplace.

"Get me some aspirins," Mama said to Fay. Mama kept her aspirins on the shelf in the closet with the herbs and other medicines.

"I don't think aspirins will do any good," I said.

"Moody, bring me some of your liquor," Mama said.

"Who says I got any liquor?" Moody said.

"Bring the jug here," Mama said.

We all knowed Moody kept some liquor near the house. Sometimes he hid the jug in an old boot, and sometimes under a pile of old quilts. When Moody brought the jug and handed it to Mama he said, "You're welcome," and then he turned to me. "Now you've got a good excuse to drink my liquor," he said.

I'VE ALWAYS THOUGHT the small hours was a deep, tender, and terrible time. Late at night all the fat and sweetness of things are gone, and you feel hard up against the cold bare facts. If you think too much in the wee hours your life don't seem worth nothing. Late at night you feel stripped down to the bone and facing the emptiness and awfulness of the world.

After everybody went to bed, the aspirin took away some of the pain, but it didn't take away the scare and trouble in my mind. Everything I thought of was terrible, my traps rusting in the water of Grassy Creek, muskrats and mink rotting in their jaws. I thought of all the things Mama had said to me about wasting my time, and they wasn't as bad as the things I'd said to myself. I didn't know what I wanted to be, and I didn't know what I could be.

Wherever I cast my mind, I couldn't find any hope. There was nothing on Green River that had any hope in it. Even if I done everything Mama wanted me to do, it would just mean working on the place, hoeing corn and splitting wood, like Daddy did. There was nothing interesting I could foresee. And long as I stayed there I'd be fighting with Moody and angry with Mama.

I was going to have to get away, to the North, to Canada or Alaska, to Minnesota, where I could start over, where the fur was better and more plentiful, where there was all kinds of fur, beaver and lynx, marten and otter, wolverine and bear. I wanted to go as far as I could from Green River. I had to change the way I was doing things, if I was ever going to amount to something.

To pass the time that night I got two of Grandpa's books off the mantel. One was an old book by James Gibbs called *A Book of Architecture*. It had designs for churches with very high steeples, and drawings of other fancy buildings too. Since I was a boy I had liked to look through that book. I especially liked to study the drawings of churches with steeples that went up to the clouds. The other book was one Grandpa had ordered just before he died. It was called *Mont-Saint-Michel and Chartres* and was by somebody named Henry Adams. It talked all about the fancy buildings of the Middle Ages, about cathedrals in France and how they was built and why they was built. I liked to browse in the book just to hear all the fine things he had to say, though I had never read the book all the way through.

I opened the Adams book to a page: ". . . and then, with pain and sorrow, you will have to toil till you see how the architects of 1200 subordinated every other problem to that of lighting their spaces. Without feeling their lights, you can never feel their shadows." It was the kind of sentence I liked, about feeling shadows, about buildings as living things.

I flipped through the book and come to another passage Grandpa had marked a few pages later: "The spire is the simplest part of the Romanesque or Gothic architecture, and needs least study in order to be felt. It is a bit of sentiment almost pure of practical purpose. It tells the whole of its story at a glance, and its story is the best that architecture had to tell, for it typified the aspirations of man at the moment when man's aspirations were highest." That was my favorite passage.

I turned the pages and seen Adams talking about cathedrals "flinging stones against the sky." I looked at the drawings of floor plans in the book and listened to the wind troubling the hemlock trees. If only I could build something myself and not just waste my time. Even the pain in my foot would be worth it, if it showed me the right thing to do.

S e v e n
Ginny

MOODY NEVER WOULD talk about what happened that night down at Peg Early's. He wasn't the kind of boy that would tell you how he felt when he was hurt or angry. He would always try to act rough, like nothing had happened. Ever since Tom died it was like he lived his life in secret, hiding even from hisself.

After we brought him home that day from Possum Holler and U. G. and me helped him out of the truck into the house, Moody just stayed in the bedroom and wouldn't come out. When I went in with a pan of warm water and a rag and towel to clean him up, he rolled over and laid there with his legs together.

"You got to be cleaned up," I said.

"Leave the pan," Moody said. "I'll wash myself."

"You ought to see a doctor," I said.

"Won't see no doctor!"

I told Moody he was too sore to wash hisself, but he didn't answer. I knowed he'd lost a lot of blood and was too weak to do anything but lay there. I left the pan on the night table and brought him some aspirins. It was the only thing I had for the pain except liquor. I didn't want to give Moody any liquor.

It grieved me to know he was hurting so bad and there was so little I could do. Muir and Moody slept in the same bed, but I told Muir to sleep on the sofa while Moody was in such awful shape. Moody needed to rest, and he needed to not be bothered.

"How did Moody hurt hisself?" Muir asked.

I didn't feel like I could tell Muir, who was only thirteen and not liable to understand such things. If Moody didn't want it knowed and bruited about, I would say as little as I could and still tell the truth.

"Moody got in a fight in Chestnut Springs," I said.

"Did Moody get cut with a knife?" Fay said.

"Maybe he did," I said.

I never seen the cut on his groin because Moody wouldn't let me touch him. He wouldn't let anybody touch him. He was sixteen years old and tall as a man, and I couldn't tear his clothes off to see his wounds. He was like a dog that has crawled into a cellar to either die or heal itself. I reckon he might have wanted to die them first days and nights he was home.

I woke in the middle of the night and heard a sound like water running. Had it started raining in the night and the water was spilling off the eaves? I listened and didn't hear no rain on the roof. There wasn't no rain pattering on the window. The springhouse was too far away to hear the water spilling from the pipe. And the branch was much too far away to hear the water rippling and bubbling between its banks. You could hear the waterfall over on the creek sometimes at night, but this wasn't a roar like a waterfall.

The mumbling and murmuring stopped and then started again. I got up and put on my robe and went out to the hall. Muir was asleep on the couch and breathing steady. The sound was coming from the other end of the house, not the kitchen or living room. I tiptoed down the hall to the other bedroom door and listened. The noise was coming from there all right.

Was Moody talking to hisself? Would he be praying on his own in the dark? I put my ear to the door and my heart stopped when I heard a sob. It was a sob muffled by blankets. It was a sob held in as much as it could be held in. I couldn't go away and just leave Moody crying to hisself in the dark. I opened the door and stepped into the room. The crying stopped.

"Moody," I said, "is there anything I can do?"

There wasn't no sound from the bed. I reckon Moody laid as still as he could. I wanted to reach out and touch him in the dark. I wanted to hold him in my arms the way I done when he was a little boy. I felt my way to the edge of the bed and set down on it.

"I feel for your hurt," I said.

"Don't matter," Moody said, his voice hoarse.

"It matters a lot to me," I said.

"Don't nothing matter no more," Moody said, sounding like his nose was snuffed up.

I thought, This is a change in Moody. Now he is going to open up and talk about what happened to him. Now that he is letting out some of the pain, he'll feel better. I knowed the best way to heal the sorrow was to grieve hard as you could and tell somebody how bad it felt.

"You matter to us that love you," I said and reached out to Moody in the dark. But soon as he felt my hand on his shoulder he jerked away. He covered hisself up with the blanket and wouldn't let me touch him.

I thought if I said the right thing to Moody I could pick the lock in his armor. I thought if I could melt just one little clot that was blocking the flow of his feelings, he would pour out his grief to me and begin to heal. But he never said another word. The more I tried to comfort him the more he closed hisself off. He had just spoke twice, then closed hisself up again like a terrapin. I seen there was no use to try to pester him or beg him to talk. He would have to decide to talk hisself. I set on the bed for nigh onto an hour and Moody never moved or spoke again.

AFTER A FEW days, when Moody was feeling a little better, I seen Muir carrying a pencil and piece of paper from a school tablet into the bedroom. When he come out I asked him what the page was for.

"Moody wants to write a letter," Muir said.

Now Moody never was one to write letters, though he could pen a fine neat hand when he wanted to. In school he had the best hand-writing of anybody in the class, and he had the best hand of anybody in the family. I asked Muir who Moody wanted to write to, but Muir said he wouldn't tell. Muir said Moody had made him promise not to show anybody the letter.

I was curious because I thought Moody might be writing to the sheriff or the revenue or to Peg Early. I didn't try to ask Moody or Muir about the letter, but I kept my eyes open. Everything Moody did was a mystery, but I needed to find out what was going on. I didn't hear no more about the letter, and when I went into the bedroom that evening to take Moody his supper I didn't see the pencil or paper. But the next morning, when I passed Muir's coat where it hung on a nail beside the kitchen door, I seen an envelope in the pocket. I looked around to see if anybody was watching, and I slipped the envelope out. The address was wrote in pencil in Moody's neat hand.

To: Josie Revis
At Peg Early's
Chestnut Springs, South Carolina

I slipped the letter back into the coat pocket, careful to not bend or wrinkle it. My throat got tight, thinking of Moody writing to that girl that got so bad beat up for helping him and loving him. My heart felt like somebody had stomped it with their boots.

The week after Moody wrote the letter and Muir mailed it, I went to the mailbox every day to get the mail. There never was no letter from Josie, or anybody else, not that I seen. It's possible that Muir got up to the mailbox before I did and took whatever letter come for Moody, but I doubt it. I don't think Josie ever got his letter, and if she did she never answered it. If there had been a letter I would have seen it in the bedroom or throwed out in the trash. A letter might have cheered Moody up. But Moody just stayed sullen and angry and never did talk about his condition. He had scabs on his face and arms, and the scabs got hard and peeled off.

Now, both Drayton and Wheeler come to see Moody a time or two, and they could have brought Moody a letter without me seeing it. But I don't think they did. If they had brought a letter Moody would have acted different.

What they did bring Moody was a drink, for when I went into the bedroom after they left I could smell it. It was that musty smell of old plums that has fell into the grass and rotted. And Moody seemed a little happier. He must have had the bottle in the bed, for I couldn't find it when I come in to sweep the floor and dust the shelf. I opened the curtains to let sunlight fill the sickroom, and I swept the dust balls from under the bed. I reckon he had the bottle under his pillow or between his legs, for I never did see it.

When Drayton come back to see Moody, I pulled him into the kitchen. "Now you ain't going to give Moody no liquor, are you? He don't need no liquor."

"No ma'am," Drayton said. But the next time I went into the room the smell of liquor was even stronger. I figured the liquor might be helping Moody get well, so I let it go.

After about a week Moody got up and started walking. He walked stiff like his joints was made of cardboard. And it hurt him to set down, I could see that. He winced and grabbed hold of the arms when he set down in the rocker. But he limped out to the porch and back, and then out to the barn and back. He limped as far as the springhouse. He must have had some liquor hid out there, for I could smell it on his breath when he come back in. But there was never no letter come for him.

Eight

Muir

IT SURPRISED ME as my foot healed to see how helpful Fay was. She brought me coffee, and she brought me dinner where I set in the chair. She had always seemed to favor Moody before, but I reckon my sprained foot made her feel friendly toward me. Before, she had just teased me and made fun of my drawings and my planning. Maybe she was just growing up a little. But she was still so skinny she didn't fill out the new dresses Mama made her.

When she drove to town with Moody in the Model T, Fay bought me a tablet of drawing paper and some colored pencils at the dime store.

"Now you can draw a castle in Alaska," Fay said, "or maybe a tower like the one Rapunzel is locked in."

For several days I sketched plan after plan, until my foot was well enough to hobble on.

I'd been thinking about how I was going to get back to my traps. The Model T was half mine. I'd paid a hundred dollars on it, all the money I'd saved from selling pelts and ginseng the year before. Moody didn't have but seventy-five dollars and Mama had paid for the rest. It was my car and Mama's car as much as it was his, but because Moody was older and because he'd learned to drive first, he got to use the car more than me. The Model T set in the shed by the crib where we used to keep our buggy, and whenever he felt like it, Moody cranked the car up and drove down to Chestnut Springs to get liquor or to gamble in one of the joints there. Sometimes he come back with another black eye or a cut on his face or arm.

By Saturday I could walk pretty good on my right foot. It itched and was sore a little. I could get around, but there was no way I could walk all the way to Grassy Creek and back. I seen that what I should do was drive the Model T to Blue Ridge Church or Cedar Mountain. From there I could walk the two or three miles to the creek and check all my traps, or at least some of them. And it was better to go on Saturday and not wait till Monday, when whatever was in the traps would be in even worse condition.

When I told Moody I was going to take the car, he said, "You ain't, no way in hell."

"That car's half mine," I said.

"I've got to go to Chestnut Springs," Moody said.

"You go to Chestnut Springs every Saturday," I said.

"And I'm going this Saturday too," Moody said.

"I have to check my trapline," I said.

"Then you walk it, little brother."

"I paid more on that car than you did," I said.

"I'm the driver of this car," Moody said.

"You think nobody but you can drive it?" I said.

Moody looked me hard in the eye. "That car is going to Chestnut Springs," he said.

"Not on Saturday," I said. I was as big as Moody now, and I was determined not to let him run over me no more.

Saturday morning when I went out to start the Model T I seen all the tires was flat. The casings had been slashed with a knife. I looked at the tires, and I looked at the patching kit. Even if I took the tires off to patch the inner tubes there was only three cold patches left.

When I went back to the house and told Mama what had happened she set her mouth in a grimace and shook her head. "The devil is having his way with Moody," she said.

"Moody is the devil," I said.

"He gets mad and can't help hisself," Mama said. Like any mama, she always tried to see the good in her children. When Moody done something bad she always said it was because he couldn't control hisself. I figured he was mean because he wanted to be.

Moody was nowhere to be found. He must have left early in the morning to walk down to Chestnut Springs, or he might have got a ride with one of his buddies like Wheeler Stepp or Drayton Jones.

"What are you going to do?" Fay said. It scared her when me and Moody got in a fuss, but it also seemed to thrill her a little.

"Somebody ought to teach Moody a lesson," I said.

"Don't talk like that," Mama said. "Moody is your brother. He needs your prayers, not a fight. Forgiveness is the test of a Christian. Moody has got anger in him. He blames the world, and he blames me."

"Don't matter how he got that way," I said.

MOODY WAS GONE all that Saturday. I thought he must have walked to Chestnut Springs or Gap Creek with one of his buddies. It was a mystery where he got money for liquor and gambling and carousing at the joints in South Carolina. Except for selling molasses and a few eggs for Mama, he never did anything to raise cash. But he always seemed to have enough in his pockets to get what he wanted, and he was gone a lot.

I spent all morning patching three of the tires while Fay walked down to U. G.'s store to sell some eggs and get new patches. I could have rode the horse down to the store, but it was better not to jump on or off the horse with my ankle still stiff and sore. I always hated patching tubes because of the stink of the rubber and the glue. I was slow at it and had to keep reading directions on the box. As I worked I got madder, thinking of what I was going to do to Moody when he come back.

Setting out in the sun where I could see the rubber better, I found the knife cuts in the tubes and one by one stuck the pink patches over the slits. But when I got the first one done and fitted the tube in the casing, and the casing over the wheel, and tried to pump it up, the tube still hissed air. Had to take it off and find the extra slit, put another patch on that, and try all over again. I got so mad I throwed the patches and the inner tube into the weeds, then had to crawl around on my knees in the stubble to find all the pieces.

By the time the tires was fixed it was late afternoon, too late to drive to the Flat Woods and check my traps before dark. Hard enough to see traps and reset them in daylight, much less after dark with a stiff, healing ankle.

Soon as I got the tires fixed I heard somebody walk into the yard. Turning around, I seen it was Moody. He'd been drinking. I could tell by the glitter in his eyes and the way he walked.

"I'm surprised you got gall enough to show your face," I said.

"Now hold it," he said and waved his arm like he was trying to slow down an oncoming car.

"Ain't you a fine son of a bitch," I said.

"Now just hold on," Moody said.

"You have showed your ass," I said.

"I know, I'm just a dog," Moody said. "Ain't nothing but a dog." He didn't show any fight like I expected. He was good and drunk and loose as a rag doll.

"You ought to have your ass kicked from here to the river," I said. I looked to see if he had a knife in his hand.

"Here, kick it, go ahead," Moody said. He unbuckled his overalls and pulled them down and turned his bare hind end to me.

"I wouldn't dirty my toe on your rusty ass," I said.

"Come on, kick me," Moody hollered. He almost fell over but caught his balance and then lost it again. He crawled with one hand and his overalls down around his ankles. "If there was a manure pile here I'd roll myself in it to show what a dog I am," he said.

"Quit acting stupid," I said. "My trapline is ruined. Don't matter that you're sorry."

"Ain't no money in furs," Moody said.

"More than in drinking," I said.

Moody staggered to his feet but didn't pull up his overalls. He hobbled across the yard, closer to me. "You can make ten times what you do with furs," he said.

"How?" I said. "By stealing it?"

"I'll show you," Moody said. "I owe it to you."

"You owe me for the tires and for all the furs in my traps," I said.

"I'll show you how to make ten times that much," Moody said.

"By bootlegging?" I said.

"Who said anything about bootlegging?" Moody said. "All you have to do is drive a car."

"Get away from me," I said. I hit him with my fist. I hit him hard as I could, in the chest, right over the heart. And it was like he was expecting it, like he wanted to be hit. He staggered back and fell to the ground with his overalls still around his ankles.

I didn't go after him again. He had took me by surprise by not trying to dodge or hit back. I looked again to see if he reached for his knife.

"You can hit me all you want," Moody said, like he was too drunk to care about pain. "I'm going to do the Christian thing. I'm going to help you out."

"You can't help me out," I said.

"You can make enough to buy new traps and a new rifle," Moody said. He looked at me sideways, like he was cross-eyed he was so drunk. "And you can make enough to buy a tool set, or more drawing paper." It was like the liquor had made him think, made him smarter. "Or you can make enough to leave here," he said, "to go someplace else like Canada and trap." It was like he could read my mind. I hadn't thought Moody paid enough attention to know how much I dreamed of buying a .30-30 rifle and of leaving Green River.

"I won't have nothing to do with bootlegging," I said.

"You don't have to have nothing to do with bootlegging," Moody said. He set in the dirt with his overalls below his knees. I'd never seen him look so ridiculous. But he didn't seem to care. I had to laugh. I pointed at his dirty long-handles and laughed.

"How much can I make?" I kept laughing.

"Ten dollars."

"Just for driving the car?" I played along, like I was considering it.

"Just for driving the car," Moody said, and laughed too. "You couldn't make ten dollars in a month of trapping."

"And what if I'm arrested?" I said.

"You can't be arrested for driving a car," Moody said, "unless you drive into a police car, or kill somebody."

"Why do you think I'd go with you?" I said.

"Because you need the money," Moody said. "And because you want to help me out. We're brothers, we help each other out."

"Since when? Are you in trouble?" I said.

"Ain't no trouble," Moody said, "if I can get to Chestnut Springs. Get me out of this and I won't ever ask you again. There ain't nobody else I can ask, except my brother."

"What if I don't help you?" I said.

"Then it will be on your conscience," Moody said.

MAMA WAS SURPRISED when I went into the house and told her I was going to drive Moody down to South Carolina. I was surprised too. I'd never gone with him to Chestnut Springs or Gap Creek. I don't think I agreed just because I needed the money. I think it was mostly that I wanted to patch up the quarrel with Moody. While he was being so agreeable I wanted to be friends, even if he was drunk. We had fought so much, I needed to patch it up. I felt guilty because I'd hit him and he hadn't fought back. And I was curious to see what he was doing.

I reckon Mama seen Moody was in no condition to drive hisself. He never even come in, but leaned on the gatepost waiting for me.

"You be careful," Mama said. She was frying up tater cakes for supper.

"Ain't I always careful?" I said.

"No, you're not," Mama said.

"Don't let Muir go," Fay said.

"Nobody asked you," I said to Fay.

"He'll just get in trouble," Fay said.

But I think Mama was relieved that Moody and me wasn't fighting no more. She was so pleased to see us making plans and working together she didn't really raise a fuss.

"Don't you want to come?" I said to Fay.

"Ha," Fay said.

I CRANKED UP the Model T, and Moody got in the passenger seat. He had buckled up his overalls and his mood had got better once he knowed I was going to take him to South Carolina. He pulled a jar out from under the seat and took a drink. Then he held out the jar to me, but I shook my head.

"That's right, little brother, stay away from demon rum," Moody said, "especially when you're driving."

It was just getting dark. I switched the headlights on. A rabbit bounced into the road, saw the headlights, and bounded along in front of us like it was afraid to leave the road. I felt scared as that rabbit, and I didn't know what I was doing any more than it did.

As WE TURNED down the highway toward South Carolina I wished I hadn't come. I wished I'd gone to my traps and was setting by the fire skinning muskrats and mink and stretching the hides on boards.

Once we crossed the state line the highway looked like it was going down into a pit. Poplars hung over the road where it run down the edge of Possum Holler, toward the curves and switchbacks of the Winding Stairs that led down into the holler of Chestnut Springs.

"Turn here," Moody said.

"Turn where?" I said.

"Right there, damn it," Moody said. He pointed to a little dirt road that connected the highway to Gap Creek.

"Thought we was going to Chestnut Springs," I said.

"You thought wrong," Moody said.

The road to Gap Creek was rough as a gully. It was washed out in places and had big rocks standing up in the middle of the routes. And even in flat stretches it was pitted as a cob. The Model T hammered on the ruts.

"What if we break an axle?" I said.

"Then we'll have to walk home," Moody said. He took another drink from the jar.

We passed a few houses with lamplight in their windows, but it was wild country we was driving into. It was the edge of Dark Corner, the wildest section of the mountains. We passed deserted cabins. In one place a creek run right across the road.

"Stop here," Moody said. All I could see was a big rock leaning out over the road with laurel bushes thick around it. I stopped the car and Moody got out and walked back up the road. I heard him talking to somebody. They spoke in low voices, and then I heard Moody holler out, "You damn right!" There was more mumbling, and then he yelled, "You're damn straight!"

I wondered if I should get out and see what was going on, but I knowed Moody wouldn't want me to take part in whatever argument he was having. And I didn't want to be seen by whoever it was either. Then the passenger door opened and Moody said, "Help me load these." I left the car idling and got out.

In the dark behind the car I couldn't see nothing at first. The woods closed over the road and there was a waterfall close by. In the glow of the taillight I expected to see whoever Moody had been talking to. But there was nobody in sight except Moody. He struck a match, and then I seen the big cans, the size of milk cans. They was five-gallon cans like dairies put milk in.

"Put these in the back," Moody said.

"On the backseat?" I said.

"No, on the back bumper," he snapped.

I lugged one to the car and hoisted it into the backseat. It was heavy, more than eighty or a hundred pounds. "What are you going to do with these?" I said. I knowed it was liquor in them.

"You don't need to know," Moody said. He was all business now, all sobered up.

We loaded the cans in the car and then I turned the car around and started back up the rough narrow road. Never did see who Moody bought the cans from. The Model T hesitated on the bumps with its new load.

"You're going to have to help me carry them," Moody said when we got almost to the highway.

"You said all I had to do was drive," I said.

"The plan has changed," Moody said.

"I won't do it," I said and gripped the steering wheel.

"You ain't got no choice," Moody said.

"I don't have to do nothing," I said.

"We can't drive out on the highway with this load," Moody said. "The law will be waiting for us."

I SEEN MOODY'S plan all along was for us to carry the liquor across the mountain into North Carolina so he would not be caught crossing the state line with the blockade. It was the South Carolina sheriff he was afraid of.

It was hard to carry those cans up the ridge and down the other side. It would have been a man's job to carry one up the steep trail in the dark. But two was work for a giant. I was out of breath and sweating before I got a third of the way up the slope. And my foot was still sore. But Moody carried a can in each hand ahead of me and never did stop. We couldn't use a light and had to let our eyes get used to the dark. Carrying a heavy weight in the dark is twice as hard as carrying it in daylight. I stumbled on rocks in the steep trail and banged into trees. But Moody knowed the way and he kept on going. That's when I seen again how tough he was. He was lighter than me, and he'd been drinking all day, but he kept going up the mountain like the cans didn't weigh nothing. He was doing what he wanted to do, what he had to do. I couldn't even catch up with him.

By the time we got down the other side of the mountain to the highway, I was plumb wore out. I set the cans down in the bushes and Moody dropped down on the ground. "You go back for the car and drive it up here," he said.

"What are you going to do?" I said.

"I'm going to wait right here," Moody said, "to make sure nothing happens to the merchandise."

"I don't even know the way back," I said.

"The great woodsman and trapper can't find his way?" Moody said. "All right, you've got *twenty* bucks at the end of this trapline."

I started back up the ridge, feeling my way a step at a time, pulling myself up on trees and laurel bushes. It was impossible to see the trail, but if I hit brush or deep leaves I stopped and changed direction. There was a little traffic on the highway below, and that helped me keep a sense of direction. When I got to the top, I rested again and looked at the stars above the trees. It seemed so strange to be doing what I was. I wished I was out in the woods on my own, camping.

When I finally got back to the Model T, I cranked it and turned on the lights. The little road looked bleached and sparkling to my eyes that had got used to the dark. It was only a few hundred yards to the highway, and I had no sooner turned onto the paved road than I seen the black-and-white car parked on the shoulder. It was a police car. The spit froze in the back of my mouth. I steered careful past the car and seen the siren on top. I'd always heard you had to pay off the South Carolina sheriff. It didn't look like Moody had paid them anything, since we had to lug the cans all the way across the mountain into North Carolina.

I'd just got beyond the police car when its lights come on. Never seen such bright lights as them that flared in my mirror. They was so big they seemed to scorch away the night and blind me. The car with its scalding lights followed me and come up close.

Now what am I supposed to do? I thought. And then I remembered there wasn't any cans in the car. Unless Moody had left his jar under the seat there wasn't any liquor in the Model T. But he probably had left the jar there. I'd never been stopped by a deputy sheriff before. My life was changing all upside-down that night.

A red light started flashing, and I heard the siren like a squawk turning into a shriek that become a whistle. I didn't see no place to pull off the pavement, so I slowed down but kept going. The siren screamed louder. I put on the brakes and stopped in the road. My feet was shaking on the pedals.

A man in uniform come to the window and I rolled it down. "Out of the car," he said.

I turned the key and got out on the highway. My knees was wobbling so bad I was afraid I would fall. The climb up the mountain had strained my healing ankle. There was two deputies, and they both had flashlights.

"Thought you would head back to North Carolina?" one of them said.

"Yes, sir," I said.

"With a little product of Gap Creek," the other one said.

"No, sir," I said.

They was both big heavy men, and they acted like they was used to giving orders. They looked in the backseat, and they looked under the seats. They found Moody's liquor jar under the passenger seat, but it was empty. They searched in the glove compartment, and they looked under the hood and under the car.

"Where have you got it hid, boy?" one said.

"Nowhere," I said.

The other one opened the gas tank and sniffed.

"You didn't go down to Gap Creek for an empty fruit jar," the first deputy said.

"Got friends down there," I said.

"I think we got a sassy boy here," the other one said.

"Are you a sassy boy?" the first deputy said.

They made me lean up against the car and they patted me down and searched my pockets. All I had in my pockets was my knife.

"Are you related to Moody Powell by any chance?" the other one said.

"Might be," I said.

"Where is Moody tonight?"

"Don't know," I said.

"This is Moody's car," the first deputy said.

"Me and Moody own it together," I said. "He's my brother."

"We're going to keep an eye on you," the first officer said. "Like we keep an eye on Moody and Wheeler and Drayton." Before I knowed what was happening he kicked my feet out from under me and I fell hard on my knees on the pavement. My ankle hurt like a nail had been drove through the bone.

"You don't want to come back to Gap Creek," the second deputy said.

"Now get out of here," the other one said.

• • •

WHEN I REACHED the gap and turned off under the poplars there, Moody didn't appear until I switched the lights off. Suddenly he was at the window. "Where the hell you been?" he said.

"Been talking to the deputy sheriffs," I said. "They was looking for you."

"They didn't find nothing," Moody said.

"I ought to beat the hound out of you," I said.

"Is he mad?" Moody said in baby talk. "Is my widdle bwother going to cwy like a baby?"

"What if I'd been arrested?" I said.

"Be good for your preaching career," Moody said. "Lots of preachers have been to jail."

We loaded the cans in the backseat and waited for a big truck to groan and grumble up the mountain, gearing down for the worst grades and then gearing up again. The truck seemed to take forever to reach the gap and pass, but it finally did and we watched the taillights as it started down the other side.

"Now where?" I said.

Moody took a drink from a bottle he had in his pocket. "Go where I tell you," he said.

"Where are you telling me?" I said.

"I'll tell you when you need to know," he said.

"Do I go north, boss?" I said.

"No, we're going to take it back to South Carolina, you fool," Moody said.

I pulled onto the highway and started up the long grade toward the Green River valley. The Model T rode smooth and low with the load in the back. I figured Moody was taking the cans up to Cedar Springs to unload somewhere near Wheeler's house. Or maybe up on Mount Olivet, closer to where Drayton lived. We was rounding the last curve before you go straight down toward the river when I seen the police car in the driveway of the summer house built by Mr. Leland, the cotton mill big shot from Spartanburg.

"I thought that car turned back," I said.

"It's the North Carolina sheriff, you idiot," Moody said.

The patrol car turned on its flashing lights just as we went around the bend.

"Faster," Moody hollered.

"Now what?" I said as the police car got closer and turned on its siren.

"Step on it!" Moody hollered.

"This thing won't outrun the police," I said. I seen the South Carolina deputies had called the Tompkins County sheriff. I felt like I'd been hit in the belly by the end of a two-by-four. The little motor of the Model T *tut-tut-tutt*ed but wouldn't go any faster. I double-clutched and shifted down to second. The road ahead looked steeper than a roof, and in the headlights it stretched out longer and longer.

"When you get to the top you can go faster," Moody said.

"We'll never get to the top," I said. The police car was getting closer and closer. I seen it was a Dodge and could outrun us any day. With its red lights flashing it looked like a dragon blowing fire. I pushed the gas pedal to the floor, but it didn't do no good. I wished I was dead. I wished I was home in bed. I wished I had ignored Moody when he come back drunk and humble.

"Faster!" Moody shouted.

"Why don't you get out and push," I said.

I stomped down on the pedal again, wishing I could pedal the car like a bicycle. A sour brash belched up into my throat.

"When you get to the top, turn onto the logging road," Moody said.

"That don't go nowhere but in the woods," I said.

"It goes to Terry Creek," Moody said.

"What if they shoot out our tires?" I said.

"Won't make no difference on that road," Moody said.

When we finally got to the top of the grade the Dodge was closer than a hundred feet. As it got nearer, a spotlight played over the Model T. The police car got so close its flashing lights seemed to be inside our car. I thought they was going to ram our back bumper. But suddenly the car whipped around and come alongside us. I seen a deputy in the passenger seat holding a pistol and pointing toward the shoulder, ordering me to stop. The police car pressed up against our car, not more than a foot away. The powerful Dodge made the Model T look like a buggy.

"Now what, big brother?" I yelled. There was no way I could turn off on the haul road with the patrol car on my left. The dirt road was only a few hundred yards ahead. If I was arrested with all the liquor in the backseat, I'd be sent to the pen in Atlanta same as if I'd been bootlegging for years. Wouldn't make any difference that I'd never done it before.

"You're so smart, tell me!" I hollered at Moody. He set like he was in a daze and he didn't know what to say.

The sheriff's car was easing ahead, and I seen what they was going to do. They was going to cut us off and force me to stop. I hit the brakes and the police car sailed on past. When we come to a stop I seen what looked like the logging road to the left.

"That's it!" Moody hollered. "Turn!"

The patrol car screeched to a stop a hundred yards ahead, but I didn't wait for it to turn around. I whipped the wheel to the left and run one tire in the ditch and hit a sumac bush. But it was the haul road all right, narrow and growed up with briars. Limbs reached out across the ruts and I shifted down to low.

"Don't slow down!" Moody hollered.

"You want to run through a tree?" I said.

The road was just a faint parting of the brush in places. It turned quick around stumps and rocks. In the yellow headlights it was hard to pick out the routes. Limbs brushed against the windshield and scratched the sides of the Model T. I drove fast as I could, and the car bucked over rocks and potholes like a wild horse. I got banged so hard my foot flew off the pedal several times. I was shook so bad I couldn't see nothing in the mirror.

"Do you see them?" I said to Moody.

He turned around and looked back. "Don't see a thing," he said.

"I ever get out of this I'll never do anything you say again," I said.

"And you'll say your prayers three times a day and read your Bible and kiss Mama good night," Moody said.

The road run across a branch, and water splashed out in feathers on both sides of the car. I thought we must be close to where the logging road run into Terry Creek. The Johnson boys had logged off these woods and the Lewis place three or four years before, and there was rotting logs and stumps and scrub all along the road.

I don't know who seen it first, but there was a glimmer in the rearview mirror just as Moody screamed, "Shit!" The sheriff's car was a good ways behind but still following. I was hoping they'd give up on the logging road. Through all the brush and scrub I could see their lights flashing.

"Damn!" Moody hollered and pounded the dashboard.

"Any new ideas?" I said.

"When you get to the road, turn the lights off," Moody said.

"I can't see where to drive," I said.

"Ain't no other way," Moody said. "Unless you have some wonderful inspiration."

I couldn't tell how far behind the police car really was. It might be half a mile, or it might be a few hundred yards. The lights bounced in and out of sight like they was tossed on waves. The lights turned this way and that way.

"Thing is," Moody said, "don't go near our house, or Wheeler's house."

"I'm not worried about Wheeler," I said.

"If they arrest Wheeler he'll lead them to us," Moody said. "Or his mama will."

For once Moody was thinking clear. Whatever happened, I wanted to stay away from the Green River Road. I never wanted Mama to see me driving a load of corn liquor and running away from the police. And I didn't want Annie, or nobody else, to see me either.

When I finally got to the Terry Creek Road I switched the lights off and turned right. If I could get to the Bobs Creek Road I could head over to Cedar Springs and maybe get from there to Mount Olivet. Or I could lose the police somewhere on the little winding road up to Pinnacle. On the rough narrow roads they couldn't go much faster than we could.

At first I couldn't see a thing in the dark in front of me. It was just a wall of black. I slowed down and eased forward.

"Don't hit the brakes," Moody said.

"I thought of that," I said.

It was like picking out shadows in a deep murky pool. I knowed where the road was but I really couldn't see a thing. It would take a while for me to get my night eyes again. I let the car slow down on its own. A brake light would give us away for sure.

Just as I was beginning to see the gray fringe of the road a little bit, the flashing lights come into view behind. Would they follow us or turn south? I reckon I was holding my breath. My hands was stuck to the steering wheel with sweat. The lights stopped behind me and then disappeared. I started to breathe again. And then all the headlights and flashing lights come into view. They had just gone behind a clump of trees.

"Shit!" Moody screamed and pounded the dashboard again.

"What's your next idea?" I said. I seen I was going to have to think of something quick. Moody was not able to help me. I heard a door open and a breath of cool air washed into the car. I turned to see what had happened. Moody had jumped out of the car while it was rolling slow.

"Hey!" I hollered, but Moody had leapt over the bank and disappeared into the dark.

Now you're really on your own, I said to myself. You have twenty gallons of blockade liquor in the back, and you're driving a car registered in your name as well as Moody's. If you jump out and leave the car, they'll still find you. They'll come to the house and arrest you. I didn't have no choice but to keep going. And I didn't have no choice but to turn the lights on again and drive as fast as I could.

But as the road lit up ahead and the lights shot forward into the night, I had an idea. It probably wouldn't work, but at least it was an idea. I had to stay far enough ahead of the sheriff's Dodge so they couldn't shoot my tires out. And I had to stay far enough ahead so they couldn't see when I turned my lights off again. There might be time for me to get all the way to Mount Olivet.

I drove so fast the Model T leaned on curves and the cans of liquor shifted and rung against each other. I hit rocks and bumps and potholes that sent the car off the ground. I had to stay a good ways ahead of the police. I run up on the bank in one curve below the Shipman place and almost tipped over. And I run out into the edge of Stanley James's field before I found the road again. But I held on like I was on a bucking sled going down a mountainside. I had to make it to where Bobs Creek crossed the road before the patrol car caught up with me. I was thrilled more than I expected to be. I had to beat those cops.

Where the road forded the creek it was shallow, with a rocky bottom. I had crossed there before, I'd waded the creek fishing for trout, and I'd trapped the upper reaches of the creek. I knowed the bottom was mostly bedrock for a quarter of a mile before the first shoals at the foot of the mountain. Soon as I splashed into the ford I switched off my lights, stopped, and turned right.

You damn fool, I thought as the Model T reared up on one side and dropped on the other. The logging road had been a smooth highway compared to the creek bed. The tires jarred on shelves and dipped and banged on separate rocks and over logs. You can't do this, I thought, and pushed the gas harder.

The cans in the backseat leaned and banged against each other. If there had been room they would have tipped over. The car's front end heaved over a lip of rock and then dropped with a splash. If I hit deep mud or quicksand I was finished. The little car shivered and the engine coughed. I let it roll to a stop and waited to see if the patrol car went past.

I figured the ford was maybe a hundred and fifty feet behind me. If the deputies stopped and shined their spotlight down the creek, they could see me. In the dark I didn't dare go any farther. If I hit a really big rock I'd break an axle or the engine block.

I waited for the flashing lights to appear. Had the police turned back? Had they turned out their lights and was they looking for me on the creek bank? I waited and waited so long I had to let my breath out and breathe again. Finally the flashing lights appeared and descended into the ford. The car seemed to stop there. I ducked down my head like they could see me. But when I looked up again the lights was climbing up the other side, and then they went behind the trees. I rolled down the window and listened. The roar of the siren got lower and lower, and then all I could hear was the mumbling and humming of the creek.

Jumping out of the car, I stepped into the creek. The cold water come up to my sore ankle and made it ache. But I didn't have time to worry about my sore foot or favor it. Flinging open the back door, I grabbed one of the cans. There was hazelnut bushes all along the creek, and I backed into the brush and felt my way to a little opening where I put the can down. Splashing through the cold creek, I got the other three into the brush. There was briars and thorns there too and I got raked and cut on my arms and legs.

But what a relief to be rid of the liquor. Without the jugs in the car I didn't even care if the cops stopped me. I backed the Model T up the creek slow as I could without stalling. Every jolt of the car hurt my foot and ankle. Every time a tire dipped into a pool I thought I was stuck. I had to open the door several times and look back to see where I was going. The rearview mirror was useless in the dark.

When I got to the ford I paused and listened for another car. But there was no sound except the murmur of the creek. I swung to the right and turned the lights on and then headed back down the creek road. I knowed it was after midnight. It might have been two in the morning. There was no light in any of the houses I passed. The only lights was flecks of mica in the road, and the eyes of a cat or coon I passed.

But when I reached the forks and turned toward the river, I seen a man ahead. He was walking in the middle of the road, and from the way he lurched I thought he was an old man. As I got closer and slowed down I thought he might be very old or sick from the way he limped and stumbled. And then I seen it was Moody. I stopped with the lights shining on him and hollered, "Get in the car."

He turned and shaded his eyes like he couldn't see a thing. There was blood on his nose and chin. He studied the lights like he didn't know where he was. I pulled on the parking brake and got out to help him into the front seat.

"Where you been?" Moody said, like he couldn't believe I was there. I guess he assumed I'd been arrested.

"I've been around," I said.

"Where is the cans?" he said, like he suddenly remembered.

"Ain't going to tell you," I said.

"Where did the cops go?" he said.

"They're probably to Mount Olivet by now," I said.

Moody shook his head like he still couldn't believe I was there, that I had not been arrested. He had abandoned me, and here I was free as a buzzard.

"Where is the liquor?" Moody said.

"I'll tell you when you pay me," I said.

Moody must have drunk the rest of his liquor, for I didn't see any bottle. "You old son of a bitch," he kept saying, and went to sleep before we got to the Green River Road.

Nine
Muir

IN THE MORNING when I woke up and limped out to the kitchen, Mama looked at me hard, and I felt little as a worm. She looked at me and she looked back at her Bible. "I won't ask where you'uns went last night," she said.

I felt like I'd been beat with a stick, and I felt like I hadn't had a wink of sleep in a week. I wasn't used to being out that late at night, and my ankle was sore like it had been sprained again. I couldn't walk without favoring it.

"You'd have done better to walk to your traps," Mama said.

I poured myself a cup of coffee. I didn't want Mama to know what I'd done. But I figured she had a pretty good idea where we'd been.

"You don't look fit to go to church," Mama said.

"I'm going to church," I said.

"Won't do you no good if you go to sleep during the sermon," Mama said.

"Ain't going to sleep," I said.

"Never thought I'd see both my boys laying out in Chestnut Springs on a Saturday night," Mama said.

"I'll go to church," I said.

"Just going to church is not enough," Mama said. "Your heart has to be open."

I was going to say something silly about cutting open my heart with a knife, but I didn't. No use to make myself even more ashamed.

IT WAS STILL partly dark, but as I passed the shed I could see the mud that had splashed up on the car. Creek mud stuck to the wheels and fenders like dried manure, and dust and trash was stuck to the sides that got wet with creek water.

It was warm and smelly in the cow stall. I looked down into the bucket as I started milking the Jersey named Alice. The smell of the manure and the heat of the cow stopped my head from spinning. I leaned against the cow's side and listened to the rumbling of the belly as I milked. "*Oooooo,*" it said in there under the warm hide.

I'D NEVER LIKED to go to Green River Church any more than other boys did. I liked the hymn singing and I liked the excitement of a good sermon, like everybody does. But most of Preacher Liner's sermons was long and hard and downright sad. Most days you set in church while he rambled on and on about how sinful everybody was and how miserable everybody would be at Judgment Day.

The main reason I didn't like to go to Green River Church was I'd made such a fool of myself trying to preach there. I'd told everybody I wanted to be a preacher, but when I got up there behind the pulpit I couldn't do nothing but sweat and stammer.

Another reason I didn't like Green River Church was the way they'd treated Mama years ago, when she used to attend the Pentecostal Holiness meetings in tents and brush arbors. Before I was born they had a vote at the church and turned her out of the membership. They turned out Uncle Joe and Aunt Lily, and they turned out Grandpa too, and he was the one that give land for the church and had built it in the first place. Who belonged to a church more than the one who give the land and built the church house with his own hands? I wished he had built a bigger church and made it out of rock. A real church ought to be made out of rock.

Mama and Grandpa had kept going to church like nothing had happened, kept paying their tithes like they'd never been throwed out. Eventually the whole thing blowed over and everybody seemed to forget it. And then when I was about seven years old there was another Pentecostal Holiness preacher come through and held meetings in a brush arbor up toward Mount Olivet. Soon as Mama started going to the revival there, the deacons of the church held another meeting and they churched her again. And again she didn't pay them any mind and kept right on going to services same as before.

MAMA TOOK ME to one of those meetings in the brush arbor, and I was scared because I didn't know what was going to happen. I knowed it was the kind of meeting a lot of people didn't approve of and that the pastor warned people against. It was scary walking up the road to Mount Olivet in the dark and turning down the trail into the holler where the brush arbor was. There was lanterns hanging on posts, and horses tied to trees. A bucket of water with a dipper set on a bench.

The brush arbor was a kind of shed made of poles with pine and cedar limbs nailed to the frame. In the lantern light the pine needles gleamed like copper and glass.

The benches in the brush arbor was just boards laid on stumps and blocks of wood. Sawdust had been sprinkled on the ground, and the smell of pine rosin sweetened the air. I set down by Mama on a bench and fished my knife out of my pocket.

"Don't get out your knife in church," Mama said.

"This ain't church," I said.

"It's the same as church," Mama said.

When the preacher stood up in front of the benches he looked like the tallest man I'd ever seen. His name was Preacher Allison, and he was supposed to be a timber man and a Melungeon from over in Tennessee. He had dark skin and black hair, and eyes that darted around.

"When the Spirit moves, it can move a whole population," Preacher Allison said.

"Amen," somebody hollered behind us.

"When the Spirit moves, it can move a whole valley," the preacher said. "For when the Spirit comes it can change the earth and sky like the weather."

"Amen," somebody hollered again.

"When a great revival lights up a valley you can't walk into the place without being touched by the holiness," the preacher said. "A sinner can feel the stirring of the Spirit and conviction as soon as he enters the community. The ground is charged and the air is charged with the spark of the Spirit. And you can feel the joy in the sweet wind over the creek, and in the sunlight on a cornfield and in the wind at night. The water that comes out of the spring in the rock is blessed, and the path you walk to the orchard is blessed."

Preacher Allison didn't wave his arms or walk around the front of the brush arbor. He leaned over us and talked in a quiet steady voice, and it give me the chills. It was the quietness that was scary. I couldn't stand to look at his eyes that was dark and close together as holes at the end of a double-barreled shotgun. I looked away from his face, and then I looked back at his stare in the lantern light.

"You have forgot the joy, and you have forgot the presence of the Savior," Preacher Allison said. "For the Lord said, 'Lo, I am with you alway, even to the end of the world.' And I can feel him right here and right now. Can you feel him? Can you feel his presence? He ain't way off yonder somewhere with the rich people and the powerful people in Washington. No sir. He is right here with you and with you and with you." The preacher pointed at people on one side and then people on the other side. I shivered when he pointed at me.

"Glory," Mama said, and raised her hands on either side of her head. "Glory hallelujah!"

"The sister feels the presence," Preacher Allison said.

I looked at Mama and then I looked away. I'd never seen her act like that. Her eyes was on the preacher and she looked like she'd seen the most wonderful thing. I couldn't see nothing where she was looking but the ugly old preacher. But Mama looked so pleased with what she seen. She rose up and screamed, "Thank you, Jesus, thank you for your blessings!"

The preacher kept looking at Mama, and Mama started talking in a stream. But I couldn't tell what she was saying. It was the strangest talk I'd ever heard, and I knowed it must be speaking in tongues. I'd heard all my life about the gift of tongues. It was what Daddy hated most about the Pentecostal Holiness services. It sounded so awful. The words that come out, the sounds that come out, was like the teeth of a saw in my ears. I put my hands over my ears and looked away. But I could still hear the things Mama was saying.

I looked down at the sawdust, and then I looked at Mama and looked away again. Mama kept talking and I couldn't understand nothing she said. I seen I had to get out of that place. Women was hollering, "Bless you, Ginny!" and men was saying, "Thank you, Jesus," and "Bless the sister in Christ." I couldn't stand the preacher's stare, and I couldn't stand what Mama was saying. It was like she was saying, "Gobble, gobble, gobble."

I reached into my pocket and got my knife out. I opened up the blade and held it in the lantern light. But I didn't know what I meant to do with the knife. I pointed the blade at the preacher, and I pointed it at the lantern beside the preacher's head like it was a gun. I don't think anybody even noticed me or the knife. They was looking at the preacher, and they was looking at Mama. I run between Mama and the pulpit and pointed the knife at Preacher Allison. The knife was my protection against the scariness, but it didn't do no good. And then I run on out into the night.

I must have been sweating in the brush arbor, for when I stood under the trees looking back at the people in the lantern light, I found I was wet like I'd come out of the creek. I shuddered in the cool night air and jerked, I was so scared. I heard Mama shouting, and then I seen her do a kind of dance in front of the preacher. And she fell down on the sawdust. She rolled on the sawdust like she was having a fit. She rolled on the ground the way a horse will wallow in the dust. I didn't want to look no more. I put my face against the bark of a tree and cried.

I never went back to the brush arbor with Mama. And I never forgot the way her face looked when she was speaking in tongues, and the way she quivered and shivered when she stepped toward the preacher. She didn't act like Mama at all, but like something terrible had come out of the air. I couldn't stand to look at her for days after the meeting. I hung my head at the table and walked past her in the kitchen.

After a week Preacher Allison closed the meeting and moved on to another revival in Pickens, South Carolina. And Mama went back to church, same as before.

IT WAS SO busy in the house as Fay and Mama got dressed for church, I had to find a place to get ready myself. After straining the milk and carrying it out to the springhouse, I got a cake of soap from the shelf on the back porch and headed toward the river. I had to favor my right foot and walk slow because my head was still spinning a little. But I gulped the fresh air of the winter morning and walked over stubble and weeds to the riverbank.

At the stream I slipped off my clothes and hung them on the limbs of a birch. A crawfish backed away when I stepped into the shallows. I had humiliated myself, and I needed to be cleansed. I felt only scorn for myself. The water was so cold it burned like turpentine and made my ankle ache. Only thing to do was jump right into the cold water. Clutching the soap, I rushed into the pool and slapped water on my back like I was trying to put out a fire. I slapped my skin and attacked myself with soap. The water bit and stung and made my bones numb. I slapped the soap under my arms and on the back of my neck and rubbed between my legs. Then I dropped into the water up to my neck. Needles stuck into my skin and gouged every pore. I jumped up like I was shot out of a barrel and run to the bank.

Ain't nothing better than the feel of drying off in the sun after a plunge in the cold river. The air and sunlight seemed like a gift of comfort after the pain of the water. Where your skin has gone numb it wakes up with goose bumps and itching. As I slipped my clothes on, they felt like fur and goose down after the crushed ice and broke glass of the river water.

At the house I put on my one suit. A lot of men wore overalls to church. But it showed more respect to wear my suit. And I hoped to see Annie. I didn't want Annie to see me in overalls on a Sunday morning.

Moody woke up while I was getting dressed in front of the mirror in the bedroom. His face was gray like he was sick. "Where you going in your trick pants?" he said.

"Where do you think, on a Sunday morning?" I said.

"Going to hear the preacher mumble and grumble?" Moody said.

"Might be," I said.

I put on my brown tie that made the suit look a little like a uniform.

"You ain't going to hear no sermon," Moody said. "You're just going to see that Richards girl."

"Could be," I said.

I WAS PLANNING to drive Mama and Fay to church in the Model T, but while I was waiting for Fay to finish primping in front of the mirror in the kitchen, and while Mama was reading her Bible by the fireplace, I heard the car start. It sputtered and barked and then went *tut-tut-tut-tut*. I run out the door, but by the time I got to the shed Moody was already driving through the gate and up the hill toward the spring. I knowed he was going after the cans I'd left by the creek. I was sorry I'd told him where they was.

I slammed the door as I come back inside.

"Won't hurt us to walk," Mama said and closed her Bible.

"Now I'll get my shoes dirty," Fay said.

"Hope he has a wreck," I said.

"That's no spirit to take to church," Mama said. "Preaching won't do you no good if you feel like that."

I'd wanted Annie to see me driving the car. Thought I might ask if she wanted to go for a drive that afternoon. I didn't know what I'd planned to do, but I wanted the car just in case.

"Let's go," Mama said.

"At least we used to have a buggy," Fay said.

"We have always walked to church," Mama said.

PREACHER LINER WAS a loud preacher. He had a harsh voice with a rattle and slap at the top of it. When his voice rose to a high pitch you felt like you had been smacked. He preached long sermons that had a lot of pressure in them. He preached like he was pushing the air tight and close around your head. I was already ashamed of myself. I figured his sermon would make me more ashamed.

I hoped Annie Richards would look around. I wanted to see the pure perfect skin of her cheek. I wanted to see if she had an earring on her delicate little ear. Even though she was only fourteen, she sometimes wore earrings. Her hair had a sparkle to it even in the dim light.

"You may think you can hide your ugly sin in a new car or a fine buggy," Preacher Liner shouted. "You may think you can outrun your sin on a fast horse, or by climbing to a mountaintop in rain or snow. You may think you can hide your sin behind good deeds and charity and helping others. You may think you can hide your sin behind a smile, behind hard work or money, behind a fine house and a new barn. You may even think you can hide your sin in church, setting up front and listening to a sermon. Well, I'm here to tell you the Lord has found you out. Your sin is black and foul. Your sin is stinking in the nostrils of heaven. You couldn't hide such sin in the deepest well; you couldn't hide your sin at the bottom of a coal mine or under the ocean. The Lord sees your heart and sees your sin like it was laid out on a table in front of a courtroom."

I looked at Annie and she turned her head to the right. She didn't turn far enough to see me watching her. But I seen the gray of her eye and the faint redness of her cheek. Her features was sharp and delicate at the same time. She knowed I was looking at her. She knowed I always looked at her when I went to church.

"You may think you can hide your sin at the back of your mind under a new hat," Preacher Liner said. "You think you can hide your filthy heart under new clothes and fine jewelry. You think you can hide your sin behind a fine singing voice or a musical talent. You may think you can run to the end of the world and get away from the Lord's work."

The preacher paused and glared at us.

"Well, I'm here to tell you the Lord has found you out. The Lord has looked into your polluted heart and found you out. The Lord knows your vice and your corruption. The Lord knows your every move and weaselly evasion. The Lord will cut you off like the diseased branch of a tree. The Lord will smite you like the wicked of Sodom and Gomorrah. The Lord will whip you out of the temple as he drove the money changers out of the synagogue. The Lord will cast you into the outer darkness with his fallen angels and wipe your name from the book of life."

Annie was too young to be courting, but sometimes her papa, Hank, would let her walk home from church with a boy. She was already the most popular girl in the community, even though she was just fourteen and beginning to show her womanly shape. Sometimes she would flirt, and sometimes she would just ignore you. She was the only girl I knowed that would act like she didn't even see you or hear you if she didn't feel like talking. Just the fact that Annie was in the church, and that I could see her, give the church a sparkle and a glow.

"When you come to the end of the way," Preacher Liner said, "when you come down to the threshold of death, what will you have to say for yourself? Will the Lord look into your heart and see the cancer of sin growing there? Will your sin be wrote across your forehead when you stand before the Judgment? Will the Lord say, Cast him into outer darkness, I never knew him? Will your sin weigh you down as you try to rise at the Second Coming?

"My friends, many of you setting here in church will never see death. For the end of time is near, and the Second Coming is near. And the day will come not too far off when the Lord will bust through the eastern sky with all his host of angels and call for his own. And the saved will be lifted up, and them washed in the blood will be lifted up, and them that has repented will be took up to heaven. And the rest will be left on this cold earth."

Preacher Liner paused and wiped his brow. He'd been preaching so loud the church still rung with the sound of his voice. The air was stirred up by the awful words. The air had shadows and needles in it. I looked at Annie but she didn't turn around. The sight of her was the only sweet thing in the church. The color of her hair was the only soothing thing in sight. I didn't want to think about what the preacher was saying. I felt little as a cockroach. I didn't want to think about what I'd done the night before. All I wanted to think about was Annie.

One time when I was about fifteen I was passing through the orchard behind the Richards house on my way up the mountain to pick blackberries. Mama wanted blackberries for a cobbler for Sunday dinner, and the berries was gone in the pasture down by the branch. As I skirted between the apple trees and plum and pear trees I heard somebody singing. It was Annie's voice. Even then she had the prettiest voice in church. I stepped closer to hear better.

When I come to the Golden Delicious tree at the edge of the orchard, I seen Annie standing by the table beside the washpot. She was washing her hair in a pan, and she had only a slip over her bare shoulders. I stepped back behind a tree and then got behind a rose of Sharon bush before she seen me.

I hadn't meant to spy on Annie, but I knowed she'd be embarrassed if I walked up on her wearing nothing but a petticoat. I couldn't help myself. I stood behind the rose of Sharon bush and watched her pour dippers of water over her hair to rinse it, and then start to comb it. In the sun her hair looked bright even though it was wet. Her shoulders was slender and perfect, and her arms was white as cream. Her new breasts was showing under the petticoat.

I can still remember how Annie sung to herself an old song called "Gentle Annie." It was a sweet tune and she sung it in a low voice. As she sung she rubbed the drops from her neck and shoulders and wiped the wetness from her arms down to the wrists. Then she spread her hair on her shoulders so it would dry fast in the sun. And she combed out each strand slow so it dried even quicker in the Saturday sun. The hair got brighter and brighter as she combed it out.

Annie set down on a tub and shook her hair so it spread out again around her neck and shoulders. Her voice was pure as the ring of one glass on another. It was pure as the sound of springwater pouring into a pool.

Annie was so beautiful it was hard for me to look at her. But I couldn't look away. It seemed impossible she could ever love anybody like me. I knowed I would always love her, whether she loved me or not. I promised myself I would always love her.

When her hair was dry she stood up and lifted a basket to gather clothes in. She walked to the clothesline and with her slim white arms unpinned sheets and pillowcases, shirts and underwear, from the line. She folded the clothes into the basket and started singing again. I breathed out and realized I'd held my breath for a long time.

"FOR WE KNOW where the wicked shall go," Preacher Liner said. "They are bound for the fiery pit. They're doomed to the lake of fire. They are throwed into the everlasting darkness. If you think a match will burn you, if you think a hot stove will burn you, imagine a lake of fire hotter ten thousand times than burning gasoline. Imagine a lake of fire hotter than a furnace, hotter than a forge that melts steel."

Preacher Liner stopped and leaned over the pulpit. We waited for him to go on, but he didn't. He just looked at us, and everybody was froze, like their joints had turned to chalk, like they was bracing theirselves for a blow in the face. But Preacher Liner didn't say nothing for a long time. He looked over the congregation like we was filth and he didn't have no hope for us. Finally he motioned to the song leader to start the invitational hymn.

As the choir sung "Just As I Am" I sung along too, but I looked down at my hands on the bench in front of me. And I tried to think about sunlight on the pine trees and the north side of the pasture hill where the frost stayed on the grass all day. I looked up but couldn't see Annie because of big fat Ruthie Tillman in front of me. I wanted to see the sweet color of Annie's hair.

"Is there anybody here troubled in their heart?" Preacher Liner hollered above the singing. "Is there anybody here that feels the need to get right?"

I was glad church would be over in a few minutes and I'd be out in the cool breeze and sunshine. I tried to think what I'd say to Annie when she come out of the church. I would stand at the steps and when she come out the door I'd take off my hat and speak to her.

"Don't listen to the devil whispering in your ear to hold back," the preacher shouted. "Hell is full of procrastinators. Hell is packed with them that couldn't make up their minds."

I'd have to get out of the church and stand close to the door, or one of the other boys would ask Annie first. Only walking with Annie would help me redeem myself. And if there was two asking at the same time, Annie would just ignore them both. I'd seen her do it. She'd walk right on by and not let nobody walk her home.

"The Lord might bust through the eastern sky any minute," the preacher yelled. "With his host of angels he'll split the blue sky in two and call up his saints to heaven. Will you be left standing on this sorry earth? Will you gnash your teeth and cry out for the rocks and mountains to fall on you?"

As Ruthie Tillman swayed with the song I caught a glimpse of Annie's hair. It was the color an angel's hair would be, so fine and glistening in the dusky church air. Her hair had sunlight in it.

"If you end up in hell, don't blame this church," Preacher Liner hollered. "Don't blame the members of this church and the deacons of this church. If you end up in hell you have sent yourself there, same as if you struck a match and set the fire yourself."

I could tell Preacher Liner was winding down. The service was about over. The song was in its last chorus and I joined in, singing louder than before. I was almost free of the dread and sadness of the church, but not of the dread and sadness inside me. In another minute or two I'd be outside. And I would speak to Annie.

Soon as the hymn was over, Preacher Liner started praying. "May the Lord go with us as we return to our daily lives. May the Lord guide us as we go about our work to earn our daily bread. May the Lord look into our hearts and help us to avoid the sin of pride and the sin of lust. May the Lord forgive us our secret faults and our public hypocrisies. And may the Lord give us peace. Amen."

"Amen," said a number of people around the congregation.

When I stepped out into the open it was like the world exploded in my eyes. Light swelled so bright it made my eyeballs hurt, but the fresh air on my face was soothing. I blinked and shaded my eyes. And then I seen Moody standing right beside the steps. He was standing right where I had planned to plant myself. And he stood there like he'd just come out of church with everybody else. He was smiling at me when I seen him.

"Howdy, Brother Muir," Moody said and tipped his hat.

"You ain't got no business here," I said.

It was like Moody to think of what would rile me the most. He had drove off to get the liquor and take it to Wheeler. And then he'd come to church and waited till the service was over. I seen the Model T in the parking lot.

"You get away from here," I said.

Moody tipped his hat and smiled at everybody coming out of the church. He smiled like he'd been at the service and heard the sermon. I looked around to see if there was any other boys waiting near the door. I saw Sam Willard standing back by the arborvitae, and Calvin Simpson on the other side of Moody. They was standing way back because Moody was there. Moody had too much of a reputation as a knife fighter for the other boys to want to argue with him.

More people come out the door, and I figured it was time for Annie to come out. Mama and Fay stepped out into the sunlight. Mama seen both Moody and me standing on the steps. "Let's go home," Mama said to both of us.

"Be home later," Moody said.

"Time to go now," Mama said and smiled. Everybody in front of the church was listening. They was waiting to see what would happen between Moody and me. I thought I seen Annie in the doorway, and then she disappeared. Her mama come out, and I said, "Howdy, Mrs. Richards." And Moody tipped his hat and said, "How do, Mrs. Richards."

But Annie was not behind her as I expected.

Then I knowed where Annie had gone. I don't know how I knowed it, but it come to me in a flicker. I stepped back and walked past Sam Willard. And when I got around the arborvitae and around the corner of the church, I run to the back. Annie had seen both Moody and me standing by the church door, and Mama talking to us, and she'd turned around and gone to the back of the church. There wasn't a door in the rear of the building, but there was a low window that as a boy I used to climb in and out of when Grandpa was mowing the churchyard. The back of the church lot joined the Richardses' cornfield on the mountainside, and I knowed Annie was going to climb out the window and walk home across the field so she wouldn't have to be bothered by Moody and me and the other boys either.

Sure enough, as I run around to the back, there she was, crawling backward through the window. "Let me help you down," I said and grabbed her under the arms.

"Where did you come from?" Annie said. On the ground she pulled away from me and brushed the hair out of her eyes. Her cheeks was flushed a little.

"I thought you might need some help," I said.

"Did it look like I needed help?" Annie said.

"That ain't the usual way to leave the church," I said.

"Better than being pestered by a bunch of fools," Annie said. She straightened her sweater where it had got twisted. Her figure was slender and young and perfect.

"Better let me walk you home," I said.

"Nobody's stopping you," Annie said. She stood like she was waiting for me to leave. She was embarrassed, I reckon. I knowed I had to say the right thing.

"Let's walk down to the spring and get a drink," I said.

"Ain't thirsty," Annie said.

"All that talk of hell made me thirsty," I said.

"Then go yourself," Annie said.

"We can go through the pine trees and nobody'll see us," I said.

WALKING DOWN TO the spring was what courting couples had always done after church. Mama and Daddy had walked down to the spring when they first met way back in the 1890s. It was maybe a quarter of a mile through the pine trees and along the edge of the pasture down to the hemlocks that shaded the spring. Late in the day, before evening services, boys and girls walked down to get a drink and they would stop to kiss in the shadows of the pines and hemlocks. Sometimes they took a bucket from the bench in the back of the church and filled it for the rest of the congregation to drink from. A lot of couples had got engaged walking down to the spring and back. A lot of marriages had their start when a boy and girl took the long way back from the spring.

I wondered if I was going to kiss her. I'd never kissed Annie before. And I couldn't tell if she was in the mood to be kissed. Her hair sparkled in the sunlight like it had crystals in it. The shade of the hemlocks was almost like night after the blinding sun. I took her hand as soon as we got into the shade. I had to say something because I had took hold of her hand.

"How would you like to go to Mount Mitchell?" I said.

"You ain't been to Mount Mitchell," Annie said.

"But now that I have a Model T we could go," I said.

"I thought the Model T was Moody's," Annie said.

"It's half mine," I said.

"Then why does Moody drive it all the time?" Annie said.

The trail was cushioned with spruce pine needles and wound down to the rocks in front of the spring. The spring basin was more than a yard across. White sand covered the bottom, and spring lizards shivered in the edges of the pool. Flecks of mica winked like stars.

I took the gourd off the stick and dipped up a drink for Annie. She took the shell and sipped from it, then throwed the rest out. "Water tastes better from a poplar spring," she said.

"No better than a hemlock spring," I said.

I took the gourd and scooped up a drink for myself, rolling the cold water on my tongue the way I'd read wine tasters roll wine. "Hemlocks give the water a spicy taste," I said.

"I don't taste no spice," Annie said.

With my lips wet I leaned over and kissed her. I brushed her lips so her lips got wet. "Don't you taste that?" I said.

She turned away. "I got to go home," she said. "Papa will come looking for me, or he'll send one of my brothers." She started back up the trail. I hung the gourd on the stick and followed.

Just as we come through the pines to the road, I heard the *tut-tut-tut* of a Model T. When we stepped out into the sunlight I seen it was Moody. He must have been waiting in the churchyard for us to come back. He swung the car out of the parking lot into the road in front of us and stopped. A big smile crawled on his face, like he was mighty pleased about something.

"Want me to drive you home?" he hollered to Annie.

"Annie is walking home with me," I said.

"Don't look like you've been walking home," Moody said.

"We was just on our way," I said. I put my foot on the running board and my hand on the window like I was going to push the Model T away.

"You should let Annie speak for herself," Moody said.

"Nobody asked you to stop," I said.

"Now don't get all bothered, little brother," Moody said. "You ain't walking so good yourself on that ankle, last time I noticed."

"I'm walking fine," I said. "Go on, get away from here." I slapped the side of the car.

"Speak for yourself," Moody said. "Come on, get in," he said to Annie and opened the passenger door.

Annie climbed into the car before I could say anything. I was going to tell Moody to get out of our way. But she got in and slammed the door. Moody revved up the motor, and as he pulled away, the wheels spun on the gravel and flung rocks back at me. A rock hit me in the knee, and the tires made two troughs of dust as he went down the road. I watched the Model T bounce on the ruts and washboard until it was out of sight around the bend.

Ten
Ginny

AFTER YOU LOSE a husband you grieve for a few weeks or months, and then you tell yourself that it's over, you will go ahead with your life with a new will and a new freedom. And you tell yourself loving is a habit you'll get over and forget with your mourning. You have got beyond such things, in the dignity and wisdom of your widowhood.

If you thought that, you will turn out to be wrong. For when you're least expecting it, seven months later, or seven years later, the memory of your loved one will come to you and catch you in the throat. And it will be like he is with you again. After Tom died, months after he was buried, I would be turning a corner or milking a cow, and something would remind me of his voice, of the way he dug with a hoe or nodded by the fire. I would feel his touch, and the tears would come to my eyes. I might be ironing or even walking up to the mailbox and think of the first time I seen him, or the way he went to sleep trying to read the paper by the fire, or the way he broke wind in his sleep, and my throat would lock and feelings stir deep in my stomach.

For I found that those we love never go away completely. They come back in the moments of our greatest sadness, and our greatest joy. And they always come unexpected. We are struggling to finish cutting hay, or watching a sunrise, and they are there with us. They are somewhere just behind us, and to the side of us. Sometimes they are watching through our eyes and listening through our ears. They are close to our ears, and close to the I that is behind the eyes.

The loved dead are with us and walk with us, and come to us in our awful moments, and in our sleep and in our dreams. They come to us in our prayers and pray with us. They are in our work and in our sweat. The dead loved ones haunt the breeze under poplars in broad daylight, and the night wind in the hemlocks, and the murmur of sparkling water.

When I was a girl I would have thought an old woman would have give up all thought of loving, but I was wrong. It's true, loving night after night and week after week is a habit that can be give up, has to be give up when your lover is gone. But the need to be loved, the yearning to be loved, never goes away from you.

After Tom died I would wake up in the night and feel the emptiness and coldness of the bed, and the emptiness of the house. We had quarreled and slept separate often through the years of our marriage. Sometimes we slept apart for months. But always there had been a reunion. Always there had been the rapture of reconciliation. There was the promise that a quarrel would end and we would be one flesh again. Even apart I would know Tom was laying just above me on his pallet in the attic. And one night he would look at me long in the lamplight and be ready to join me in the bedroom like it was our first night and we was one flesh again.

But after he was gone I would wake up in the middle of the night and imagine I had been touched. I'd lay there feeling a hand had been run over my skin, over my breasts and my belly. That's how much I needed to be handled and pressed. There was too much in me that needed to be brought out by loving. I was not that old yet. My hair had some gray, but I was not too old to need love.

You act your age, I said to myself. Act your age in front of your children and Pa and Florrie. Act your age in front of the preacher and the community, and in front of the Lord.

The need for love filled me like the need for fellowship with the Holy Spirit. I needed to be loved so bad I walked along the river and up the hill to the top of the pasture. The wind whispered crazy things in my ear and I rubbed my hands together and put my hands on my hips.

And I found out I talked to myself. I had talked to myself when I was young, but had got over it. A few months after Tom died I was scouring out milk pitchers with boiling water from the kettle and Florrie, who was helping me to dry them, said, "Ginny, what did you say?"

"Didn't say nothing," I said.

"You did," Florrie said. Florrie always liked to be stubborn and critical. "You have been talking to yourself."

"I reckon I know when I'm talking and when I ain't," I said.

"You said something about how a catfish wouldn't eat what Lily fixes for Joe," Florrie said and giggled.

I guess my face turned red, for that was exactly what I had been thinking, how uncertain a cook and housekeeper my sister-in-law Lily was. I was embarrassed to have said my thoughts out loud. I wondered what else I had said, thinking I was only thinking it.

"You talk a lot while you're working," Florrie said.

"Just muttering to myself," I said. But I wondered what else I might have revealed, for I often thought about love things. In spite of myself I thought about men and women together. I thought about good-looking young men and the way they talked and the way they was built. I thought about Hank Richards that had moved from Gap Creek to the little house that my brother Locke had built out beyond the church before he went back in the army. Hank had shoulders as strong as Tom's was and he was a good-looking man. Already he had been appointed a deacon. He was seven or eight years younger than me, and he had the strongest neck and arms. His black hair was wavy where it fell across his forehead. And his eyes was blue as the October sky.

Shame on you, I said to myself. Hank is another woman's husband, and he is younger than you. And he wouldn't give you a second look even if he was single. I had always thought Florrie was the lustful one in our family, and here I was having love thoughts about a married man, only a few months after Tom had died.

What is the cure for wandering thoughts for a middle-aged woman? I guess I learned from Tom that the cure for most things in this world is to work harder. If you are worried or distracted, just bring your mind back to the work at hand. For sweat and the feeling of accomplishment will go a long way toward curing most worries that settle into our minds and don't want to go away.

But sometimes even the hardest labor won't clear your mind of daydreams. Sweat only spirits up the blood more. And what makes you tired makes you daydream more. I thought of young men in overalls and no shirts working along beside me. I thought of what they would say as we worked. I thought of how we would walk to the spring for a drink in the hottest part of the day.

And not even praying helped. For when I prayed I thought of a young preacher saying the words of the Bible that had always thrilled me. I seen a young man with long curly hair and a thin blond beard like the pictures of Jesus saying my favorite words from the New Testament: "I am the true vine." "I am the way, the truth and the life." "I am the root and the offspring of David, and the bright and morning star." "Before Abraham was, I am."

Such praying just made me more excited. I thought of the young song leader at the revival I had attended at Crossroads. When he sung it was like he put every muscle of his body and every ounce of strength into his voice, in the notes and words of his singing.

On Jordan's stormy banks I stand,
And cast a wistful eye . . .
O who will come and go with me?
I am bound for the promised land.

And when I prayed to the Lord to show me a sign to cure my loneliness and the hopelessness of widowhood, and when I tried to study on the higher things, what come to me was a picture of the millennium, of the New Jerusalem foretold in Revelation. And what I seen in my mind was a world of trees and meadows along creeks where boys and girls in thin gowns walked and danced in the shade of trees and grape arbors. In paradise they walked hand in hand and kissed on top of a hill where they could look out on a crystal sea. It didn't help my problem to think such thoughts.

BUT THEN I learned to worry about my younguns more than myself. I seen I had been a selfish mama when Tom was alive, and I had cared too much about myself and my own feelings. And I thought more about Pa and how his heart had gone weak and sore on him. I thought about the sick and needy in the community. When the air got too thick and close in my head, I remembered how my younguns would be raised with no daddy, and how I had to love them enough for two parents. I thought how prideful my oldest girl, Jewel, was, and I thought how angry and resentful Moody was, and how mean to Muir, and I wondered what I had done to make him that way. And I thought how confused and excited Muir was in his mind, even at the age of nine or ten. And I thought how young Fay was and how I'd never done anything to make her less ashamed of me. She blamed me for the quarrels with Tom, and for the death of Tom. And I thought how they would have to grow up with no daddy. I didn't know then that Jewel would die in the 1918 flu. I didn't know what was coming.

It was when I worried about my children that my own little problems withered down to size. And I thought how I had always sought my own pleasures first. But the truest pleasure was to think of them first. It was simple advice, but it was the only advice that worked.

You have been tried in the fire of desire, I said to myself. You have wandered in the desert and in the flames of your bereavement. And you will turn all your loving and all your work toward those around you, them closest to you. You will rededicate yourself to your family.

But even so, it give me a thrill to watch the strong young men that worked with the rye thrashers in August. They labored in the heat and streamed with sweat. I watched them rub off the chaff that stuck to their shoulders. And I thought of the Cherokees that had camped on the same land by the river. I thought of braves that had played their ball game for hours in the fields until they got so hot and sweaty they had to jump into the deep, whispering pools for a swim.

SECOND READING
1922

Eleven
Muir

I COULD HEAR rain on the roof when I woke early in the fall. It was not a pounding or even a tapping on the shingles. It sounded more like a peck and murmur along the eaves. When steady rain runs off a roof it sounds like the gutters are swallowing. And the house feels isolated, far out in the ocean of rain.

When I come back from milking, my shirt and hat was dripping. My shoes left wet tracks on the kitchen floor. Mama told me not to drip on the dough. She was fixing to make pies and had dough rising on the stove. Soon as I strained the milk I tied a cloth over the pitcher to carry it out to the springhouse.

"You ought to put on some dry clothes," Mama said.

"Muir don't want dry clothes," Moody said. "He likes to live like a fish."

"At least I don't drink like a fish," I said.

"You're a working fish," Moody said.

I was glad to get back out in the rain, away from the close air of the kitchen. When it rained in fall weather I preferred to be outdoors. The world of rain is clean and soothing. But I don't know what it is about rain that draws me into it. Maybe the fresh drip off every weed and leaf and needle of the pines clears and cleans the seconds and minutes. Maybe rain is the purest counting of time. I had hated myself since I went down to Gap Creek with Moody. Maybe the rain would wash me clean.

After leaving the milk in the springhouse I listened to the rain on the cedar shingles there. It was dark and musty in the springhouse. The world outside looked brighter when I stepped back into the rain. The light on a rainy day is so gloomy it reminds me of a church, and the gloam of twilight, and the light in groves and thickets. The light of a rainy day is easy on the eyes and calms me. In the dim light I felt sheltered and private.

At the barn I took a tow sack off the pile and flung it around my shoulders. A tow sack will turn off a lot of rain from your back and keep you warm on a rainy day. With the sack over my neck and upper arms I felt I was wearing a cape or the vestments of some kind of service. The rough cloth, rough as bark or binder's twine, would get heavy as it soaked up the rain and weigh like armor on my shoulders.

Moody and Mama had always teased me about working in the rain. But I couldn't help myself. I didn't want to help myself. When it was raining I couldn't just set in the house and listen to the drip on the eaves and watch the fire. I could set and look at magazines or the architecture books or *Pilgrim's Progress* for maybe an hour, but then I had to do something else. I had to be outdoors where the rain was. If I stayed inside I'd get a headache and feel I was missing something important. I couldn't stand myself if I just set there.

With the sack around my shoulders and my hat dripping from the brim, I got a hammer and some nails from the feed room in the barn. It was the perfect day to fix the fence around the pasture. You don't want to get out in the fields while it's rainy and pack down the mud between rows. But it don't hurt to work in the weeds along a fence, if you don't mind getting wet. I took the pliers and a coil of wire so I could patch the broke places in the fence.

Some strands of barbed wire had come loose, and I nailed them back to the posts. Other places a strand was broke, so I had to splice it. You stretch fence wire with a pole for a lever, so I cut a hickory sapling to use as a stretcher. It was good to see wire straight and tight on the posts again. Made me feel there was some order and hope in the world.

"Nobody but you would be out here," a voice said. It was Aunt Florrie. She'd walked across the hill to help Mama and Fay make pies. Florrie was the only person I knowed besides myself that liked to be out in the rain. She had an old coat throwed over her shoulders, but her head was bare. Her hair was soaked and dripping, and it stuck to her temples and forehead. Aunt Florrie had sharp features and black eyes and her skin was dark as a gypsy's. There was not a wrinkle on her face, and she could work like a man when she wanted to.

"You're your daddy's son," Aunt Florrie said. "Tom ever did like to work out in the rain."

"Did Mama quarrel at him too?" I said. I could ask Aunt Florrie about Daddy easier than I could ask Mama.

"Ginny couldn't help herself," Florrie said. "I don't reckon she ever did understand Tom."

There was a post leaning over where the dirt had washed away around it. I pushed it upright and begun to pound it into the wet ground with the axe. "Here, let me hold that," Aunt Florrie said. She held the dripping post with both hands while I pounded it.

As I drove the post deeper into the ground the wires tightened like guitar strings.

"Tom was a mighty good man," Aunt Florrie said. "You remind me a lot of him."

"He worked harder than I do," I said. Water splashed from the top of the post as I drove it in.

"You'll work harder when you find what you want to do," Aunt Florrie said. She held a strand of wire tight against the post while I nailed it in place. Drops of rain run down her cheek.

We walked along the fence to where it run into the pine woods. A post was leaning over and needed bracing. I looked around for a sapling to cut for a pole. "I hate for you to get wet," I said.

"The rain makes me feel young," Aunt Florrie said. She sounded like a little girl. I chopped down a yellow pine and trimmed off the limbs. Then I sharpened one end so I could drive it into the ground.

The brace was a makeshift repair, but it was the best I could do without putting in a new post.

Aunt Florrie warned me against getting myself tied down to any girl. "You have big plans," she said. "You go on ahead with your big plans."

Just then there was a flash, and a click of lightning in the air. The crash of thunder was so close it sounded like the air was turning inside out and doors was slamming above us. The ground was so wet it sucked at our shoes as we walked along the trail, staying back away from the fence. There was another flare of lightning.

"I don't want to be struck before I can have a drink and warm up by the fire," Aunt Florrie said.

"I've heard working in the rain makes you thirsty," I said.

"Only crying will make you thirstier," Aunt Florrie said.

THE NEXT MORNING I got up early and milked the cow for Mama. And I strained the milk into pitchers and carried them out to the springhouse. Mama fried eggs and boiled some grits. But even as I set down to eat I knowed what I was going to do. I'd made up my mind during the night. Moody had not come home all night and he'd left the Model T in the shed.

"I'm going to Canada," I said. I poured some molasses on my plate and sopped it up with a biscuit.

"How're you going?" Mama said.

"I'm driving the Model T," I said, and took a long drink of coffee.

"Moody won't let you have it," Mama said.

"Moody can't stop me," I said.

"Then I'll stop you," Mama said.

"I've made up my mind," I said with all the firmness and calm I could muster.

"Well, you can unmake it," Mama said.

I finished my coffee and stood up. I'd made my plans during the night and knowed what I had to do. Nothing had been right for me since I'd helped Moody drive the liquor up from Gap Creek. "There ain't nothing for me here," I said. "I'm going where the fur is better."

"You're going to lose everything," Mama said. "Your family, your friends. You're going to get yourself killed."

"I could stay here and get myself killed," I said.

Mama turned away and stood in front of the water bucket on the counter. I could tell she was crying. Mama had always expected me to do something important, like being a preacher, and she depended on me to do the things she wanted around the place. She didn't depend on Moody for anything. She fussed at me and she argued with me, but she expected me to do what she said. For once in my life I was going to do what I wanted, what I had to do.

FROM SELLING MOLASSES I'd saved seventy-one dollars, which I kept in a can in the shed where Moody couldn't find it. I knowed just what I had to take if I was going to trap in Canada. I got my mackinaw and my hunting boots from the bedroom. I packed my long underwear and my wool socks and my heavy shirts and pairs of pants. I packed my gloves and my hunting knife and my winter cap.

The gear almost filled the backseat of the Model T. I put my traps on the floor of the car and slid the shotgun under the clothes on the backseat.

"You'll freeze to death up there," Mama said. She come out to the gate and watched me load up the car. "And nobody'll know what happened to you."

"I'll write you a letter," I said.

"Send me a picture postcard of a Mountie," Fay said. Fay had come out and stood beside Mama.

"Let's have a prayer before you go," Mama said.

I bowed my head while Mama prayed. But I didn't listen to what she said. I didn't close my eyes and I looked at the red dirt in the yard and at the moss under the closest hemlock. It was early fall and the periwinkles on the bank was blooming again. Cones from the hemlocks sprinkled the yard like little eggs. I wondered if I'd ever see this red dirt again.

When Mama said amen I looked up and seen how worried she looked. "First my husband dies of typhoid, then my pa dies, and my oldest girl dies, and my oldest son goes into the liquor business, and now my youngest son is going off to Canada," Mama said. She come forward and hugged me, and Fay hugged me too.

"I'll come back next summer," I said, and hurried to start the car. I didn't look Mama in the eye. When I climbed into the driver's seat I patted my pocket to see if the money was still there. Mama and Fay waved as I drove out of the yard. My heart was jumping under my collarbone, but I set my teeth and said to myself, Calm yourself, you idiot, if you want to make it all the way to Canada.

I stopped at the gate, got out and opened it, drove through, then stopped again and latched it. I drove by the molasses furnace and the pine thicket, by the edge of the orchard on the hill, and around the holler where the spring was. I drove by the old house place where my great-grandpa had built the first house on the property.

At the church I turned right to drive out by the Richards house. I wasn't sure why exactly. I was still mad at Annie, but maybe I wanted to catch a glimpse of her as I drove past. Maybe I hoped she would see me and know I was leaving Green River and she would feel sorry she'd treated me bad. The sun was just coming up and there was nobody on the porch of the Richards house. I seen a cat crouched in the weeds by the road. And then I seen Mrs. Richards milking in the hallway of the barn. I waved to her, but she was bent to her work and probably never even seen who was going by.

I watched the Richards place lit up in an orange glow by the sunrise in my rearview mirror.

At the highway I turned north and drove past U. G.'s store. It looked closed, but I hit the horn anyway, in case U. G. was there early, unpacking and sorting things on the shelves. There was smoke coming from the chimney, so he'd already started a fire in the stove.

I'd studied out the route I was going to take many times. Highway 25 that passed right by U. G.'s store went all the way to Toledo, Ohio. From Toledo I would drive to Detroit and then across into Canada. The same ribbon of pavement would take me all the way, going mostly straight north through Tompkinsville and Asheville, through Marshall along the French Broad River, and across Tennessee to the Cumberland Gap.

From the Cumberland Gap the highway plunged north through Berea, Kentucky, into the Bluegrass country, through Lexington, and on to Cincinnati. It was a cool autumn day, and I drove with joy away from my troubles, away from Green River. The little car *tut-tut-tutt*ed up mountainsides and speeded up on the down sides. I passed people cutting cane and people boiling molasses. I passed people gathering corn in wagons and people curing tobacco in long sheds on the sides of the mountains.

You just stay calm, I said to myself, and patted the steering wheel. As I wound up into the Cumberland Gap I remembered that was where one of my great-grandpas had died in the Confederate War. I remembered that when Daniel Boone had crossed into Kentucky a hundred and sixty years ago he'd come the same way. "You're driving through history to the future," I said. I liked the sound of that and said it again. "You're driving through the past into the future." And I thought of Sergeant York, who lived not too far away in the Cumberland Mountains of Tennessee.

As it started getting late in the day I wondered where I was going to stay the night. I was driving into the sunset north of Lexington. If there'd been woods I would have stopped and camped in them. But I was in the Bluegrass country and all the land was fancy farms with white fences and painted barns. It was the first place I'd ever seen that looked exactly like it was supposed to. The white fences, the stone gates, the lanes running back to mansions with white columns among oak trees, the painted stables with weather vanes, the tall slender horses, looked just like all the pictures I'd seen in magazines. There was no rough, unpainted barns, no gullies, no rocky cornfields. It was hard for me to imagine the wealth that must support such farms. The Model T kept rolling and rattling along. I was getting tired and my back was stiff and sore from setting all day. I'd not got much sleep the night before.

After the sun was down and I was driving along the dark highway, getting worried, I seen a sign that said TOURIST CABINS 75 CENTS A NIGHT. It didn't look like I was going to find a place to camp and I couldn't keep driving all night. I was so stiff my neck hurt when I turned my head. I drove into the yard where the sign pointed.

The office was in a regular house, and after I paid my seventy-five cents the woman in charge give me a key and pointed to a row of little houses in the pine woods. "You're in number six," she said.

"Where can I get something to eat?" I said.

"There's a hot plate in the room," she said and closed the door.

A string of lights run along the road beside the row of cabins. I was so stiff from driving I couldn't hardly walk. And I was so tired nothing seemed real. Even though I was there looking for number six, I didn't feel like myself at all.

I found my door and opened it and turned on the light. You never seen such a bare little room. The place wasn't much bigger than the bed, and all the furniture was a dresser with a flaky mirror and a hot plate on a little shelf. The bed looked thin and lumpy. The toilet and shower was in another building, and I hurried out into the night to use the toilet. There was people going in and out of the building and I spoke to them, but they didn't seem interested in being friendly.

"Do you know what the weather is like north of here?" I said to a man washing his hands at one of the sinks.

"Haven't the slightest idea," he said without even looking at me. I was glad to hurry back to the room and close the door.

I got some raisins and crackers out of my packsack and eat them, setting on the shaky bed and looking in the mirror. In the light from the one bulb my face looked gray, a kind of yellow gray, and I looked older than I was. I'd been awful hungry, but as I started to eat my appetite went away. I just wanted to lay down and rest. I was tireder than if I'd walked my trapline or pulled fodder all day. I was tired just from setting still and worrying about the road ahead. My back was sore like it had been beat with a stick.

Maybe it was the excitement of being away from home for the first time, or maybe it was because I was so tired from driving, but I didn't fall asleep like I expected to. I was so weary I thought I'd just drop off. But as I laid there I kept feeling I was still driving. I could feel the bump and rattle of the Model T. I kept thinking I was steering on winding roads and watching out for trucks in curves. It seemed like everything was magnified and stretched out of shape and then shrunk by turns.

Lord, I prayed in the dark, if you don't want me to go to Canada I won't go. If you want me to go back home and help Mama and Fay, just show me a sign. I'll do whatever you want, if you'll just show me what it is. I laid in the dark hoping for some kind of sign. I must have floated off to sleep still thinking about a sign, for the next thing I knowed there was daylight and it was already eight o'clock.

I went to the bathhouse and shaved and washed my face, and I didn't even try to be friendly to the other people. Then I went back to the cabin and gathered my things and got on the road.

There was a guesthouse down the highway about a mile with a sign in front that said BREAKFAST 25 CENTS. I stopped there and had eggs and grits and coffee, and biscuits with jelly on them. Once I got the coffee and grits in me I started to feel better. As the coffee warmed me up, and the grits and eggs and jelly started filling me up, the world got firm again and the morning fell into place. I seen I was doing something I had to do. You are going toward something better, in a long zigzagging way, I thought.

By ten o'clock I crossed the great bridge into Cincinnati. I knowed it was a bridge built by the same man that made the Brooklyn Bridge. It was the biggest manmade thing I'd ever seen. But I didn't have time to look much because the traffic was so thick and fast and crazy. And traffic was so loud and close I didn't have time to look at the city when I got to the other side. I just drove right on down the wide street, trying to miss the cars that weaved in and out in front of me. There was horns honking and lights flashing at intersections. I just stayed on Highway 25 and stopped at lights with all the other cars, then rushed forward when the lights changed. I didn't even have time to glance at buildings and parks, I was so busy trying not to hit other cars and looking for road signs. I seen a great church to my left but didn't have time to look at it.

Through my open window I could smell the city. It was a stink of oil and car exhaust and rotten things, like rotten cabbage and sour meat. But it was a stink of burned things too, scorched hair and chemicals on fire. The roar scared me. The noise of horns and slamming brakes sounded like the world was falling apart, or falling on top of me. A policeman blowed his whistle and pointed at me, or beyond me. I seen a man whose face was nothing but scabs laying on the sidewalk. I gripped the wheel and told myself that I'd come back to the Queen City and look at Cincinnati another time. I drove on past light after light and corner after corner. I felt a little sick at my stomach as I drove up into the hills past fancy estates. And then I was beyond the city.

I was so relieved to get through Cincinnati without having a wreck, I felt like hollering out. Once I reached the farm country beyond, I pounded the wheel and laughed, knowing I was in the North for the first time, that I had at least made it across the Ohio River. I was the first member of the family that had been in the North since my grandpa was took a prisoner to Elmira, New York, in the Confederate War.

The farm country of Ohio was so pretty it smarted my eyes to look at it. The corn was gathered and the fields was already plowed for the winter. Fields run back to hedgerows of oaks and ash trees. Barns was neat and painted red. I seen teams of great Percherons doing the fall plowing. The soil looked like black silk turned a thread at a time. At home we never plowed till early spring. But I'd heard it was better to open up the soil before winter and let it breathe in the cold months.

I drove on through the town of Lima. The country beyond was flat as a stove top, and the plowed soil was dark as snuff. There wasn't a hill or even a river in sight. I seen stacks of pipes along the sides of fields. I guessed they used them for drainage.

About two or three miles north of town I noticed a big red sedan following me. It come up close behind and I seen it was a Duesenberg. The big car pulled around and passed. I thought if I had a car like that I'd be in Canada already.

But when I drove on about a mile I seen the shiny red car stopped beside the highway. It was pulled over on the shoulder and the hood was raised. As I got closer a man in a brown suit run out into the highway and waved his hands at me. I pushed in both the clutch and brake and slowed down, but even as I stopped I wished I hadn't. I wished I'd just kept going. The Duesenberg had several people in it, and the man that flagged me down wore the most expensive-looking suit I'd seen in a long time. He run over to my car and leaned in the window.

"Hey, sport, would you give me a lift to the next filling station?"

he said. The way he said *sport* made a nerve somewhere in my belly feel sick. But now that I was stopped I couldn't just drive away.

"What's wrong?" I said.

"Fan belt's broke. Got to get a new one," he said.

There was no excuse for not helping somebody in trouble on the highway that I could think of. I heard a woman laugh inside the sedan.

"Sure, get in," I said. But the man had already opened the door and was climbing in. I throwed my mackinaw coat into the backseat.

"You're a peach, sport," the man said. He smelled like some kind of aftershave. He had a jaw like an anvil and a neat mustache, but there was something twisted about his face, like one eye was lower than the other, or a cheek had been crushed and the nose turned wrong.

As I drove away from the red Duesy, the woman inside laughed again. It was hard to imagine what was so funny about a fan belt breaking.

"Well, sport, where you heading?" my passenger said. He lit a cigar and offered me one.

"Thanks, but I don't smoke," I said.

"Good for you," he said.

"Northern Michigan, Canada maybe," I said.

"Going up there to get some Canadian hooch?" he said and cuffed me on the shoulder.

"No, I'm going to trap fur," I said.

I wondered if the man had a gun under his chocolate brown suit. My shotgun was in the backseat under all my gear.

"Trap what?" the man said.

"Mink and muskrats, maybe beaver and otter," I said.

"You'll freeze your ass, sport," the man said. He knocked the ash off his cigar out the window and let the wind make the tip glow for a few seconds.

"Hey, you got a girl back in Carolina?" the man said.

"Not anymore."

"Ah, you must have got somebody, big handsome hunk like you," the man said.

"I used to think I had a girl," I said.

"You been getting any lately?" he said. "That why you going to Canada? Those Eskimos will give you their wives if you come visit."

"No, I just want to catch fur," I said. The man made me feel I was in a stupor and couldn't hardly talk.

"Fur's just another name for pussy, sport," the man said.

"The fur's better up there because of the cold winters," I said.

"The fur's better, ha, ha, ha," the man said.

Looking in the mirror I seen the big red car. It appeared behind us and was gaining quick.

"Hey, ain't that your car?" I said.

The man didn't even look back. "Might be," he said and puffed on the cigar. "What do you care, sonny?"

"I thought you said the fan belt . . ."

"Them is smart guys; they must have fixed it already," the man said.

I gripped the wheel, wondering what was going to happen next. The Duesenberg come up behind and followed for a few seconds, then whipped around, and in a few more seconds was far ahead.

"Ain't they going to wait for you?" I said.

"Don't you worry about me, sport. Just keep on driving," the man said.

My palms was sticky on the wheel, and my foot trembled on the clutch when I had to change gears. I drove on for several minutes and seen the big car stopped at a crossroads ahead.

"Well, professor, just let me out right up there," the man said.

"Where the car is?" I said.

"No, on the other side of the moon," the man said.

I pushed down on the brake, and before the Model T had come to a stop the man jumped out and slammed the door. "Take care you don't catch no social disease from that Canadian fur," he hollered back at me. "And stay away from Canadian booze, you hear?"

I jammed in the clutch and shifted down to first and drove on fast as I could. I got ahead maybe half a mile when I seen the big sedan pull into the road again. It swept up behind me and passed in a gush of wind. Nobody inside give any sign that they seen me. Soon the Duesy was out of sight ahead and I felt the wetness on my forehead and under my arms, and my feet trembled on the pedals. It was several minutes before I noticed again the fine farm country I was driving through.

I stopped for lunch at a drugstore in Findlay. It was the first time I'd set foot on the ground of the North. But the pavement didn't look any different from that in Asheville. The people acted busier but was no better looking or better dressed. The buildings, the cars, the clothes, did look new and expensive. I set there eating hotdogs and telling myself how lucky I was to be alive. I asked myself what I would have done if the man in the brown suit had pulled a gun. The news of gangsters in the North, especially around Chicago, was in the papers every day. There was even supposed to be gangsters following their enemies into the mountains of North Carolina.

I STAYED THAT night in another tourist court in northern Ohio. But the cabin in this one was a little fancier than the one in Kentucky and it cost two dollars. After the long day on the road, I set on the bed in the little cabin and counted my money. I'd started out with seventy-one dollars. But at the rate I was spending money for gas and lodging, eats and oil and new inner tubes, I couldn't travel for more than another few days. And then I wouldn't have enough to get started trapping. I'd have to find a job wherever I went. And if I was going to turn around and go home I'd have to do it while I still had enough money to make it back to Green River.

I laid awake much of the night listening to traffic on the highway. It was strange to think I was in the North. But I wasn't sure I felt really there. Maybe I was just thinking about being there.

When it was daylight I packed up my cheap suitcase and pointed the Model T north again. As flat as the land was, I could feel it sloping steadily toward water. The air was cooler, with a damp wind out of the northwest. Farms got fewer and smaller the further I drove. And every little town seemed to have a factory of its own. The sun was out, but the air had something in it, something faintly lavender or red. Soot, I guessed, from the smokestacks and trains. The traffic on the highway got heavier, with many more trucks and buses. The highway got wider, with two lanes going each way. I gripped the wheel and hoped I didn't have a flat.

By the middle of the morning I crossed a great bridge into Toledo. You never seen such a place as I was driving through. Along the high-way was three enormous mills high as little mountains, and one rail-road yard after another. There was long warehouses made out of tin, with loading docks like porches. I'd seen places like that in pictures, but what you can't get from pictures is the size of things. There was brick buildings covering a hundred acres. I passed grain elevators high as Meetinghouse Mountain. Some silos was so tall they throwed shadows across the highway.

I drove on, as far as it was from Green River to Tompkinsville, without seeing anything but mills and warehouses, elevators and gantry cranes. Where did all the people live? There was switching yards that glistened like new-plowed fields. How many people had it took to make all this? And how many did it take to keep it all going?

The city of Toledo itself, when I finally reached it, was disappoint-ing. It was just like the other cities I'd drove through, maybe a little bigger than some. I'd planned to stop, but instead I just kept going with the traffic. I stopped at red lights with all the other cars and trucks and buses, and then rushed forward with the stream like wa-ter breaking from a dam. I felt like I couldn't pull over if I wanted to. I told myself there was no place to park. I knowed that if I did stop I would turn back and the trip would be over. Something pulled me on to keep going with the roar of the traffic. The most important thing was not to have a flat tire out in the river of traffic, for then I would drown. I looked out for the lights at the corners and for policemen giving directions. I wanted to look just like everybody else.

Nobody had told me a city was so loud. With so many horns blar-ing and brakes screeching and sirens, I didn't feel at myself. I couldn't remember what I wanted to do. A truck pulled in front of me, and I couldn't see where I wanted to go or needed to turn. A trolley rung its bell and just missed my fender. Even if I had wanted to stop, I couldn't have. The air smelled like rotten eggs and burned motor oil. There was a stench of melted rubber. A woman dashed in front of the Model T chasing a child, and I just barely missed her. Two sol-diers was fighting in front of a café.

After what seemed like twenty-five miles I found myself driving through factories and railroad yards again. There was long warehouses and big storage bins. There was mountains of coal and gravel with loaders reaching like goosenecks to the tops of the piles. I was near the lakefront, for on my left I could see piers and wide ships and gantries and loading cranes. It was the Great Lakes. I'd reached the Great Lakes and wanted to stop and have a look. But there was no place to pull off the highway and look. Many of the yards and docks had fences along the highway.

Traffic got faster than it had been in the city and I had to keep moving with it. The road swung back to the northwest, away from the harbor, and there was only one more warehouse and beyond that was marshland. I could smell mud and foul water. I wanted to look at the lake, so I turned quick into the loading area beside the long building. A platform run along the side of the warehouse out into the water. There was piles of rope and spools of cable heaped on the platform.

"Hey mister," somebody called.

I looked around to see who was hollering. A man stood at the door of the building with a clipboard in his hand. "What can I do for you?" he said.

"I just wanted to look at the docks," I said.

"What do you mean, 'look at the docks'?"

"I just wanted to have a look," I said.

"Then I suggest you look someplace else," the man said.

"I just wanted to look," I said. I couldn't think of nothing else to say.

"Keep moving, buddy," the man said. "Get out of here."

I felt like he'd knocked the breath out of me. My gun was in the back under all the gear. I wished I had it out to pull on the Yankee smart-talker. I stood by the car several seconds trying to think what to say. The wind off the lake was deadly cold and made me shiver. It was right out of Canada, I thought. If I kill a Yankee I'll never see Green River again. I won't see the graveyard where Grandpa and Daddy is buried, or the south side of the pasture hill on a warm winter day. My knees shook a little.

"You ain't got no right to talk to me that way," I said.

"What way?" the man with the clipboard said. He stepped off the platform and come closer to me. He looked at the tag on the Model T. "You tell Metcalf he better send somebody smarter if he wants to spy on us," he said.

"I just wanted to look at the lake," I said.

The man with the clipboard kicked the tire of the Model T. And then he looked at me like I was a hobo. "Maybe you *are* as dumb as you look," he said.

"Listen here, mister," I said.

"You better get in that flivver and beat it," he said, "if you ever want to see Carolina again."

A boat was pulling into the dock. It was bigger than a speedboat. I guess it was a cabin cruiser.

"Get out of here!" the man hollered.

I got into the car and shifted into low. The man leaned in the window and yelled right in my ear, "You tell Metcalf he can kiss my ass!"

My hands shook as I turned left onto the highway. I had to drive all the way back through the miles of warehouses and salvage yards and braiding tracks. There was smokestacks giving off yellow smoke that burned my skin. A gray-and-purple haze hung over the highway.

Now where are you going? I said to myself. The traffic churned around me, and horns blared and *oogah-oogah*ed. I drove without looking back, into the city and through the city. I gripped the wheel and watched out for red lights. I kept thinking of stopping and going back to shoot the man with the clipboard, or at least hitting him upside of the head. He'd insulted and humiliated me. I owed it to myself to shoot him.

And then it come to me that the boat arriving at the dock must have been coming from Canada, carrying liquor from Canada. That's why he'd wanted me out of the way so quick, why he had got so mad. He was afraid I'd see what they was doing. He thought I was a spy for another bootlegger named Metcalf. Metcalf was a competitor, or even a revenue agent for all I knowed. I kept driving without hardly thinking where I was going. The stench of car exhaust and smoke from the factories filled the Model T and made my head feel light.

I knowed there was other people, regular people, in the North, but they was hid away behind walls and I couldn't get to them. There must be churchgoing people, decent people, in the cities and small towns, preachers and builders, teachers and architects, but I didn't know where to find them.

Now, I had been cramped up in the car for the past two days and hadn't took a good shit. I was used to working and walking miles every day. And I was used to eating more than I had in the little diners and restaurants I'd stopped at. Getting mad at the man with the clipboard must have stirred something inside me, for I felt a pain and a dull restlessness in my guts.

But I was in the middle of traffic in Toledo, Ohio, and there was no place to stop and no place to pull off. I tried to think where people would go when they traveled through a city. Some filling stations had toilets behind them, but I didn't see any filling stations. In the country, churches had toilets behind them, but in the city I didn't see any toilets near the churches.

I crossed the Maumee River and there was more factories and brick buildings beyond. I tried to remember how far it was to open country south of the river. I'd been so excited driving toward Toledo that I hadn't noticed the miles as the countryside had give way to the outskirts of the city.

My compass laid on the seat behind me. I'd planned to use it in the woods of the Far North. Its blue needle quivered and pointed away from where I was going. The blue sliver trembled like my hands on the steering wheel. I wished I could just pull over and empty myself.

In the woods you don't have to worry about looking for a toilet. In the woods you can just go behind a tree and find comfort. Out on the highway I didn't even know where I could stop and park. There was stores and houses everywhere. I could be arrested just for stopping.

The pain wrenched inside me, a dull sad pain that felt like grief. And then it got sharper, and I gripped the wheel like it was pulling me on. I drove faster and sweat dampened my temples. It seemed like the buildings and stores and offices would never end. Finally I seen a clump of pine woods ahead. It wasn't more than an acre of trees, bigger than a clump, but not a real woods. But it was big enough and there wasn't any houses close to it. I pulled off on the shoulder of the road and into a haul road. Soon as I stopped the car I jumped out and run into the thicket. And soon as I was out of sight of the road I dropped my pants and squatted.

It was like there was an explosion inside me. A thunderstorm boomed and tore open in my guts and everything busted loose. I felt like everything I'd ever eat rushed out of me. It felt so good it hurt. I was sweating I was so weak, and I held on to a little pine bush. Just having a quiet place to shit was heavenly.

I'd left the world of the Blue Ridge Mountains, where a toilet was wherever you needed it, and where you could stop and look as long as you wanted to.

My insides was inflamed with release. They hummed with relief and freedom so intense I felt a little numb. And I felt like I'd been reborn.

Twelve

Ginny

I ALWAYS HOPED something would come of Muir's talk of building a house or even a castle. I knowed he wasn't going to build a castle, but if everybody's home is his castle, then Muir might build a home. From the time he was a little boy he had studied Pa's old architecture book. It was a book Pa had bought a long time ago on one of his trips down to Greenville, and it had pictures of churches and other fancy buildings in London. From the time he was a boy Muir had copied floor plans and drawings of churches from it.

Muir would take a pencil and any old piece of paper, the back of an envelope or a scrap of a paper bag, and scratch out the lines of a house or bridge, a tower or a steeple. He liked to draw castle walls, and he drawed straight lines with a length of lath took from the shed. He measured and he erased. He would get mad and throw the page away. And the next thing you know he'd be scratching on a paper again.

I knowed Muir would always have trouble working with other people. Maybe he took it after Tom a little bit. And maybe he took it after me. Tom never did like to take orders, and he always wanted to be working at his own plans and projects, on his own land. From the time Muir was a little boy he liked to work, but only at something he had dreamed up. He wanted to work in his own way, at his own grand schemes. If I put him and Moody to gathering corn or fixing a fence, they might gee-haw for a little while, but next thing you knowed, Muir would have lost his temper because Moody was bossing him around and teasing him. Muir never would do what nobody told him to do.

I wanted Muir to find his life's work, but I knowed it wouldn't do any good to push him in any one direction. He was stubborn and contrary if he thought you was telling him what to do. I had wanted him to be a preacher. I thought he had a natural gift to be a preacher, that he was born to be a preacher. And look what come of that. I had always wanted him and Moody to work together, and they had fought worse than ever. Only thing they had done together was go down to Gap Creek for a load of liquor in the Model T. Muir was ashamed of that and didn't think I knowed about it. I knowed he wasn't going to become a bootlegger like Moody, but I worried about his guilt and confusion.

So when Muir packed up the Model T and headed for Canada, I told myself it might be for the best. Of course I was scared, with him leaving home and him so young and uncertain. And going off in that car he could have a wreck or be robbed by gangsters. Canada was a long way off, and people froze to death there. I had read Jack London and remembered "To Build a Fire."

When Muir started loading up the car to go north, my heart felt trapped in ice. I seen there was no way I could stop him. He was so unhappy and desperate to strike out on his own. He was so sick of hisself and ashamed of hisself. A mama can't do much with a son that is drove by demons.

A man has to find his work in his own way. Tom had taught me that. All I could do was look on and pray that Muir would be safe, and that he would return to us.

The morning after Muir left for Canada, the house felt empty, even though Fay and Moody was still there. It was early fall and I went out and gathered eggs and milked the cows. As I strained the milk I thought, Everything on the place feels loose and distant. I was used to having Muir there going about his work. I was used to complaining to him. He was the child I had put my hopes in. He was the son that give a shape to the things I had wanted and the things I had expected when I was young.

"Who is going to dig the taters?" I said to Fay and Moody.

"Muir will dig the taters like he always does," Moody said.

"How will Muir dig the taters while he is in Canada?" Fay said.

"Because he will be back before his tracks are gone from the yard," Moody said. "He'll run out of money and come straight back home," Moody said.

I wanted to take up for Muir. I wanted to say he could make it on his own and find his way to Canada, if that's what he wanted. Much as I hated to see him go, and much as I wanted him to come back, I didn't want to think Muir would come home out of failure and weak nerve. I didn't want to think he'd be defeated again. A mama is divided that way. I didn't want Muir to fail in his ambitions, and I didn't want to lose him either. I was pained and tore both ways.

"Who is going to churn today?" I said. The crock of clabber set by the hearth was ready to be stirred and brought off.

"I'll churn if I can set on the porch and sleep while I'm doing it," Moody said. Moody had already had a drink that morning; I could smell it on him. He surprised me by volunteering.

"The crock is ready to turn," I said.

It warmed my heart to think that Moody was so accommodating. Was it because he was glad to have Muir away? Or was it because he missed Muir already? I was old enough to know a person can feel two or three ways at the same time. But whatever the reason, it was a pleasure to see Moody willing to help out.

That day and the day following, Moody done more work on the place than he had in years. He picked enough fox grapes in the trees by the river for me to make twelve pints of jelly. He fixed the gate to the pasture so it didn't creak and scrape the ground when it opened. He even hitched up the wagon and helped me carry the tops Muir had cut from the cornfield to the stack behind the barn.

I seen Moody had been so contrary because Muir argued with him. And he was ashamed, now Muir had gone, maybe for good, and was trying to make up for it. Muir and Moody had brought out the worst in each other all these years.

I had always showed Muir favor, and I reckon that had kept Moody riled up and lashing out. I had favored Muir in my heart. Moody was feeling more at home and at ease with his younger brother gone. I was the guilty one. I was glad for his help and for his change of heart, but I felt guilty too.

Moody helped me pick up apples in the orchard to make cider. We gathered all the apples that had fell in the grass and washed them in a tub by the springhouse, then crushed them in the cider mill. The air was filled with the scent of ripe and busted apples. Moody sweated and the smell of liquor on his breath mixed with the scent of ripe apples.

"Where do you reckon Muir is by now?" I said. It was the third day since Muir had left.

"He's probably holding to the North Pole by now and trying to kiss a polar bear," Moody said.

"I hope the car don't break down," I said.

"The Model T is so simple you can fix it with chewing gum and a tin can," Moody said.

"He will need heavy clothes in the North," I said. As I turned the screw on the press, golden juice foamed out through the cracks and gathered in the groove and run to the spout. Fresh cider has the most mellow smell.

"Muir can kill a polar bear and sleep under its hide," Moody said. He was in a jolly mood, and the more he worked the more cheerful he got. I'd never seen him work so long and steady.

"I hope Muir will go to church in the North," I said. Juice bubbled and seethed out of the cracks in the press and run to the bucket beneath the spout. Flies and yellow jackets buzzed around us.

"Maybe he can preach to the wolverines," Moody said as he dumped more apples in the grinder.

"It broke his heart that his preaching failed," I said.

"Maybe he will be a preacher yet," Moody said.

I thought how Muir was really just a boy still.

THAT NIGHT I had a dream about Muir. He was faraway but I seen him pushing the Model T, like it had run out of gas or broke down. He was pushing the car down the road in flat country with briars and bushes on either side. And then I seen it wasn't a road but a river he was pushing the car in. He was wading in water up to his knees and pushing the Model T. It was a muddy river and the current was fast, and I heard a roar of shoals or a waterfall ahead. But he was so busy pushing he didn't hear the noise. Watch out, I hollered, and tried to touch him. But he couldn't hear me, and he just kept struggling through the muddy water. I reached out again but couldn't touch him. And I seen there wasn't any wheels on the Model T. And then I woke up and heard the crickets on the pasture hill.

T h i r t e e n
Muir

I PULLED INTO a diner between Dayton and Cincinnati. It was near dark and the light inside was so bright I blinked as I set down on a stool. I ordered coffee and two hotdogs all the way. I was hungry for onions and chili on the weenies.

A salesman in a shiny striped suit set down beside me and laid his soft gray hat on the counter. "How you doing, buddy?" he said. I nodded and kept eating. I didn't want to have nothing else to do with strangers, but he sounded like he was from down home. He leaned over and asked me where I was headed.

"North Carolina," I said and kept chewing.

"That's where I'm from," he said. He told me he was from Raleigh and that he sold advertising for Mail Pouch tobacco. It was good to hear a friendly voice.

"What you doing way off up here?" he said and winked. "If you don't mind my asking."

I told him that I had planned to trap in Canada but changed my mind.

"Why would you freeze your butt in Canada when we have the most fur in North America right in North Carolina?" he said.

"Where?" I said.

"Why, on the Tar River, east of Raleigh," he said. "I come from that area, and where the river runs from Rocky Mount to Tarboro and then to Greenville, there is so many muskrats they're a nuisance to farmers."

"Don't nobody trap them?" I said.

"Sure, people trap them," he said. "But there's so many it don't make no difference."

He described the pine woods along the Tar River, and the muskrat tunnels in the banks of the stream. He said the winters was mild down there, and I'd be a fool to go to Canada when the Old North State had more fur than anybody could catch in a hundred lifetimes. When I got up to leave he give me his card.

I got back in the Model T, and as I drove toward Cincinnati I kept thinking about the muskrats on the Tar River, and about the level pine woods in eastern North Carolina. I thought about the mild winters there, and the hundreds of dollars worth of fur I could catch in one season. Everything Mr. MacFarland had said had took me by surprise. I stopped for the night in a little tourist court just north of Cincinnati. All night I dreamed about hundreds of muskrats with glistening fur.

I reached Green River in the middle of the next night. It was two o'clock in the morning as I turned onto the Green River Road. The dirt road was rough and rocky and jolted me awake. A possum run across the ruts in front of me. When I seen that grizzly possum I knowed I couldn't go back to the house. It hit me that sudden. If I went back to the house Mama and Moody and everybody else in the community would see I was defeated. I was defeated again. I had failed as a preacher, and I had failed as a trapper in the North. I had drove bootleg whiskey for Moody. I couldn't go back to face U. G. knowing I still owed him money.

What I did was stop the Model T at the gate to the pasture. I turned the motor off and the lights off and set there in the dark. The motor creaked and ticked as it cooled. Katydids and crickets was loud in the pasture and in the trees above the road. In Toledo I had wanted more than anything else to be home. I had wanted to set my feet on the ground of Green River. But now that I was there I couldn't bear to face Mama. I couldn't face myself either if I just drove up into the yard and admitted I had been defeated. I was still ashamed of myself.

I wanted to be a trapper, and I wanted the freedom of the woods and creek banks. I could not be satisfied with just working around the place knowing I was a failure and a coward. I set in the dark and listened to the blood behind my ears.

A plan started taking shape in my head as I set there in the car. Instead of going back to the house in disgrace, I would head down to the Tar River to trap that winter. I could make hundreds of dollars in a few months catching muskrats. The winter was mild there and I could camp out in the pine woods by the river. I could live on rabbits and squirrels and save my money, and see a part of the state I'd never seen. And when I come back I would not look as foolish as I did now. Maybe I could respect myself.

I set in the dark and shivered, thinking what a good plan it was. I still had forty dollars left, enough for a train ticket to get me down there. I wouldn't take the Model T but would leave it for Moody and Mama to use. I'd have to carry my traps and things to the train depot and leave them to be shipped to Rocky Mount on the Tar River. And then I would leave the car by the gate with a note and walk back to the depot.

I got my map of North Carolina out and studied it by match light. The Tar River run through Rocky Mount and Tarboro and Greenville. I could take the train and be there in a day. I could camp out and catch hundreds of muskrats. Why hadn't I thought of that before? I knowed everything about catching muskrats. The Lord was showing me how to get away from Green River, and how not to be such a failure.

I would be living in the woods, and I would need a boat to trap on the river. But I could buy the boat once I got down there. I already had my traps and scent bottles, mackinaw coat and boots. I would pack them all up in a box to ship to Rocky Mount. I would leave a note in the car at the gate saying I was trapping on the Tar River and would be back in the spring. I was so tickled at the plan I grinned in the dark.

I'D NEVER TOOK a long train trip before. I'd been to Tompkinsville and Spartanburg and Asheville. I'd never seen the eastern
part of the state, but I'd seen pictures of the flat fields and lazy
swamp-lined rivers, the wide pine forests of the coastal plain. I kept
thinking about Annie as I rode the train to Asheville, about how
she'd look when she was growed up a little bit more. I was still mad
at her for flirting with so many boys.

I had to make that journey. I was thrilled and sad at the same time.
You have to go far away before you can return and start again, I said
to myself. You have to go east to go west. It sounded like something
I'd read in a book about Columbus.

I looked out the train window at the trees on the mountainside,
the yellow poplars and gold hickories, the red and orange maples.
The world through the window looked like a painted picture. I wished
I could draw a mountainside of colorful fall trees. I patted the bills in
my pocket. The crisp money felt alive.

THERE WAS A two-hour layover in Asheville. My suitcase and
shotgun and coat had to be carried into the station. The big box of
equipment was being sent on as freight. I set in the station surrounded
by my gear and looked around the crowd in the station for faces that
I knowed. Everybody that I seen was a stranger. Everywhere I went
I'd be looking for faces that I knowed, like I was still on Green River.

The train east finally left around ten o'clock. I wrestled my stuff
on board and settled in a seat. This is a long trip away that will give
you months of freedom, I said to myself as I watched Asheville drift
away. After swinging around the end of Beaucatcher Mountain, past
the many summer hotels and cottages, past the TB sanitarium at
Oteen, the train begun the long climb up the Swannanoa River to the
crest of the Blue Ridge.

There was brief stops at Swannanoa and Black Mountain before
we slipped through the nick of the mountain wall and begun winding
down into the Piedmont. A tunnel passed us under a ridge. I have read
that building the railroad into the mountains was one of the most
spectacular construction jobs east of the Rockies. The state of North
Carolina started the railroad several times before the Confederate

War and tried for ten years after the war to complete the line. But the grade was too steep and a lot of the ridge was solid granite under a thin covering of soil and trees. Twice, the money was raised and then embezzled by officers of the railroad company. Finally the road was built with convict labor. The state was too poor to afford blasting powder, so they heated the rock face with giant log fires and then doused the spot with floods of cold creek water. That cracked the granite and they was able to pry and hammer a few feet loose at a time. There was riots and knifings in the convict camp, and a lot of prisoners died while building the high trestles. Finally in 1879 the rails from Morganton and the east connected in the middle of the tunnel with the tracks coming down from Asheville.

As we come out of the tunnel I could see the engine puffing in a curve far below. The tracks coiled down the mountain through eight or ten curves. Ahead I could see out fifty miles or more over the foothills and the autumn woods to where fields of shocked corn and red clay gullies disappeared into the haze. It was like I'd passed through a barrier and there was a new world ahead, at my feet. I felt joy mixing with the sadness as we turned and twisted down the mountainside and roared through smaller tunnels. I seen the great fountain at Old Fort raising its sheaf of feathery water against the breeze in the station yard. I watched a river winding as it descended and split apart over a rocky bed.

All day long, as we stopped in Hickory, Statesville, Winston-Salem, and then Durham and Raleigh, I kept thinking what a big wonderful state this was. The towns was almost like northern cities I'd seen. There was tall buildings in the centers of the towns, and big shining cars around the stations. And there was many warehouses and tobacco-scented districts of factories and storage buildings. The smell of tobacco hung over the towns like clear smoke.

It was between Burlington and Durham, late that afternoon, that I set behind a group of college boys. From their talk I understood they'd been to a debate at Davidson College and was returning to Trinity College. They must have won, for they sounded loud and full of theirselves. All wore blue jackets and little white-and-blue caps. When the conductor was not around they passed a thin flask among theirselves. I couldn't tell from the talk what the debate had been about.

"I could have died with pleasure when he said, 'It's part of the modern *consciness* to be concerned about the poor.' I couldn't believe my sweet ears. I wondered if he was confusing *consciousness* with *conscience*."

"That was choice," another boy said.

"Then after he said it once he couldn't seem to stop repeating it. He must have said it ten times."

"Oh, that was rich, really rich," another boy said.

"No, that was choice; let's say really choice."

"If you must say so."

"I once had a science teacher," the first boy said, "who couldn't say the word *oxygen*. It seemed impossible for him. Something like *okigen* was the best he could manage. He would avoid saying *oxygen* as long as he could, referring to 'element number sixteen' or 'O_2' and 'the element we breathe.' But since it was a science class he eventually had to say the word again, and it always came out *okigen*."

"Oh, that's rich."

"No, choice, my boy, choice."

"Oh, you're drunk. Be careful or we'll get thrown off the train."

"And this same science teacher couldn't say *debris* either. He always pronounced it *derbis*."

"Oh, come on, you're giving lying a bad name."

The conductor eyed the boys as he passed through the car, but he didn't say nothing. I reckon I'm as smart as any of them, I said to myself as I listened to them giggle.

IT WAS NIGHT before the train reached Raleigh. There was another two-hour layover there before I could catch the train going further east. I checked my suitcase and shotgun into a big locker and walked out to look at the state capitol. I wanted to see the monument I'd read so much about. I wanted to see the capitol building itself. But when I found the building I was a little disappointed. The dome looked like something unfinished, no bigger than many courthouse domes. I was in a kind of stupor from the long day of travel. I walked over to the Confederate monument and read the inscription below the marble statue: FIRST AT BETHEL, FARTHEST AT GETTYSBURG AND CHICKAMAUGA, LAST AT APPOMATTOX. It was after midnight, and I studied those words in the floodlights and thought of Grandpa at Petersburg and Chickamauga.

I GOT OFF the train at Rocky Mount between three and four in the morning. There was a few lighted streetlamps, but everything was closed up. I hoped there'd be somebody to give me directions. According to my map the river run right through town. And since the town wasn't all that big I figured I couldn't be more than half a mile from the river. But I didn't know which way to go. I took out the map and tried to study it under a streetlight but couldn't read the fine detail. There was no point in hunting around in the dark anyway. I wanted to get out in the country as soon as possible, but I'd need help carrying the box of traps and supplies. And I wanted to get something to eat before I left for the river also.

In the early morning damp I walked back and forth on the station platform to keep warm. It was damp and bone chilling. My suitcase and shotgun was stacked on the cardboard box by the station door and I stood by them shivering before I started walking again. My clothes didn't seem to give any protection against the chill. I looked at the clock above the station door and seen it was almost five.

There was a stink I'd been smelling without noticing it, a muddy and rotten smell like old rags that had got wet and soured. And there was another smell, not so much of fish as of earthworms, and maybe rotten eggs. It must have been the river and the smell of the toilets behind the shacks along the river. And there was a smell of wet ashes and of rancid bones washed by rain.

I stood on the platform and stomped my feet and beat my hands together. So this is what you have come to, I said, freezing to death and starving in a strange place at five o'clock in the morning? And all to trap muskrats, to make money, to keep away from Green River. It was hard to follow the reason of it all as I shivered with the dampness.

Around five-fifteen a mail wagon drove up and a man in uniform got out, lifting a sack down from the paneled van. When he seen me he said, "Yes sir, are you waiting for the train?"

"I got off the train," I said, my teeth chattering, "more than an hour ago."

"Do you need help with anything?" he said.

"Need help carrying my stuff to the river," I said. "I'm going to camp by the river."

"In this weather?" the man said.

"I'll be trapping muskrats," I said. "Maybe some mink too."

"Not much fur in these parts, boy. You have come to the wrong place."

"Not according to the reports," I said.

"What reports?" the man said. But before I could tell him what the salesman had said, he climbed into the wagon and drove away. I felt tireder and colder than ever as he rattled out of sight. What did he mean, there wasn't any fur here? Would the salesman have lied? Most likely the man was a trapper hisself and wanted to keep others away from the river. Or maybe he had friends and relatives that was trappers. Or maybe he was just an unfriendly person. Some people hate for trappers to come into their territory.

A café down the street opened at five-forty-five, but I was afraid to leave my gear on the platform. It was too heavy for me to carry all of it to the café. The mailman had made me feel uneasy. I wanted to get out on the river as soon as I could.

Just then an old black man drove by in a wagon pulled by a mule. He had several sacks stacked in the wagon bed, like he was going to mill. I run down the steps and called to him.

"Whoa now," the old man said as he reined up the mule. He looked surprised to see me.

"I'll give you a dollar to drive me and my equipment out into the country," I said.

"Where out in the country?" the old man said. "I was on my way to mill."

"Give you two dollars to drive me out to a good camping spot on the river," I said.

The old man backed the wagon up to the platform, and him and me loaded the box and suitcase and shotgun beside the meal sacks. Then I climbed up on the seat beside him. "Powell's my name," I said and held out my hand.

"So's I," the old man said and flicked the reins.

"You mean your name is Powell?" I said.

"Sho is," the old man said.

We drove out of town just as there was beginning to be light in the east. I seen the town was street after street of small houses, most with a tree or two in the yard. The streets run out on very flat bottomland. Just at the edge of town we passed a little store and I asked the driver to stop. The store was just opening, and I run in and bought several cans of pork and beans, a bag of rice, coffee, and sugar. That would get me started, until I had time to shoot a squirrel or catch some fish.

"How you gone trap on the river?" the old man said after we got started again.

"Have to get a boat," I said.

"Where you gone get a boat?" the driver said.

"Do you know anybody that builds boats?" I said.

"Trammel build boats," the old man said.

"Where does Trammel live?" I said.

"Two, three miles up the river. I show you."

"Has he built many boats?" I said.

"Oh, Trammel, he build boats all his life," the old man said. "Five, ten dollar he build a right good boat."

After buying the train ticket, I had twenty-six dollars left. I patted the money in my pocket. We rattled past a tobacco warehouse and a tanning yard. After that we was in open country. The road turned down along the river and I got my first glance of the Tar. The river rushed fast as a flame below the weedy bank. I hadn't expected such flow in the flat country. There was no rocks above the surface or on the bank, like there was in mountain streams. The whole body of the river seemed to roll and splash in one solid rush of flow. There was houses in sight and it was too close to town for me to camp.

"Where you want to go?" the old man said.

"Need a place in the woods to camp," I said.

The road swung back away from the river and didn't get close to the bank again. I could tell the driver didn't want to go much farther. I guess he needed to get his corn to mill.

"That Trammel's house," he said and pointed to a place far across the fields toward the river.

The wagon creaked and rolled on and I seen some swampy-looking woods ahead. The river must have been about a quarter of a mile away. "You can let me out here," I said when we got to the pine woods. The ground was low, but at least there was some cover from the wind. The old man and me unloaded the box and carried it into the brush.

"Is there any muskrats here?" I said as I give him two dollars.

"You find muskrats anywhere they plenty of mud," the old man said.

"This looks muddy enough," I said.

The old man folded the bills and slid them in his bib pocket, then climbed onto the wagon. He slapped the reins on the mule's back and drove away with his sacks of corn.

HAD TO MAKE several trips into the woods, carrying first my suitcase and shotgun, then half the contents of the big box, then the box itself. I had to find a place to camp, and it didn't take me long to see it would have to be back a ways from the muddy stream. Creek banks in the mountains was firm and rocky. The banks here was low and mushy ground.

Took me half an hour to find a fairly dry spot, two or three hundred yards from the river. I wished I'd asked the old man where the nearest spring was, for without clear water I couldn't make coffee. I was tired and needed some sleep. I got a fire going and warmed a can of pork and beans. After eating the whole can I unrolled the blanket and laid down. I was so tired I felt sore all over. Even my joints was sore from the long train ride.

As I laid there I heard a crow somewhere off in the woods. Crows sounded the same everywhere. A wagon creaked by on the road a few hundred yards away, but I didn't bother to raise my head to look at it. I hoped they couldn't see my camp from the road. And then I heard a train whistle not too far away, going west toward the mountains.

When I woke it was the middle of the afternoon and the sun was warm in the thicket. The air felt like August instead of early fall.

With weather that warm the fur would be thin. And thin fur brought a lower price. I would have to catch more muskrats to make up for the thinness.

I was stiff from sleeping on the ground and still sore from the night on the train. And it was like my head was numb from being in a strange place and waking up at that time of day. I figured it would take me a few days to scout the river and to get a boat built. I might as well take my time. It was too warm to feel like trapping season. Maybe it would turn cold soon. I hoped it would be a cold winter, even though I'd be camping outdoors.

After eating another can of pork and beans, I gathered up my stuff as best I could and heaped it together. And I sprinkled leaves over everything so it wouldn't be noticed in the undergrowth. Then I took my canvas bucket to look for water. I had to have water. That was the first thing to find.

I figured the Trammel house was about a mile away, and I decided to look there. I crossed the scrubland to a ditch, and beyond the ditch was a field. And beyond the field was another field. Instead of a mile it was more like two or even three. But finally I saw a weathered clapboard house across the stubble of a cornfield.

As I got closer, more than a dozen hounds come out from under the porch. They begun a symphony of barks and bellows as I got near. By the time I reached the yard they had sung all the parts and traded tunes and sung them again. An old black man and two younger black women, and a number of children, come out on the porch and stood there watching me walk up.

"Shut up," the man said to one of the hounds and kicked at it. The dog easily dodged his foot.

I asked him if I could fill my bucket at the well.

"Why, help yourself, sir, just help yourself," the old man said.

The well was at the side of the house, and the dogs nosed around my feet as I approached it. I drawed up the wooden bucket and filled the canvas pail. Holding the water high so the hounds couldn't lick it, I returned to the front of the house. The whole family was still standing on the steps and in the yard.

"I understand you build boats," I said to the man.

"Nah, too old to build no boats," the old man said.

"I heard different," I said. "I need a boat for trapping on the river this winter." One of the bigger dogs jumped up and put its paws on my chest.

"Get down there, Luther," one of the women said. "You get down." She picked up a hoe handle from the porch and hit the dog. "I teach you jump on folks," she said. The whipped dog yelped and slunk away to the side of the house.

"How much did you charge when you did build boats?" I said.

"In the old days about six dollars," the old man said. "But I got rheumatism in my shoulder now, make it hard to hammer and saw."

"I'll give you seven dollars for a johnboat," I said, "if you make it quick before trapping season."

Trammel kicked at the dirt in front of him. He was stooped and his neck wrinkled. But you could tell he'd been a strong man in his time. One eye was swole almost shut. His overalls was faded but had creases ironed in the legs. "Couldn't vex this shoulder for less than ten," he said.

The hounds sniffed their way around me, and chickens pecked here and there in the yard. The yard had been swept clean with a besom. You could see the marks the switches had made in the sand.

"I'll give you eight," I said. "How soon can you do it?"

"Gots to have at least nine," Trammel said.

"How soon can you have it ready?" I said.

The old man studied for a while and spit on the ground. The chickens rushed to the gob. "Can't work on Sunday," he said. "Maybe a week, five or six days. Nigh onto a week."

Before I left I asked where there was a good spring in the woods, not too far from the river.

"Ain't they one near the old Coggins place?" one of the women said.

"No, that's all kiver with mud from the big freshet," the other woman said.

"They one down the river on the other side," Trammel said, "about three, four miles I reckon."

As I walked away with the bucket of water I could feel them

watching me, the old man and the two women, all the children. But I didn't turn to look back, and I didn't stop until I crossed the cornfield and reached a row of trees. And when I did turn to look back the house was out of sight.

The next day I spent the day whacking through thickets and swamps looking for a camping spot near a spring. The springs I did find was in such marshy places I couldn't set up a camp, or so near a cow pasture I was afraid to drink the water. The springs was full of rotten leaves and mud and needed to be dug out and cleaned in any case. When I looked at the muck and scum on the water I thought of typhoid. Typhoid fever killed my daddy. Springs in the mountains was bold, with cold clear water throbbing out of the ridge or hillside. Here a spring was sluggish, just a seepage, a swamping up through trash. In places puddles was covered with rusty mucus and metallic-looking purple-and-blue slime, and a jelly coating. Gnats fizzed up around rotten logs.

My boots got scratched and muddy, and my pants picked by briars. I didn't know where I was going to wash clothes. I had parted brush and looked for solid dry ground. Everyplace I walked along the river I looked for muskrat sign but didn't see any. Was I on the wrong side of the river, or along the wrong stretch of the river? According to the salesman, I should have been right in the middle of muskrat country.

Late that afternoon I hiked several miles downstream to a bridge and crossed over to explore the northern bank. It was getting up toward dark, but in some yellow pines I found a pretty bold spring, and some dry ground within a hundred yards of the spring. It was almost directly across the river from where I left my things in the morning. I'd have to wait until the boat was finished to carry my gear across, rather than lug the stuff down to the bridge and back up the other side. I'd seen only a few muskrat tracks, and no mink tracks at all. Once I glimpsed a coon track on a side branch, and I let a polecat pass far down the trail in front of me.

FOR THE NEXT four days I was busy looking for muskrat sign. I was beginning to wonder where the fur was. I slept in the thicket near the road, and every morning I walked down to the Trammel house to fill my canvas bucket. The old man didn't get the planks from the sawmill until Monday. He completed the frame of the boat Wednesday. Maybe it was his rheumatism that slowed him down, but he sure didn't seem to be in any hurry.

I was getting wore out by waiting for the boat. And I still hadn't found enough muskrat sign to spit at. The next day I walked all the way into town for new supplies. In the store there was men setting around the stove, just like they would be at U. G.'s store. There was two old fellows playing checkers. They didn't appear to even notice me.

With my sack full of cans and loaves of bread I walked back along the dusty road and across the fields to the camp in the thicket. If I was home Mama would be talking over the news with me and Fay, and with Aunt Florrie. And Moody would be making fun of somebody. We'd be setting by the fire talking about what was in the newspaper. Mama liked to read the paper and keep up with the news. If there was a bad story she would point out that such ruin is foretold in the Bible, in Revelation.

As I walked through the tobacco fields and cotton fields and pine woods, and along the wide muddy river, nothing out there seemed to notice my problems. Leaves blowed off some of the oaks and poplars along the river and scattered out into the fields. Ducks flew creaking and squawking far out over the river. A single cloud high above me was lit by the late sun. I hoped my money didn't run out before I started catching and selling pelts.

I'd planned to live by my gun and fishing. But I'd spent almost a week looking for a camp and carrying water from Trammel's well, and looking for muskrat sign. I hadn't seen much game, but I'd killed several squirrels and fired once at a quail and missed. I was going to have to start supplying myself with meat, now that I'd spent so much money on flour and coffee, sardines and pork and beans, and the candy bars I couldn't seem to resist when I went to the store.

THE NEXT DAY it took me an hour to find and kill a rabbit that made only one meal. There was so many dogs in the area the rabbits was kept thinned out. But there was squirrels in the oaks and hickories, back away from the river, and while I waited for the boat to be finished I lived more and more on squirrels stewed with taters or fried in flour. A few I shot had wolves in their skin, big fat grubs squirming in the fur, and I throwed those away. The sight of so many fat grubs near the tender flesh begun to kill my appetite and taste for squirrels.

The fishing I tried in the muddy river was mostly useless. In the mountains I growed up casting for trout in Green River and the clear feeder creeks, or using worms in the deeper pools after a rain. But in that dirty bigger stream I found it hard to find the holes. The water was so murky it was hard to judge the depth. I figured maybe the still places was deeper. I cut a willow pole and tied my line to it, and I caught nothing but hog suckers and one ten-inch bass. The brown smelly river turned my stomach against eating anything caught there.

I'd heard the Tar River got its name from the tar kilns on the banks farther down toward the coast. But somebody else said the river was called that because of the dark stains that seeped into the current from swamps. Wherever they got the name, it appeared to be the right one, for the thick black mud and silt looked like tar even if it did smell like rotten eggs and rancid grease. The mud stuck to everything the current touched, and pushed up fat cushions of slime in eddies.

FINALLY FRIDAY AFTERNOON old man Trammel had the boat ready and brought it up to my camp in his mule-drawn wagon. The craft looked a little rough to me. Not all the joints was even. The lumber hadn't been sanded, and only the tar in some of the cracks would keep the water out.

"Is this wood green?" I said. The planks didn't look seasoned.

"Gots to swell closed," Trammel said. "All new boats leak a little."

We carried the little boat down to the river and set it in the mud. I paid Trammel the nine dollars, and I didn't have but fifteen left. I'd have to start catching fur soon. But even if I caught muskrats the next day it would be another month before the hides would be cured enough to sell.

I took the two freshly carved oars and launched my new craft into the muddy current. I had to row up to the camp in the thicket and carry my gear across the river to the higher ground in the pine woods. But once I got out into the current and pointed the boat upstream, I seen I had a lot to learn about rowing. I'd paddled a canoe on the river and on the lake below the cotton mill. But I'd never really rowed a boat before. It looked so simple. But I found myself going around in a circle while the river carried me quick downstream. When I finally straightened out and headed back upriver I seen how much ground I'd lost. Trammel stood on the bank beside his mule watching me.

By the time I'd been carried down the river two or three hundred yards I seen the complications of the job at hand. Not only was I going to have to balance the pull of one oar against the pull of the other, matching the depth of stroke and speed, while at the same time offsetting the push of the current, but there was something about the shape of the boat that was wrong. The boat was slightly lopsided and tended toward the left, unless I pulled harder on the left oar. By the time I'd drifted another hundred yards I begun to work with the combination of current and spin and stopped turning in circles. I got the boat under control and slowly started making headway against the river.

Rowing steady and hard, I finally made it back to the launching place, but old man Trammel was gone. There was an inch of water on the floor of the boat. By the time I pulled up in the mud near the camp, even more water was washing across the bottom, into my shoes. Not only was I rowing a lopsided boat, but I'd have to row and bail at the same time. My only hope was that the wet planks would swell together overnight.

I did carry all my belongings to the new camp across the river that afternoon. But even as I set up the little tent, I seen that if I had much of a trapline I'd be moving up and down the river and camping wherever I happened to be at nightfall. If I carried everything with me and the boat turned over I'd lose all my gear. I'd have to leave some supplies at the camp in the pines so I wouldn't be wiped out.

That evening, just as I finished another fried squirrel and started to

wash the pan in springwater, it begun to rain. I moved everything under the piece of canvas stretched between two saplings. The rain con-
tinued in a steady downpour. The rain was quiet but never seemed to
let up. The air got so cold and damp I was shivering in my blankets.

THE NEXT MORNING everything I had was soaked, in spite of
the tent. I laid in the damp blankets in the early light, wishing I didn't
have to get up. I was nearly out of money and three hundred miles
from home, and so far I hadn't caught a single muskrat.

I wasn't sure I could start a fire, because everything was soaked
and dripping and I hadn't thought to put any kindling under the canvas. Lord, show me what to do, I prayed. Show me what is your will
and your plan. If I've been vain, punish me. Let me go farther down
the river and look for muskrat sign below Tarboro. Let me see if I
can find some fur. Don't let me be a complete failure. Give me something to respect in myself.

In the gray drizzle I folded my wet blanket and started to pack my
gear. If it was going to rain all day there was no use to set and wait
for better weather, feeling sorry for myself and thinking about a hot
meal. My matches was dry, but there was nothing else in the woods
dry enough to start a fire with.

A hound bellered not more than fifty feet away. I looked through
the drip from my hat brim and seen a big yellow-and-tan dog standing between two pine trees. The dog shook the tags on its collar and
bellered again. The howl was magnified by the damp air.

"Here, boy," I said and held out my hand, rubbing my thumb on
my fingers. It was always a good idea to make a friendly sign to a
strange dog. "Here, boy," I said again. The dog looked at me and
bellered again and didn't show no interest in being friendly.

Just then I seen two men approaching through the trees. They carried rifles pointed out in front of them. I reckon I seen them before
they spotted me. I thought of ducking and trying to hide in the
brush. But it was too late, for the dog had already found me.

"There he is," one of the men said and pointed at me.

"Hold it right there, mister," the other one hollered. I seen the
badge pinned to his raincoat. The men come up to me with caution,

and the dog bellered again, then whined and whimpered. "Shut up, Digger," one of the men said.

"What are you doing here, boy?" the man with the badge said.

"Camping out," I said. My mouth was dry and jerked a little from the cold.

The sheriff poked with his foot among my gear. He looked at the traps and the shotgun. Rain splashed on everything. "What else are you doing here?" the sheriff said.

"Trapping for muskrats," I said.

The sheriff turned over a pot and looked in my water bucket. "You got a trapping license?" he said.

"I've got one," I said, and reached into my shirt pocket for the slip of paper.

"That's OK," the sheriff said. He poked with the tip of his rifle through the sack of supplies and cooking utensils.

"I ain't caught any muskrats yet," I said. "I was waiting for my boat to get built. I've shot a few squirrels."

The sheriff stepped closer and looked me hard in the face. "We heard you was making liquor with Trammel," he said.

"What?" I said.

"We heard you was helping Trammel make moonshine," he said.

"That sounds crazy," I said.

"That's what people say," the sheriff said. I didn't like the way the deputy held his rifle pointed at me.

"Who told you such stuff?" I said.

"Never you mind who told us," the sheriff said. He kicked over my bag of provisions and the sack of traps. The deputy cut the lines of my tent, and the wet canvas settled to the ground.

"Now, you get away from here," the sheriff said. "We don't want any bootleggers in this county."

"I ain't made nothing," I said.

"Now get," the sheriff said and pointed his rifle at me. I seen I didn't have no choice but to do like he said. He had the badge and he had the rifle on me. The sheriff and his deputy watched as I gathered up my scattered things in the rain. My mackinaw coat was soaked and the canvas was muddy and stuck with trash and pine needles. I carried everything to the boat and seen that the bottom of the boat was covered with more than an inch of water. The boat would have to be bailed out. Suddenly, in a jolt of rage, I turned and faced the sheriff. "You got no right to run me off!" I hollered.

"This is my right," the sheriff said and patted the rifle. "You wouldn't want to fall into the river, would you?" I knowed he must be in the liquor business hisself and was afraid of somebody new horning in.

I took an empty bean can and started to dip out the boat.

"Never mind about that," the sheriff said. "Now get going."

When I shoved off and climbed into the boat and started rowing, the sheriff and his deputy come down to the water's edge and watched me. The hound bellered again, and the deputy raised his rifle and fired into the water beside me, making an ugly *thunk*. I stared hard at them as I pulled on the oars and the boat rocked in the current. I bent over low till I thought I was out of rifle range.

RAIN DIMPLED THE water behind me as I rowed. The river was rolling and chopping in flood. It must have rained a lot upstream in the night. Everything, water, sky, trees, shore, all was the same dull gray as the mud on my boots and the water in the boat. The mud was on everything, blankets, pants, hands, shotgun. Everything smelled sour, like the river itself was spoiled and rotten. The river looked infected, as if thousands of outhouses and barns had emptied their runoff into it. And there was no rocks or white water to thrash and clear the flow. The silt on the bottom and the muddy banks melted into everything.

I stared hard at the sheriff and deputy, expecting them to shoot at me, until I swept around the bend of the river. Then I looked down at the mess of my belongings at my feet. Everything had been throwed in piecemeal, and water sloshed over my boots and the bags of pots and pans. The meal bag had broke and spilled cornmeal in the dirty water. The blankets was as wet as wicks. I shivered with cold and with anger.

But the boat was not leaking as bad as I'd feared. The swelling overnight must have partly sealed the joints. I rowed far out into the river, into the fastest current, and then I tried to row downstream ahead of the current. I looked over my shoulder for snags, but the water seemed to have swept away all planters and sawyers. I thought about stopping somewhere ahead and looking for muskrat sign, but I wasn't sure exactly where the county line was. Would the sheriff of this county tell the sheriff of the next county to watch out for a stranger in a boat? He knowed I was going downstream in the high water. I thought maybe once I got to Tarboro I'd be in Edgecombe County, but wasn't sure, and I didn't know where my maps was. The river was now so high that most of the places I could have set traps was underwater anyway.

After I rowed several miles in the rain, some ducks flew off the river. I reached for the gun, thinking a roast duck might taste pretty good. But just then the boat swung around in the fast current and I lost my chance. I rested for a minute on the oars and floated past thick pine woods. I passed more tobacco fields. Nobody seemed to be out because of the rain. The river was pricked by the steady downpour, and I was soaked to my armpits. The hunger pains in my belly was getting worse. With the woods and brush dripping on either shore, it would be near impossible to start a fire even if I did put in.

Finally I seen a village maybe half a mile off from the river. At least there was a cluster of houses beyond the river brush and fields, and a church steeple stuck up into the gray sky. Just seeing the church made me feel better. I rowed in close as I could and run the boat up into the mud and tied it to a root. I was so stiff I couldn't hardly stand up when I got out of the boat, and knowed I must look like a wet dog, unshaved and soaked. But at least there was still money in my pocket that could buy something to eat, if there was a store. I tried to wipe the mud off my boots as I walked closer to the first building.

The biggest building in the village had gas pumps in front and a sign that said HEARTSEASE GROCERY. I remembered the village of Heartsease from the map. It was between Rocky Mount and Tarboro.

The men inside looked like the men gathered in any country store. They eyed me as I bought cheese and crackers, sardines, and three candy bars. They looked exactly like U. G. and Hicks and Lon and Charlie setting there by the stove.

"Reckon you're a ways from home?" the man behind the counter said.

"A little ways," I said, knowing I looked wet and miserable.

"When the state of North Carolina goes bust, maybe we won't have to pay taxes," one of the men by the stove said.

"They'll make us pay more taxes," another man said, "to get the government out of the hole."

The heat of the stove felt good, but I knowed I'd better get away before they started asking questions. I crumpled the top of the bag in my fist and slipped out the door. Rain hit my face as I headed to the river. On the boat I eat the sardines and cheese and crackers and tried to decide what to do. I spread the mackinaw coat over my head in a kind of tent and eat the candy bars.

The river was getting higher. It had rose two or three inches since I'd pushed the boat up in the mud. There was no choice but to go on downstream, to Tarboro, or the county east of there. Maybe I could camp in the pine barrens down near Greenville until the rain stopped and the river went down. Surely that was in another county. Maybe if I put my tent deep in the woods I could wait out the wet spell and start looking for muskrat sign again. Maybe things would look different when the rain stopped.

By the time I'd eat the candy bars the rain had slacked, and as I pushed off into the river a wind sprung out of the north. The clouds was churning high above, at different heights, moving at different speeds. As I rowed, the wind begun to chop up the water, splashing me with spray off the oars. In the wind my wet clothes felt full of holes. I had to stop and try to start a fire soon. If I didn't I might take pneumony. But the thought of looking for something dry enough to burn on the muddy banks made me keep rowing. My hands was getting numb on the oars.

By the time I reached Tarboro that afternoon I had a bad chill. I was trembly and almost too weak to guide the boat to shore. The wind had swung hard and straight out of the north and I couldn't stop myself from shaking. I watched two black men in a lumberyard on the shore shifting around a pile of planks.

Then the bow struck something hard underwater, either a rock or a log. The boat almost turned over, and it took in the top of a wave. I dug the oars in deep, trying to balance the boat. But the current was too fast, and it spun me around again. The town with its bridge and lumberyard and the backs of stores whirled by me. The river had got higher and faster. I was already even with the town and passing it.

My left hand was so numb the oar slipped out of it, and as I lunged to catch the shaft I almost fell out of the boat. Water sloshed from end to end over my feet and through my traps, pushing the suitcase around. I wondered if there was shoals ahead that made the river faster. I grabbed the other oar with both hands and tried to paddle closer to shore. But the blade was too heavy and too narrow to get any grip on the water. I drug the oar behind like a tiller to at least make the boat point ahead and not rock so bad.

Already the town had gone whirling by, and I was no closer to the bank than before. Waves leapt up like paws trying to turn the boat over. The boat tilted so bad it felt like I was looking down at the lashing water one second and up at it the next. I thought of Mama standing by the kitchen counter, quietly kneading bread. She didn't even know what had happened to me. Lord, I prayed, it looks like I won't get out of this river alive.

I thought, I could be home setting by the fire. And I heard myself laughing at myself. The wind burned my face like ether and the little boat rocked on the whitecaps as waves twisted it around from one side to the other. I shoved the oar in deeper and deeper. There was six inches of water in the boat, but I couldn't bail and paddle at the same time. The boat rode low in the water. I was going downstream fast as a stampede.

Lord, I prayed, I don't want to die in this filthy river. If it's your will for me to die, I know that I will. But if you spare me I'll go back to Green River and help Mama on the place.

The boat spun around in the raging tide and I stabbed at the waves with the oar. I thrust the oar down like it was a pole to find bottom. The boat tilted and plunged and I seen the water was coming up to get me. I leaned back and then bent low to keep from falling out.

I drove the oar into the ugly water one more time and finally found the bottom. I pushed hard as I could to pole to shore. The boat swung this way and it swung that way, but finally I wrestled it into the shallows and run the prow into the mud and weeds. I figured I must be a mile below the town. I was so wore out I was shaking, and it seemed an astonishment I was still alive at all.

I clawed my way up the bank to see where I was. I was in the yard of a tobacco barn. Two men come out the door and looked at me like somebody that had rose from a grave. I tried to speak, but my teeth chattered so bad it was hard to explain my situation.

"Do you think I could leave my boat here while I go back to the station?" I finally said.

"Don't hear nobody saying no," one of the men said.

"Will you keep an eye on my things?" I said.

"Somebody might tote them away even with my eye on them," the other man said.

"I'll trust you all," I said and tried to grin. I got the suitcase and the shotgun out of the boat. Everything was covered with mud.

"You look like you fell in the river," one of the men said.

"I come close," I said, "mighty close."

I carried the shotgun and suitcase to the road and looked toward the town. Couldn't see where the train station was at first, but as I got closer I seen the tracks and just followed them. And then I could hear the pant of an engine beyond the tobacco sheds. As I walked along, my boots squished they was so full of water. People turned to look at me. I knowed I looked wet and dirty, and when I passed a store window I didn't even recognize myself at first. My hat was ruined by the rain and my face was black with a beard and campfire smoke. My clothes was wrinkled and muddy. I looked worser than a tramp, but there was nothing I could do about it. I walked right into the station carrying the suitcase and the broke-down shotgun.

THE SKY WAS completely clear by the time the train pulled out of Tarboro near dark. My hands shook from the chill and the moving of the train. From the window I could watch the tobacco fields and pine woods and the river in the distance go by, gold in the late sun. But however gold the river might appear at a distance, I could still smell the mud and filthy water on the suitcase and my boots. The stink of the river and its silt seemed to have soaked into my skin and under my nails. I would never forget the rancid grease smell of the river. The Tar River smelled like the muck around the slop chute of a hogpen.

As I set on the train my bones begun to warm up. I could still smell the brown river water and greasy silt somewhere in the back of my head. The train slowed and stopped in Heartsease and I looked out to see the country store where I had bought my dinner, but it was too dark to tell one building from another. I blowed my nose again and again. Mama or Fay would be milking out at the log barn, or throwing corn to the chickens. It was still light that far to the west.

I hadn't hardly noticed the man and woman on the seat in front of me, until their voices rose so loud that other people in the car begun to look toward them. The man was a skinny little feller with a week's growth of beard. The woman was heavy and had her hair pulled tight in a ball on top of her head. Her lips didn't look like they had smiled in years.

"I just want to know where it is!" the woman hollered. She looked hard at the man beside her.

"I told you," the man said. He looked around like he wished nobody was listening.

She turned away and stared out the window. We was on the stretch between Rocky Mount and Raleigh, and the train was picking up speed.

"It's the onliest dollar I had," the woman yelled.

"I told you," the man said. He took out a cigarette and lit it with trembling fingers.

"You told me shit!" the woman said.

"Couldn't help it," the man said.

The train passed a siding where a locomotive and several flatcars loaded with pulpwood waited on a spur. A water tank shot by.

"You couldn't help it," the woman mocked and made a face. He looked away from her and around the car. "Bought yourself a drink," the woman said. "That's what you done. You can't shit me."

"I told you already," the man said, not looking at her.

Suddenly the woman screamed and begun beating the side of the man's head with her fists. He tried to dodge and his cigarette was knocked to the floor. "Ain't nothing to eat!" the woman shouted. She grabbed a purse from her lap and swung it at the man's face.

The man fended her off with his elbow, then turned and shoved her back with the heel of his palm in her face. The woman's head slammed against the window. "You pissant!" she hollered.

I seen the conductor coming down the aisle. Everybody in the whole car was watching to see what he would do. I knowed that anybody misbehaving on a train could be throwed off. The conductor could stop the train and put them off beside the track if he wanted to. Conductors could do whatever they felt like.

I reached into my pocket and pulled out my damp folded bills. I took a one and put the rest back in my pocket. As the conductor got closer I leaned forward and tapped the man on the shoulder. "Is this your money?" I said.

The man wheeled around, startled. "What?" he said.

"I found this behind your seat," I said. "Is it yours?"

The woman grabbed the bill out of my hand before the man could answer.

"What is this?" the conductor said. He prodded the man on the shoulder with the ticket puncher. "What's going on here?" The conductor's belly was so big his coat wouldn't button over his belt buckle.

"Ain't nothing," the man said.

"What was you all hollering about?" the conductor said.

"We was just talking," the man said. He rubbed the back of his neck with a scarred hand.

"They lost a dollar and I found it," I said.

The conductor glared at me, at my beard, my dirty clothes. "Don't allow no trash to fight on this train," he said.

"We was looking for something," the woman said. She stared down at her lap.

"Did you find it?" the conductor said.

"Yeah," the man said, "we found it."

The conductor looked at the man and then at the woman, and then he looked at me. The man stared straight ahead and the woman looked at her purse. The conductor stepped forward and ground out the smoking cigarette on the floor. "Any more trouble and you all are off," he said.

Fourteen

Muir

THAT WINTER AFTER I got back from the Tar River I laid low and worked on the place, like I'd promised the Lord I would. I split rails and built a new fence for Mama around the orchard. Mama frowned and encouraged me by turns, and Moody ribbed me, but I never did tell them I'd nearly drownded on the Tar River. I figured nobody needed to know that. I worked on the road above the spring, and I trapped a little. I couldn't think of any other way to make money. Since I had left my traps on the Tar River, I had to buy new ones from U. G. on credit.

But it was a bad winter and I caught almost nothing in my traps. In February I had to take my pelts to U. G. He was playing checkers by the stove in the back of his store when I brought him the measly pile of furs I had. I still owed him for the traps and a box of shotgun shells I'd got the winter before that. I was ashamed to ask him for more credit.

"What say, Muir?" U. G. said. He glanced up from the checkerboard. He was playing with old Hicks Summey, who claimed he was the champion checkers player in the valley. Hicks liked to take a drink, and he liked to set at the store and play checkers.

"Not much, U. G.," I said and laid my little bundle of furs on the counter.

"Mink didn't run to your traps?" U. G. said.

"It was a poor season," I said.

"Fur ain't worth nothing anyway," U. G. said. "There's too much fur from Canada coming on the market."

I owed U. G. about twenty dollars, and I hadn't saved but five from the molasses money.

U. G. jumped his checkers over several squares on the board and picked up some pieces. "Let's take a look at them skins," he said. U. G. walked behind the counter and inspected each pelt I'd brought and run his fingers through the fur. "Can't give you but eighty-five cents," he said.

"That's not even enough to pay what I owe you," I said. "Ain't got but five dollars to my name." I took out the five-dollar bill.

U. G. looked at the furs and he looked at the bill.

"Wish I could pay you off," I said.

U. G. stared at me so the electric light reflected off his glasses. "You look like a store clerk to me," he said. "You can count and you're honest. You can work off your debt, dollar a day."

It was the last thing I expected. I never had seen myself clerking in a store. But I seen working was better than owing money to U. G. And it was better than staying home and fussing all the time with Moody. Abraham Lincoln had started out as a store clerk. And if I saved my money I could buy a ticket to get away from Green River again for good, if I wanted to.

"Here, let me get you an apron," U. G. said.

"Are you going to play checkers or not?" Hicks hollered from the stove.

"Do I have to wear an apron?" I said.

"Apron'll save your good clothes," U. G. said. "Besides, an apron will make people trust you. Trick of the trade."

SATURDAYS WAS ALWAYS the busiest days at U. G.'s store. Beginning at seven o'clock in the morning people from all over the valley and ridges up the river started stopping by in wagons and buggies, on foot, and some in cars. They brought baskets of eggs and cakes of butter wrapped in waxed paper. Sometimes they brought crates of young fryers, or old hens that had stopped laying, to trade for bolts of cloth or flour and coffee. Most people with their own cars and trucks drove on to town where their eggs and produce brought a better price and the goods they bought was a little cheaper.

As I stood behind the counter I dreaded for Annie to come into the store and see me working there. And I dreaded to see Moody too, for I didn't want him to bother me and rile me while I was working in public.

U. G. trusted me to do everything except weigh up ginseng. He weighed ginseng hisself on his delicate little scales. "Wild sang is worth twice what cultivated sang is," he said.

"How can you tell the difference?" I said.

"*You* don't need to," U. G. said.

"What'll I do if somebody brings some in?" I said.

"Tell them to wait for me," U. G. said. "Dug ginseng is hard and firm when it dries, and smooth as a seed. But sang growed in a patch dries faster and wrinkles more. Don't have the potency of the wild."

While U. G. played checkers, and when the store was quiet, I took a pencil and drawed on a sheet of brown wrapping paper. I drawed houses and castles and churches. I drawed steeples five and six stories high. I drawed stone walls and pointed windows.

"What are you scribbling there, Muir?" Blaine said.

"Drawing me a map to Canada," I said.

"Thought you'd already been up north," Blaine said.

"Might go again," I said, "when I have the money."

U. G. LET ME take care of about everything besides ginseng. I sold pocketknives and penknives and hunting knives out of a case in front of the counter. I sold candy bars and chewing gum to boys and girls that come in with pennies and nickels. Because he was down on the highway U. G. had electricity, and I sold cups of ice cream out of the freezer. I sold dripping Co-Colas from the cooler in the corner. There was cookies in the big clear jar on the counter, and strings of licorice, and pickles in a crock of brine.

I sold sausages too, and boiled eggs from a jar. But most of the sausage I sold was the little cans of Vienna sausage on the shelf beside the sardines. I sold soda crackers and wedges of cheese off the wheel. I sold canned salmon and sometimes canned beef. I sold taters out of bushel baskets, both sweet and Irish.

From kegs in the back of the store I scooped up nails of all pennies and weighed them. I sold hammers and hoes and shovels, picks and mattocks, scythes and swing blades. I sold pliers and wire cutters, hedge clippers and carpenter levels and saws. In the dark space in the back of the store there was sacks of dairy feed and laying mash, shorts for hogs and cottonseed meal. I liked the smell of molasses in dairy feed. I sold bags of crushed oyster shells for chickens and scratch feed for little chicks. There was oats for horses and mixes of sweet feed.

It was early spring, and U. G. had brought in a supply of seeds and fertilizer. I sold bags of guano and ammonium nitrate and nitrate of soda, 5-10-10 and 10-10-10. There was bags of bean seed and corn seed, sweet corn and field corn, pole beans and bunch beans. There was tobacco seed and squash seed, pumpkin seed and seed potatoes. There was flower seeds in little envelopes with pictures painted on them, and bulbs for dahlias and glads.

Now, there was a case behind the counter where U. G. kept medicines for sale: bottles of castor oil, Doan's kidney pills, Black Draught laxative. There was medicines for worms, bottles of cough syrup and soothing syrups, boric acid for sore eyes, and peroxide for cuts, along with Mercurochrome and bismuth of violet for dressing cuts. U. G. sold rubbing alcohol and camphor, iodine and mineral oil, witch hazel and wart medicine. There was oil of cloves for toothache and ointments for piles and aching muscles.

But the things I enjoyed selling most was fishhooks and trout flies, fishing lines and coils of gut leader. U. G. sold little tin boxes of sinkers and corks for lake fishing. And there was also boxes of red and green shotgun shells, 12, 16, and 20 gauge. There was boxes of rifle cartridges, rimfire and center-fire. I sold ammo for .32-, .38-, and .45-caliber pistols.

Locked in a special case was rifles and shotguns and pistols, some new and some traded. U. G. served as a kind of pawnbroker for the valley, taking rifles and shotguns for groceries, sometimes loaning money outright on the security of a watch or a pistol.

U. G. sold watches too, both men's and women's, as well as alarm clocks. He sold steel traps and coils of barbed wire, clotheslines and binder's twine. He sold tater diggers and pitchforks, turning plows and cultivators. He even had in stock a hillside plow that could be turned either right or left. He sold horse collars and trace chains, singletrees and leather harness. He sold bridles and plowlines and halters for bulls.

There was bottles of bluing and a dozen kinds of soap and washing powders on the shelves. There was bleach and lye and disinfectant. There was sewing machine oil and neat's-foot oil, cottonseed oil and coal oil in a barrel out back. We sold scissors and thread and needles, thimbles and crochet hooks. We sold pinking shears and cloth off big rolls.

But the strangest thing I sold in U. G.'s store was kept in a chest of drawers in the back of the building. There was boxes wrapped in tissue paper where the shiny fittings for coffins was packed. If somebody making a coffin needed brass handles and hinges and corners, they come to the store. We sold shiny brass screws also, and nameplates for nailing onto the lid. In the attic of the shed behind the store U. G. even had a few factory-made coffins, but I didn't find out about them until Aunt Alice Herrin died on the mountain and they wanted to bury her in a hurry because the weather was hot and she had gangrene.

U. G. LET ME play the radio in the afternoons if there wasn't too many customers. When I was unpacking boxes or counting eggs into paper cartons for shipping, I wasn't supposed to listen to the radio. "You'll lose count if you're tapping your toe to a banjo," U. G. said.

But in fact the radio stayed on most of the time. I think some customers come to the store just to hear the radio. They wanted to gather by the stove and listen to country music and to gospel music. They wanted to listen to news about baseball, about Babe Ruth. I liked to listen to reports from London and from the Philippines. I even listened to sermons some afternoons and sometimes to a symphony orchestra.

I was listening to organ music on the radio one day and dusting the shelves with a feather duster when somebody walked into the store. I looked up and seen Annie and her mama. The spit caught in my throat and I had to swallow.

"Howdy, Mrs. Richards," I said. Mrs. Richards had light brown hair that was dusted with gray. And she still had fair skin. You could tell how pretty she was when she was younger. But she had big rough hands that showed how much work she had done.

"I brung you some butter and eggs," Mrs. Richards said.

I glanced at Annie, but she was looking at the candy bars inside the glass case. Her mama placed two baskets on the counter. One was filled with brown eggs and the other with butter wrapped in waxed paper.

I hadn't tried to go with Annie since she rode back to the house with Moody that day. She had done it just to spite me, because she hadn't gone with Moody since. If she had I would have heard about it. Moody would have told me.

I got an egg crate from behind the counter and begun counting the eggs into its cups. Mrs. Richards usually brought about ten dozen at a time.

"How you doing?" Annie said. She leaned against the counter in front of me. "We missed you at prayer meeting," she said.

"Had to work late," I said.

I figured if I was just polite with Annie, that was the thing to do. I'd show her I was too growed-up to be mad. She liked to flirt with everybody and tease everybody. It was just her way. But I was determined I wasn't going to be fooled by her again.

After I counted out eleven dozen eggs and wrote the number on a sheet of brown wrapping paper, I got out U. G.'s little scales and weighed the butter. Mrs. Richards always packed her mold extra full, so each cake weighed more than a pound.

"That's almost seven pounds of butter," I said. I figured with a pencil on the sheet of brown paper. "That comes to four dollars and seventy-five cents," I said.

"I need sugar and coffee and baking soda," Mrs. Richards said. "And some raisins and a new sifter."

"I want a Hershey's bar," Annie said.

"Might make you fat," I said. I knowed Annie was awful proud of being slim. She was slimmer than any girl in the valley.

"Do I look fat?" Annie said. She turned sideways so I could see how slim she was and how her sweater come down over her hips. She was slender as a flute and she had the prettiest figure I'd ever seen.

I measured out the coffee and sugar into bags and tied them up. And I got a can of baking soda and a box of raisins.

"Ain't seen you driving your car lately," Annie said.

"What else can I get for you?" I said to Mrs. Richards.

"Hank wants some shaving soap," Mrs. Richards said.

I looked on the shelf near the front of the store where the soaps and toilet articles was. Annie followed me on the other side of the counter. "The circus is coming to town two weeks from Wednesday," she said. She leaned on the counter and watched me sort among the soaps and tooth powders, jars of face cream and bottles of shampoo and lotion. I didn't look back at her, but I could feel my face getting hot. I found the shaving soap and turned around.

"I have to work at the store," I said.

"It only comes once a year," Annie said.

"I might be able to get the car," I said. It just come out. I didn't mean to say it. I put the shaving soap in the basket and added up Mrs. Richards's purchases on the sheet of brown paper.

"I owe you a dollar and twenty-one cents," I said.

"And give Annie a candy bar," Mrs. Richards said.

I reached into the case for a Hershey's bar.

"I don't want no candy," Annie said. "I want a Co-Cola."

I give Mrs. Richards a dollar and sixteen cents from the register. Annie took a bottle from the cooler and opened it and followed her mama to the door. Just before she went out she turned back to me. "I hope you can go to the circus," she said.

Fifteen

Ginny

I HAD KEPT Moody's letter in a drawer of the bureau for years. I took it out again to read it.

July 17, 1918
Dear Mama,

I take up pensil in hand to right you a letter on the fine tablet I paid the guard a nickel for. Somebody has likely told you already where I am. But I figured you would never know the truth unless I rote you.

I cutt one of the Willards in a fight at Chestnut Springs. He needed to be cut is all I cann say and I done it. It's simple as that. Reckon I sliced his guts deeper than I meant to was all.

You can tell fokes I've gone off on a vacashun if you want to. You can tell them I've gone tramping in the woods and camping like Muir does. You can tell them I'm gone out west to dig for gold. I don't care.

But the upshot of it was that after I fit with Sandy Willard and cut him the deputies arrested me and took me heer to the Greenville jale. They couldn't have arrested me. They wouldn't even have knowed about the fight unless Peg Early or one of hers had told them.

Sometimes I think Peg Early and the Willards are in cahoots against me. That's what I think.

But the upshot was that cause Sandy was so bad cut and had to be sewed up by the doctor in Traveler's Rest, they give me thirty days in jail heer. That was Peg Early's doing, if I don't miss my guess.

The Greenville County jale is not hell. These July days it's worser than hell and hotter. It's so hot you have to lay still on a bunk just to keep your hed from swimming. I reckon if you moved around you'd just lose your breth.

Ain't complaing about my commodations. But whatever anybody done they don't deserve the Greenville County jale. Rations is some stale bread and watery otemeal that tastes like rotten newspapers. And for dinner they give you pinto beans that are half raw and a cup of stumpwater for coffee.

I won't tell you about the smell heer, with all us men inside and the sweat and no water to wash with. The place smells like pee and puke when they bring a drunk in and he throws up his guts. The stink of this place would make you sick, even if you was well, which I ain't.

Now I'm just a dog. I admit I'm just a dog. Ain't never done nothing but get in trouble and get looked down on. I've been a shame to you ever since I was a youngun. I don't give a damn.

After Daddy died it was like I never done nothing rite again. That's a fact. Daddy would sometimes take up for me, but after he was gone nobody else did.

I don't want you to try to get me out of heer. And don't get U. G. to try. The judge said it would be thirty days, and by God it will be. Don't spend none of Daddy's money on me. I have got free room and board from the people of Greenville County and I will take them up on it. Don't spend none of Daddy's molasses money on me. No sir.

If somebody here gives the guard any sass they get rapped with a billy club drove into their gut. You don't answer a bull he'll ram you with a club in the belly. If they want to they can wait a day to

bring you any water. In this heat you sweat out every drop in a
few hours, and then you are so weak you just lay still and feel the
air has teeth.

I was laying heer righting this and somebody grabbed my pensil and broke it in two. I had to pay a guard four cents for that
pensil, and now I have to right with the stub. Since they took my
knife I can only sharp the led by rubbing it on the floor. I naw
away the wood and rub the led on the seement to give it a point.
Never thought a little peece of pensil would be so dear. When I
get out of heer I'm going to buy a box of yellow pensils.

The big feller that broke the pensil has it in for me. He has a
grudge cause I'm from North Carolina. He says people from
North Carolina ain't Tarheels they're shit heels. He's a big feller
named Warren that will blow snot on his hand and wipe it across
your mouth. He was caught peeping into people's windows is
why he is heer.

"I will teach you a lesson before I'm done," he will say. I
would fite him except they took my knife when they put me in
heer.

A drink of licker would sooth me. A drink of licker would be
like a frend to comfort me. But I don't want to get any more
licker till I get out of heer. The other day Wheeler and Drayton
come to see me. Now I knowed Wheeler had something in his
shirt cause of the way the shirt pooched out at his side. I kept
looking at his shirt and when he leaned up close to the bars he
reached into his shirt and brought out a half pint bottle.

I stuck that bottle in my own shirt fast as I could, but another
prisoner had seen it. Soon as Wheeler and Drayton was gone, and
soon as it got dark, Warren started in on me. "Ain't you going to
be sociable?" Warren whispered in my ear.

I pulled away from him and pushed myself up against the wall.
His breath stunk like the floor of a chicken house.

"Powell don't want to share with his buddies," Warren said to
the others. He muttered something to the other prisoners and
they grabbed hold of me. Sixteen hands held me to the bunk
while Warren twisted the bottle out of my shirt.

In the dark he drunk most of the licker hisself, and then he give

*the others a little sip. And when the bottle was empty they held
me against the bunk and crammed the neck of the bottle in my
mouth.*

*"Now you have something to piss in," Warren said. "Save your
piss and drink it." In a fair fite he knows I could beat him easy.
And when I get out of heer I will.*

*I will see you uns in a month, after my vacashun, your son,
Moody*

After I got the letter me and U. G. drove down to Greenville and
paid Moody's fine. We got him out of jail and brought him back. I
never showed nobody the letter. When I mentioned the letter to
Moody he said he had never wrote a letter. He said he wouldn't
know how to write a letter while he was in jail, even if he had
wanted to. But I had seen the letter, and I remembered every word of
it. It was the year Jewel died of the flu. I remember it well.

Sixteen
Muir

"YOUR FRIEND HICKS died last night," Mama said.

"Hicks?" I said.

"He died when he was milking. They found him in the stall with the cow standing over him."

"I don't believe it," I said.

I had seen Hicks the day before at the store. He had been playing checkers with U. G. as usual. He was a good friend and was somebody you could always depend on to say something funny and friendly. He liked to play checkers, and he was always ready to take a drink, and he was always ready for a laugh. But he wasn't a mean drinker. Far as I knowed he'd never hurt nobody. He loved a good story as much as anybody you ever seen, and he never teased me about trying to preach. People said he stayed at U. G.'s store so much because him and his wife, Jevvie, quarreled. Every time he took a drink she run him out of the house. But I never seen him quarrel with nobody else. I remembered how tall and stooped Hicks was, and how he made a little extra money sharpening saws for people. He could sharpen a saw until it melted the wood it touched. And he took pride in his checkers playing.

Mama said Hicks's funeral was tomorrow evening.

Hicks lived up on Mount Olivet, and though I hardly knowed the rest of his family I seen I had to go to his funeral. I'd spent too many hours with Hicks at the store to stay away from his burial service. I would go and wear the old suit I had bought to preach in.

"I'm going to need the car tomorrow," I said to Moody at supper.

"You may need the car, but I need it worser," Moody said.

"I have to get to Hicks's funeral," I said.

Of course Moody got up before daylight and drove away in the Model T, and I ended up walking to Mount Olivet on that November afternoon. The church was right on top of the mountain, and it was about five miles from the house. I knowed it would take about an hour and a half, and I give myself plenty of time, since the funeral was to begin at three. I started out right after dinner.

The walk up to Mount Olivet was easy. It was a calm and mild afternoon with gathering clouds. The haze on the far mountain hinted there might be rain. People setting on their porches after eating Sunday dinner spoke to me as I walked past. Everybody knowed it was the day of Hicks's funeral. But most wasn't going to the service, maybe because Hicks was a drinker and wasn't a regular churchman.

I liked the way the suit fit over my shoulders and hips as I walked. I hadn't wore if for a long time, but it still fit. The sun gleamed on the delicate herringbone pattern. I turned up the dirt road that run along Freeman Creek and started climbing.

"Hey, Muir, going to your wedding?" somebody hollered. I looked back and seen Blaine walking behind me. I stopped to let him catch up.

"That's a humdinger of a suit," Blaine said. "You going to preach the funeral?"

"Only if they ask me," I said. "A man needs one good suit in his life."

"So they'll have something to bury him in," Blaine said.

"Hope to wear it a few times before that," I said.

"Better hope it don't rain," Blaine said.

"It rains, I'll just stand under a tree till it stops," I said.

I expected to see more people on the road going to Hicks's funeral. But we didn't run into anybody else till we come around the bend a few hundred yards below the church. There was a cluster of men and boys gathered by the road. One was pulling the wire of a kind of trolley that carried buckets of water from the spring far down in the holler. "Howdy," I said.

"What say, 'fessor?" one of the men said.

"You boys getting any?" Blaine said.

"Getting any what?" one said. And everybody laughed.

"Getting a drink of water," one of the Jenkins boys said.

"That's what I meant," Blaine said.

I watched one of the MacDowell boys pull on the trolley contraption. It was strung on pulleys attached to trees right down the steep mountainside. The buckets was wired to hooks and they filled theirselves in a reservoir of rocks down at the spring. It was a fancy device. The bucket in the reservoir filled, and then it took the MacDowell boy several minutes to reel it up the mountainside to the road as the other bucket was lowered to be filled.

"I never seen one of them before," Blaine said.

"Old Hicks invented it," the MacDowell boy said. "Thunk it up and built it."

"Then we should have a little ole drink in his honor," the Jenkins boy said.

"Not of springwater," Blaine said.

"Branch water and bourbon," somebody said.

"What if we ain't got no bourbon?" Blaine said.

"Then just plain liquor will have to do," the MacDowell boy said. He reached into the water bucket and pulled out a dripping jar.

"Why, you sneaky son of a bitch," the Jenkins boy said.

"I wouldn't want ole Hicks to be funeraled without a toast," the MacDowell boy said. He passed around the bottle and everybody had a sip. I pretended to have a taste, just enough to wet my tongue, because I didn't want to show no disrespect by refusing a drink in Hicks's honor. And I didn't want to show no disrespect to the family or the church by coming to the funeral smelling like corn liquor neither. I dampened the tip of my tongue and passed the bottle on to Blaine.

"Here's to Hicks, wherever in hell you are," Blaine said and raised the jar in the air.

"I hope they have good drinking liquor in hell," the MacDowell boy said.

"If they have good liquor, then it ain't hell," I said, and everybody laughed.

"Wherever Hicks is there'll be a drink of liquor," the MacDowell boy said.

I took a dipper of water from the bucket and drunk it. "We better get to the church before we miss his funeral," I said.

"Don't reckon Hicks would grudge us a little sip," Blaine said.

SEVERAL MEN IN suits stood outside the door of the little church. One that I recognized as the pastor at Mount Olivet stepped forward to meet me. I was surprised he knowed who I was.

"Hey buddy," the preacher said, "could you help us out?"

"If I can," I said.

"We seem to be short a pallbearer," the preacher said. "Could you fill in? After all, you was a friend of Hicks."

The pastor showed me where to stand, and I found myself opposite to U. G. I nodded to U. G. and he nodded back. I nodded to the other pallbearers too. There was the MacDowell boy, a Willard, a Freeman, and somebody I thought was a Griffith.

The pastor told us what we was supposed to do. When they brought the casket in the wagon we would slide it out and carry it to the table in front of the church. Then we would set on the left front bench while the family set on the right. After the service was over we would tote the casket out and the family would follow.

I stood in line and nodded to the people as they walked into the church. I tried to look dignified and clasped my hands in front of my waist. I had been to a lot of funerals but never served as a pallbearer before. I stood up straight as I could.

A wagon with the coffin in it come creaking up the road. When it reached the churchyard the driver turned the wagon and backed it almost to the church steps.

"Here goes, boys," the pastor said. I took hold of the cold brass handle on the right side of the coffin and pulled. The box slid out over the rough boards and I passed the handle on to the Freeman boy and grabbed the second handle and pulled again. When I took hold of the third and last handle it felt like the whole weight of the casket fell on my fingers. But when I lifted up I found the box was already moving in the grip of the other pallbearers. I had to skip to catch up and take the extra weight as the casket tilted up the steps.

Rain started to fall just as we went into the church. A drop hit the arm of my suit and made a dark spot.

Mount Olivet Church was the smallest sanctuary I'd ever seen. It was really just a little clapboard chapel with a steeple no bigger than an outhouse. Inside was maybe ten benches on either side of the aisle. The preacher had cleared off the communion table in front of the pulpit where the offering baskets and the communion platter usually set. We rested the casket on the table and turned it around lengthwise to the congregation. I was sweating with the effort in the muggy air. I was going to set down with the other pallbearers on the left, but the preacher tapped me on the shoulder and pointed to a screwdriver on the floor beside the pulpit.

After thinking for a second I seen what he wanted me to do. Without looking back at the congregation, I picked up the tool and started loosening the screws on the lid of the coffin. There was four on either side and one at each end. The screws come out of the pine easy, but I was careful not to loosen them too much. The screws must not fall out of the lid when it was took off, or they'd be hard to find in the dark church. Me and the preacher lifted off the cover and carried it to the corner, but the screwdriver slipped out of my grasp and went clattering to the floor. I scooped it up and laid it by the pulpit again.

As I straightened up beside the coffin, I seen Hicks's face for the first time. He laid with his eyes closed and his skin looked dark as a bruise. And there was a smell coming from the box. Somebody had put cologne on the body, and talcum powder. And there was the scent of camphor from the cloth that had laid all night on his face. And there was a faint smell of whiskey, and another smell too, like Hicks had already started to rot, as any animal on a trail might smell after being dead two days.

After I set down, the family on the right come forward to view the corpse. Hicks's widow, Jevvie, had to be helped by her son Lamar.

Jevvie limped to the front of the church and stood with her hands on the side of the box. She looked inside and sobbed loud and deep. The sob filled the church like a gong had been hit. It felt like the whole church had been struck dumb. Everybody froze because Jevvie's sob sounded so complete and final, like that was all there was to say about Hicks, about his life and his death. Everybody knowed that Jevvie and Hicks had quarreled about things all their married lives. Jevvie looked down at him in the coffin and shook her head. It was as if all the sadness of her life was summed up in that sob. Finally Lamar led her back to the front bench on the right, and the rest of the family filed forward, other sons and daughters, the grandsons with their hair combed for the first time in their lives and their shirts buttoned tight around their necks.

As the rest of the congregation come forward to view the remains of Hicks, I listened to the rain on the roof get louder and louder. It was a tin roof and it banged and chanted with every drop. The little church house rung inside like the sounding box of a piano. The church was just a cabinet of sound. It was raining hard as a summer storm. I thought how the people of Mount Olivet needed a bigger, more solid church. There was a rap of thunder like a big shirt had been tore. The roof clapped and clattered, and thunder fired another salute for Hicks.

The pounding on the roof was so loud it was hard to hear the preacher when he stood up and led the congregation in "We Are Going Down the Valley." It was a mournful song and I joined in in a low voice. But the music was mostly drowned out by the throbbing on the roof. The preacher prayed, and next we sung "On Jordan's Stormy Banks," which was more mournful still. I shivered, just listening to the music and the cold rain. If the rain kept up, the new-dug grave would be full of water. How could we carry the casket up to the graveyard in such a storm?

" 'In my Father's house are many mansions,' " the preacher read, " 'if it were not so, I would have told you. I go to prepare a place for you . . . that where I am, there ye may be also.' "

I shuddered, feeling the dampness on my skin and in my stomach. The banging on the roof sounded like it was in my head. The crease in my pants was straight and sharp as a knife blade. I run my fingers along the crease. The cloth was smooth and hard and without wrinkles.

"In the midst of life we are in death," the preacher was saying.

The roof sounded like drums and cymbals and castanets. It was loud in the church as Fourth of July fireworks. I looked at U. G., who had his head bowed.

WHEN THE SERVICE was finally over, the rain had not stopped. If anything the storm sounded louder. The congregation stood up and sung the "Battle Hymn," and it sounded like the shingles above was clapping. Then the preacher prayed again. And soon as he finished he motioned for the pallbearers to come forward and take the coffin. I got the casket lid from the corner and laid it over Hicks in his Sunday suit. In the dark I had to feel the screws to twist them down with the driver until they groaned.

We turned the coffin crossways on the table and each took hold of a handle. Walking slow as we could we headed toward the door and I heard the family rise and follow. There was a clap of thunder just as we got to the door. As we come outside, the horse and wagon at the door, the road and the cemetery on the hill, was all lit up in a flash of lightning. The ground was a river of splashing and racing water. Water leapt up and water at the bottom of the steps looked four or five inches deep.

I hesitated for a moment. But the pallbearers behind me pushed forward and I stepped right out into the downpour. The dignity of the occasion demanded it. There was nothing else to do. Rain dashed in my face like it was coming sideways. Water hit my eyebrows, and I was blinded by lightning. At the bottom of the steps I walked right into water like it was a creek. Water soaked down my neck and under my tie.

"Slide it right in the wagon, boys," the preacher said. He had an umbrella and he held it over the end of the coffin as we loaded it into the wet wagon bed. Then he held the umbrella over Hicks's wife.

Soon as my hand was free I took out my handkerchief and wiped my face. But it didn't do no good, since even more water run down my forehead and into my eyes. We fell in step behind the wagon and followed it through mud and running water across the yard and up the haul road to the cemetery on the hill. Water run off my suit at first like it was a raincoat. But by the time we begun to climb the hill, I could feel the dampness soaking through the herringbone cloth around my shoulders. Water come right down my back and under my collar. My suit is going to be ruined, I thought. Just for paying my respects to Hicks I'm going to ruin my only suit.

Several people behind had umbrellas, and Lamar held one over Jevvie as we walked up the hill. None of the pallbearers had umbrellas. But it didn't make much difference because the rain was coming so hard and blowing so fast even an umbrella didn't do much good. By the time we got to the top of the hill where the fresh grave had been dug, my wet suit was molding to my chest and shoulders, sticking to my back. Both pants and coat was heavy.

As we slid the casket out of the wagon I tried to steady myself, but my foot slipped on the mud. Down I went in the dirt, and the coffin handle tore out of my grip. The wet coffin hit my leg and turned sideways, and the lid popped off. I must not have screwed it down tight enough. Hicks's body rolled out onto the mud beside the grave. Everybody gasped, and then they looked at me as I hauled myself up, caked with mud. My leg felt like it was broke, but I hardly noticed it.

I was so ashamed I couldn't look at nobody as I tried to wipe the mud off the suit and off my hands and wrists. The clay stuck to the herringbone like red shit, like grease. Jevvie was looking at me with pity, as if I was a little boy that had messed hisself. Lamar held her elbow and glared like I was the last straw that ruined his daddy's funeral. I was so confused I kept slapping at the mud on my pants and on the sleeve of the suit. The rain spit gobs in my face.

I wanted to wallow in the mud to show how humiliated I was. I hated myself as I seen the disgust on the face of the preacher. U. G. looked embarrassed for people to know we was cousins. The pain in my leg was awful, but I wished it was worser.

There is a kind of shame so bad it's almost a thrill of shame, a fit and a spasm of shame. When I seen the pity for me on the widow's face I shuddered in my bones. I wanted to hurl myself off the hill into the lowest pit of hell, or into a sewer. You have showed your sorry ass again, I said to myself. You have showed what you really are.

My hands was too filthy to help them lift the body back into the casket. My face burned as I tried to wipe my hands off on my dirty pants. Rain throwed itself in my eyes.

I stood with the other pallbearers soaking up the rain as the preacher read from the Bible beside the grave and we sung "Beautiful, Beautiful Zion." Rain dripped from my dirty cuffs and elbows. There was another crash of thunder and everything got lit up again. The coffin resting beside the grave had water puddled on it. Nobody there would ever forget how I had slipped in the mud and dropped Hicks's coffin. They would tell everybody.

" 'As for man, his days are as grass,' " the preacher read. " 'As a flower of the field, so he flourisheth. For the wind passeth over it, and it is gone; and the place thereof shall know it no more.' "

When it was over I couldn't look at anybody. I started walking back down the hill and found U. G. beside me. My suit could not have been wetter or dirtier if I had fell in the river. The cloth pulled and weighed on my legs. Mud was caked like manure on my knees.

"Hicks never did like things dry," U. G. said.

"I bet he's having a good laugh at us right now," I said. I was ashamed to look at U. G., and I was ashamed to look at myself. As I walked away from the cemetery I thought I could hear Hicks chuckle in the pouring rain.

Seventeen

Muir

IT WAS AFTER Hicks's funeral that the circus come to town. I told
Mama I was going to drive Annie to the circus, and Mama said I
had to take Fay. She said Hank and Julie wouldn't let Annie go unless I took Fay. So I had no choice but to take my little sister. I asked
U. G. if I could have the afternoon off to drive Annie and Fay to the
circus. To my surprise he said I could. U. G. had never mentioned
me falling down in the mud at Hicks's funeral.

They always had a parade through town to advertise the circus,
and some people said the parade was a better show than the circus itself. Maybe that was because everybody in the county turned out,
and it was like a holiday and a carnival rolled up into one. I always
did like a parade, and to see all the animals and the prancing, dancing ladies going right down the middle of the street was a special
thrill.

As we drove to town Annie set in the seat beside me, and Fay set
by the window. I noticed that Annie's hands was red from doing
washing that morning. She kept them folded in her lap so the redness
wouldn't show.

Fay wanted to park in front of the feedstore on the south end of town so we could watch the parade from the car in case it rained. But I told her there wouldn't be any room there, and besides, we couldn't see from the car with people standing all along the sidewalk.

We found that Main Street was blocked off anyway. I had to drive up King Street and park in front of Brookshire's Livery Stables and car lot, where me and Moody had bought the Model T.

"I wish Mama would have come," Fay said. "She would have liked the circus."

As we walked the two blocks up to Main Street, Annie kept her arms folded so her hands was hid. Everybody in town seemed to be going in the same direction. We got to Main just in time as the band music started in the distance. We could hear snatches coming down the river of the street. But those snatches of trumpets and trombones, and the beat of drums, was sparkling and thrilling. People lined the sidewalks and we had to push our way through to see anything. Finally we found a place just above the feedstore and across from the courthouse. The dome of the courthouse rose silver in the sun.

The excitement in the crowd was like music too. There was a beat and a hum as people stretched to see and shifted their feet and children darted out into the street.

"Where is the lion?" a little girl hollered.

"Hush up," her mama said.

People packed both sides of the street, and kids run out on the pavement to see what was coming and got jerked back by their mamas. Annie stood on tiptoe to see better, her hands still folded on her chest. A policeman walked by and blowed his whistle and waved the crowd back.

"Yonder they come!" a boy hollered. But I couldn't see much over the heads of all the people. Since Annie was a good bit shorter than me she probably couldn't see at all. I wished there was something she could climb on. I wished I could hold her up in my arms.

The music got louder, and it was like the music I'd heard on the radio for a military funeral one time. As the band got closer it sounded like bright metal and silk cloth was tearing across the sky. Drums bruised the air again, again. I put my hands under Annie's arms and helped her stand on tiptoe.

It was the fireman's band from Asheville, a banner proclaimed. There was a big fat fellow with a red face carrying the drum and punishing it. There was a row of trumpets and trombones, blasting the sky with echoes and sweet barks.

After the fireman's band I seen this man prancing in a tall hat and uniform. The tall hat had a tassel on it and as the man strutted the tassel danced around. The man carried a silver baton, which he throwed high in the air and caught. I don't know how he could catch the spinning stick so neat.

There was another band behind the major. It was the city high school band, dressed in maroon and gold. The crowd cheered because they knowed all the boys and girls in the band, I reckon. There was sons and daughters and cousins and neighbors puffing on the horns and slamming the cymbals together like pot lids.

But everybody was looking up the street now. For just behind the high school band was the swaying elephant, and all of us turned toward the elephant. It was so big it didn't look like anything alive, except that it was moving. There was a kind of painted rug draped across the elephant's forehead, with a star on it. And several people rode on a big rug on the elephant's back. The animal was so high it was like looking up at a tall building to watch the riders. A man in a silk top hat, and a pretty lady in a dancer's short skirt, set just behind the elephant's head. And a midget or dwarf set behind them and waved to the crowd. He looked tiny as a child, except his head was big.

"How did they get up on the elephant?" Annie said over her shoulder.

"Must have climbed a ladder," I hollered in her ear. Her ear was pink with excitement.

And then I noticed the elephant's eye. It was the size of a big lightbulb and looked dark as prune juice. The elephant appeared to be crying, for liquid run down the side of the leathery face. What could make an elephant weep? I wondered. It should be happy, wearing its colorful bedspread and marching in front of the cheering crowd. Its tears was the color of tobacco juice.

A man strutted in front of the elephant carrying a stick, a kind of wand. He appeared to be the man that was in charge of the elephant. He appeared to be the master of ceremonies, maybe the boss of the circus, striding out in front and waving his hat to the crowd. I guess he was the ringmaster in charge of the show.

As we watched, the elephant behind him stopped marching and turned toward where me and Annie and Fay stood.

The man with the stick yelled up at the elephant, but the animal ignored him and started toward us on the sidewalk. I seen it was crying out of both eyes, tears sliding down to the elephant's mouth.

"Hey!" the man in the top hat yelled, but the elephant didn't pay him any heed. The animal stared right at me and over me. I turned around and seen the elephant was studying its reflection in the window of the storefront. It took a step closer to us.

There was laughter on the other side of the street, but I couldn't tell what the people was laughing about until I seen the great clods dropping behind the elephant and knowed it was doing its business right in the street. And what a big business it was! Chunks and pieces the size of grapefruits plopped down on the pavement. A pile of dark wads and chunks stacked up like cannon balls. The crowd tittered and clapped.

"The Lord gosh," Annie said.

"Whew!" Fay said.

A big wagon with cages of lions and tigers had to stop on the street behind the elephant. But the band kept on playing and somebody blowed a whistle. The elephant flung its trunk out like a whip and the crowd pushed us back. It was looking at itself in the store window and must have thought it was facing another elephant as big and sad as itself. The elephant let out an awful screech that sounded like the squall of a sawmill when the blade hits a knot or a nail.

"Get back!" the man in the top hat hollered, and hit the elephant on the trunk with his stick. The animal flung out its trunk again like it was trying to shake off a fly. Boys whistled through their fingers and throwed papers and apple cores and things at the elephant.

Suddenly the elephant started toward us, and everybody pushed back from the curb. Annie screamed and I stepped back, still holding her under the arms. A blue roadster was parked on the street and we all rushed to get behind it. The man on the elephant's back rapped his stick on its forehead and grabbed a floppy ear.

When the elephant got to the roadster it reared up, just like in the pictures I'd seen where a circus elephant climbed on a stool or a bar-rel. The animal put one foot on top of the roadster, and then its other front foot. The car creaked and lurched and something broke inside. The top wrinkled and caved in.

"Oh no!" Annie screamed.

"Let's stay back," I said.

The elephant's eye looked panicked. The big eye was full of dark liquid and it widened till it seemed ready to bust. People pulled away from the car as glass popped and shot out of the windows. A man in a gray suit, who appeared to be the owner of the roadster, run around the front of the car like he was trying to shoo the beast away from the hood. He looked frantic, and hollered, "Get back! Get back!" and placed his hand on the radiator cap like he was protecting it.

The elephant turned and come down with a foot the size of a stove on the man's head. The head hit the hood and popped like a terra-cotta flowerpot. It happened in a second, but everybody on the street seen or heard it. The elephant brought down its other foot, crushing the man's shoulder against the grille of the roadster. Blood spurted over the car and over the people standing close by. A drop hit Annie's dress and she tried to brush it away.

As sudden as it had reared up, the elephant lowered its front legs to the street and backed away with a scream. The animal turned and started marching down the street again, and the man in the top hat had to run to get in front of it. The circus wagons and the prancing horses behind the elephant went past, but the crowd hardly noticed them. A clown doing tricks rode by on a little bicycle, and there was jugglers on stilts and a man breathing fire. But we didn't hardly pay any attention. Nobody could take their eyes off the man on the hood of the car.

The body rolled off the radiator onto the sidewalk, but there was no head, just pieces of scalp and bloody bones, rags of a head. Annie turned away and put her red hands over her face. Then she took her hands away and looked. Everybody looked and gasped.

Women was crying all around and Annie sobbed against my chest. Somebody bent over the body and touched the shoulder, as if to see if it was still alive. But there was no life there, not after what the elephant had done. The crushed pieces was wet and sticky. People crowded in closer to get a better look.

We was locked in by people on every side and couldn't hardly move. I put my arms around Annie and Fay as the crowd pressed tighter and closer. Somehow a dog had squeezed between the legs of the crowd and was licking the blood off the sidewalk.

"Get away!" I hollered at the dog.

A whistle blowed, and then another. "Stand aside!" somebody yelled. "Stand aside!"

A policeman pushed his way through the crowd, trying to find out what had happened. "Stand back!" he yelled and blowed his whistle again. He seen the man laying on the sidewalk with only scraps in place of a head, and he bent over him. "Who done this?" he yelled.

"The elephant," several people shouted.

"How?" the policeman said.

Just then another man in a uniform pushed his way through the press of people. He was a fat cop with an officer's cap. He acted like he might be the captain. "What is this?" he shouted. Then he bent over beside the other policeman. They shouted in each other's ears, and then the first policeman stood up.

"Arrest the elephant!" the big man said.

"You can't arrest an elephant," the other officer said.

"Just like a dog that has bit somebody," the chief cop said. "You have to secure it."

THE CIRCUS WAGONS rumbled past, but nobody paid them much mind anymore. Another band come marching and blaring by, and then an open car with the mayor and another man in a top hat. They rode in a long black car and waved, but nobody much noticed them. I guess they wondered why everybody was looking at the sidewalk beside the busted roadster. I recognized the other man was Congressman Wilson, who was coming up for reelection.

But the spirit had gone out of the parade. People stood back and stepped aside like they didn't hardly know what to do. Others kept pushing on through to get a good look at the body on the curb. When they seen the man's crushed head they turned away.

After the last car went by, and the high school band from Canton kaboomed and bugled past behind it toward the south end of Main Street, two men in white uniforms shoved their way through the crowd, carrying a stretcher. "Go away!" one shouted. "Stand aside!" the other yelled. They dropped the stretcher on the sidewalk and lifted the body onto the canvas. One picked up the pieces of hair and skull and placed them on the stretcher beside the crushed head.

Annie tried to turn away but couldn't with all the people crowding on every side. "I want to go home," she said. "I don't want to see no more."

"Me too," Fay said.

"You don't want to see the circus?" I said.

Soon as the body was wrapped up and carried away, the crowd started shifting down the sidewalk in the direction the parade had gone. People begun thinning out like snow melting and trickling away. Me and Annie and Fay was left standing on the sidewalk near the bloodstains and crushed roadster. A great heap of elephant dookie stood in the street like a cairn placed there as a marker. The courthouse beyond looked deserted.

Annie's face was white as a pillowcase as we walked back to the car parked at Brookshire's. I felt a little sick at my stomach too, and nobody had much to say as we waited for the traffic jam to loosen up so I could drive home.

AT THE HOUSE Fay rushed in to tell Mama what had happened. I followed her and just come through the screen door when I heard her blurt out, "Mama, you wouldn't believe what we seen in Tompkinsville."

Moody asked what we had seen when we walked into the living room. I told him about the elephant and the man with the roadster.

"Sounds like you have seen the elephant," Moody said.

THE NEXT MORNING when I got the paper I found the elephant story was the headline. There was a picture of the man who'd been killed, and there was a picture of the elephant looking wild, its eyes streaked like they'd been crying blood. The article said the elephant was twenty-six years old and had never hurt anybody before. "Mr. Salvanti, the owner and trainer of Jumbo, says he has always been a friendly, gentle animal," the reporter said. "No one can explain why the young animal suddenly stopped in the parade and turned on the blue Ford roadster and killed its owner, Mr. Raymond Foster of Mills River. The elephant had not been sick, or provoked in any way that was noticed. Some suggested that Jumbo saw his reflection in a store window and thought he was confronting another elephant."

The story went on to say that Sheriff Walton and Chief of Police Howard had arrested the circus animal and was holding him until an inquest was completed. "State law requires that any animal causing injury or loss of life be secured and put down," the reporter said. "Sheriff Walton says the case is in his jurisdiction because the circus is camped at the county fairgrounds. Chief Howard claims it is in his jurisdiction because the death occurred within the city limits.

"Meanwhile Jumbo is confined to his quarters at the fairgrounds under a guard of both the sheriff's department and the city police. Chief Magistrate Walker of the county court has already ruled that the animal must be put to death if it is proven it killed a man. But so far the appropriate means of execution has not been determined. Chief Howard says the execution will take place on Saturday afternoon at the fairgrounds."

"Who ever heard of executing an elephant?" Fay said. "An elephant ain't a person. An elephant don't know right from wrong."

I told her a destructive animal had to be put down. The paper said the idea was not to punish the animal but protect society.

"Do you want to see the execution?" I said.

"Do you?" Fay said.

On Saturday afternoon we drove over to the Richards house to ask Annie if she wanted to go to the fairgrounds to see what would happen.

"I don't see how they can kill an elephant," Annie's daddy, Hank, said. "Nobody has a gun big enough to kill an elephant. At least not in these parts."

"If they just wound it, the elephant might go crazy and kill more people," I said.

Annie's younger brother, Troy, pointed out they would have to bury the elephant where it died. Nothing was strong enough to pick up a dead elephant.

"They won't kill Jumbo," Annie said. "They'll just put him on the train and ship him away."

"The circus has already gone," Hank said. "I heard at the store they loaded everything on the train last night and pulled out for Greensboro."

We all got into the car, Annie in the front beside me, and Fay and Troy in the back. I drove out the Spartanburg Road to the fairgrounds. But we hadn't gone much past the hosiery mill at East Flat Rock when I seen the road was jammed with cars. There was cars parked on both sides of the road and cars in yards and driveways and fields. It looked like the whole county had turned out to see the elephant. I pulled into a little side road near the hosiery mill and parked.

"We'll have to walk at least a mile," Fay said.

"Just hope it don't rain," I said.

The fairgrounds was covered with people. The circus had gone and the fields was muddy in places and scattered with straw and manure and sawdust. There was a few empty pens where they had livestock shows in the fall, and a big pen where they was holding the elephant. Several bales of straw was piled beside the pen.

I pushed my way through the crowd, and Annie and the others followed. It took a while to even get close enough to see the elephant. The animal stood in the pen panting, shifting from one side to the other. It looked like it was scared by all the people crowding close on every side. There was a lot of deputies and policemen beside the pen, and they carried rifles and shotguns. It looked like they was trying to decide what to do. "Ain't you going to kill that crazy thing?" somebody yelled.

There was newsmen with writing pads and cameras and flash attachments. There was boys throwing peanuts and apples at the elephant.

Jumbo's eyes looked wetter than they had before. He appeared to have been crying all night and brown stuff was crusted on the skin below his eyes. I wondered if he was crying now because his trainer was gone and he was among strangers.

"If they shoot that animal it'll go crazy," Troy said.

When we got closer I seen the elephant's foot was tied by a big rope from one of the fence posts to an iron collar on its ankle. Sheriff Walton in his wide-brimmed hat come to the fence, and just behind him followed the chief of police. I wondered if they was planning to shoot the elephant at the same time, to show they was each in charge of the situation.

And then we heard a train whistle and the *chuff-chuff-chuff* of a locomotive. The crowd got quiet and turned toward the railroad tracks that run right along the edge of the fairgrounds. There was a spur track and siding where they unloaded wagons and animals and tents for the circus. The spur run not far from where the elephant was penned. The train got closer and the whistle louder. "Maybe they're going to load Jumbo up and ship him away," Annie said.

The crowd shifted toward the tracks and everybody got pushed along. Finally I seen the smoke from the locomotive, and then the eye of the locomotive itself. It was coming up the grade from the direction of Spartanburg. At first it looked like a regular engine, and then I seen the thing behind it.

The engine was pulling a big car that had a cab and a long crane reaching behind. The arm had a wheel and a strand of cable at the end of it.

"It's a railroad crane," I said. "It's what they use to lift locomotives that have wrecked and gone off the tracks. I bet they brought it all the way from Greenville, or maybe Atlanta."

A gasp went up from the crowd as they watched the engine haul the crane into view and then slow down and pull up alongside the pen. People stepped back from the tracks as the engine hissed out steam from its wheels and the engineer leaned out his window.

The crane was longer than the locomotive, and one of the train-men climbed up into the cab of the crane and started its motor. Black smoke and steam started puffing out of the stacks of the crane. As people backed away, the crane begun to turn, roaring and creaking on its long car. The back of the crane reached out over the grass. It was the biggest and heaviest piece of machinery I'd ever seen. The crane swung around on its turntable until the arm was almost over the elephant's head.

I was beginning to have an inkling what was going on.

There was a cable with a heavy ball and hook at the tip of the crane. The cable run right over the pulley wheel at the end of the boom. One of the sheriff's men started crawling out the long crane with a piece of rope in his hand. He cooned along the boom until he got to the wheel just above the elephant. Then he pulled up the rope from the ground and we seen there was a heavy chain attached to the end of the rope. The elephant squealed as the chain rattled past its ear.

The deputy slipped one end of the chain over the hook on the cable and swung the big chain over Jumbo's head behind the ears. Somebody throwed the other end of the rope up to him, and he pulled the opposite end of the chain up and hooked it tight as he could around the elephant's neck.

I had noticed before that when you see something awful you don't always understand at first. And then it hits you like a fist of electricity that hurts your bones down to the soles of your feet. I felt my breath tighten and the nerves in my teeth ache as I watched the men pull the chain tight around the elephant's neck. The elephant screamed and tried to break away, but it was caught. It seemed odd that such a huge animal had such a high-pitched scream. I felt silly to be there watching the elephant be punished.

The deputy sheriff cooned back down the long arm of the crane, jumped onto the cab, and climbed down a ladder at the back to the ground. Smoke and steam blasted from the engine of the crane and the boom begun to rise, pulled by cables from the windlass in front of the cab. The man inside operated it by levers.

It was strange to think of the elephant as a murderer, but not as strange as what was happening now. The crowd got quiet, and the big crane roared like it was straining to lift the long arm. The cable went taut and the chain tightened around the elephant's neck. The elephant was pulled over so it was leaning, and its eye opened wider. The animal screamed worse than a pig and its gray hide wrinkled around the chain, crimped where the pressure was.

A deputy with an axe pushed his way through the crowd and started chopping the rope that tied the elephant's foot to the post. The animal tried to break away from the crane and stumbled sideways, knocking over a section of the fence. People hollered and backed away.

"Stand back!" a deputy yelled.

"Who's in charge here?" Annie said.

"The sheriff, I reckon," I said. But I thought about her question: Who was really in charge? Was it the mayor of the town, or the board of county commissioners? Was it the sheriff? Or was it the chief magistrate that had made the ruling? Was it the law itself? Was nobody really in charge?

"Can't you stop them?" Annie said. She had tears in her eyes. She banged on my chest with her fists. "You've got to stop them!" she cried.

My knees was trembling. I felt like a coward. I knowed somebody ought to take charge and stop them.

"Do something!" Annie screamed and banged on my chest harder. There was more tears in her eyes, and her face was white.

"No!" I hollered.

Little by little the front of the elephant was pulled off the ground. The front feet kicked at the ground and at the fence. They kicked the air like the elephant was trying to swim. He swung his rear sideways and knocked over another section of the fence. The elephant was trying to run away from the chain. He was trying to pull loose, and he kicked out like he was dancing.

When Jumbo turned his rear toward us I could see all the scars on his hide. The elephant's skin was wrinkled and dusty. Up close you could see a few hairs like big whiskers. The skin looked like he had been cut and hurt a lot of times, maybe with chains while he was pulling things, maybe from hitting sharp limbs and nails. The rump was a mountain of wrinkles and scars. It looked like the skin didn't fit the elephant but was too big and had got twisted on the elephant's frame. The legs danced like logs tamping dirt.

"*Errr!*" the elephant roared. Its head got pulled sideways as it tried to wrench away. It was panting and snorting. The pant sounded like the flame in a furnace, or a chimney on fire. A big stream of yellow liquid squirted from the animal as it struggled. People yelled and pushed away.

"Get out of the way!" a deputy shouted and waved his shotgun.

Annie asked me again wasn't there something I could do, but I shook my head. There was nothing.

The front end of the elephant lifted higher and higher, and I heard a crunching sound, like bones breaking or flesh tearing inside the neck. But it could have been skin breaking under the chain, for there was white places and pink places with blood on them on the elephant's neck. The last time the elephant screamed the squeal got turned off like the air had gone out of a whistle. The throat puffed out and went limp. There was a gurgling and panting in the chest.

The crane pulled higher and higher. It seemed impossible anything could lift an animal that big. As the crane raised up, the elephant appeared to stretch, like it was made of rubber or something heavy in a wet sack. The back feet kicked and drug the ground, and the wheel turned on the end as the boom raised higher.

"It won't work," somebody hollered. "The elephant's too heavy."

Annie put a handkerchief to her mouth. My own stomach felt like the bottom had dropped out of it.

The motor on the crane roared louder and louder and steam blasted from the top.

"Get back!" a deputy shouted, and waved us further back with a shotgun. Soon as Jumbo's hind feet was pulled off the ground it was clear what he was warning us about. The elephant swung like a pendulum at us and everybody stumbled back to miss the feet and the manure that was flung over the ground. The swinging feet knocked down the rest of the fence.

And then I heard the awfullest sound as the engine went quiet for a moment. It was a whimper or wheeze inside the animal's throat. Maybe as the chain slipped tighter the big head bent sideways. But the noise was no louder than a puppy whimpering or some little furry thing caught in a trap.

The crane blared its motor again and pulled the elephant higher and higher. The legs kept kicking like he was swimming or treading water and the big body swung above the pen and over our heads. I seen the elephant's eye blink as it swung back and forth and round and round.

"Look at the trunk," Annie said. The elephant's trunk was flopping around like a snake caught on a hook.

The deputies and policemen gathered to one side and waved the crowd farther back. The sheriff took a rifle and aimed at the elephant's head.

The sheriff fired, and then fired again. And all the other men in uniform started firing at the elephant's head. Annie and Fay put their hands over their ears. It was deafening. They must have shot twenty times, and then twenty more. The smoke of gunpowder drifted over the crowd. When they finally stopped shooting you could see blood dripping from the elephant's trunk and from the mouth and running back down the elephant's shoulder. The big eye was still open.

"He's not dead yet!" somebody yelled.

I seen the hind leg move, but it might have been from a breeze or the jolt of the crane. The policemen fired several more rounds into the elephant's head. After what seemed like an hour the body was still. Once it was dead, the elephant didn't look as big as it had before. It hung like something ugly wrapped in canvas or a shroud.

I COULDN'T HARDLY drive the Model T home. I nearly run off the road twice between East Flat Rock and the depot, and Annie screamed. Fay was crying and Troy didn't say nothing except, "Boy, it took that elephant a long time to die."

After I let Annie and Troy off I drove on back to our house. But I wasn't hardly aware of what I was doing. I kept hearing the elephant squeal, and the wheeze in its throat as the chain tightened. I seen the great body swung on the chain like a mountain tore loose, a hunk of the earth ripped out. I kept hearing the shots the deputies fired one after another.

Instead of going to the house with Fay to tell Mama what had happened, I headed toward the river. Without looking where I was going I banged into cornstalks and weed stubble. I stepped through cockleburs and Spanish needles. I felt like I couldn't breathe until I got away from other people. And I kept seeing the elephant's eye, swole up and wet, a bulb of fear.

Where are you going? I said to myself. I knocked a cornstalk out of my way. At the river I walked beside the hazelnut bushes and under the sycamores. The leaves was wet and my good shoes was getting soaked. The river muttered like it was teasing me.

I felt silly for going to the fairgrounds to see the elephant die, and I felt sillier for having took Annie. Instead of making a good impression and showing her a good time, I had showed her something awful, something I was ashamed to have seen. I was ashamed to have been seen there. I was sick in my guts and in my bones. I hated that I had took Annie and she had seen it all.

But something bothered me even more than shame. Something about the death of Jumbo had seared through me and scalded me and scorched the marrow in my bones. More than being ashamed, I was scared. I kicked the leaves under the sycamores and put my hand on a river birch. The birch bark curled like pieces of dry skin.

The elephant is just an animal, I said. You have killed muskrats and mink, wildcats and foxes and deer. You have killed hogs and a sick dog one time.

As I walked out of the trees into the edge of the field I seen something gleaming in the pine thicket across the pasture. It was hard to guess what would be shining so among the pines. I tried to think if we had throwed away any bottles or jars there. Had a piece of tinfoil blowed across the pasture and lodged in the brush of the thicket?

My daydreams and ambitions was big and awkward as the elephant, and I was just as trapped. I had tried to turn this way and that way. Nothing I'd tried had worked. I had fell down in the mud at Hicks's funeral and spilled his corpse out in the rain. It was the panic in the elephant's eye that I recognized. Its helpless terror stirred and chilled me.

What was that flashing like a signal from the edge of the pines? I wanted to keep walking, but if the sun moved, whatever it was wouldn't shine no more and I wouldn't be able to find it. I crossed over the end of the cornfield and headed toward the pasture. I climbed over the bars of the milk gap and aimed myself at the flashing light. Whatever it was must be under or between the bushes and was catching the late sun that come through a gap in the thicket.

You are clumsy as the elephant, I said to myself. And like the elephant you blunder around and hurt people. You are guilty and you are trapped, and nobody is able to help you.

As I got closer, the light under the pines seemed to throb and shift. And then I seen there was a limb stirring that made the light twinkle. At first I thought it was a pile of old jars and rubbish that had been uncovered by the rain. I got down on my knees and crawled into the thicket, pushing aside some briars and honeysuckle vines.

It was glass that was shining, jars and jugs washed by rain and catching the late sun. But there was also something in the jars that made them sparkle, like they was full of water. And then it come to me: This was where Moody hid his blockade liquor. This was where he kept his supply, close to the house so he'd always have some to sell and drink hisself.

The jars was heaped in a low spot, and they'd been covered with pine needles. But the rain had washed the needles off, and Moody had not been back to cover them yet. There must have been thirty or forty fruit jars of corn liquor, clear as springwater. I unscrewed a lid and smelled the contents. The scent was subtle and surprising, not as fruity as I expected. It was a scent with dignity in it. I sniffed the fumes like there was a message in them.

Brushing off the remaining needles to get a better look, I seen what appeared to be a square of folded cloth. It was covered partly in leaves and dirt. It was oilcloth folded like a tight envelope. I opened it up slow and seen money, some fives and tens and twenty-dollar bills, as well as several gold pieces. This was where Moody had kept his bootlegging money all along. He always claimed to be broke so he wouldn't have to spend any or pay Mama for his board. He had kept it out here wrapped in oilcloth. I counted out the money. There was a little over seventy dollars. Moody didn't have much to show for all his bootlegging, but at least he wasn't as broke as he had claimed.

I was so tired and weak I set down on the pine needles, and I was so thirsty I wished I had a dipper of cold water. But there was no water in the thicket, only the mason jars heaped there. The fear and guilt for watching the elephant die had parched me. I held up a jar in a beam of late sun and unscrewed the lid. The scent filled and inspired the cool air. Maybe I'll try a little sip, I thought. I'm so tired and scared I'm about to crack. A drink might ease my anguish. I took a sip and it burned my tongue. Swallowing quick, I felt the flare and flush in my throat and belly. But it felt good too, warm and uplifting.

I took another drink and it seemed the colors of the thicket and late sun got mellower. Though I was setting in the pine needles, I felt raised. I could think clearer.

As the liquor worked its way into the veins of my arms, I felt lighter. And I felt both shielded and naked at the same time. So this is why Moody likes to drink, I thought.

I looked out across the pasture, beyond the house, toward the church and Meetinghouse Mountain. The little steeple was just in view between the tips of the hemlocks. The mountain rose beyond, high against the deep blue sky.

I seen a church on the mountaintop, one you could see from all over the valley, a church with a steeple so high it caught the first and last light of day. I took another sip from the jar. The liquor whispered and hummed in my ears. The sun was gone from the thicket, and the air was getting cool, but I didn't care. I was warm inside the stove of my skin. Late sun touched the top of Meetinghouse Mountain with rose-and-lavender light, like it was bleeding, like the peak was a chosen spot.

I am afraid, and I'm afraid of being punished for my awkwardness and my daydreams. I am clumsy and helpless. I must do something right. I will not just wallow in the mud. I will not be penned in and hung. I could die before I get anything done. In the great curve of centuries I am already dead.

The late sun touched the very tip of Meetinghouse Mountain with copper, rose and copper. They was the colors of a stained-glass window. I had seen pictures of cathedrals built on hilltops. The great churches of the Old World was on hills where they could be seen for miles around. I had read about Chartres Cathedral in the Adams book, about how it was built on a hill on top of the ruins of a pagan temple. The high ground, the mountaintop, was the place for an altar and a place of worship. A church was shadowy like a grove. A grove on top of the hill was the most sacred place.

I sipped and seen the first star pop out over the mountain. The star snapped in the blue-and-lavender sky like a thought. I am seeing from a whole new angle, I thought. I have a new vantage point to think from.

My grandpa had built the first church on Green River out of the materials he had. I would build a new church out of what I could find available.

Lord, show me what to do that will have meaning and will last, I prayed. Show me what to do to quell my fear and lostness. Show me how to work for a purpose, and not just to blunder and fail. Don't let me be a complete fool. Don't let my spirit be killed.

Looking at the sky above the mountains, I felt like I seen the curve of the world stretching far as I could look, and the curve of time stretching beyond that, far as the curve of thought. The blood whispered in my ear: This is what you was meant to do, to pray in the woods and to build a church in the woods. The stars coming out above whispered in the dome of sky, like the whole sky was a whispering gallery.

I tried to stand up but felt my nose mash against the pine needles. I reached around, but the thicket turned faster than I did. The prow of a great ship plunged sideways through my head.

A voice whispered way back behind my ears: You will build a church. Upon that mountain you will build a church. You will place an altar in the wilderness. You will make a place of prayer and praise high in the wilderness.

I looked behind me in the thicket and seen nothing but darkness. I looked at the mountaintop under the new stars. And it come to me that the Lord had whispered to me his message, and he had whispered to me his covenant. I was to build a new church on the mountaintop. The old church was little and drafty. What the congregation needed was a new church, and it would be the work of my life.

I would build a church on the mountaintop with my own hands and on my own land. That was what I had been born to do. If I couldn't preach with words I would preach with my hands. My sermons would be in wood and stone. For I seen the new church had to be built with rock that would last through the ages, like the churches in Europe. I would build a steeple that would inspire all that seen it in all weather and all seasons, as it pointed to heaven.

A church building was a kind of scripture and a kind of sermon. A church would inspire people when they wasn't even thinking about it. A church was a sign to people of the covenant of grace.

I got on my knees and held on to a pine tree and thanked the Lord for showing me my purpose and my future. I felt an ease and strength I had not felt in a long time. The sky above the thicket leaned and swimmed a little, and the trees swayed and rocked a little. But my head was steady and clear. I seen what I had to do, and what I was going to do.

Eighteen
Muir

THE NEXT MORNING Mama said she thought it was a wonderful idea when I told her what I planned to do. But she said I couldn't build a church without asking the preacher and the board of deacons. I told her that of course I planned to ask the preacher.

"In a Baptist church it's up to the congregation," Mama said. "The preacher ain't supposed to have any more say-so than any other member."

Fay said she had always thought the preacher was supposed to be the boss. Preacher Liner acted like he was the boss. All I could think of was that a new church would change the spirit of the community, and Mama agreed. But she said the whole membership would have to vote, after I told them what I was planning.

I hadn't thought of that before. I hated to ask the very people who had seen me make a fool of myself trying to preach to vote for a new church I wanted to build. I doubted they would have any confidence in me.

"They're not building the church," I said. "I'm going to build the church myself."

But I was pleased that Mama showed enthusiasm for my plans.

She said a new church could give the Green River valley a new start. She seen that a new church could bring the people together and make them want to work together. But she warned me I would need a lot of help. And that I would need the support of the congregation.

"What if Grandpa had waited for a vote to build the first church?" I said.

But Mama just argued that was in a different time and before there was a congregation. And Mama said, as she always did, that I shouldn't get carried away with my plans. I couldn't deny I'd made a fool of myself more times than one. But this plan was different. It was something I would do at home. The land on the mountain belonged to us, and the rocks on the river belonged to us, and the trees on the mountainside. I told her it would be my sweat that put the rocks in place on the mountaintop.

"You couldn't carry that many rocks to the mountaintop in forty years," Fay said.

"If it takes forty years, then I will work forty years," I said. I knowed there was churches in Europe that had took hundreds of years to build.

"Son, I hope you can do it," Mama said.

"You're just doing it to impress Annie," Fay said.

Just then Moody come into the kitchen. He must have been listening on the porch. "Sounds like Muir wants to build a Tower of Babel," he said. Moody knowed more Scripture than he let on. I hadn't told him I'd found his stash of liquor and money in the thicket.

"I'd rather build something up than tear down what everybody else has done," I said.

Moody lit his cigar and leaned on the mantel, grinning at me. I told him I would need his help in carrying the rocks from the river to the top of the mountain, and in cutting the trees.

"Don't expect me to aid your foolishness," Moody said. But there wasn't as much sarcasm in his voice as I had expected. I think the idea of the church on the mountaintop had caught his interest too.

"Muir wants to bore with a big auger," Moody said to Mama.

I would build a church with a steeple so high it would be the first thing people seen when they stepped outside in the morning.

The old church set at the foot of Meetinghouse Mountain. The new church would set on the top, higher than the peach orchard on Riley's Knob. I crossed the pasture and walked through the Richardses' field on the side of the mountain. The Richardses' land joined ours, and our property run to the top of the ridge. I climbed up the mountainside behind the church to the steep part where Uncle Joe and Uncle Locke and Grandpa had dug for zircons in the 1890s and caused a landslide. Their pits was full of leaves and rainwater, and the big piles of dirt was still bleeding rocks and mud down the side of the mountain. Above the pits was a kind of shelf with more laurel bushes. But the very top was covered with white oaks and poplars.

I climbed to the peak and looked out through the trees. From there you could see all the way up the river valley to the Banes' land and the Morrises' land, to Chimney Top and the far end of the Cicero. To the right you could see far as Pinnacle and Mount Olivet. To the east you could see Tryon Mountain, which Grandpa used to call Old Fodderstack. And to the south you could glimpse Corbin Mountain on the South Carolina line.

Out of the river valley and the creek valleys and the branch coves, the ground gathered itself up to the height where I stood. The ground I stood on was like an altar next to the sky. This is the place the church has to be, I thought. I've hunted turkeys here, and I've found ginseng here, but this is the spot the church was meant to be. This is the place of worship. It was far from the rocks in the river that would be used in the walls, and it was far from the spring. But rocks and water could be carried up the hillside. Climbing up the ridge, people would climb out of their ordinary lives into purer air.

I went ahead and talked to the preacher about my plans. I talked to him after prayer meeting on Wednesday night. After the service let out I took the preacher aside and told him there was a project I wanted to discuss. We stood on the steps of the church in the dark while the wind was roaring on the slope above. I was so nervous I felt sweat dripping under my arms.

"What is troubling you, Muir?" the preacher said. "I've felt for some time that something was troubling you." The preacher leaned over me like he was pushing me away.

"What was troubling me was that I didn't know what I wanted to do," I said.

"The Lord will answer if you pray for guidance," the preacher said.

"The Lord has showed me what he wants me to do," I said.

"Not everybody is called to preach," Preacher Liner said. Preacher Liner was such a big man you always felt he was pressing up against the air around him. I always felt like I was going to smother when I was around him.

"I'm not studying on preaching no more," I said. "I'm going to build a new church." The preacher didn't answer. The wind on the mountain was so loud it sounded inside my ears and inside my blood. The wind chanted and pounded inside my head.

"Why do you want to do this?" the preacher said. He shifted in the dark the way a boxer or wrestler might.

"I feel led to do it," I said. "I feel it's what I was meant to do."

"Might be the devil's work," Preacher Liner said. He was not pleased like I expected him to be. There was a stiffness in his voice. Preacher Liner was a big man with a face that got red when he preached. His eyes was the color of tobacco juice. He stood too close when he talked to you, like he was trying to drive you back.

"It's not the devil's work to build a new church," I said. My voice was weaker than I hoped it would be.

"It's the devil's work to split up a congregation," the preacher said. "The devil splinters churches all the time."

"I don't want to splinter no church," I said. "I want to build a new church for all of us, on top of the mountain."

"Oh," the preacher said. The wind got quieter on the ridge above, but louder in the trees in the pasture below the church. The wind was like a chorus shouting its disapproval at me. Sweat run from my forehead and dampened my temples.

"I want to build a rock church, a bigger church, right on top of the mountain there," I said. "I want to put the church up high where everybody can see it, and I want a steeple that shoots up into the sky. It'll have a bell to ring to the farthest coves of the valley, calling everybody to worship."

"How do you know the Lord is leading you to do this?" Preacher Liner said. He didn't sound pleased; he sounded irritated.

"I can feel it," I said. "I had a terrible feeling after the elephant died, and I prayed and the Lord showed me I was to build a new church, for we need a new place of worship."

"We ain't got money to build a new church," the preacher said.

"I will build it myself," I said. "My grandpa built the first church in these parts, and I will build this one."

"You can't build a church all by yourself," the preacher said.

"I'll build it with rocks out of the river, and planks from the trees on the hill," I said. "I will build it one rock and one nail at a time."

"Beware of the sin of pride," Preacher Liner said. He didn't talk at all like I thought he would. Here I was, offering to build a new church with my own hands out of my own materials, on my own land, for his congregation. The least he could do was show a little appreciation. He didn't like my plan because it wasn't his idea.

"I want to make something I can take pride in," I said. "Maybe I'm called to preach in work, and in stone. The church will be my gift to the community."

"A church is not made with just rocks and mortar," the preacher said. "A church is in the hearts of people. A church is in the will of the community to come together in fellowship."

I seen it wouldn't do any good to argue with the preacher. He didn't like my idea yet because it was new to him. And he didn't believe I could build such a church. How could he, since I had never proved myself? I'd failed at or quit everything I'd tried so far. It was up to me to prove I could accomplish something. I didn't need anybody's permission to do my work. I just needed the patience and the sense and the time to get the work done.

"There ain't even water on the mountaintop," the preacher said.

I told him we could carry water from the spring in buckets, and there was no need to have baptizings on the mountain. But the preacher was quiet for a long time. It was scary for him to just stand there in the dark without saying nothing. Wind roared on the mountain, and I shivered with the sweat under my shirt.

"I won't let you divide this community with some crazy scheme to build a church," the preacher said. "All my life I have fought off Pentecostals from breaking up my church, and I won't let it happen again."

But I had already made up my mind.

THERE IS A rage that comes on you when you look at woods that need to be cleared. Oak trees and poplar trees stand in the way of the open place you want to make. Trunks hard as masonry have to be chopped through. And stumps have to be dug out of the ground or burned any way you can to get rid of them. A man with an axe looks at the woods all around him and above him and hears the roar of an ocean in his ears and feels the tightening of a fight in his guts. It must be the way our grandfathers felt when they faced the raw wilderness a hundred years ago.

The shadows of the thickets make you mad. The must and mold of the leaf floor rile you. With your two hands and an axe you want to let in the sunlight. You want to chew up the forest and spit it out as mulch. Saplings wave and tremble when you swing against them. Dry leaves and sticks break up when you trample them. The rotten dirt underneath is exposed. Cobwebs and vines need to be tore away and roots tough as gristle ripped from the ground. The ground is laced with secret roots that have to be jerked out like stitches.

When I looked at the trees on the mountain I seen ten thousand licks of the axe that stood in the way of ever starting the church. There was fifty thousand strokes of the saw and a thousand digs with the grubbing hoe. There was bushes and log fires and leveling that stood in the way of my idea.

It was Saturday evening before I got out of the store and come home to work on my plans. As long as I worked for U. G. I could afford to buy tools and supplies a little at a time. But I wouldn't have time to work except on Saturday afternoons. It would take me weeks to get the mountaintop cleared. It would take me months to dig the foundation and pour the footing. It would take me years to build the church.

I knowed there was no reason to be in a hurry. Yet I felt in a hurry. Better to go slow. Since nobody was supporting me, I would have to go slow. But as the building rose, people would get used to the idea.

The preacher would come to approve, and Mama was already enthusiastic. It would take years for people to warm to the idea of the new church, and it would take me years to build it. But when the community saw the beautiful building take shape they would be proud of it.

That first Saturday I chopped down the biggest poplar on the mountaintop. I seen it was better to start with the big timber and clean up the little stuff later. The hardest work should be done first. But as I chopped and watched the yellow poplar fall, and as I slashed limbs and piled laps in a heap right on top of the ridge, I thought how much money I would need just to get started, once I got the trees cleared off. I could borrow Mama's axe and saw and use our horse, Old Fan. But where would I get a leveler to lay off the foundation? And where would I get the trowel to smooth the footing? I needed new hammers and chisels for shaping rock. I'd need a longer level and try square.

After I got rocks out of the river and out of the creeks, after I heaped them in piles by the streams, I'd still have to build a road up the mountain before hauling them in the wagon to the mountaintop. To make the road I needed a pick and shovel and mattock. I needed a drag pan and turning plow. To pour footing I needed bags of cement and I needed lumber to make a mortar box. I needed a cement hoe, and I needed to haul sand from the bend of the river.

I trimmed limbs off the big log, and then I took the crosscut and sawed the tree into sections before it got dark. Pulling a crosscut saw wears you out in the legs and the back, as well as the arms, for you have to stoop down or squat down to draw it through the log. And when you're working by yourself you have to push the blade back through the cut, then pull it again. Chopping and sawing is about the hardest work there is. You wonder how the first settlers was able to clear so much woods so fast. I was wore out in an hour.

Nineteen
Ginny

ONE OF THE best ways we had to make a little money was selling molasses. Sorghum was the one crop you could depend on, for no matter how bad the weather was, hot or cool, dry or rainy, cane seemed to thrive along the river. We had always growed cane for ourselves, but it was my husband, Tom, that started planting a whole acre, then two acres, and some years three, and selling syrup by the gallon down at the cotton mill. Tom built the new molasses furnace in the pasture, and every year he sold a hundred dollars', or sometimes two hundred dollars', worth of molasses.

Sorghum making is hot and dusty work. You go out in the field and break your back stripping the leaves from the cane. And then you have to cut the stalks and haul them to the mill. Somebody has to feed each stalk into the crushing rollers while the horse walks round and round turning the mill. Then the juice, drawing hundreds of flies and yellow jackets, is carried to the pan over the furnace. The worst job is stirring the pan with the skimmer while it boils down. And you have to dip the shiny scum off as you stir. You stand smothering in the smoke and steam, for molasses can't be cooked a minute too long or they'll be rubbery and thick. If they're not cooked enough they're watery and green.

Every year me and Muir done most of the work. I'd ask Moody to help out, but like as not he'd find an excuse to be gone on the day it was time to strip a field and carry the stalks to the furnace. "Moody, we could use an extra hand," I said one September morning in 1919 when Moody was seventeen. It was the fall the typhoid come back to the river and fever broke out in houses all down the valley. Hank Richards's oldest boy was took sick. Typhoid likes hot dry weather, but I figured that if we worked and sweated enough we would sweat out the germs if we got any. Moody had always hated to work with molasses since he was a little boy. It was tedious bone-wearing work.

"Ain't got time," Moody snorted.

"The rest of us has got time," I said.

Muir and me went ahead and done all the stripping and cutting of the acre of early cane. We hauled the stalks to the pasture in the wagon. It was hot as it can get in September. Even though he was still a boy, Muir had split a wagonload of wood for the furnace, and I lit a fire under the big steel pan. Muir hunkered down under the turning shaft of the mill as Old Fan walked around and round. And soon the juice was trickling into the bucket and drawing flies. It would take us at least two days to crush the stalks and boil the sap down to syrup. I figured there was over fifty gallons to be made, and I had to wash out the jugs with hot water and dry them in the sun.

Hard as the work was, it was satisfying too. For boiling the juice was like taking the sweetest extract from the summer, from the soil and sun and rain. The syrup was the pure essence of the harvest, the sugar of the big sorghum grass. The molasses we would store up in the jugs was the very sap and marrow of the grass, concentrated till it was dark and smooth as oil.

"Let me do that," somebody said. I looked up and seen Moody with his sleeves rolled up.

"Thought you didn't have time," I said.

"Give me that skimmer," Moody said.

If he had decided to work, I wasn't going to argue with him. His daddy had showed him how to make molasses same as the rest of us. I needed to be carrying jugs out of the smokehouse and scalding them by the springhouse. "Here," I said, and handed Moody the skimmer.

The three of us strained and sweated all that day, and the next, to make molasses. Moody bent over the smoking pan and skimmed off the dirty foam. He dug a hole in the pasture and poured the scum there. Molasses scum looks both green and purple and shines like it was boiling metal. Moody cussed when he spilled some on the knee of his overalls, but he kept on working. I was so tickled to have his help, tears come to my eyes.

When we finished up, there was seventy-two jugs full of molasses. It wasn't the best syrup we had made, because Moody was out of practice and let some cook too long so they was thick and strong. But most of the jugs was good and we set them in the smokehouse to cool.

The usual thing was to load twenty or thirty jugs in the wagon and drive down to the cotton mill village. Tom had peddled molasses door-to-door there and made some regular customers among the mill hands. You could also stop the wagon in front of the company store, and people would come by and buy jugs from you. But the fastest way was to go house-to-house. Once you started knocking on doors, women down the street would hear you coming and be ready with seventy-five cents for a gallon of syrup.

Muir and me drove the wagon down to the village two different days. I hated to do it and felt my face get hot when I walked up to a house to knock. But I done it anyway. I done it for the memory of Tom, and I done it to help Muir, who needed the money for his traps and guns and his big plans. A woman has to help out her children if she can.

We sold forty gallons and got thirty dollars, and I give half to Muir. There would be a late cane field to cut in early October, but we would keep that syrup to sell a gallon at a time through the winter. There was two jugs in the wagon we hadn't sold, and when I carried them back into the smokehouse I glanced at the row of jugs we had left. There should have been thirty-two, including the jugs I brought back. But it looked like there was less. I counted only twenty-six jugs in the gloom. The place smelled of salt and smoke and grease, and the ashes of old fires.

Had somebody stole six jugs since we made them? I counted them again and six was missing. And then I thought Moody must have took them. I was going to give him ten dollars for helping us, but he must have already took some of the jugs to sell as part of his pay.

When Moody come to the house that night I give him five dollars. "Is that all I get?" he said and set down at the table with his hat still on. I had tried to teach him to take his hat off when he come through the door.

"You have already took some of your pay in kind," I said.

"It's the only kind thing I get," Moody said. He could always quip when he felt like it. But that's all Moody would say. He didn't tell where he had sold the molasses or how much he had got for them. I tried to think if there was some way to make liquor out of molasses. I reckon you can make liquor out of anything sweet. But with all the corn growed around the valley it would be a waste and a shame to use up good molasses that way.

I was coming out of the henhouse the next day when I seen Moody walking toward the smokehouse. Now, I never was one to spy on my younguns, but I was curious to see if he was going to get a jug of molasses. I had seven eggs in my apron and I laid them on a shelf in the shed and stood under the hemlock tree while Moody entered the smokehouse and come out carrying a jug of molasses. He closed the latch and started out the trail to the pasture. It was late in the evening and shadows stretched out from the pines like trains behind brides.

I didn't want to spy on my own son, but I couldn't help myself. I figured he was hiding jugs in the pasture where he could get them later. I always wondered where Moody hid his liquor on the place. I expected it was in the pine thicket. I kept trees between me and Moody as I followed him.

But he didn't turn into the pine thicket. He crossed the branch and climbed right up the trail on the other side. And he followed the trail through the Richardses' pasture. The Richards family had been quarantined because of typhoid. I wanted to holler out and tell Moody not to go there. But then he would see I had followed him. Surely he knowed Billy, the oldest boy, had the fever. Their spring had been condemned by the county, and they was having to dig a well.

No! I hollered in my mind. But I didn't say nothing. I'd be ashamed for Moody to know I had followed him. I'd be ashamed for anybody to know I was spying on my own flesh and blood. I crouched down behind a Ben Davis apple tree.

Moody walked straight to the Richards house and climbed the steps. There was nobody in sight. He set the jug down beside the front door. He didn't knock and he didn't open the door, but turned and walked back down the steps to the road.

My heart thrust up into my throat, for I knowed he would see me in the apple trees if he come back toward the pasture. How would I explain that I'd watched him bring a jug of sorghum to the Richardses? I was ashamed of myself, and yet I was thrilled to see what Moody had done.

Instead of returning across the pasture, Moody turned on the road toward the church. In the shadows I couldn't hardly see his face, but it appeared he was smirking, like he had a secret. I wanted to call out to him. I wanted to run to him and hug him and tell him how proud I was he was giving molasses to the Richardses. I wanted to beg him to forgive me for spying on him. But I stayed behind the tree and watched him disappear around the bend.

When I seen U. G. next time at the store he said, "Molly Bane asked me to tell you she was mighty grateful for the gallon of syrup you sent her." The Banes had had two cases of typhoid fever that fall.

"What gallon?" I said.

"The one you had Moody bring them," U. G. said.

"I'm glad it was useful," I said.

There was five other families in the valley that was struck with typhoid that fall. All but two of them lived. It turned out Moody had took every one of the families a jug of molasses without telling me. It was a side of him I knowed was there but didn't see too often. It was a side I hoped he would show more.

"It's a good thing you done," I said to Moody one night, "taking the jugs of syrup to them that needed it."

"What jugs?" Moody said.

"Them you took to the Richardses and Banes and the others," I said.

"Ain't no charity," Moody said.

"It was a good thing," I said.

"I don't know what you're talking about," Moody said.

Before Christmas the typhoid fever had died out in the valley and I thanked the Lord it had passed over us.

Twenty

Muir

THE CORN WAS still standing in the fields, and Moody hadn't lifted a finger to get it in. I told U. G. I would have to stop working in the store. I couldn't help Mama and build the church and work at the store at the same time. I only had time to do what had to be done. I hitched up Old Fan to the wagon and gathered all the corn and throwed it into the crib and into the barn loft. It was so easy to hitch up the wagon and gather corn. Work seemed easy. I gathered every ear in the bottom fields and heaped the unshucked ears in the shelter of the crib and barn. I would shuck them later, a bushel or two at a time to take to mill. The work was smooth as a dance. All you had to do was go ahead with it. Work was the easiest and cleanest thing in the world. It was a year since I'd gone to the Tar River. I was glad to have the corn to gather so I could put off working on the church a few more days.

Soon as I got the corn all in, I gathered up a pick and shovel and crowbar to take down to the river. The most rocks was in the fast stretch at the end of the bottom, and in the creek just above where it run into the river. I needed thick rocks, and big rocks, but rocks not too big for me to carry. I needed rocks that would fit together in a wall. They could be any color or kind, as long as they could be joined together at the right thickness in a foundation and in the walls.

Now, to get rocks out of a river you have to work in the cold water. To reach some of the best rocks you have to wade right into the pools. But mostly you can stand on other rocks to pry and lift out one at a time. A shovel is too thick to slide under rocks, and the tilt and curve of the blade don't help. A pick can be used to pry rocks loose, but its handle is too short. Soon as I waded out in the cold river and started picking out rocks, I seen that what I needed was a pry pole, something you could shove under a rock to raise it. I got the axe and cut an oak sapling and used that for a while. But what I really needed was a steel rod. Finally I found an old Model T axle in the gully below the church, and that turned out to be my best tool.

When you're looking for rocks to build a wall, you search for pieces of a puzzle that ain't even made yet. Maybe that's not the way you think of it, but that's what you're doing, figuring how round rocks and three-cornered rocks, square rocks and long rocks, flat rocks and bulging rocks, can be fitted together. Mostly you're looking for the right thickness, for you'll have to worry later about how the shapes will fit. Anything can be fitted together with mortar and a little hammering to the edges.

When you pry out rocks from their sockets in mud or a riverbed, you can try to roll them to the bank or slide them over other rocks. But if a rock ain't too big, you just pick it up and carry it to the shore. You wrestle a rock out and hold it on your lap streaming water on your knees and stagger to the bank and toss it on a pile in the weeds. I got out three-cornered rocks and five-cornered rocks and rocks so irregular you couldn't name what their shape was. I got out granite and flint and milk quartz. I even got out some orange quartz and rock that looked like it had flashing garnets and isinglass in it.

In ABOUT A week I heaved out several piles of rocks on the riverbank, and I toted out several more on the bank of the creek, working my hands raw and water-sobbed in the river. And I was cold and wet every day when I got back to the house. I'd set by the fire, but it took hours for the chill in my bones to melt away. The coldness seemed to get into my blood and stay there.

"I don't think the Lord expects you to build a rock church with your bare hands," Mama said.

"What else is worth doing?" I said.

"Nothing is more important," Mama said. "But you could build us a new barn if you wanted to get some practice."

"I'll build the barn after I build the church," I said.

"Building a barn is as worthy as building a church," Mama said, "if it's done in the right spirit. The best work is to do what's needed."

"People won't know they need a new church until they have it," I said.

TALKING WITH MAMA reminded me I couldn't go no further until I had a way to carry the rocks and other materials up the mountain. I had to open up a road before anything else got done. I didn't have much money, and I didn't have any tools except a shovel and pick and mattock. I had several piles of rocks by the river and by the creek, but they was a long way from the top of the mountain.

"Maybe you could pray the rocks to the top of the mountain," Moody said.

"I'm going to pray that you'll help me," I said.

"I'll help you roll them off, once you carry them up there," Moody said. He slouched against the doorpost, swaggering the way he always done when he'd had a drink and was beginning to feel better.

"How big a church are you going to build?" Fay said.

"Big as I can," I said.

"As tall as a town church?" Fay said.

"Taller," I said.

"Be careful you don't punch a hole in the sky," Moody said. He drove his finger up into the air.

I TRIED TO think how I would build a road up the mountainside. How would I start it? Where would I put it? The road couldn't be too steep, or the horse couldn't pull a wagon up it, or the wagon would run away going down. I would have to swing the road around at a gentle grade but make it as cheap and fast as I could. I didn't want to tear up any more of the ridge than I had to, or cut down any more trees than I had to, or move any more rocks than I had to.

I didn't have a transit or surveying equipment. I just had a tape measure and an axe. I knowed the road had to go up from the parking lot of the church, and I knowed how steep the pitch could be. So what I did was just walk up through the woods marking trees out along the slope at an easy grade. After about a hundred yards I turned at a switchback and started up higher. It took four switchbacks to get to the top. But by the end of the day I had a reasonable route. And for the most part I went around and between the big trees so there wouldn't be too much felling to do.

"Muir Powell the Roadmaker," Moody said when he come up to see the route I'd marked out. He couldn't seem to stay away from where I was working, but he wouldn't help out.

"Wish I had a sow like old Solomon Richards did," I said.

"This road ain't wide enough for a sow," Moody said.

"It can be widened and improved later," I said.

"Do you figure to build a road to heaven?" Moody said.

"That's the road we all want to build," I said. My plan to build the church had snagged Moody's interest. Even though he ragged me, he kept mentioning the church, and he come to see what I was doing. I think he was tired of just laying out with Drayton and Wheeler. He was getting older, and the new church was such a good idea even Moody seen it was interesting.

I had a plan for the ditching and the rounding of the switchbacks. I would have to use a pick and shovel. But for most of the roadway I was going to use the light turning plow, not the big turning plow for deep plowing, but the little one we used for the tater patch and the hillside garden.

Soon as I'd cleared brush from the right of way and cut down the trees that had to be felled, I hitched up Old Fan to the plow and drove her up to the churchyard. Annie's papa, Hank, was working in the field beyond the church when I got there. It was one of the rare times he wasn't away on a construction job. "What are you going to turn?" he hollered at me.

"The mountain," I hollered back, and Hank chuckled.

"Then you must have a lot of faith," he hollered.

"I'm going to plow me a road," I said.

"Watch out for roots," Hank called back. It was well known that plowing new ground, many a man had near about castrated theirselves when the plow hit a root or buried rock.

Old Fan was confused when I guided her into the woods and started bearing down on the handles of the plow. The blade cut into the leaves and into the leaf rot underneath and started rolling over black dirt. But I hadn't gone ten yards when the plow point snagged on a root and the handles jolted out of my grip. And after another twenty yards the plow snagged again and a handle rammed into my belly. I recalled the story of Bowen Ward up the river that had hurt hisself so bad with a plow he died of the bleeding in his belly.

Go slow, I said to myself. "Whoa," I called to Old Fan. "Whoa there." I held the plow at arm's length and when the point hit a big root, I stopped and backed up and went over it. The roots could be cut later with the axe. Silly as it looked, I plowed a rough furrow from the bottom of the mountain to the top. And then I turned the blade over and started back down. On the way down I seen my plan was going to work. The thing was to loosen as much dirt as I could and later level it with the shovel. Going down, the plow went deeper. All the plow did was move dirt out of the hill and shift it over a little bit. But that's what building a road was, digging dirt out of the slope and setting it aside on the shoulder. If I plowed the furrow again and again, I'd have a road.

As we plowed back up the ridge I seen we'd already made a trail. With four or five more sweeps I would have a narrow road. With a dozen or twenty trips to the top and back I'd have a rough wagon track.

It's a pleasure to tear into a mountainside and shape it to your will. I tore deeper and deeper with the plow, opening the fresh dirt, the red clay under the topsoil, the mealy soil. I chopped out roots wet with sap as ripe fruit, and I tore rocks out of their sockets. Some of the rocks I set aside to carry later to the top. The biggest rocks I just pushed aside.

I'll tame this mountain a foot at a time, I said to myself. Old Fan and me are conquering the height an inch and a shovelful of dirt at a time. I stopped the horse and chopped away roots and saplings. There was a seep spring halfway up the mountain, and I cut a little ditch for it to run along the side of the road to the switchback. The raw dirt gleamed in the woods like it was red-hot. The new dirt smelled like perfume and ether from a long time ago, like fumes buried deep in the ground.

The switchbacks are levers, I said to myself. They are wedges with which I'll raise tons of rocks to the edge of the sky. The switchbacks will raise the weight of a church a rock at a time until it touches the stars. If I'd had the money I would have hired help and machines. But this way I knowed every foot of the road, as I knowed every rock I'd got out of the river. And I'd know every nail and every board and pane of glass I would put in the church later.

"Lord, this mountaintop is your altar," I said as I worked.

For three days me and Old Fan plowed open the road on the mountainside. We went up and then down. We plowed deeper and deeper into the ridge until the bank was a yard high. I jerked out rocks and ripped out roots white as grubworms. The furrows begun to look like a road. The way was wide enough and level enough for a wagon to make it to the top with a load of rocks.

After I finished the road I laid out the foundation. I stretched my tape measure over the ground to mark the size of the church, and I drove stakes at the corners and tied strings to show where the trenches should be dug. It made the church seem more possible, to see where the foundation was to be, what the shape was going to be.

Digging out the foundation was both rough and delicate. It was hard work, digging through roots and rocks into the subsoil of the mountaintop. But the trenches had to be exactly twelve inches wide, and level. I didn't have a transit or leveler. I just had my carpenter's level. I shoveled out the floor of the trench and laid my level on the dirt. This is where my church will be joined to the earth. This will be the hidden seal between the church and the mountain, I thought.

And then I thought how I was opening the earth to plant a seed. The church was the seed of all the worship and all the sermons and songs, and of all the inspiration that would happen there. I was a farmer planting a great seed in the soil of the mountaintop. I dug out the design of the trenches as exact as I could in the uneven dirt, following the plan I had drawed.

EVERY DAY HAS its own flavor, I thought. Every morning when you get up is different, and the curve and feel of every day is different. You look forward because you're curious and because you hope for a surprise, for firmness, an easy glide.

But the day I started hauling rocks up the mountain it felt like nothing would go right. I hitched up the wagon, but Old Fan didn't seem eager to work that morning. She seemed to know what we was going to do, the way horses sometimes guess what you need them for. I think they can sense the worry in people, and that makes them anxious too. She stalled when I tried to back her between the shafts. "Whoa, there," I said. "Back, back."

"That horse don't want to carry the riverbed to the top of the mountain," Moody said. He had got up early and was patching a tire on the Model T. I hoped he would help me, once he seen I had got the road plowed up the mountain. ,

"How would you know?" I said.

"Have you got a hair in your ass?" Moody said.

"Thought you might be going to help me," I said.

"Never told you that," Moody said.

"I thought this would be a family project," I said. "A gift to the community, like the first church."

"What has the community give to me," Moody said, "except a kick in the butt?"

"We only get back what we give, like Mama says," I said.

"Then I should kick the whole community," Moody said.

When I finally got Old Fan hitched to the wagon, I drove her down to the river. The piles of rocks looked heavy and clumsy. I couldn't believe I'd pried and wrestled that many rocks out of the riverbed. The wagon suddenly looked awful flimsy, fragile and weak. I lugged a cold rock over and laid it in the bed. If I put more than ten in at once, the wagon would be too heavy for Old Fan to pull up the mountain. It would take a lot of trips to move the rocks to the mountaintop.

I had over four hundred rocks in my piles by the river and creek. If

I carried only ten at a time that would be forty trips. And if I made
five trips a day that would take eight days just to move the rocks. It
would be getting up toward Christmas before the job was done.

We started up the road and Old Fan worked fine, pulling the
wagon up the hill and around the foot of the mountain to the church.
She was a horse that was always willing, to be fair, even when she
was worried or didn't feel like working. She was a horse that would
do her part, as long as she wasn't too tired.

But when we turned into the road we'd made up the mountain behind the church, and when the grade started getting steeper, I seen
her slow down. For one thing, the dirt in the road was still soft and
the wagon wheels sunk down, making the wagon harder to pull. But
on the incline the pile of rocks in the wagon bed looked heavy enough
to break the planks.

"Giddyup," I hollered to Fan. "Giddyup!"

The mare kept going but she got slower and slower. It was like
time slowed down as I watched her. Now, a wagon gets harder to
pull in rough ground the slower it goes. The more speed you have the
easier it is to pull over roots and rocks. I'd tried to make the road all
at the same pitch, but there was a place after the second switchback
that was steeper than the rest. I guess I'd got in a hurry when I laid
that off, or I'd lost my sense of the grade. As we come through the
second turn and started up again I seen the wagon get slower still.
Fan's flanks trembled and her feet was unsteady and danced a little
bit sideways.

"Giddyup!" I hollered. "Now giddyup."

But the little horse's flanks shivered like she had the chills. If she
stopped it would be harder to get going again. If I had to throw on the
brake I didn't know how we'd start up again without rolling back.

"Giddyup!" I hollered, and put my hand on the right front wheel
and pushed. I shoved hard and thought of the way people talked
about putting your shoulder to the wheel. Old Fan pooted with the
strain and snorted and kept going. I kept pushing but the wagon got
slower again. My eyes burned I was heaving so hard. There was
about twenty more feet of the steepest part and then the grade gen-
tled off again.

"Giddyup!" I hollered. "Get your lazy ass up!"

But it didn't do no good. The wagon come to a stop and Old Fan's hooves shoved into the dirt and sidestepped to hold her place. I run around to the right side and slammed the brake shut. The wagon set still and the horse stood still. "Whoa there," I said. "Whoa there."

There wasn't a thing to do but throw off two or three of the rocks to make the wagon lighter. I laid them on the side of the road where I could get them later. But one rock was almost round, and it tipped over the shoulder and started rolling. Before I could grab it the rock was crashing through the leaves and banging on trees below and bouncing over logs. I watched it roll out of sight into some laurel bushes.

That rock wants to go back where it come from, I thought. It wants to go back to the riverbed. But all the rocks come from the mountaintop first. The rocks was cliffs and mountains that got busted up and washed down into the valleys. Rocks didn't want to be on mountaintops. They didn't want to be laid in the sky. They wanted to go down so they could sleep in the riverbed and dream the long story of the river. What I was doing was against nature. Setting rocks in new shapes and combinations in the sky was against nature. That's why it was so hard and why it was so important. Anybody could let things wash downhill with the drift. The hard thing was to make something strong and firm and straight, something with a will and purpose in it, something with an idea that would stand against the wash and waste of the elements. It was up to me to do the work because I was the one that had the idea.

With the wagon lighter I hollered giddyup and released the brake. I pushed on the wheel and we made it past the steepest place and labored to the top of the mountain where I'd cleared away the trees and dug the foundation. I decided to pile the rocks in several places around the site, close to where they would be used. But by the time I got the wagon unloaded I was tired out, and so was Old Fan. I seen that instead of five loads a day I'd be lucky to haul four, or maybe even three. With only the one mare to pull the wagon, there was no way to do it faster. Instead of eight days it would take ten or even twelve days just to haul the rocks up the mountainside.

That evening when I was bringing up the third load I seen a man standing in the clearing on the mountaintop. He held his hands behind his back and he was looking at the foundation I'd dug. When I got to the top I seen it was the preacher. He'd come up from South Carolina for the prayer meeting that evening.

"Evening, Brother Muir," he said when I stopped the wagon. I was sweating from the pushing and the climb.

"Evening, Preacher Liner," I said.

I was glad he'd come to see what I was doing. But at the same time I had a feeling. He'd not made the climb up before. I figured he'd not come to give me any good news.

"Looks like you're hauling the riverbed up here," the preacher said.

"All I can," I said. Didn't seem polite to start unloading with the preacher standing there.

"You have worked hard," the preacher said. He was holding his hat behind him and he brought it around to the front and studied the brim. "I know you have worked hard," he said.

"This is only the beginning," I said.

"I come up here because I want to talk to you," the preacher said.

"Figured you did," I said.

"Brother Muir, sometimes we feel we're called to do things, and it's only our pride calling us, not the Lord." What I felt about Preacher Liner was his weight. He was a heavy man, but he willed hisself to be heavier still. He made his voice heavy, and he put all the weight he could gather against anybody else's ideas or opinions in his voice. He wanted you to feel he could crush you.

I felt my breath getting short.

"I'm doing what I feel led to do," I said.

"That's what I want to talk to you about," Preacher Liner said.

"If I don't know what I'm led to do, then who does?" I said. I was tired and sweaty and I wanted to get the wagon unloaded.

"The Lord works in mysterious ways," the preacher said. "Sometimes we have to listen to those older than us to know what to do."

"Who am I supposed to listen to?" I said. I was madder than I expected to be. I couldn't help myself.

"We have to listen to them with experience," the preacher said. "I will not have my church split up by some foolish notion."

"I believe the Lord asked me to build this church," I said. "He showed me a vision of what needed to be done."

"Maybe you misunderstood the vision," the preacher said. "Maybe you didn't get the message right."

"I'm not building this church on my own land just to please you," I said, my voice trembling.

"All my life I have fought Pentecostals," the preacher said. "This church has been my work, and I won't leave it to Pentecostals."

"I ain't a Pentecostal," I said, "and I don't need nobody's permission to build a new church."

"People are worried about you," the preacher said.

"Who is worried?"

"Your mama is worried about you, I know," the preacher said. "You're so all fired up to do things, and you keep changing your mind."

"How do you know Mama is worried?" I said.

"Because she asked me to pray for you," Preacher Liner said. His face was splotched red and pale in different places. I noticed there was circles under his eyes.

"Who are you to tell me that?" I hollered. Anger was swelling up in me and sweeping me away. Anger rose from the center of the earth, and from the beginning of time, and roared through my bones and belly. Lightning flashed behind my ears.

"I think we should pray about this," the preacher said.

"I've done prayed about it," I shouted. I wrapped the reins around the brake handle on the wagon and started walking toward the woods. I wasn't going to argue with the preacher no more.

"Pride cometh before a fall," Preacher Liner called after me, but I kept on walking.

I DIDN'T GO back to church for almost a month after I argued with the preacher. I was busy building the foundation on the mountaintop. That was my worship, I told myself. I had got the foundation wall up almost two feet. But I couldn't stay away on

Christmas Eve. I wanted to hear Annie sing and her mama, Mrs. Richards, sing. And I wanted to see the little Christmas pageant that Mama had the younguns put on every year. When I was a boy I had took part in the play and carried a shepherd's crook or a box wrapped in tinfoil that was supposed to look like a Wise Man's gold.

It was a cold clear night and the service had already started when I come into the church. There was no place to set except on the back bench where the backsliders and drunks and rough old boys set.

"What say, Muir?" Wheeler said when I slid in next to him. He had a week's growth of beard.

"Not much," I whispered.

"You getting any?" Wheeler said.

"Not much," I said.

"Shhhh," Will Stamey said.

I couldn't see the choir from the back of the church, but I knowed they was setting behind the curtain on the left. An angel wearing paper wings climbed up a stepladder under the star above the pulpit. " 'Behold, I bring you good tidings of great joy,' " she said. " 'For unto you is born this day in the city of David a saviour, which is Christ the Lord.

" 'And this shall be a sign unto you; ye shall find the babe wrapped in swaddling clothes, lying in a manger.

" 'And suddenly there was with the angel a multitude of the heavenly host praising God, and saying,

" 'Glory to God in the highest, and on earth peace, good will toward men.' "

I felt my skin get stiff with chill bumps when the little girl said them words. She was John Fisher's girl, I think. They was among the first verses I'd ever learned in the Bible. Mama read them to us younguns at Christmastime.

Will Stamey lit a match and throwed it into Wheeler's lap. Wheeler knocked the match onto my lap. There was nothing to do but slap the match to the floor and stomp on it. My boot made a loud bang when it hit the bench in front of me. People turned to look back toward us.

"Shhhh," Monroe Anderson said.

The women started singing "O Little Town of Bethlehem" behind the sheet stretched in front of the church. I listened for Annie's voice. I could hear her mama's fine alto. Annie had a clear soprano voice.

O little town of Bethlehem!
How still we see thee lie!

It was the best song there was. The thought of the silent stars going by, and the hopes and fears of all the years, made me shiver. And I thought I could hear Annie's voice, such a pure note with all the others. Such a rare voice.

Somebody on the back bench belched as the song come to an end. It was just a belch and wouldn't have amounted to nothing, except people started giggling. All the boys in the back row snickered and giggled till you couldn't hear what the younguns was saying at the front of the church.

"Shhhh," I said.

But they kept on laughing among theirselves until it near about ruined the service. I looked to the end of the bench and seen Moody staring at the window. I hadn't noticed him before. He wasn't paying any attention at all and he wasn't laughing. He looked like he was way off in his own world of worry.

SOON AS THE play was over they called out the names of the kids with presents under the tree, and the choir sung "Joy to the World." When the preacher said the final prayer I was the first to get outside.

"Now shake hands with everybody," Wheeler said as he followed me out, "like a real preacher would."

Moody come out and stood in the shadows of the churchyard, but I didn't pay him any mind. There was a moon floating high over the church and over the mountains.

"Hey, Romeo," Moody said to me.

I looked at the moon high over the juniper trees and knowed I was not going to wait and ask Annie if I could walk her home. I hadn't had the money to buy her a present anyway. After the Christmas play and the carols, I wanted to be alone. I wanted to climb up the mountain in the moonlight and see the work I'd done on the church. That was what I wanted to do for Christmas.

"Who is Romeo?" I said to Moody and walked past him in the dark.

It was the prettiest night you ever saw. Moonlight flooded over the mountains, making them look like folds of blue-and-purple velvet. There was lights in the houses up and down the valley. When I reached the top of the ridge I heard a firecracker go off, and then another. A dog barked somewhere, and I could hear the shoals over on Bobs Creek. People going home from church carried lanterns down the road and along paths to the hollers.

Just then there was a squall from the thicket on the north side of the mountain. Sounded like it come from the laurels. I answered with a squall of my own. And then the wail come again, a high wawl that rose to a scream and sunk away to a growl. It sounded closer than before.

"Come on, wildcat," I said to the dark. "I wish I had your hide."

More firecrackers was popping in the valley, and then a shotgun boomed. And I heard a crash beyond the clearing, like something had jumped out of a tree into the leaves.

"You're just a kitty cat," I hollered at the dark.

And then I seen two lights at the edge of the clearing. They was eyes so bright they reflected the moonlight. They shined and blinked.

"Come on, tiger," I yelled. The eyes blinked again and then they was gone. I heard something bound away through the leaves down the side of the mountain.

The breeze on top of the ridge was icy. I shivered as I looked down on the lights in the valley. The moon was so bright you couldn't see too many stars. This is where people will come out of church after a service and see moonlight on the river fifty years from now, I thought.

I stepped to where I thought the door was and stumbled on rocks. Had I forgot where I had put the door of my own church? I felt my way to the wall, but the top seemed rougher and lower than I expected. I took another step and banged my foot on more rocks.

What had happened to the foundation? It felt more like a rock pile than a wall. I took out a match and struck it. There was rocks scattered every which way. It was like my wall had melted down. I thought I must be at the wrong place or looking at the site from the wrong angle. Had I forgot how much work I had done?

I bent over and seen there was dried mortar on the rocks, and pieces of busted cement on the ground. I struck another match and seen sockets and nests of cement where rocks had been knocked loose. I looked closer at a rock and seen a white dent. Somebody had took a sledgehammer and knocked down the top row of my foundation wall. It didn't seem possible. I stomped the ground and walked around to the other side and struck another match. There was rocks busted loose and broke on that side too.

It didn't seem like Christmas anymore, and I didn't care about the moonlight shining on the mountains that looked like satin. Anger flushed through me and burned my temples. Even the shadows under trees turned red. It must have took somebody a whole day to destroy my work.

I throwed down the match and started down the mountainside. I was so mad I didn't look out for limbs and brush, and they slapped me in the face. I was so angry I didn't care where I was going. I must have reached the road and walked down to the river and back without even noticing. I don't know how much time passed as I walked around the pasture and up the creek.

When I got back to the pasture fence I crossed it without thinking. The grass in the pasture was almost white with moonlight. The ground glowed with moonlight and my anger glowed. I was so mad the shadows seemed lit with red sparks, and when I closed my eyes I seen red shooting stars. Wasn't but one person mean enough to do that to my work. It was a cold night, but I was so mad I was sweating.

Mama had left a lamp burning in the kitchen for me. Otherwise the house was dark and quiet. I was going right to the bedroom to find Moody. I was going to let him know I'd seen his Christmas present to me.

But there was still a little fire in the fireplace. Some logs had burned down to glowing coals. I seen a boot in front of the fire, and then I seen a leg in the boot. I looked closer and seen Moody laying on the floor in front of the fireplace.

"Get up, you son of a bitch," I said. I was so mad the words almost stuck in my throat. When I got closer I smelled liquor like toilet water on him. He must have come in from celebrating with his buddies and passed out in front of the fire.

"Wake up," I said, and prodded him with my boot.

"What hell?" Moody said and rolled over. "What the hell?"

"Merry Christmas," I said and kicked him in the hip.

"What hell?" he said again and set up.

"I seen what you done," I said and pulled him to his feet. He still had his coat on. "You bastard," I said and smacked his cheek.

Moody raised his knee and hit me in the side. I think he was aiming for my crotch and missed.

"You blackguard trash!" I said and shoved him against the mantel. A flower vase fell in the dark and broke on the hearth.

"I've put up with your doings before," I said. "But not this time." I hit Moody in the face and he slid down the wall beside the fireplace. There was something sticky on my hand. He held up his elbow to protect his face and I hit him on top of the head and on the chin.

"Crazy fool," he said and spit.

"You ruined my work," I said and hit him on the side of the head. My hand was numb and bloody.

Mama come into the living room with a lamp. Her hair was in a braid. It looked grayer in a braid than it did loose.

"He's drunk," Mama said. "He don't know what he's doing."

"Drunk ain't no excuse," I said.

Fay come out of the dark hallway with a blanket wrapped around her shoulders.

"You've got to do the Christian thing," Mama said.

"I ain't done nothing," Moody said, and wiped the blood from his mouth. "But I might know who did."

I asked Mama what was the Christian thing to do. I was so riled I couldn't hardly feel my feet on the floor.

"To forgive seven times seventy," Mama said.

"I have forgive Moody a thousand times," I said.

Moody had already set back down on the floor. He patted his lip and looked at the blood on his hand. He was awful quiet, like he was studying on something that puzzled him, unable to see it clear.

• • •

ON CHRISTMAS DAY I walked along the river and stayed away from the house. I was embarrassed, and I felt guilty. Since my own brother had tore up the work on the church, it was almost the same as if I'd done it myself. I can't explain it, but that's the way I started to feel. Like I'd almost done it myself. And I felt guilty for hitting Moody when he was drunk. But mostly I felt guilty for losing my temper. Every time you get angry and hurt somebody you feel bad about it, no matter what they've done. Mama was right: it was the Christian thing to forgive seven times seventy. I had failed Mama and I had failed myself. I thought how my good intentions and my grand ambitions had caused only trouble. I wondered if I should quit working on the church. I wondered if I should just give up and leave Green River for good, as I'd planned so many times.

In the bright sun of that Christmas Day I walked along the river and heard beagles bellering in the fields above the Bane place. Somebody was rabbit hunting on Christmas, enjoying theirselves the way they was supposed to. The boom of a shotgun echoed off the mountain above the river. Somebody was enjoying Christmas as a holiday.

When I got to the forks where Rock Creek comes into the river I stopped and stood in the pines. I didn't want to go no farther. The beagles was yipping and yelping way up on the ridge, sounding like a flock of geese up there. Their noise rose above the noise of the creek. I dropped down on my knees in the pine needles.

I listened to the wind in the pine trees that sounded like an ocean a long time ago, and the mumbling of the creek water, and the beagles inflaming the air with their yaps. Who was I to impose myself on the world? Who was I to make requests of the Lord? What right did I have to take up space and air and water from other people? Who was I to demand an answer to my prayers?

My defeat was so total I felt cleansed by it when I stood up. As I stepped down the trail I felt baptized with shame. I was stripped to the bone and humiliated and there was nothing to do but start over again. I was as free as if I had been born again. Anger and defeat had cleaned me out and made me feel light as I walked down the trail and across the creek. I walked by the river feeling naked as a baby. I could go anywhere I wanted to. I could escape from Green River.

THIRD READING

1923

Twenty-one

Muir

I HEADED TOWARD the west, for that seemed to be the direction of freedom. To start all over again you went to the west.

The woods smelled of wet leaves rotting in the middle of winter, and mud along the river give off a musky scent. It was a smell of sinkholes and swamps. By nightfall I'd be on much higher ground. I stomped the ground I was so glad to be on the trail.

By dark I reached the Flat Woods and camped there. It was my old trapping ground. The trees was familiar as friends. It felt good to sleep there by a fire under the stars, except the night was so cold I had to keep getting up for firewood. I dreamed about walking all the way to Black Balsam and maybe beyond, toward the Smokies and the blue wilderness to the west where ridge rose beyond ridge and peak above peak. The ground I laid on could take me anywhere I wanted to go, to the Rocky Mountains if I wanted to walk that far.

Whoa there, I said to myself in my half-sleep. Easy does it, Muir, old boy. Don't go flying off like you done before. For a long journey it's better to go slow at first. Take one step at a time, and travel one day at a time. If you hurry you'll find nothing at the end but wore-out legs. All roads lead to the same end, so what's the use of hurrying? Slow down and be peaceable in the peaceable kingdom.

I GOT UP before daylight, and by the time the sun rose over Chimney Top I was already in Transylvania County. I stayed away from the big creeks and roads and cut straight across the mountains toward Brevard. By the middle of the day I reached the village of Brevard and stopped at a store to buy four cans of sardines, a box of soda crackers, and some candy bars. No need to use my camping supplies before I had to. But I kept walking. I didn't stop till I reached the Davidson River that come tumbling and foaming clean and singing out of the high hollers below Pisgah. On the bank of the stream I set down to open a can of sardines.

The key fitted over the tongue of tin and I rolled back the metal top to reveal the tray of oily fish. Wished I had the fork out of my packsack, but I didn't want to take the trouble. I could eat with my fingers and then scrub them with sand and river water.

I'd almost finished the sardines when I seen this old man watching me. He was hid by some sweet-shrub bushes along the river and dressed in a rough gray coat and crushed hat. He peeked around a tree not more than fifty feet away.

"Howdy," I said, like the old man was not hiding or spying on me. I acted like he was in the open and I'd just seen him.

The man pushed his gray head around the trunk and peered like he wasn't sure he'd heard me.

"How do?" I said.

The old man stepped out quick from behind the bushes and come closer. All his clothes was ragged and he carried a pistol in his belt. "Are you fit?" he said.

I wasn't sure that's what he said, but I couldn't make any other sense out of the old man's words. "Fit as I'll ever be, I guess," I said. I wished the man didn't have the pistol in his belt.

"Having a picnic, eh?" the old man said. He looked hard at the sardine can in my hand.

"Would you like some sardines?" I said. I could smell the old man. He smelled like rags that had laid in an attic for years.

"Don't look like you've got none to share," the old man said. He put his hands in his pockets.

"Got plenty," I said and pulled a can of sardines out of the paper bag. "Here."

It took the old man several tries to get the key fitted on the lip of tin. But once he did he soon rolled back the top and begun eating sardines with his fingers. He set down on the bank beside me and I passed him the box of soda crackers.

"Much obliged, young sir," the old man said. He eat like he hadn't had a bite for days. Suddenly he wiped his right hand on his pants and took the pistol out of his belt and laid it on the ground at his side.

"You ain't planning on settling here?" he said and looked hard at me. Drops of oil and cracker crumbs had caught in his beard.

"Just stopped for a bite," I said.

The old man looked at the packsack on the ground, at my .22 rifle and blanket roll. "I couldn't let you do that," he said. "I wouldn't let you settle here."

"Who are you?" I said.

"I look after this settlement," the old fellow said.

"What settlement is that?" I said.

"The river, Davidson River." He gestured toward the woods upstream and the woods downstream. I looked around expecting to see a house or clearing I'd missed before. There was nothing but trees.

"They're all gone now, but they'll be back," the old man said. "I'm what you might call a caretaker, looking after the place till they come back."

"Where did they go?" I said.

"Some went to Texas, and some went west to Ar-kansas, and some moved all the way to Montana, I reckon. The Whites moved to Asheville, but they'll be back."

I looked around again, like I was trying to find something in the woods along the river I'd missed before.

"Couldn't let you settle here," the old man said. "It's my job to look after things."

"I see," I said. The old man picked up the pistol but didn't point it at me. He held it straight out in front of him.

"Do you see, boy?" he said.

"So you're the caretaker?" I said.

"My daddy was the preacher, Charlie Pyle," the old man said. "When they left to go to Ar-kansas I stayed here."

"Why did you stay?" I said.

"Stayed back here to hunt and fish, I thought. And then after they was all gone it come to me little by little over the years what my job was. That's the way it comes to a man, to see his purpose little by little. I seen I was left here not just to hunt and fish and trap muskrats out of the mountains. I was chose to stay behind and look after things till they all come back. Right over yonder is where the school was." He pointed through the sycamores along the riverbank. But I didn't see nothing except more trees in the flats.

"When are they coming back?" I said, keeping my eye on the tip of the pistol. It was an old cavalry .45 model, scratched and dirty. I couldn't tell if it was actually loaded.

"They're coming back anytime," the old man said with a challenge in his voice like he thought I might not believe him. "The Partridge house was right over there below the spring. I was sweet on Mary Alice Partridge. Me and her will marry when they come back."

The old man turned and looked me hard in the eye. "You can't settle here, boy," he said.

"Just passing through," I said, "on my way to Black Balsam."

"This land is took," the old man said.

"I can see that," I said.

"Me and Mary Alice used to play by the spring," he said. "Do you know what an ebbing and flowing spring is?"

"Can't say I do," I said.

"It's a spring that'll gush out all at once like it's in spate and then after a few minutes goes dry, or nearly dry. And then after a while it'll start gushing again."

"Why does it do that?" I said. The pistol on the old man's lap was aimed almost straight at me.

"Mr. Bailey that used to teach school here said it was some kind of siphon," the old man said.

"A siphon?"

"Like a holler place in the mountain that'll fill up, and when it's full a drain at the lip that acts like a siphon will empty it." The old man finished his sardines and throwed the can into the bushes. He wiped his hands on leaves and then on his pants.

"Let me see your pistol," I said.

"Couldn't let you settle here," he said, "even though I can tell you're neighborly. No spare land here to settle."

"Just passing through," I said.

"Couldn't let you do that, if you tried to claim and clear a place," the old man said. "Much as I'd admire to have your company."

"I'm on my way to Black Balsam," I said. "But it's a good thing you're looking after the place."

"You're welcome to camp here," the old man said. "I'm staying here myself till my folks come back."

"Have you heard from them?" I said.

"Not in the last few days," the old man said. He looked at his hands like he was trying to remember.

"Maybe they'll write soon," I said.

"They'll come back," the old man snapped, like I had disputed him.

"Yes," I said, "and they'll be grateful you've looked after things." I put my hand in the bag, took out two candy bars, and handed one to the old man. He tore off the wrapper like a little kid opening a Christmas present. Then he eat the candy slow, savoring every crumb of chocolate and caramel, every peanut and chewy clot.

"You're not a preacher?" the old man said.

"No, I ain't a preacher," I said.

"We already got a preacher," he said. "My daddy's a minister of the gospel."

"I've got to get going," I said. I reached for the packsack and the .22 rifle in the leaves. The old man picked up the pistol and aimed it at me. I reached out to brush it aside but realized he was handing it to me.

"It's a Colt forty-five, like cowboys carry," he said.

The revolver was heavy and dirty. It was so old the edges of the cylinder was rounded. I spun the cylinder and seen all the chambers was empty. I pulled back the hammer and seen the spring was broke. From the dirt caked in the action and in the barrel, it was clear the pistol had not been fired for years. "That's a real Colt," I said and handed the gun back.

"Got to finish my patrol," the old man said. He licked the chocolate off his fingers. "Every week I go from the mouth of the river to the highest spring up yon side of Looking Glass Rock. Do you know where the Pink Beds is?"

"I've heard of them."

"I look after the Pink Beds too," the old man said, "where people used to camp out in summer with their wagons and tents, and even their cows and chickens, among the pink flowers. People from Asheville and down in South Carolina."

I stood up and put on the packsack with the blanket roll tied over it. I cradled the rifle under my arm. "My name is Powell," I said.

"My name is Pyle," the old man said. He watched me walk away. When I'd gone maybe a dozen rods he called out, "Watch out for painters in the Balsams." I walked another few paces, then turned to wave at him, but he was nowhere in sight. He'd vanished into the brush along the river.

I FOLLOWED A wagon road along the river past several old homesteads with standing chimneys and cellar holes full of leaves. There was a few log buildings sunk in like they'd been pushed down. I seen patches of periwinkles and old boxwoods in the yards, set out by women long ago. I passed a mill and seen a millstone laying in the leaves like the wheel of a stone cart. There was a log church at the forks with its steeple wrecked by a blowed-down tree.

Where are these families now? I thought. The old man is patrolling this ghost community day after day and decade after decade. I passed an old schoolhouse where a rusty bell still rested on its post, ready to ring children in from recess. It looked like everybody had been snatched away, the way the Bible said the saved would be took at the Rapture, when beds and graves would be emptied.

Where the road turned up one of the tributary creeks, I seen a little patch of tombstones in the woods. They was hand carved, with rough letters, and some had leaned so far they'd toppled over. Catbriars covered some of the stones. I could see the name JONES on one and IN GLORY scratched on another. Broke jars was scattered in the leaves where flowers had been brought years ago.

I thought I was past the old community when I come to one last cabin in the woods. The house looked so little I thought at first it must be a shed or cow stall, maybe a lean-to hunters used. But there was an old window cut in its gable where a loft had been and where children must have slept on pallets. Vines growed out of the windows.

The door of the weathered cabin was gone, but I could see the rags of leather hinges that once held it in place. And then I noticed something else on the doorpost. There was a rag tied all the way around the post like a bandanna. It was faded and dirty with mold. Stepping closer, I lifted the edge of the cloth and it tore in my hand. But I could see it had once been red, a kind of red scarf knotted around the wood. I remembered that when there was smallpox or typhoid in a house in the old days they tied a red cloth on the door to warn those passing to stay away. If there was an epidemic, a red cloth would be tied to a tree by the road to warn travelers not to stop. I jerked my fingers away from the rag and rubbed them on a nearby tree. I knowed germs wouldn't last on a rag all those years, but even so, I brushed my hand on the bark.

FOLLOWING THE WAGON road up the narrow creek valley, I seen the sheer face of Looking Glass Rock ahead. It was a mountain of solid granite with a great bald dome and half a scalp of trees on its top. The mountain rose straight up for a thousand feet before curving back to a brow. I'd never seen anything as steep or as big. Who needs to build a church when a rock that big is already set in the wilderness? I thought. And then I thought, No, what is in nature is not the same as what is made by hands. The fact that something is made with human design gives it a special kind of beauty and meaning.

The road run right up under the foot of Looking Glass Rock, and I seen straight above me little streams that run through grooves down the solid rock. Names was carved at the bottom, and pictures that looked like signs from an unknown language. Fires had blacked the base in places. Bushes growed out of cracks in the big rock. Everything was on such a grand scale. The rock was bigger than any cathedral. Hemlocks growing out of the wet soil at its foot was eight or ten feet in diameter. The laurel bushes rose high as trees out of the rotten leaves beneath the rock.

Looking at my contour map, I seen I'd need to leave the road just beyond Looking Glass Rock. Got out my compass and found roughly what direction I needed to go in. The peak of Big Pisgah was to the right, steep and pointed as a fodder stack across the distance of clear air. I needed to go west along the chain of ridges. I was looking across the valley of the Pink Beds to the shoulder of Clawhammer Mountain. A trail bent off to the left and I followed it.

There is something comforting and thrilling about walking toward the west. I had always wanted to see Black Balsam and the higher mountains to the west. The west is like a magnet that pulls you toward something big and new.

Climbing with the pack and rifle slowed me down pretty quick. As I climbed I felt the power go out of my chest. Long before my legs was tired I felt tired in my chest and throat. The blood knows when you're tired, I thought. As I climbed I thought how time was like the force of gravity, pulling you down, dragging you down, wearing you out. Preacher Liner and the board of deacons, Moody with his sarcasm, Annie, they all wore me down.

Climbing is so simple it's hard to understand why it's so tiring. You just lift one foot ahead of the other and step a little higher. The muscles behind the knees raise you an inch at a time, half an inch. One little step at a time and you raise yourself out of the creek valley and into the sky. It's the leverage done with your feet on the great wedge of the mountain.

I slowed down and plunged my toes into the leaves step after step. I walked sideways, zigzagging up the steepest places. My boots sunk in the soft dirt under the leaves, making toeholds there.

Finally I come around the end of the ridge and seen a cliff far above me. It was a vast rock that jutted out in layers like a face, with chin and lips, nose and eyebrows. In the late sun the face looked coppery and shiny. Reminded me of pictures of the Sphinx. The cliff hung high as a cloud, dark and threatening.

I got out my map and searched the lines and names. Where I

thought I was, was the name Devil's Courthouse and the eleva-
tion 5,740 feet. The only other name along the ridge was Black
Balsam. I was looking right up at Devil's Courthouse. I knowed the
place had been named by the Cherokees, but the cliff didn't look
much like a courthouse. It resembled an ugly face sticking out of the
mountain.

The valley was almost dark. I took off the pack and looked for a
level place in the leaves. I found a kind of shelf and made a fire and
then cut some pine boughs for my bed. Instead of cooking anything I
decided to eat more of the sardines and crackers. But I boiled some
water for coffee. It was already cold in the valley under the cliff, and
I could see ice on the rock high above me. Soon as I eat I washed my
hands in a branch and wrapped the blanket around me. Then I set by
the fire sipping coffee till I was too sleepy to hold my eyes open.

Once in the night I heard a boom like a shotgun or a cannon.
There was an echoing chain of booms like a train makes in a freight
yard. But I didn't hear it again and wasn't sure but what I dreamed it.
All night the cold air from the cliff slid down and gathered close
around me.

NEXT MORNING THERE was ice along the branch and in my
canteen. Even wrapped in the blanket and in my mackinaw coat I
was cold in my bones. The fire had burned out and I had to scratch
in the leaves for twigs and sticks to start it again. My hands trembled
when I struck a match, but I kept them cupped around the flame till
it caught on one little sliver and then another, lighting the shadowy
woods floor.

I'd ground my coffee at home and put it in a waterproof can. I set a
pan of water beside the coffeepot to boil for grits, then gathered more
sticks to make the fire bright. Nothing'll make you appreciate houses
like camping out in cold weather, I thought. The most common things
like tables and stoves suddenly become valuable and wonderful.

As I eat steaming grits from the pan, I begun to wake up and
gather strength. The soreness in my back and legs from the day before was still there but mellowed by a night's sleep. I put on clean
socks and laced up my boots. The cliff above, facing west, was still

dark. I could barely see its features. I kicked the remains of the fire out, rolled up the blanket, and strapped on the packsack. I took one short step, and then another and another. A deer bounded away, flashing its tail like a lantern.

By the time I'd climbed halfway up the ridge I was sweating and out of breath. I stopped to rest and seen a tree beside me that was not a white pine or a hemlock. Its needles was short and glittered like blue crystals. The tree was almost black. That was a balsam, the first balsam I'd ever seen in the wild. I touched the sharp stiff spines. The bark was scaly and covered with lichens and moss. I looked out along the ridge and seen others pointed like steeples. They was trees out of the North. I'd read they'd been stranded on the peaks here since the last Ice Age.

I broke off a twig and sniffed the incense of the sap. It smelled sweeter than a white pine and reminded me of Christmas and the Wise Men's frankincense and myrrh. The black trees was scattered on the slope above, getting thicker and thicker, until at the top the ridge was covered with them.

It was hard to push through the balsams, they was so stiff and scratchy. I picked my way from open space to open space. Limbs broke and stung my hands like released springs. Litter sifted down my collar. Needles raked my cheeks.

When I got to the top of the ridge I couldn't see a thing. The spruce and firs was so thick I couldn't even be sure I was on top. Wind hummed in the trees above me, and I heard a distant roar on the other side, far below. Could it be wind in the gap? And then I heard a *hoof-hoof-hoof* sound, and a boom like two buildings had crashed together. Was the mountain making noise inside? I'd heard of mountains that groaned and roared and boomed in their guts. Was that the reason the Cherokees had been afraid of this ridge and thought it was haunted by the devil?

I tore my way left through the terrible thicket. Finally I saw sunlight ahead and pushed out into the open. It was a clearing with weeds and mountain ash and sumac. I shaded my eyes against the rising sun and looked far down the mountainside. At first I just seen smoke and couldn't tell what I was looking at. *Hoof-hoof-hoof,* come the sound from below. Then I seen the train engine puffing up the valley. Hadn't seen a railroad on the topographical map.

All at once I seen the valley below clearer, and I smelled the scent of timber on the wind coming up the ridge. And I smelled smoke and seen all the hollers and slopes below had been stripped of trees. There was tangles of logs and stacks of logs and piles of burning brush. I seen steam shovels spurting smoke, and trucks and cranes on the slope. The mountainside had been slashed and looked ugly as a mangy dog. There was rough bridges on stilts across branches, and roads cut into the slopes. There was so much litter of logs and brush, the mountainside looked chewed up and spit out.

"Hey, bud, what are you doing here?" somebody yelled.

I turned and seen a man in uniform pointing a gun at me. He wore a hat like an army sergeant's, with a wide flat brim. "What are you doing here, buddy?" he said, stepping closer.

He had a thin mustache and a fat gold ring with a white stone on the hand that held the rifle. "This land was leased by the Sunburst Lumber Company," he said. "Trespassers will be prosecuted."

"I'm just hiking to Black Balsam," I said. I hated to be questioned. He had took me by surprise.

"You just hike right on," the man said. "Where you from?"

"Where are you from?" I said, suddenly angry.

The man stepped back and cocked the .30-30, aiming the deer rifle at my chest. "I'm from the other end of this rifle. Now get!" he said. He pushed the tip of the rifle at my belly and I backed away. He pushed it again and I stepped further back into the little clearing.

"Go back where you come from, bud," he said.

I hated to have a rifle pulled on me that way. I felt helpless as a child threatened by a hickory switch. Tears come to my eyes as I turned and walked toward the thicket of balsams. My will had been bent in the most unexpected way in the most unexpected place. At the edge of the trees I turned to face the man in uniform.

"Get on away from here!" he yelled. "Are you too dumb to understand English?"

As I plunged into the thicket, tears broke from my eyes. I pushed aside limbs and was knocked sideways by the heavy pack. Briars and twigs clawed at my clothes. A needle hit me in the right eye. When I'd gone about a hundred yards down the slope I stopped. Bits of bark and twigs stuck to the tears on my cheeks. I wiped my eyes with the back of my left hand.

If I climbed back up to the little clearing and shot the ranger with the .22, nobody would know who done it. Nobody knowed where I was in the mountains. I could shoot the guard from the edge of the trees and the bastard would never know what hit him. Or I could blast him in the belly so he'd die slow and painful, looking at his bloody uniform as he bled to death.

Get away from here. Now get. I kept hearing his ugly voice in my mind. I was sick of people talking to me that way. The guard had scared me and humiliated me, like the sheriff and the others. I stopped to rest, thinking I might go right back up the ridge and shoot the ranger. But more than likely he was waiting for me. In fact, he probably expected me to come back. I thought of just calling off the camping trip and going home. But there was nothing back home but the mess of my church foundation on the mountaintop. There didn't seem to be any place to go to. I thought of ambushing the man in uniform and burying his body in the thicket. Nobody would ever know what happened to him.

Taking the map out of my pack, I unfolded it on the ground and studied its sections. I was in the gap west of Devil's Courthouse and just a few miles from the high peak of Black Balsam. What I could do was circle back around the thickets and then climb up on the peak itself. It had not appeared that the logging operation reached that high. If I was careful to stay in the fir trees nobody would see me. I could reach the peak and camp there and think about what to do next.

It took me all morning to drop back down into the hardwoods and work my way back along the chain of ridges toward Black Balsam. I kept the map in hand and took out the compass several times to check direction. Every time I thought of the ranger I stomped the ground and kicked the leaves. At dinnertime I didn't stop to build a fire, but eat the last can of sardines and the last candy bar.

After washing my hands in a seep spring and drying them on bark,

I begun to climb the peak of Black Balsam. Starting slow, going steady from step to step and rock to rock, I swung past beech trees and hickory trees. There was patches of snow on the ground as I got higher. The air was thin and cold. When I reached the fir trees I walked slower, trying to skirt the thickest clusters of balsams. I wondered if I could point a gun at the ranger. I wondered if I could shoot him.

The trees on the summit had not been cut. But when I reached the top I could hear the *chuff-chuff-chuff* of the steam engines and the shouts of men and whinnies of horses. The edge of the cut timber was only a few hundred yards down the other side of the peak. I took off the pack and left it at the very top. With the rifle in my left hand I crawled to where I could look down on the slashed and stripped mountainside and valley.

I was afraid I'd see the ranger standing in the clearing waiting for me. And I was hoping I would see him there. But what I seen instead was dozens of men sawing logs with crosscuts and chopping off limbs. Teams of four and six oxen pulled the logs out of the hollers below. A steam shovel swung the logs up on a platform. I looked for the dinky engine I'd seen from Devil's Courthouse. I could still hear the *hoof-hoof-hoof* of the locomotive, and its whistle, but it was miles below the oxen and sawing crews. There was trails and haul roads cut here and there through the tangles of logs and piles of brush.

And then I seen how they got the logs down the mountain to the railroad. There was a cofferdam on a branch up near the head of the valley, and a trough made of planks running down from it. The trough was raised on stilts across gullies and draws. Water splashed and flashed in its course as the trough shot over trestles and hollers down the mountainside. At several platforms beside the flume, logs was piled by steam shovels to be rolled one at a time into the chute of rushing water. A log put in the trough darted down the mountainside, bumping and knocking the planks of the chute until it was out of sight.

It was a clever way of carrying logs down the mountainside to the railroad. I had to give them credit for that. They'd ruined the mountain, but they showed they was experts at their work. Men with peaveys and pry hooks rolled logs one after the other into the rushing flume. As I watched, I seen a log get stuck in the trough. Maybe it was an extra-big log, or maybe it had a knot on it. I couldn't tell. Maybe there was a loose nail on the chute that caught the end of the log.

Water splashed and sprayed in a rooster tail out of the trough where the big log was jammed. Water moved so fast in the trough it sprayed up ten or fifteen feet. There was a rainbow on the plume of spray. Several of the men climbed out along the rim of the flume to dislodge the timber with cant hooks. A man in a brown uniform stood below the flume waving his arms like he was shouting directions. He looked like the guard that had pulled the rifle on me. I raised my .22 rifle and put the bead on him. But he must have been a quarter of a mile away. I lowered the barrel.

The man in uniform climbed up the braces of the trestle into the splashing water and grabbed a cant hook from one of the other men. He tried to wrestle the big log free.

Out of the corner of my eye I seen the crew at the highest platform on the flume roll another log toward the trough. Surely they could see what was going on below them. Surely they wasn't going to put another log in the shooting water. Three men on the top platform got behind the log with their peaveys and started rolling it. They prodded and levered the log to the lip of the trough.

The log rolled into the chute like a bullet had been dropped into the chamber of a gun. It shot away, slowed at a turn, then speeded up again. I seen that the trough curved around the slope just enough so the men on the second platform couldn't see the top one.

The man in the brown uniform climbed into the trough far below to get a better purchase on the jammed log. He was not looking up the mountainside. He appeared to be hollering at the other men and giving them orders. In the splash of the spray he probably couldn't even see the flume above or hear what anybody said to him.

The new log swung to the long curve and dropped in the flume like a mink darting for a kill. I wondered, If I holler will he hear me, or if I fire the rifle will he hear the shot? But it was too far away, and I didn't even try to warn him.

When the rushing timber hit the jammed log, the ranger in the uniform went flying off to the side. He rose like he was throwed by dynamite, and then he fell into the valley far below. The clashed logs spun in different directions, throwing off splinters. Men come running from all over the mountainside. The trough stood intact, the water fast and sparkling in its groove.

I was almost too weak with fear and excitement to crawl back into the thicket and climb up to the summit. My hand trembled as it held the rifle. When I reached the packsack I set down on the cushion of needle litter to rest.

Later a steam whistle blowed and blowed and blowed below. I guess they was carrying the body of the ranger down the mountain toward Asheville. I was sure he was the same guard who had threatened me. I smelled the moss and mold under me, and the balsam rosin above me. I would camp just under the rim of the peak that night and boil three or four of the eggs I'd brought with me. I was sure there was enough water in my canteen. But I would start for home in the morning.

Twenty-two

Ginny

I HAD NEVER thought I would know pain worse than the death of my husband, Tom, and the death of my daughter Jewel, and I didn't till I seen my boys filled with hate and enmity toward each other and fighting right in the house on Christmas Day. It was the saddest hour, and the saddest sight, to watch Muir kick Moody on the floor and Moody so drunk he didn't hardly know what was happening.

If Moody had done what Muir said he had, it was a terrible thing. To destroy the work of another, especially work on a church, shows a disrespect and hate, a destructive rage, that is hard to forgive. Muir had already worked so long and sacrificed so much for his vision of the church house. He had tried so long to find his way as he blundered and stumbled and come to dead ends. And now he was humiliated to have his work ruined.

WHEN MUIR FIRST said he was going to build a church on top of Meetinghouse Mountain my quick thought was fear. For he had been disappointed so many times and he felt like such a failure after wanting to preach and driving to the North and trying to trap on the Tar River. I was his mama and I didn't think he could stand any more disappointment. I didn't want him to be humbled and humiliated again.

But my second thought was: What a wonderful ambition he has. What a wonderful idea and vision for the community and for the future. Pa had built the church that stood now when most of the valley was woods with just a few cabins. Pa had raised a place of worship and a place of prayer in the wilderness. It was such a necessary and such a hard thing to do.

You can manage to worship and pray out in the woods or under an open sky. The Lord will hear you wherever you are. But that's not the same as having a consecrated place, a place set aside for fellowship and communion with the Creator, for song and praise. A church makes a community come into meaning. A church raises a collection of houses and homesteads into a community. A valley ain't whole until it has a patch of consecrated ground.

But my boy Muir was too young for such a job. He had built walls of rock, and he had built a little chimney for the molasses furnace. In his heart he was a builder. I could see that. But I was afraid a church, a rock church like he had in mind, on top of the mountain, was too much for him. Almost too much for any one man, much less for a boy in his late teens. But I wanted a new church too. I didn't know what to say.

"Can you do so much heavy work by yourself?" I said.

"I have always done heavy work," Muir said.

And that was true. Muir could only work by hisself. He got riled up and argued if he tried to work with anybody else. He wouldn't take orders, and he wouldn't take any criticism. But he had always done the heaviest work on the place, the chopping and digging, the lifting and plowing.

I knowed also that to do the Lord's work is a privilege. To do the hard work that is give to us is an honor. It was the only way for Muir to get beyond his confusion and his pain, to do the work he was called to do. What greater happiness is there than to do the work we are give?

But Muir was young and he was only human. I seen there was a lot of pride and vanity mixed up in his plans, like there was in his

ambition to preach. He wanted to impress Annie. He didn't only
want to build a church; he wanted to build a big church, like he had
seen in books, and in pictures in magazines. It was a prideful ambition, to build a white steeple that shot higher than the trees, that
could be seen from one end of the valley to the other and maybe
beyond.

Yet nobody done anything of importance unless they had some
pride, and some ambition in their vision. Pride was all mixed up with
the calling and the will to make and to achieve. I seen that, and I seen
I had to be careful what I said. A mama has more influence than she
realizes sometimes. A mama can hurt the confidence in her child
without hardly knowing it.

From the first I planned to help Muir at the right time. I had to see
if he could start the church on his own and get it going. He had
started so many things and dropped them. And then I would help
him with money, and help him do the work. But I had to find out if
he really meant to do the job or was just dreaming, the way he had
about going to Canada. If I helped him out and made it too much my
project, he might lose interest. If it seemed like I was telling him what
to do, I knowed he would lose interest.

But on Christmas Eve, when somebody busted up the foundation
Muir had laid, I seen it was time to help. If Moody had done the
dirty work it was my job to help get the work started again. And if
Moody had not done it, as he said he hadn't, it was still my place to
help. I felt an enthusiasm for the work on the mountaintop, and I felt
drawed to it the way I was drawed to brush arbor services when I
was young. The destruction of Muir's work made me angry, and it
made me want to be a part of the work. The thought of the white
steeple pointing up into the sky on the summit stirred my heart more
than anything had in years.

I made up my mind to tell Muir I was going to help him start
again after he left with his packsack. If he come back, I would tell
him I'd buy tools and lumber and nails for the church. I'd help him
any way I could.

I DIDN'T HARDLY know what to say to Moody once Muir
had packed up his haversack and took his rifle and gone off to the

woods. Moody was my son and I loved him, but he just seemed to get angrier. I thought I had seen signs in him of softening. I knowed there was good in him, if he'd just let it come out. But if he had ruined Muir's work, he was worser, not better. It was like he was trying to get revenge for what he thought the world had done him.

After Muir was gone I seen Moody putting on his boots and coat. He had a little .32 pistol which he kept in the closet, and he slipped that into his coat pocket. He had a grim, almost ashy look, like he was sick at his stomach.

"Where are you going?" Fay said.

"I have a little job to do," Moody said.

"You're not going to tear up Muir's work even more?" I said. I felt sick at my stomach to hear myself say that.

Moody turned to face me, the way he hadn't in a long time. There was a set to his jaw. He was completely sober. "Is that what you think of me?" Moody said. "I can see you have a high opinion of me."

"Did you do it?" Fay said.

"I don't know what to think," I said. The change in Moody's manner was alarming.

"I think I know who done it," Moody said.

"Who?" I said. "Who would do such a thing?" It give me hope that he seemed to be denying it. Moody snuffed his nose the way he done when he was sober and serious. "I have an idea," he said.

"Don't you go get in trouble," I said and pointed to the pistol in his pocket.

"There is already trouble," Moody said.

What had happened on Christmas Eve had scared Moody. I could see that. Muir's anger had scared him, and Muir's accusations. There was more going on than I could understand. Whatever had happened to Muir's church foundation had something to do with Moody, even if Moody hadn't done it hisself.

I asked Moody what he knowed that he wasn't telling. But he just said he was going to find out. He had some suspicions. I told him I was sure Muir hadn't hurt nobody.

"Nobody but me," Moody said.

"Watching you all fight is the saddest thing I've ever seen," I said.

"It's sad for me too," Moody said.

My heart jumped up in my throat, to see the change in Moody. There was something really different about the way he acted.

"Everybody is against him, and his big plans," I said.

"He thinks I'm against him," Moody said.

I was so pleased and hopeful about the change in Moody I didn't know what to say. I had been right about the signs of a growing and a sobering in him. The great black weight on my heart lifted a little.

"Nobody else in this whole valley wants to do nothing," Moody said. "Muir is crazy, but he is the only one here with an idea in his head. His schemes may be foolish, but at least he tries."

I didn't know what to say.

"There is some business that has to be attended to," Moody said. He took some biscuits from the top of the stove and put them in his coat pocket. He patted the handle of the pistol. "A gun talks even when it don't say nothing," Moody said.

But no good could come of seeking revenge. Everything I'd ever seen told me that. Vengeance is mine, saith the Lord. Only the spirit of forgiveness could win in the end.

EVERYTHING WAS SO quiet in the house with both Muir and Moody gone. I was thinking about how I planned to help Muir with his church when somebody knocked on the back door. It was Hank Richards.

Hank was a neighbor I never seen much of, except at church, because he was always off building houses at the cotton mill and around the lake, or down in South Carolina. He was a deacon of the church and a close neighbor, but I seen little of him.

I was took by surprise and asked Hank to come in and set by the fire.

"Ain't got but a minute," he said. He had broad shoulders and a handsome face and forehead.

"How are you doing?" I said.

"Same old sixes and sevens," he said and laughed. "Feel too old to work and too young to retire." Hank looked into the fire and he looked at me. He held his hat on his knee and fingered the brim with his big strong hands. He said what he had come for was to talk about Muir.

I hoped he hadn't come to complain about Muir paying attention to Annie. I told him Muir was somewhere off in the mountains.

Hank said he was awful sorry to hear what had happened to Muir's church.

"I wanted to ask if it was all right for me to help him on the church," Hank said. That took me by surprise too, for I didn't think anybody was interested in building the new church except Muir and me. I told him he didn't need to ask me.

"Preacher Liner said you disapproved," Hank said.

I told him I didn't disapprove. I was just worried about Muir taking on such a big project, and him so young and flat broke. Hank spit tobacco juice into the fire and said he thought Muir had a good idea, and that he wanted to help him.

"You don't need my permission," I said. It made me mad that the preacher would tell others I disapproved of the new church. "I mean to help Muir myself," I said. Hank's words thrilled me. It meant a lot that somebody else seen the worth of what Muir was trying to do. I didn't know Hank all that well, but I seen there was more to him than I had recognized before.

"When I was young I had big plans," Hank said. "But nothing come of them. It's a wonderful thing when somebody can see beyond the bare needs to what might be."

I told him that Muir had always been a dreamer and a builder. He had always lived through his imaginings.

"This valley could stand a new church," Hank said. "I've always wanted to build a church, and I've never had a chance before. I've worked on cotton mills and even built a schoolhouse or two."

Especially after others had destroyed his work, it made all the difference in the world if just one other person shared Muir's vision of what could be built. And if one person could understand what he was doing, then others could too and would in time.

I could have kissed Hank I was so grateful and pleased. I could have took his hand and kissed it. But that would have just embarrassed him. I was older than Hank, with gray in my hair. I knowed better than to make a show of my gratitude.

"I won't be able to help for a few days," Hank said. "Building is slow in the middle of winter, but I have a little job in Saluda still to finish up."

It was three days later and almost dark when I heard some-body on the porch. I thought it must be Muir come back from his hike into the mountains. I figured he would be cold and hungry, and I was frying up some shoulder meat and had grits boiling in the saucepan. Nothing will warm you up like hog meat and hot grits.

But when the door opened I seen it was Moody. He looked pale and gaunt, like he had been tired and scared for a long time.

"Where have you been?" I said.

"Been around," Moody said.

"That don't tell me much," I said.

Moody stepped to the fire and held out his hands. He looked like he had been shrunk by the cold and by walking a long way. He looked thinner than ever.

"What did you find out?" I said.

Moody turned to me, and his eyes burned with a black soberness I hadn't seen before. "I'm going to have to leave home for a while," he said.

"What have you done?" I said. An icicle of dread drove down my spine.

"Found out who busted up Muir's foundation," Moody said.

"Who?" I said.

"They done it to get back at me," Moody said.

"Why would they get back at you?" I said with dread in my voice.

"Long story," Moody said.

"Supper's almost ready," I said. "You can tell me while we eat." I thought if we could just go ahead and eat, things might turn out all right.

"I've got to run," Moody said.

"What do you mean?" I said.

"I think I may have killed one of them," Moody said.

"One of who?" I said.

"One of the Willards that done the busting up," Moody said.

"You didn't kill nobody?" I said.

"I didn't mean to," Moody said. But he wouldn't say any more. He asked me and Fay to fix him some biscuits and side meat, some corn bread. He filled a sack with pans and cups and stuff.

"Boil some eggs," I said to Fay. I fried some sausage to go with the eggs.

"The law will be after me," Moody said. "They will ask you where I went."

"Just tell them the truth," I said.

"They will put me in jail," Moody said.

"Not if you was in the right," I said.

"I ain't waiting around to find out," Moody said.

LORD, DON'T LET it be a fact, I said under my breath after Moody left. Let it all be a mistake.

It was a cold clear night, and when I stepped out on the back porch I seen how bright the stars was. The moon hadn't come up yet, and the stars was so fired up they sparkled in the river and on the branch. Because the air was so still the cold didn't sink in at first. Cicero Mountain loomed black as a sleeping bear across the river.

Just then I seen lights shoot onto the sides of the hemlocks out by the springhouse, and I heard the rattle of a car. *Tut-tut-tut-tut,* a motor went, and a jolt of chill shocked through me. Nobody ever drove to the house after dark.

The car stopped at the gate and then come on down the hill. When the lights flooded against the shed I seen the car had a siren on top. The man that got out carried a flashlight. I went back in the house and put the dishpan on the table, then met him at the front door with a lamp.

"Sorry to bother you, ma'am," the man said. He was wearing a uniform and a trooper's hat. I did not invite him in.

"We are looking for Moody Powell," he said.

"He ain't here," I said.

"But this is where he resides?" the officer said.

"Sometimes," I said. "But he ain't here now."

"Moody has finally got hisself in real trouble," the trooper said. "What kind of trouble?"

"Can I come in, ma'am?" the officer said.

I stood back and let him step through the door, and then I led him to the fireplace.

"I'm Deputy Sheriff Otto Jenkins," the man said and took off his hat.

"What kind of trouble is Moody in?" I said.

"Moody has killed Zack Willard," the deputy said.

"How do you know it was Moody?" I said.

"Because Zack's three brothers seen him," Deputy Jenkins said.

What could I say that would help Moody? I figured the longer I talked to the officer the more time Moody would have to get away. It was so quiet in the house I could hear a creak and pop in the attic as the house shrunk with cold. The clock on the mantel tapped like time was dripping out of it.

"Moody wouldn't go to kill nobody," I said.

"Ma'am, a man is dead and Moody pulled the trigger. It won't do him any good to run."

Just then there was another knock at the door, and another deputy that must have been waiting in the car come in. He was a young man, but he was so fat his uniform looked stretched on him.

"This is Deputy Henry Thomas," the first man said.

"Why would Moody kill one of the Willards?" I said. "It don't make sense."

"Might have something to do with liquor," Deputy Thomas said.

"Why would the Willards bust up Muir's new church?" I said.

"Don't know about that," Deputy Jenkins said.

"Moody said he knowed who broke up Muir's rockwork," I said.

"All I know is, the Willards didn't want nobody horning in on their bootlegging," Deputy Jenkins said.

"Moody wasn't trying to hurt nobody," I said.

"Ma'am, is Moody here?" Deputy Thomas said. The fat deputy had scars on his face, so his cheeks looked bumpy as oatmeal. I tried not to look at him. His shoulders was too thick for his uniform, but he looked me hard in the eyes like he was an important man.

"He ain't here," I said.

"I hate to ask you this, but could we search the house?" Deputy Jenkins said.

I was going to say, Why don't you take my word for it? or Do you have a search warrant? I felt myself get stiff, and anger washed through me. But getting mad wouldn't do Moody any good.

"Go ahead, if you want to," I said. "But you won't find him here. Neither of my boys is here."

"Much obliged to you, ma'am," Deputy Jenkins said.

They took their flashlights and looked in the kitchen and on the back porch. They poked in the closets and in the bedrooms.

"They ain't got no right," Fay said to me.

I felt naked with them looking into our things. They found the ladder to the attic and Deputy Jenkins climbed up. I hated for him to see the books and magazines and old furniture scattered up there. The place was nothing but dust and cobwebs, and Pa's old books and Muir's drawings laying everywhere.

When Deputy Jenkins come back down there was cobwebs stuck to his hat. He took the hat off and brushed the spiderwebs away. "How many outbuildings do you have?" he said.

"Smokehouse and springhouse, corncrib and shed and chicken house," I said. "And an old log barn."

Fay and me stood at the window and watched their flashlights circle and lift as they opened the smokehouse and springhouse. After they searched the barn they come back to the house and asked where the cellar was.

"You won't find nothing hiding in the cellar but taters," I said. Taking a lamp from the mantel, I led them out the back door and down the steps to the basement. It was warm in the cellar, compared to the outside. Their flashlights played over the shelves of jars. Sprouts from the taters run like white snakes to the door. I half expected Moody to be hiding there. It was a relief to see nothing but buckets and old sacks and a toolbox against the moldy wall.

When we come back into the house the fire felt mighty good. I wished they would leave. I wished I could think clear about what had happened. Everything was going wrong and moving so fast I couldn't think what to do.

Deputy Thomas asked me if I knowed where Moody went and I told him I had no idea. I reckon he didn't believe me. His cheeks looked like they had raisins in the skin.

"It will go easier if he turns hisself in," Deputy Jenkins said.

"What if he is innocent?" I said. I wanted them to leave. I wanted to find out what had really happened. I wanted to tell Muir what had happened.

"Ma'am, you will feel a whole lot better if you tell us where Moody is hiding," Deputy Thomas said.

"You could be charged as an accessory if you're hiding him," Deputy Jenkins said.

"Are you accusing me of hiding him?" I said.

Deputy Thomas stepped closer and motioned for Deputy Jenkins to back away. "We're not accusing you of nothing, ma'am," he said. "All we saying is that it would go a lot easier on Moody if he turns hisself in."

Twenty-three
Muir

I HAD WATCHED the ranger get killed without even trying to warn him, which was bad enough. But when Mama told me Moody had gone after the Willards and killed Zack by accident, I was dazed. I had been wrong about everything, blinded by my anger and surprise and vanity. And now Moody was wanted by the law.

Let this be a lesson to you, I said to myself, gritting my teeth. Be slow to anger, and even slower to judge. Oh, I am a fine person to build a church.

"I ought to go look for Moody," I said.

"Wouldn't do no good if he's hiding," Mama said.

"You might lead the law right to him," Fay said.

"What do you mean?" I said.

"I read a story in a magazine where that happens," Fay said. "A man goes to help his brother and leads the law right to him."

I knowed there was truth to what Fay said. But surely there must be a way to slip into the woods without the sheriff seeing me. I knowed every branch and sinkhole in the Flat Woods and the Long Holler beyond the Sal Raeburn Gap. But I was too dazed to think straight. When I tried to help I usually made things worse. I couldn't

go looking for Moody unless I knowed for sure nobody would follow me.

I didn't know what I wanted to do about Moody. He had caused
me so much trouble I sometimes wanted to just forget about him.
And I felt guilty again for feeling that way. I would tell myself I had
to go look for him, and then I would tell myself I couldn't do that: it
wouldn't be fair to him. I didn't know what was the right thing
to do.

WHILE I WAS thinking about what to do to help Moody, I decided I might as well go back to work on the church. I was troubled
in my mind, and there was no other way to pay for my pride and my
anger. Things had gone so wrong and crazy, there was nothing to do
but climb back up on the mountain and start again. I dreaded to go
there. It was the hardest thing, just to look at the mess and start to
pick up the pieces.

THE SCENE ON top of the mountain was as bad as I expected.
There was nothing to do but look square at it. The rocks I'd laid for
the foundation was mostly busted loose from each other. A lot of flat
rocks had been broke. Rocks had been throwed off in the woods
down the side of the mountain. It had took a lot of work to do all
that damage. The mortar box had been chopped up with an axe, and
the framework I had started was knocked loose. There'd been almost
as much work of destruction as I'd put into making the foundation. I
didn't know where to start. There was so much work to do it staggered me just to think of starting all over again.

But I seen one corner had not been broke. Loose rocks had been
piled against it, but the corner itself was intact. That was the place to
start again. Beginning with that corner I would rebuild the walls. I
cleared limbs and loose boards away from the corner. I brushed
leaves away and dusted the cement. I will set these stones in order, I
said under my breath. I will take the rocks the Willards broke and set
them back in their rightful place.

I gathered the scattered rocks into piles and toted rocks from the
edge of the woods and from the brush where they had been throwed.

The rocks had to be sorted and aligned. The pieces had been tossed away by anger and ill will. Only patience and care would reassemble them into a church. As I worked I thought about Moody hiding in the woods, and I blamed myself. I knowed there was something I should do, but couldn't decide what it was.

I walked down to the pasture and caught Old Fan and hitched her to the sled. And I got a water barrel from the barn and filled it at the spring. Water sloshed in the barrel as I drug it up the rough road and then up the side of the mountain. To start again I had to have mortar, and to make mortar I had to have water. I had only two bags of cement U. G. had give me on credit, so I'd have to be careful and not waste any. I nailed the mortar box roughly together.

Mixing cement can be one of the most satisfying jobs. You pour in sand and you pour in the powder of cement, and you pour water in the box, and then you start hoeing it to mix it up. You rake it back and forth and back and forth in the box until the sand is grayish green in the batter. If the mix is too dry it'll be crumbly and mealy and won't spread. If it's too watery it won't be firm enough to stick. And if the mud is too sandy it won't set hard enough. But if there's not enough sand, it won't hold fast either and will crack and scale off.

As I worked I wondered if Moody was hiding in the Long Holler, or was he in South Carolina? Had he gone to one of the caves on the far side of Ann Mountain? Could I find him without being seen? Would it do any good if I did find him?

I hoed the mortar like I was making bread. But the slime reminded me of dung also, and the bitter smell of the cement burned my nose. Gather the rocks and hold them with slime, I said under my breath. Gather the rocks and arrange the earth in an altar.

I cleaned off the rocks that had been busted loose, chipping off the cement with my light mason's hammer. With the fresh mortar I fitted the rocks back in place again. I fitted them mostly where they'd been before, with a few small changes. It was like the rocks found their places again. I took my ruler and my level and took my try square, and I made the walls more plumb than they'd been before. Having done it once, I knowed better how to do it now. I tried to lay the foundation upright and square. I gathered rocks scattered in the woods and added new ones. To keep the mud soft in the repaired mortar box I added a splash of water and stirred it from time to time.

"So this is where you do your work," somebody called out. I looked up and seen Mama standing beside the ruined wall. It was the first time she had climbed up the mountain to see my work.

"Don't look like much now," I said.

Mama was almost out of breath, and her hair had fell across her eyes. She brushed the hair out of the way and studied the piles of rocks and dirt. "You have made a start," she said. "I will pay for whatever supplies you need."

I was so surprised by what Mama said I was embarrassed. My face got hot, and I kept raking and smoothing the mortar in the box.

"With Moody off hiding from the law, and everything so crossed up, I want this family to be doing something," Mama said, "something that counts."

Mama handed me a twenty-dollar bill. She said when that run out she would find more.

I stuffed the bill in my pocket and laid the hoe down on the edge of the box. It was like going back to when I was a boy and she showed her enthusiasm for my ideas. When you have big plans all you need is the support of one person. If one can see what you're doing, then others will follow.

I wanted to hug her I was so lifted up. But when I turned to thank her, she had already started back down the mountain. There was tears in my eyes, and my throat was sore with feeling.

EVERY DAY I worked on the foundation, and I worried about Moody. In the cold winter wind, and in patches of sunlight and cloud shadows, I carried rocks and set them in place. I smoothed and pointed joints with my trowel, lifted rocks and put in more mortar. Sometimes a rock had to be shifted around to make it plumb. Sometimes a rock had to be pushed to make it line up with the rocks around it. I wondered what I could do to help Moody. It seemed all I could do was work on the church.

I was working harder and faster than ever on the fourth day when somebody else called out to me from the edge of the woods.

"Brother Muir," they said. I looked around and seen Preacher Liner. At first I thought I wouldn't speak to him, and then I remembered my terrible pride and my repenting.

"Hello, Preacher Liner," I said. I stood up with the trowel in my hand.

"The deacons have asked me to talk to you," the preacher said.

I didn't say nothing. It didn't sound good if the board of deacons wanted to send a message to me. I dipped more mortar and slapped a tongue on the wall.

"We just want to ask you some questions," Preacher Liner said.

"What kind of questions?" I said, and spread the wet mortar like butter on the rock.

"Questions about your intentions," the preacher said.

"My intention is to build a church," I said.

"Questions about Baptist discipline," the preacher said.

"I'm not standing to be ordained," I said. "I'm going to build a church."

"I didn't come here to quarrel," the preacher said. "Only to invite you to meet with us on Saturday at three."

I picked up another rock and set it in place on the wet mortar. All the good spirit I'd felt before was gone. Anger come into my breath.

"What if I don't want to meet with you all?" I said.

"The church is not just rocks and planks and window frames," the preacher said. "The church is the membership. That's Baptist doctrine. The least you can do is come talk to us about your plans on Saturday."

AFTER THE PREACHER left I worked harder than ever. I reckon anger helped give me strength to work. I stirred mortar and slapped it in place and I heaved rocks up and worked them into the perfect position. I measured and placed the level against the wall. I was building foursquare and firm. I was building a wall that might last a hundred years. I was building a high altar on the mountaintop. I remembered that's what Peter had said when he was talking out of his head at the Transfiguration: Let's make an altar up here to remember what we have seen.

But as I worked that day and on the sunny days that followed, and wondered where Moody was, and wondered if I was going to talk with the deacons on Saturday or not, I also thought again about how the church was going to look when I got it finished. If I built a tower for the bell that looked like a castle tower, it would appear old and powerful. But a white steeple that reached up and up and up, pointing to heaven, would be the most beautiful of all, the most inspiring.

I'd seen pictures of churches in Charleston and in New England where the steeples rose through many stages, squares and octagons, round and six sided, with arches on one story and windows on the next and columns on the tier above that. Nothing was better than a high steeple for a church. And no color was better than white.

I seen how I was going to build the steeple, and it was going to have to rise in stages far above the roof of the church and far above the trees. With Mama helping I could afford the materials. A steeple is like a chimney sending thoughts and prayers and sight up toward heaven. A steeple would be the hardest thing to build, for I would have to raise a scaffold. A steeple would have ornaments and scrollwork and fancy cabinetwork. The steeple I had in mind would go up eighty, ninety, a hundred feet. The pedestal would be of rock, but the higher levels would be white wood, white to catch the early sun and the late sun, white to be seen from Pinnacle or Tryon Mountain. The white would shine in the sky.

ALL WEEK I argued with myself about whether to go look for Moody and whether to meet with the deacons. I imagined things I would say to them, and things they'd say to me. I thought about just going to look for Moody and taking him some rations. I thought about ignoring the preacher's invitation. I thought about just working until dark. But as it got close to three on Saturday I decided to go down to the church after all. I'd go in my work clothes caked with cement, in my boots spotted with gritty mortar. I decided to go because I wanted to tell them what I planned to do. I'd never explained to anybody except Mama the vision I had of the church.

But stepping into that room and speaking to those men would take my breath away. I remembered how bad I had preached, and how in school I'd stood up to debate and found I couldn't say a thing. It was like my throat locked and my mind was empty when I got up in front of people. I couldn't remember my name, and I couldn't have said it if I had remembered. It was like my tongue was still tied down and had never been snipped free.

They'll be asking the questions, I thought as I walked down the hill toward the church. All I'd have to do was answer them. And U. G. would be there. And Hank would be there. And there was nothing they could do to me. Would they try to throw me out of the church for building a church on my own property? The church hadn't give me a cent toward the building, not a nail or stick of wood.

They was all there in the church when I arrived, setting in the amen corner. There was six of them besides the preacher, as well as Riley, who was chairman of the board of deacons. I set down on the bench behind them.

"You come on up here, Brother Muir," Riley said, and pointed to a chair in front of the altar. Riley was married to my great-aunt Catherine. He raised cattle and had the best bull in the valley. I guess Riley thought of hisself as a kind of squire.

"I don't need to set up there," I said and swallowed. But I went up anyway.

I nodded at U. G. and Hank as I walked to the front of the church. My face already felt hot. Maybe I was windburned from working at the top of the mountain.

I set down and seen how dirty my shoes and pants was. They looked like they'd been smeared with cement. The preacher set on the front bench, and Riley stood up beside me like a lawyer in court. "I was sorry to hear your brother, Moody, was in trouble with the law," he said. I couldn't think of nothing to answer and just nodded. Riley cleared his throat.

"This quarterly meeting of the deacons of Green River Baptist Church will come to order," Riley said. "We have met here today to discuss one major item of business."

Most of the deacons was looking down at their laps and at their feet. They seemed a little embarrassed to be there.

"It's said that Brother Muir is building a new church on top of the mountain," Riley said. "Is this true, Brother Muir?"

"It is," I said. I glanced at U. G., but he was looking away to the side of the church.

"By whose authority are you building a new church?" Riley said.

"By my own," I said.

"A decision to build a new church has to be made by a vote of the whole congregation," Riley said. "And the motion has to be recommended by the board of deacons. That's in the bylaws of the church."

"I'm building on my own land and doing all the work myself," I said.

"Was you authorized by the board of deacons?" Riley said.

"No, sir."

"Did you ask the board of deacons for authorization?" Riley said.

"No, sir."

"Then you're building it for another congregation?" Riley said.

"No, sir," I said. "I'll give the new church to this congregation."

"But this congregation has not been consulted," Riley said. "The thing you're doing is outside the bylaws of the church and contrary to church discipline. It has nothing to do with this church."

"It's for this church," I said.

"You have broke the discipline and bylaws of the church," Riley said. "By a vote of the congregation you can be dropped from the rolls of the church."

"You didn't build *this* church!" I hollered at Riley. "My grandpa built this church when he come back from the Confederate War."

U. G. raised his hand.

"Brother Latham," Riley said.

"We're only meeting today to ask questions," U. G. said. "We didn't meet here to threaten or throw Brother Muir out of the church."

"Hear, hear," Hank said.

"I'll build the church whether you authorize it or not," I said.

"Why would you do that?" Preacher Liner said. "Why would you go against Baptist discipline?"

"Because I'd never get you all's approval," I said.

"That's right," Riley said. "We'd never approve such a foolish scheme."

"I'm building for the future," I said. "In a hundred years people will worship on the mountaintop. And a hundred years after that too."

"Are you doing this work out of pride?" Preacher Liner said.

I told them I had tried to conquer my pride, but Riley warned me the devil works in mysterious ways. I said I wanted to build an altar on the mountain where everybody could see it. Riley said then it must be for my own greater glory. But I told them the church was not for me but for them, and for their children and grandchildren.

"Do you have the funds sufficient for such a building?" Preacher Liner said. "Do you have the permission of your mama to build on her land?"

"It's not any of your business," I said. "But she does want me to build the new church. And she's helping me." Anger rose like little bubbles in my blood. My bones was feeling light. I knowed that getting mad was the worst thing I could do. But I couldn't help myself.

"You think building a new church is none of our business?" Riley said.

"Whether Mama approves or not is none of your business," I said.

"You mama is a member of this church," Riley said.

"And you throwed her out too, her and Grandpa," I said. I told him I hadn't asked for their help and I didn't need their help.

"Is that the Christian spirit?" Riley said.

I stood up. I wasn't going to be talked to like a little schoolboy they could scold. I was going to get out of there.

"Set back down," U. G. said to me. I waited for a second and then I set back down in the chair. "Everybody knows you're trying to help the church and the community," U. G. said. "You're not doing this for your personal gain. It's just that most people don't see the need for a new church. This is a country congregation, and we don't need some big church house on the mountaintop."

"I think we should hear Brother Muir out," Hank Richards said. It was the first time he had spoke, but nobody paid him any attention. He was the newest member of the board of deacons.

"It's good to have big plans," the preacher said, "as long as they don't divide the church."

"I can see you all are against me," I said.

"Let's hear more about your plans," Hank said.

"A church is made up of its members," Preacher Liner said. "In a Baptist church all authority is vested in the congregation. Nobody, not the deacons, not even the pastor, has any more say-so than the rest."

My blood was humming behind my ears. There was sweat on my forehead and around my temples. "If people choose to be stupid, what's the point of getting together with them?" I said.

"The church is the Lord's institution in this world," Preacher Liner said.

"This community does need a new church," Hank said. "I move we put it to a vote of the congregation."

"We get strength from fellowship and working with each other," the preacher said.

"I would rather set out in the woods and listen to the birds sing," I said.

"Brother Muir, we want you to be a part of us," U. G. said. "But we want you to be reasonable."

"Reasonable means doing nothing," I said.

"We appreciate your zeal," Preacher Liner said. "We only wish your ambition could be channeled to more practical goals."

It was no use to talk to them. I stood up again. "You can kick me out of the church if you want to," I said, "like you kicked out Mama and Grandpa."

"That was a long time ago," Riley said.

I walked out of there with all of them staring at me. My humiliation and my defeat was so complete I felt almost triumphant. They had destroyed everything I'd tried to do. Or I had destroyed everything. I didn't know which it was. Moody was running from the law because of my church. The community and the preacher and the deacons and the forces of nature was against my work. The law of gravity was against my work. And the rain and freeze and thaw was against my work. Only Mama, and maybe Hank Richards, didn't seem opposed to what I was doing.

My defeat was so total I felt freed by it as I stepped down the aisle toward the back of the church, opened the door, and slammed it behind me. I felt bathed with anger. I was stripped to the bone and humiliated and there was nothing to do but start over again. Anger and defeat made me feel light as I walked down the steps and across the churchyard. I hoofed it down the road by the spring feeling naked as a baby.

I decided to go look for Moody. He was in trouble and I should go find him and help him. He was my brother, and I should offer my help whether he wanted it or not.

At the house I loaded my packsack with cornmeal and bacon, with shoulder meat and a box of raisins. I put in matches and extra socks and a pair of gloves.

"Where are you going?" Mama said.

"You will lead the deputies right to Moody," Fay said.

I done the milking and I eat supper. I waited until it was good dark before heading out. Mama handed me a ten-dollar bill to give to Moody. When I left the house I went east, like I was walking toward the highway. I stopped and listened to see if anybody was following me. In the pines I turned to the river and followed the river, as I'd done so many times in the dark, all the way to its head at the edge of the Flat Woods.

By the time I got to Pinnacle it was way past midnight. I knowed Moody could be anywhere, even over in South Carolina toward Caesar's Head, or in the Long Holler beyond the Sal Raeburn Gap. But I tried to think where I would go if I was Moody. And I kept thinking of the cave on the other side of Ann Mountain, beyond Pinnacle. It was a cave where outliers and deserters had stayed during the Confederate War. It was a cave far under the mountain with a rock crevice above it that reached up hundreds of feet and served as a kind of chimney.

I felt my way in the dark through the trees around the side of Pinnacle. There was no trail, and limbs scratched across my face. I walked sideways with my arm outstretched, and stepped in branches and sinkholes from time to time. When I thought I was lost, I stopped and listened to the wind on the high ridge to my right.

The woods was just beginning to get gray when I reached the foot of Ann Mountain. It had been years since I'd visited the cave. It would take a little poking around to find it. I crossed the branch where rocks had spilled down the mountain, and started climbing. Something stung the air like a mouth organ or hornet above my head. I ducked and then heard the crack of a rifle. I dropped to my knees and listened. There was bootleggers in the Flat Woods, but I didn't think there was any still on the side of Ann Mountain. I hadn't seen any fire up there.

If it was Moody shooting at me, how could I call him? What if some deputy had followed me in the dark, like Fay had said they would?

I crawled toward the biggest rock nearby. Another bullet sung through the air with a sick twang. "It's Muir!" I hollered. And rolled behind the rock. I listened for a voice or movement farther up the mountain.

"I have brought you something!" I shouted. Pulling the packsack off, I held it up above the rock. A bullet whined like a banjo string had broke, and knocked the pack out of my hands. A hole the size of a fifty-cent piece was tore in the flap.

I set there trying to think what to do. I am my brother's keeper, I said to myself over and over. I must do what I can. It could be anybody shooting at me. But I knowed it was Moody. Moody was mad because he had told me not to come looking for him. I wanted to tell him I had come to help him any way I could. I was sure nobody had followed me in the dark.

"I want to talk to you!" I yelled.

I expected another shot to sing through the air and crack a tree nearby, but none come. I waited and listened for a shout, but the woods only dripped their morning dew. The branch below murmured through its rocks, and a hawk whistled somewhere way up on the mountaintop.

"Won't you talk to me?" I hollered.

There was some kind of movement farther up the ridge, and I strained my eyes to see better. It was getting daylight by then, and the woods was gray and brown.

"I come to help you!" I hollered up the mountainside, and there was an echo from the ridge beyond the branch: *help you, help you.* But that was all. The woods and the mountainside was quiet.

"I will leave the pack here," I yelled.

• • •

WHILE I WAS walking down toward the head of the river, I thought somebody was watching me or following me. It was an itchy, prickly feeling. I spun around and seen somebody way back behind me. They jumped quick into the laurel bushes, but I got a good look and seen it was one of the Willards; Sam or Stinky it was, I think.

"What do you want?" I hollered. But they never stepped out from behind the laurels.

"Do you want to shoot me?" I yelled. But the woods was dead silent.

When I walked on I looked back from time to time, but I never seen them again.

THE NEXT MONDAY I was hammering the old mortar off a rock when a voice behind me said, "You have your work cut out for you." I turned and seen Hank Richards. He had on his carpenter's overalls and he was carrying a toolbox.

"They didn't leave me much to go back to," I said.

Hank set the toolbox down. "That was some Christmas present," he said.

"I reckon they wanted to give, in the spirit of the holiday," I said.

"I have come to help you," Hank said.

"You have?" I said, not sure I heard him right. "I am obliged," I said. The stiffness in my throat kept me from saying more.

"When I was your age I had big plans," Hank said. "I wish somebody had encouraged me."

I told him Moody said the Willard brothers broke up my foundation.

"I heard that," Hank said. "And I heard about Moody shooting one of them."

"It was an accident," I said.

Hank said he had had his own troubles with the Willard brothers, back when he was courting Mrs. Richards.

Hank had built so many houses and barns, he knowed just what to do. "The most important thing is to get your foundation right," he said. He looked at the ruins of the west wall where the door of the church was to be.

"It may be just as well they knocked that down," he said. "The footing needs to be poured again."

I didn't argue with him, though that was my first impulse. I was embarrassed for him to see the mistakes I'd made. I got a mattock and he took a shovel, and we broke away the ruined work and dug the trench deeper. Hank was so strong he worked like a machine. We redug the ditch in no time, it seemed. I told him I couldn't believe he was helping me.

"I wouldn't mind giving Preacher Liner a surprise," Hank said.

Hank took his hammer and some nails from his toolbox and repaired the mortar box better. He hammered slow, but the wood fell into place for him. It was a pleasure to watch how sure he was with a hammer and saw. He used the tools so they seemed a part of his hands.

"I'm not much used to laying rock," Hank said. But he seemed to know just exactly what to do next, better than I did. He seemed to understand my idea for the plan of the church already.

"Have you got a blueprint?" Hank said as he laid his level on top of the new west wall.

I admitted I had only a rough drawing and showed him the sketch I carried in my pocket. It was creased and smudged. I told him I would make a better drawing that night.

As Hank worked he made building appear to be the most natural thing. He didn't waste a single move. Every time he reached or turned he got something done.

"You hadn't ought to have give up preaching," Hank said as we laid the next level of rock on the foundation that afternoon.

"I just made a fool of myself," I said.

"Everybody makes a fool of theirself at first," Hank said. He marked off the space for the door on the left side. With his help I had almost brought the wall back to where it was before Christmas Eve. Us two working together got four times as much done as me working alone.

"Not such a fool as I was," I said.

"I made a worser fool of myself at your age," Hank said. Hank said that when him and Mrs. Richards first got married and moved down to Gap Creek, there come a flood at Christmastime. The flood was so bad they had to escape from the house in the middle of the night. In the dark, in the rushing water, he had let go of Julie's hand and found the way to the barn by hisself. He was ashamed of hisself.

It was hard to believe Hank was talking to me that way. "What did you do?" I said.

"I acted crazy and cowardly," Hank said.

Hank said that just about the only way we learn anything is from our mistakes. "Everybody makes their own mistakes," he said.

"I've made aplenty," I said.

"I ain't seen nothing you've done yet that says you can't be a preacher," Hank said.

"It was prideful of me to want to preach," I said.

"I felt the call when I was young," Hank said. "But nobody encouraged me."

IT's HARD TO describe how much easier the work was with Hank helping. He understood what was to be done next and how it was to be done. I had been fumbling around and piddling around on my own. Working with him, I felt more powerful, and the rocks and boards was more firm and ready to be joined. By the end of the week we had rebuilt the foundation to where it was before, except now it was in plumb. There wasn't nothing sigodlin about the corners and walls. I was tired out and a little dazed by what all Hank done and said. After he come to the mountaintop the mess sorted itself out and the rocks got gathered back in place. Right after the worst will come the best. I had heard that said. But I kept worrying about Moody. I couldn't feel easy for thinking about Moody.

"I am humbly grateful to you," I said to Hank at quitting time.

"Next you are going to have to get some lumber," Hank said.

"I want a rock church," I said, "like the cathedrals and churches in the Old World."

"You can have rock on the outside," Hank said. "But you need a frame on the inside. You want walls and ceiling to keep it warm in winter. You want paint on the walls so the church will look bright and clean."

I seen he was right. I hadn't thought clear enough about what the inside would look like. I had thought mostly of how the church would look from the outside.

Hank took a piece of paper bag that had held nails and he got a pencil from his bib pocket and started figuring. "Thirty feet by twenty feet by twelve feet high," he said. "How steep do you want the roof?"

"Steep as a town church," I said.

He wrote down numbers and then more numbers. "You will need double sheathing," he said. "I'd say you will need at least five thousand board feet, not counting studs and sills and joists."

"And a steeple," I said.

"How high a steeple?" Hank said.

"Over the treetops where everybody in the valley can see it," I said.

"You'll have to have seven thousand board feet," Hank said.

"That's a lot of trees," I said.

"I'll help you cut them," Hank said.

When I walked back down the mountain to the river road, I stopped at the mailbox. It was already getting dark, and I knowed Mama would want the newspaper and a magazine if any had come. She was so worried about Moody she needed something to take her mind off our troubles. But there was just a bill for taxes in the box, besides the newspaper. And an envelope with no stamp on it. My name was wrote in pencil on the envelope. It was such neat lettering I was sure it was done by Moody. You would not have thought he would write such a fine hand, but he could, when he put his mind to it.

In the dim light I could just barely see, but I opened the letter and found it was scribbled in the same tiny hand in pencil.

Dear Muir,

You old rascal. I take pensil in hand to say don't come looking for me again. For you probably couldn't find me, and if you did you'd probably lead the law strate to me. For I know they must be watching the house from time to time.

*I'm writing this with a pensil stole from a schoolhouse, on a
tablet bought at a store, you don't need to know where. I'm
warning you not to try looking for me again. Killing Zack Willard
was an accident, but he got what he deserved.*

*Now I know your plan to build a church is foolish, but no
foolisher than most things people does.*

*I guess the Willards thought you was helping me bootleg, like
you done that one time, was why they broke up your foundation.
It was to scare me so they could sell all the liquor in the valley. Me
and Wheeler and Drayton was cutting into their business too
much.*

*Muir, I get mad easy, because you are such a damned mama's
boy and do everything right. I was always blamed for trouble, I
still am blamed. You thought I broke up your damned church.
You kicked me when I was drunk and asleep. You always thought
I was a dog, you and Mama together.*

*If you want to build a church, build a damn church. It can't
hurt nothing and might even help old backsliders like me. You
want to be a preacher you go ahead and be a goddamned
preacher. Just because you stumbled and flustered that first time,
and people laughed when I farted, don't mean you can't preach.*

*Hell, I heard you practicing out in the woods when I was lay-
ing drunk in the thicket and you was trying out what you wanted
to say. And you sounded good as a real preacher man to me.*

*Not that I ever cottoned to preachers. But you was calling out
the words good as any caller at a square dance. I heard you.*

*Till I get out of this you can have the Model T. All it needs is
some new spark plugs and the points filed. And a new inner tube.
You fix it up and use it to go to services when you are a famous
preacher.*

*And don't you all worry about me. I'm going to lay low for a
few weeks and watch out for myself.*

Your ragged assed brother, Moody.

I folded the letter and put it in my pocket, then hurried down to
the house to show it to Mama.

In the days after Moody sent the letter, Hank helped me saw down twenty big oaks on the pasture hill. He taught me things about felling trees I'd never heard of before. He showed me how to guess the number of feet in a tree still on the stump.

Hank told me that you measure the thickness of an oak six feet off the ground, and measure the height up to the first limbs. Then you multiply half the thickness by itself, and by three, and by the feet to the fork or first big limbs, and you get roughly the planking inside the log.

Not only did Hank show me how to figure the lumber in a tree, he showed me what trees to cut for different parts of the building. Some of it I'd heard before, and some I hadn't.

"We'll cut hemlocks for the sills," he said. "One of them hemlocks by the spring should be enough." He said termites won't touch hemlock, and moisture don't hurt it much either.

I told him I wanted the church to be made of oak, like the big oak beams I'd read about in Durham Cathedral, where you could see the axe marks made nine hundred years ago.

Hank said oak would work for the sheathing, but he'd recommend pine for the frame and studs because a nail can be drove through a one-inch oak board, but not through two or three inches of oak.

As we worked I tried to think what I would have done without Hank's advice and help. I would have just fumbled on. He moved so slow it surprised me how quick his work mounted up. Sometimes I found myself standing there watching him work. He showed me that all things, especially hard things, had to be done one little step at a time. There was no need to hurry.

We worked so steady we got the timber cut in a week. In another week it was all sawed up, and Mama paid to have the lumber trucked to the foot of the mountain. We hauled it to the top in the wagon. The stacks of lumber gleamed in the clearing beside the rock piles.

Hank showed me how to nail together two-by-tens to make the sills of the church. The floor would be about three feet off the ground, and the sills set on the rock foundation. We made joists out of two-by-eights to hold up the floor, and Hank took some one-by-fours and sawed them into lengths to nail between the beams for struts and braces. He used his level and try square at every step to make sure everything was plumb and foursquare. "A building has to be perfect at the foundation, or it will never be right later," he said again.

He showed me how to use a plumb bob.

Soon as the beams was in place it was time to lay the subfloor. "Always nail subfloor planks at a forty-five-degree angle to the walls," Hank said.

"Why is that?" I said.

"Makes the floor twice as strong," Hank said. "The subfloor acts like bracing for the bottom of the house."

He showed me how to saw planks at an angle using his try square. The subfloor took shape like the deck of a ship on the mountaintop. Like an altar.

Middle of the afternoon Mrs. Richards and Annie come up to the top of the mountain carrying a coffeepot and two mugs and some biscuits with molasses on them. "Thought you could stand some coffee," Mrs. Richards said. She poured me a cup and Annie handed it to me. My hand was sore from holding the saw so long. Annie's hair sparkled bright as the lumber in the winter sun.

I took a sip of the coffee and felt it running through my belly and out my arms like little lights to my fingertips. The boards and sawdust, the cement and rocks, got sharper and brighter.

"Who ever thought there'd be a church on this mountain?" Mrs. Richards said.

"There ain't one yet," I said.

"A mountaintop feels closer to heaven," Mrs. Richards said.

"This will be a good place to watch the sunset," Annie said. I had not tried to go with her in a long time. I reckon I'd been too busy to think about courting.

ALL MY LIFE I had heard carpenters talk about the "idea" of building, how some men naturally had an "idea" for building, and others didn't. But I'd never seen an example before I worked with Hank.

I showed Hank my new drawing for the church and he studied the page careful. And after that it was like he had memorized it. It was like he could already see the church in his head as clear as I could. He could see what would go where before I did.

After we got the subfloor down we started nailing the studs in place every eighteen inches around the sides. The upright two-by-fours made the cage of the frame, so it begun to look like a building there in the woods. The fresh lumber was white as cream.

"Can I make a suggestion?" Hank said. It was a windy day in February and his face was flushed. "Do you really want windows two feet off the floor?" he said.

"To let in the breeze during a long summer service," I said.

"That won't be a problem up here where there is always a breeze," Hank said.

"Windows have got to be low enough so younguns can raise them," I said.

"High windows will let light slant down on the pews and on the floor," Hank said. "They'll give a more sacred look to the church. People can look up and see the light streaming in."

Anger shot up in me like somebody had touched a trigger. It was my church, and I had already planned it in a hundred ways before Hank ever struck a hammer blow to it.

"Build it any way you want," I said and put down my hammer. I tried to think of something else to say and couldn't. In a mad stupor I walked to the edge of the floor and jumped to the ground. I kept walking till I got to the laurel bushes on the north side. When I stopped in the thicket I was already ashamed of myself. I stood in the winter leaves, breathing short with rage and embarrassment.

What a fool you are, I said to myself. I seen what had made me maddest about Hank's suggestion was that he was right. His idea of the church was clearer than mine. Higher windows would make a more sacred effect. Lower windows would distract the congregation while they listened to a sermon. And there was no reason little younguns would need to raise or lower the windows. Might be better if they couldn't.

I hated to go back and face Hank. I would rather be whipped with a leather strap than face somebody that had made me mad. I had showed my ass, as Moody would have said.

I turned and started back into the clearing, pushing limbs out of my way. Hank was still nailing down studs, toenailing them in. His hammer rung in the clearing like hard fast barks. He didn't stop nailing when I climbed back up on the subfloor.

"I hadn't ought to get mad," I said. "You was right about the windows."

"Always had a quick temper myself," Hank said.

"I hadn't even thought about the windows," I said.

"Short temper's a sign of a clear conscience," Hank said. "But it never does much good." He looked up and grinned. "I hit a foreman upside of the head one time and got myself fired."

I picked up my hammer and held the next two-by-four for Hank to nail. My face was hot in the wind.

LATER SOMEBODY SPOKE from the edge of the clearing. It was Preacher Liner, and he looked out of breath from walking up the mountain.

"I heard you was helping Muir," the preacher said to Hank. "I wanted to see it with my own eyes."

"Building is slow this time of year," Hank said. "I had a little time on my hands."

The preacher come closer to where we was working and stood with his hands on his hips. Hank showed him where we was going to put the doorway and steeple, right near where he was standing.

"The deacons didn't authorize no new church," Preacher Liner said.

Hank worked calm and steady. He told the preacher he thought building a new church was a good idea, and that he just wanted to help me out a little. The preacher said the only idea that counted was the one the congregation voted on. "That's Baptist discipline," Preacher Liner said.

Hank was calm as a bank teller. He started nailing again, and his hammer blows was like drumbeats. He told the preacher he didn't want to argue with nobody, and that he just wanted to build a church on the mountaintop that people could use.

"Them that break the laws of the church can be rebuked," Preacher Liner said, raising his voice a little. He hadn't even noticed me.

Hank told the preacher everybody serves the Lord in their own way. He didn't look at the preacher, but his face had got redder in the wind.

"That is not the spirit of fellowship," Preacher Liner said. "If everybody went his own way there wouldn't be no church. I won't see my church divided."

"A man has to follow his conscience," Hank said, "and do what he thinks is right."

"That's not Baptist discipline," Preacher Liner said. "A deacon must be an example to the community. A deacon is a pillar of the church."

Hank kept nailing without looking at the preacher. There was sweat on his forehead.

"I'd hate for you both to lose your letters in the church," Preacher Liner said. "Muir is just a boy, but you are old enough to be accountable."

Hank spun around so fast his carpenter's apron slapped against his hip. The calm was gone from his face, and his eyes was narrow as buttonholes as he faced the preacher. The preacher was heavier than Hank. "I would hate for you to fall off this mountain," Hank spit out.

"It's a sin to threaten a preacher," Preacher Liner said.

Hank never answered him, and the preacher turned and walked back across the clearing and disappeared down the road. I was so nervous my knees was shaking.

"Get me some more nails," Hank said like he was short of breath. I went to the box beside the pile of two-by-fours and got a handful of twelve-penny nails.

"Why is the preacher so opposed?" I said.

"Don't do no good to talk about it," Hank said. "Let's talk about the west wall."

I wanted to hear what Hank thought about the preacher. I wanted to ask him again why he was helping me on the church. But I seen asking him wouldn't do no good. "We can build the base of the steeple twelve feet by twelve feet," I said.

"There will have to be more studs on this side," Hank said, "because it's going to support the steeple."

That was something else I hadn't thought of. The base of the steeple had to be stronger than the walls to support a tower fifty or even sixty feet high. The west wall would have to be reinforced.

"I guess a preacher has pride like anybody else," I said as we nailed the extra studs.

"Let's not talk about preachers," Hank said.

But Hank did talk about preachers, a week later, when we had the frame up and was ready to nail the rafters. It was beginning to look like a real church house then, with a steep gable high as the trees. We had to make a longer ladder out of hickory poles. The hardest work was putting the ridgepole on. It was so high I was afraid. I wasn't used to working that high off the ground. When I looked around I could see over the tops of the trees far up the valley.

The roof beam was made of two-by-sixes nailed together.

"What's the news of Moody?" Hank said.

There was a special closeness, working that high off the ground in the wind with the woods and valley stretching below us.

"Ain't heard nothing from him except that one letter," I said. "He must be hiding somewhere in the woods."

"Hope he has a shack or cave to stay in," Hank said.

"Preacher Liner come to the house to see Mama," I said. "He told her that Moody's trouble was punishment for us defying the church."

"Did he really say that?" Hank said. He leaned far out to keep his balance while nailing the two-by-sixes together.

"He said the Lord punishes everybody in his own way," I said.

"Preachers is just human, even if they are anointed," Hank said. "They make mistakes same as the rest of us."

When I climbed down to get another two-by-six I looked up at the rafters against the sky. They leaned together, pointing like fingers to the center of the sky. The rafters really looked like the shape of a church, like the figure of a church. Hank carried a two-by-four on a beam easy as an acrobat on a high wire.

Twenty-four
Ginny

IT WAS U. G. that drove up into the yard that March evening. U. G. was the kind of man that always took responsibility in a quiet way. He come to the door, and when I met him his hat was already in his hand.

"Come on in," I said. I knowed the news was not good when he didn't say nothing as I led him to the fire. We hadn't heard a thing from Moody in weeks, and I was afraid of bad news.

"It's about Moody?" I said. A chill rippled through me down to the bones in my toes.

"Afraid I have bad news," U. G. said. He paused. "Where is Muir?" he said.

"Up on the mountain working with Hank on the church," I said.

U. G. shook his head and looked into the fire.

"What has happened to Moody?" I said.

"Moody has been shot by a deputy," U. G. said, almost under his breath.

"I don't believe it," I said.

"I hate to be the one to tell you," U. G. said.

"Where did it happen?" I said.

U. G. took me by the elbow and led me to the couch. He set down beside me and put his hand on my shoulder.

"The deputies stopped by the store yesterday," U. G. said. "They asked if I knowed where Moody might be. I told them the truth, that I didn't know any more than they did. The big square-jawed feller named Thomas said the sheriff wanted to make a deal with Moody. If Moody would tell what he knowed about the Willards' bootlegging with Peg Early, then he might get off light, might even get the charges dropped. Jenkins said if Moody didn't turn hisself in the Willards was going to find him and kill him anyway.

"I seen the truth in that. Moody's only hope was to leave the country or make some kind of agreement with the sheriff. He couldn't spend his life running from the sheriff *and* the Willards. I truthfully didn't know where Moody was laying out, didn't want to know. If I had to guess I'd say he was somewhere beyond Pinnacle, probably in one of the caves on Ann Mountain, but I didn't tell them that. I told the deputies I'd try to find him and talk to him, if they wouldn't follow me. They agreed and said they'd appreciate any help I could give.

"To throw them off I got in my truck and drove down to South Carolina, where they couldn't arrest nobody anyway. I drove down to Highway Eleven and cut across the foot of Gap Creek to the Caesar's Head highway. Then I drove back up to North Carolina just south of Cedar Mountain.

"To make sure nobody was following me I pulled into a haul road and waited behind the brush for half an hour. But nobody come by or stopped, so I started walking toward the branch that runs on the back side of Ann Mountain.

"That side of Ann Mountain is all boulders and rock cliffs. A man could hide out there and hold off a posse if he wanted to. There was rocks that jutted out above the oak trees like towers. There was rocks that leaned out so far it made you sick just to look up at them.

"I stood below them rocks and hollered out Moody's name. There was nothing but an echo. 'Come down and talk,' I yelled. 'I have something to tell you.'

"*Tell you,* the cliffs on the far ridge repeated.

" 'I want to help you,' I shouted between my hands.

"*Help you,* come back from the ridge.

"Something stirred behind me and I turned to see Moody holding his pistol pointed at me. He had a beard and his hair pointed every which way. He looked cold and hungry.

" 'You ain't got no right,' Moody said.

" 'The sheriff can make it easy for you,' I said.

"Moody looked weak and tired. The pistol shook a little in his hand.

" 'I wouldn't have led the law to you,' Moody said.

" 'The Willards are going to kill you if they find you,' I said. But I was no longer sure I had done the right thing in coming to Ann Mountain. What if the Willards had followed me? I had an ugly feeling in my gut, and an itch in the back of my neck.

" 'You think I don't know that?' Moody said.

" 'Moody!' somebody yelled from the laurel bushes across the branch. Moody whirled around and pointed the pistol at the laurels.

" 'Drop that gun,' they called. 'Your life ain't worth a snowflake in hell out here.' It was Thomas the deputy.

" 'You have done this,' Moody snarled at me over his shoulder.

" 'You promised to let me talk!' I shouted at the laurel bushes.

" 'You have done this to me,' Moody said again. I thought he was going to turn and shoot at me. But just then Thomas stood up and stepped out of the undergrowth.

" 'Put down your gun,' the deputy called.

"I seen the look on Moody's face. It was like the strain went out of him all of a sudden. It was a look of relief that come over his face. I reckon he was just plain wore out with hiding and waiting. He turned slow as a man about to open a door and raised the pistol toward the deputy. He didn't pull the trigger. I don't think he ever intended to pull the trigger.

"A shot come from the laurel bushes. It was the other deputy that had Moody in his sights. He shot Moody right through the chest with a slug.

"I run to Moody and tried to stop the blood with my jacket wadded up against the wound. But the blood just kept streaming out. I tied my jacket across his chest, but the jacket was soon soaked and dripping as we carried him out toward the haul road. It was long after dark before we reached the highway, and he had bled to death before we got even close."

When U. G. stopped I felt like all the blood had drained out of my heart. I was too weak to say anything.

"Moody called your name out as we carried him," U. G. said.

"What did he say?" I asked.

"He just said 'Mama' twice as we toted him," U. G. said.

I took a breath, but there was no air in the room.

I thought of Moody with his pistol in the woods at dark. He had been dead a whole day and I hadn't knowed about it. I had give life to him and suckled him at my breast. There is no greater grief than a mama's grief over her own flesh and bone. I was so stunned I watched myself in my grief like I was another person.

A truck whined into the yard and ground its gears and stopped. I was numb as I watched them open the back of the van and lift out a stretcher. U. G. held the door for them.

"Are you Mrs. Powell?" the deputy said.

"Put him on the couch," U. G. said.

They laid the stretcher down on the floor and lifted Moody onto the couch. He had several days' growth of beard and his hair was not combed. His eyes was closed and his features looked like wax. There was blood on his coat.

"Ma'am, would you sign this?" one of the deputies said, and held out a clipboard with a piece of paper on it.

I ignored him.

"It just says you received the body and will assume custody of it," the deputy said.

I turned away from him and looked at Moody. The stain on his coat had turned black. Fay sobbed on the corner of a chair.

"I will sign it," U. G. said to the deputy.

When the deputies was gone and the truck had whined out of the yard, I tried to think what to do. If I set down and let myself go I would never get up again. There was grief in me that would turn me inside out and crumble me to pieces if I give in to it. There was sobs in me that was worse than any vomiting or seizures if I let them out.

"You set down, Ginny, and I'll take care of everything," U. G. said.

"No," I said, "Moody has got to be laid out. I'll go clear the kitchen table."

Fay looked up at me, her face red and her eyes wet. "How can you think," she sobbed, "of laying him out yourself?"

"I'll do what has to be done," I said. I couldn't soften the anger in my voice. The pride and anger give me strength. Without the pride and anger I would have fainted.

I stepped into the kitchen and collected the salt and pepper shakers off the table. I gathered up the sugar bowl and the molasses jar, and the little jar of pickle relish. Taters was already boiling on the stove, and I set them aside. I pulled the oilcloth off the table and folded it on the counter by the water bucket. There was crumbs and a little dust on the bare wood of the tabletop. I brushed it off with a wet rag.

"We'll bring him in here and lay him on the table," I called to U. G. and Fay. I throwed some sticks of wood in the stove and poured the kettle full and set a dishpan half full of water on top of the stove.

"You don't need to do this," U. G. said.

"I do need to do it," I said. I rolled up my sleeves and stiffened my will against the tide of grief I knowed was coming.

Just then Muir walked through the kitchen door. His face was twisted all around as he said, "I heard about Moody." Then he busted out crying. His lips stretched every which way. He took me in his arms.

I told him we would have to lay Moody out, and it would take all of us to carry him. I led Muir into the living room and told him to lift Moody up while I pulled his coat off.

"Oh, Mama," Muir said, and took Moody by the shoulders.

Moody's arms was stiff as wood. They had been laid over his chest and it took some yanking and pulling to get the sleeves of the coat over the wrists. It was so awkward I felt myself blushing, in spite of the icy grief that soaked through me. The body was so heavy and cold it was hard to think it was my boy Moody.

As I tore the coat off, Florrie come into the room and asked me what I was doing. I didn't even know she had come to the house. I told her I was getting the body ready to lay out.

"Set down and don't make a spectacle of yourself," Florrie said.

"Since a cooling board wasn't used the back is curved," I said. I told her to help me carry him to the kitchen if she wanted to be useful.

"What are you trying to prove?" Florrie said.

Fay and Muir was both sobbing and useless. I seen I had to do what needed to be done.

"You are beside yourself," Florrie said and took my arm.

U. G. and Muir took Moody's shoulders, and me and Florrie took his legs, and we carried him into the kitchen. Water was boiling on the stove and the windows was starting to steam up.

"Me and U. G. will do this," Florrie said.

"No, Mama, I will do it," U. G. said to Florrie.

I felt my will was a dam holding back a great tide of confusion and mourning. I had to shove hard as I could. If I let the dam bust loose I would drown.

"You all go back to the living room," I said. "Muir and me will do this."

"Why are you acting this way?" Florrie said.

"I will lay out my own son in my own house," I said.

"You are on your high horse," Florrie said.

They all stood back when I brought in another lamp and set it at the side of the table. I pulled off Moody's overalls an inch at a time, and I pulled off his shirt. He had been shot through the chest and blood had dried around the hole between two ribs like brown paint. There was wet blood in the wound, and the smell of old blood.

"You leave this to me," U. G. said.

"Stand back," I said, "and bring me some camphor." I seen the only thing to do was cover the wound with a bandage soaked in camphor. When Muir lifted the body so I could strap the bandage around the chest, Moody's eyes come open. I closed them before anybody else could see. The eyes had a milky, cloudy look.

I poured hot water in a pan and got a piece of soap and started washing Moody on his hands and arms. His hands was stained with berry juice, or maybe it was blood. I scrubbed his neck and behind the ears. I hadn't washed his face since he was a boy. I was careful not to open the eyes again.

"Bring me your razor," I said to Muir.

"I will shave him," U. G. said. "You can let me at least shave him."

U. G. was a barber and used to shaving people. I let him shave Moody while I scrubbed his chest and belly. Moody's bowels had opened after he died and I cleaned that up with hot water and a cloth. I had not seen Moody's private parts since he was a little boy. I tried not to look at the scar on his groin.

This is a test of dignity and strength, I thought. This is a test of faith. I will not give in to grief yet. Moody's anger was in his blood, and his temper was beyond his control. It was like all his life I had seen this moment coming. And just as he had begun to change, to soften and grow up, he had been killed. It was too sad to describe in words.

And it was my fault. I didn't know how exactly, but I was his mama and I was responsible for him. At the very least I had failed him by not expecting enough of him. I had expected a lot from Muir, and almost nothing from Moody.

I emptied the pan off the back porch and got clean water. I washed Moody's legs and feet. With my scissors I trimmed his toenails. His toenails was long and crooked and dirty.

"Now, what is he going to wear?" I said to U. G.

"Does Moody have a suit?" U. G. said.

"All he has got is overalls and flannel shirts," I said.

"He can wear my old suit," Muir said.

"Moody don't need a suit," I said. "He never wore a suit in his whole life."

"If his funeral is going to be in church he has to wear a suit like anybody else," Muir said.

"Your suit is too big for him," I said.

I got clean overalls and a shirt out of the bedroom and we slipped them on Moody a piece at a time. I remembered how hard it was to lift a dead body from the time Tom died. The weight and the rubbery stiffness make it almost impossible to fit clothes on the frame. It took all of us lifting and pulling, pushing and rolling, to do it.

After Moody was dressed we left him laying on the table. Muir would have to make a coffin the next day out of some of his oak boards. U. G. volunteered to bring him some handles to screw on the

sides and a nameplate and some hinges. I set a lamp on either side of
the body and left it there.

"You come set by the fire," Florrie said to me. "I'll fix you something to eat."

"Don't want nothing to eat," I said.

THE NEXT MORNING Preacher Liner come while Muir was
hammering at the coffin in the backyard. I heard him talking with
Muir where he worked at the sawhorses, and then the preacher
knocked on the door.

"Ginny, I have come to be with you in your hour of tribulation,"
the preacher said, stepping into the living room, hat in hand.

I was not surprised to see the preacher, but I was surprised he had
come so early in the morning. And he was tense, like he thought he
might not be welcome. He looked at Moody's body still laying on the
kitchen table. I had put a handkerchief soaked in camphor over
Moody's face to keep the skin from turning black.

"The Lord will not put on us a greater grief than we can bear,"
Preacher Liner said. The preacher turned his hat in his hands and
looked around the living room. He looked sick. There was bags under his eyes, and his shoulders was stooped. I had never seen him
look so old and worried.

"Would you like to set down?" I said.

"I have come to ask about the funeral," Preacher Liner said.

I told him we ought to have the funeral today, since Moody was
killed the day before yesterday.

"Where was you planning to have it?" the preacher said. His question startled me. I told him we had planned on having the funeral in
the church.

"Strictly speaking, Moody was not a member of the church,"
Preacher Liner said. I seen why he was acting so nervous.

"We have always gone to Green River Church," I said.

The preacher said Moody was not a member, and that he hadn't
hardly attended church, and that he had been killed in a fight with
the law.

"Are you judging the state of his soul?" I said. There was a tremble and edge to my voice.

"All we know is his actions, and they are not the actions of a Christian," Preacher Liner said.

I patted my chest and looked at the fire. Fay stood in the doorway from the bedroom. "If Moody can't have a funeral in church, does that mean he will go to hell?" she said.

"Has the board of deacons agreed to this?" I said.

"The board of deacons has voted," Preacher Liner said.

I listened to the fire whine, the way it does in March when there's bad weather on the way. I felt like I was breathing sand.

I reminded the preacher that Moody's grandpa had built the church. The preacher cleared his throat and stepped closer to the fire. He took a deep breath and let it out. "Strictly speaking, you are not a member of the church," he said.

"I was baptized forty years ago," I said.

The preacher said he had checked the records and had found Pa and me had been dropped from the rolls and never been reinstated. I told him that was a long time ago, but he said there wasn't any record of me ever getting my letter back.

It felt like my bones was turning to ashes. It felt like some old guilt was finally catching up with me, after laying buried all those years.

"You mean we can't go to church no more?" Fay said. Tears was swelling in her eyes.

"It would be awkward to have Moody's funeral in the church," Preacher Liner said. "It would be against Baptist discipline."

"Moody took a long time to grow up," I said. "He was just beginning to change. He was just beginning to be hisself."

"I can preach Moody's funeral here at the house," the preacher said.

"So that's what you have come to tell us," somebody said from the doorway. It was Muir, who still held a hammer in his hand and had shavings on his pants. "That Moody ain't good enough for your church."

"Moody was not a member," Preacher Liner said.

"Who are you to say who is a Christian and who ain't?" Muir said. He stepped closer and his face was white.

"The church must make a stand against lawlessness," Preacher Liner said.

"This is not about Moody," Muir said. "This is about me building the new church, ain't it?"

"I am the pastor," the preacher said. "I will not see my church split by factions."

"You spend your time keeping people out, rather than bringing them in," Muir hollered.

"You are upset with grief," Preacher Liner said. "You are not at yourself."

I seen Muir was right. What Preacher Liner wanted to do was keep people out if they didn't agree with him. If they argued with him he always hid behind Baptist discipline. But he seemed sick and weak too.

"I'm at myself enough to see you clear," Muir said.

"I didn't come here to argue," Preacher Liner said.

"You come here to get back at me for building the new church," Muir said. But he didn't holler. His voice was calm as the breeze in the pines.

"I didn't come here to swap accusations," the preacher said. "I will not leave my church to the Pentecostal Holiness. I will say good day to you." The preacher hurried to the door and I followed and watched him as he cut across the yard to the springhouse.

"Does this mean Moody won't have a funeral?" Fay said.

"We will pray about Moody," I said.

"I will preach Moody's funeral," Muir said. I turned to him. His face had got red and sweaty, but his voice was calm.

"You don't have to," I said.

"I will preach his service in the new church," Muir said.

"But the new church ain't even built," I said.

"It's built enough to have a service," Muir said.

"But you are not ordained," I said.

"The Lord will ordain me," Muir said.

FAY WALKED ACROSS the pasture to tell the Richardses we planned to have the funeral on top of the mountain in the unfinished church. After Muir had said it, I seen it might be the thing to do. Moody had been killed over Muir's effort to build the new church.

The new church was on family land, and nobody could tell us we couldn't use it. And the new church was unfinished. It was really just getting started, the way Moody was just starting to grow up. It was a fitting place to have a memorial to Moody.

U. G. drove up in his truck to deliver the handles and hinges for the coffin. When I told him what we planned, he said, "Wouldn't it be better to have the service right here?"

"Muir wants to conduct the service in his new church," I said. "He wants to preach the funeral hisself."

"I understand that," U. G. said. "But the fact is there's no place to set in the unfinished church. There's no way to get the coffin up there except tromping through the mud of the new road."

I walked with U. G. out to where Muir was working on the coffin beside the shed. He was sanding the planks he'd planed and nailed together. The box was lined with an old blanket.

"Brother Muir, I have a suggestion," U. G. said.

Muir stopped sanding and looked up.

U. G. said he thought we should have the funeral at the house. But Muir said he wanted to show Preacher Liner he couldn't tell us where to conduct our service. Muir looked at the sandpaper in his hand. I knowed he was anguished by confusion and grief. So much had happened in the past few days. He was young, and disappointed in his plans.

"I will preach it the way I see fit," Muir said and slapped the leg of his overalls.

Twenty-five
Muir

I KNOWED I had to preach Moody's funeral in the new church. There was nothing up there but piles of rock and lumber, scraps and mud, and a frame on the rough foundation. None of the rock veneer was done, and there was no door or windows. Not all the sheathing had been nailed on. But in my mind the place had already been consecrated and dedicated, and it was the place for Moody's funeral. It was the place to hold the service, among the people that loved him in spite of his faults and had seen him begin to change into a better person. A funeral didn't have to be in a finished church. If you looked at it right, the whole world was a church, a place to worship and honor those that had died.

"We will find the Lord's will if we wait," Hank had said. I seen the wisdom in that, and I seen that my most common failing was hurry. I'd always had trouble waiting. But I seen I had to preach Moody's funeral. That was not just pride. After the way Preacher Liner had acted it would not be fitting for him to funeral Moody. If there was to be words said, it was my duty as his brother, and as somebody that had aspired to preach, to say them. I owed it to Moody to honor his life. Whether I was ready to preach or not was not the point. It was a necessity.

When Hank come down to the house he said he would make benches in the new church by setting planks on rocks. And he would place the coffin on two sawhorses, after he carried it up in the wagon. "But I don't know what you will use for a pulpit," Hank said.

"I won't need a pulpit," I said.

All Hank's talk about preaching while we was working had hit its mark. He had talked again and again about how he had wanted to be a preacher and never had.

"A preacher don't have to be perfect," Hank had said. "Nobody in this world is perfect. A preacher only gives what he has, all of what he has."

Hank's words had rung in my head for weeks. All through January and February we had worked together. I repeated in my mind the things he said without hardly knowing it. "What a preacher is, and what a preacher does, is as important as what he says in the pulpit," Hank had said. "And what he says to the grieved and to the afflicted and troubled in their minds, is as important as what he says at a revival meeting. For a preacher his whole life is his witness and his sermon."

"WE WILL HAVE the funeral up there at four o'clock this evening," I said to U. G. and Hank and Mama. "And we will bury Moody before sunset."

"I'll help you dig the grave," Hank said.

"I'll tell everybody to come that wants to," U. G. said before he got into his truck.

I had never seen Mama so dazed, not even after Jewel died. She had worked in a fury the night before, after they brought Moody's body home. I reckon she was trying to push back the grief that might drown her. In the morning she looked tired and shrunk, like the will had gone out of her. She even looked a little stooped, which she never had before.

"You go set down while I finish the casket," I said to Mama.

"Somebody has got to trim the lining," she said.

"I'll do that myself," I said.

"Are you sure you want to preach the funeral?" Mama said.

"I'm going to do it," I said. There was no use to try to explain my feelings.

"I pray the Lord will bless you," Mama said.

Just then Aunt Florrie arrived with a dish of ham and a pone of hot bread. "Come on in the house, Ginny," Florrie said. "I want to fix your hair."

When I was left alone with the coffin I sanded the corners and edges until they was soft as silk. We show our love through little things, I thought. I tacked the lining to the sides of the casket. It didn't really matter if the lining was neat, since nobody would really see it except for me. The work reminded me how much I cared for Moody and how sorry I was we had quarreled and fought so long. The boards of the coffin would rot in fifteen or twenty years, but it was important to show myself how much I cared, and that I was doing what was needed, what a brother could do, at this important moment in my life.

I took a ruler and measured the sides of the box, and I marked the places for the two handles on either side and at each end. U. G. had brought brass-colored fittings, his best. They was heavy solid metal. The brass would go well with the oak wood. I hammered in the screws a little and then twisted them tight with a screwdriver.

When I stood back, the fittings sparkled in the sun. The box was plain but clean and beautiful. The boards was joined so tight you couldn't see the seams. It was the best carpentry I'd ever done. The wood was sanded so the grain looked magnified. It was not a fancy coffin, but it was the best I could do with the materials and the time I had. My sermon would have to be done the same way. I would make it the best I could with what I knowed, in the time I had.

When I carried the box into the house, Florrie and Mama and Fay helped me fit Moody in his casket. We put him in careful and Florrie lifted off the camphor cloth and combed his hair. Moody's face had turned gray as pipe clay. I didn't want to look at him. It didn't feel like he was there.

"I've got to help Hank dig the grave," I said.

"You set down and eat something," Aunt Florrie said.

"Ain't hungry," I said. I was in a hurry to get to the graveyard.

"Have some ham and bread," Mama said. "I'll get you a cup of coffee."

I wanted to act calm and normal as I could. I set down and eat the sweet ham and hot corn bread. Florrie had made strong black coffee and I drunk a cup of that. But things already appeared bright and vivid. My grief and my determination made things sharp and the colors firm. The day had a long slow curve to it which I was going to follow. It was the shape of what I had to do. It was the shape of what there was to do.

"Put the grave in the row with Tom and Pa and Jewel," Mama said. "But leave a space for me."

I TOTED THE mattock and shovel on my shoulder to the family graveyard on the hill above Cabin Creek. Hank was waiting there with a pick and another shovel. The cemetery knoll was set just under the sharp ridge of Mount Olivet. Buzzard Rock loomed on the mountain far above. The first grave there was Great-Grandpa's, who died in 1871 at the age of eighty. His marker was a rough slab of granite. It was a peaceful place, with oak trees all around and a few junipers and boxwoods here and there.

"Just show me where to dig," Hank said.

"Let's line the grave up with the family row," I said. "And leave a space for Mama to be buried beside Daddy."

Sighting down the row of gravestones, I marked a spot in the broomstraw. Hank took out a carpenter's ruler and measured a place six feet by two and a half.

"Ever wonder why they bury people six feet down?" Hank said.

"Cause that's how tall people are?" I said.

"More like because that's below topsoil, below roots, even below earthworms," Hank said. "The hard clay seems clean and safe."

We dug out the soft sod and piled it up. The ground had froze and thawed so much, and soaked up so much winter rain, it was soft as dough on top. The turf cut smooth and rubbery. We piled it all to the side neat as pieces of a machine we was taking apart. Underneath, the topsoil was black and mealy. But there was only three or four inches of it. The graveyard was put on a hill where the soil was not much use for cropping.

Under the topsoil was yellow subsoil with isinglass in it. The fresh dirt glittered when we throwed it out into the sunlight. The damp clods dried quick in the breeze. As I dug, it felt like the shovel was growed to my hands. I thought, I am eating the soil with a big spoon. Moving the earth was what I was born to do.

Hank cut the sides of the hole neat as he would carve wood. He had his level and his ruler, and he shaved off dirt to make the corners plumb. As he worked, the dirt opened up to the shovel. When he hit a rock Hank took the pick and loosened it and dug around it.

"Lucky the row is turned so the graves face the east," Hank said.

"Why do graves face the east?" I said.

"So the dead will be facing Jesus when he busts through the eastern sky at the Rapture," Hank said. He heaved a big rock out of the hole.

A church faces west, and a grave faces east, I thought. The worshipers and the dead always face east.

Below the subsoil was red clay, packed hard as ice. It took the mattock or pick to loosen it. The clay carved like soft rock, and when it was throwed out in the sun it looked red-hot. We dug deeper and deeper. These are the walls between which Moody will lay for the next few centuries, I thought.

Hank took out his level and tested the floor. "Got to make the bottom level," he said, "though nobody will ever know the difference."

"We will know the difference," I said.

"This will be Moody's house for a good long spell," Hank said. "We might as well set it foursquare."

WHEN I GOT back to the house I was sweaty and dirty. It was already three o'clock.

"You ain't got a minute extra," Mama said. She was already dressed up in her Sunday dress. Moody's coffin laid on two chairs in the living room, opposite the fireplace. Aunt Florrie had found a sprig of arbutus and laid it on the box. It was early March and the only thing blooming was arbutus.

I took a cake of soap and a rag and hurried out to the springhouse. The thought of preaching made my skin feel like it was turning different colors. I took off my clothes and wet the soap in the water below the cooling box and greased myself all over. And then with the rag I washed away the sweat and dirt. The cold water stung like lye and made my skin smart and tingle.

When I got back to the house I seen Hank and U. G. had already come for the casket. The living room appeared empty, with the two chairs facing each other in the center.

My clean shirt and suit was laid out on the bed. The shirt had been ironed and the pants pressed. My mouth was dry and my lips stuck together like they was swole and glued. Lord, I will say what words I can, I prayed. Give me the words you want me to say and that will be enough.

My hands was so stiff I had to try three times before I got my tie knotted. My fingers felt too big to guide the ends of the silk through the knot. People stopped by the house before they went on up the mountain. I could hear them talking in the living room and on the porch.

I looked in the mirror and combed my hair. My Bible was on the bureau. My tongue felt stuck to the roof of my mouth. My hand shook as it pulled the comb through my wet hair. It was a hand rough from hammering and sawing, and lightly blistered from shoveling the grave. I wished I was out in the woods along the river. I wished my tongue was as certain as my hands to do the needed task.

Lord, give me the words, I prayed. For the words belong to you, not to me. Give me the words that are right for Moody, and the thoughts that will comfort Mama and Fay and heal the awful bereavement. I looked in the mirror and wiped the sweat from my brow.

The next time I look in this mirror the funeral will be over and Moody will be in his grave, I thought. However my sermon goes, it will soon be over and my life will go on. The skin prickled on my lower back. I patted the tie snug.

WITH THE BIBLE in hand I walked across the pasture and climbed up the side of the mountain. I didn't want to see nobody until I got to the top. The first person I met at the church was Frances, U. G.'s wife, setting on a chair by the door. I wondered why she was

setting by the door, but when I got to the door I seen the unfinished
room was full of people. U. G. and Hank had arranged the chairs and
the benches so they faced the coffin. There must have been thirty or
forty people in that cold, dark room. Even the shucking chair from
our corncrib had been carried up the mountain. Every chair was
filled and there was people standing by the open windows and along
the sides of the room. I didn't have time to notice them all, but I seen
Blaine and Charlie, and Mrs. Richards and Annie. Wheeler Stepp
was slouching in the back and Drayton Jones stood beside him.
From the wetness of their eyes it appeared they had had a few drinks.
I seen Florrie and U. G. and Hank and George Jarvis, and two of the
Jenkins boys. Several nodded to me. Mama and Fay set in front of
the casket. It was cool and drafty and they had their coats on. This is
an upper room, I thought. Late afternoon light poured through the
gaps in the sheathing.

I stood in the doorway for a few seconds, waiting for somebody to
say something. And then I seen they was waiting for me. It was up to
me to step to the front of the room on the subfloor and take charge.
The bones in my knees felt like water. All eyes in the church was
turned to me, scalding my face. I swallowed and I stepped to the
front of the coffin.

But those three steps changed the way I felt. By the time I reached
the front of the church I seen I was part of a ceremony. I was not
there as myself only, but as a minister in the ceremony of the funeral.
Whatever I said, it was the ritual of the funeral that was important.
In a way it didn't hardly matter what I said, because it was Moody's
life and death that was important. Anybody, almost anybody, could
be the minister, the vessel. It was the power of the occasion, and the
ancient words and everlasting truths, that was important.

When I turned to face the gathering the air got cooler. Their eyes
was not on me but on the service itself. We was all there to remember Moody.

"Let us pray," I said and held up my hand. Every head in the room
bowed, even Wheeler's and Drayton's. I closed my eyes. "Lord, we
are here to remember our brother Moody and to ask your blessings
and your mercy and your love to ease his passing. We are here to

express our love for Moody and for one another. We are not here to judge or accuse. We ain't here to place blame. For it is goodness that will be remembered. The wrongs men do pass away like last year's frost. The good they do is repeated and remembered.

"As we are gathered here to remember Brother Moody, ease our grief and bereavement. Show your mercy on Mama's sorrow and Fay's sorrow. For we have lost a son and a brother. Everybody here has lost a cousin or nephew, a neighbor or friend. Give us strength to bear this grief. Give us the wisdom to know thy will and to trust the working out of your plan in the trials and confusions of our lives."

After I prayed I asked Mrs. Richards and Annie to sing for us. I thought they would have to sing unaccompanied. But Hank took a French harp out of his pocket. I had forgot that he played a harmonica. I'd heard that when he was young he had been a banjo picker. But after he got married he played only the French harp.

Hank cupped the French harp in his hands like it was a flame he was shielding from the wind, and he blowed a low, sweet note, and then more notes, sucking in and out. And I seen it was "There's a Land That Is Fairer than Day" that he was playing. It was a sad and mystical song. I kept my head bowed as Mrs. Richards and Annie sung.

There's a land that is fairer than day,
And by faith we can see it afar;
For the father waits over the way
To prepare us a dwelling place there.

In the sweet, in the sweet, by and by, by and by,
We shall meet on that beautiful shore, by and by.
In the sweet, in the sweet, by and by, by and by,
We shall meet on that beautiful shore.

Mrs. Richards sung alto and Annie sung soprano. The voices was like two streams, one silver and one gold, weaving in and out of each other. Their voices was so pure and so simple, and the harmonica so sweet, that it was like the music inside the seconds was released. It was the music of the fresh air, the music already in the air, coming out of their throats.

I stood beside the coffin and seen it was not just talent and skill that made the music so perfect. It was the feeling and intention; it was the occasion of the gathering, the family and friends, in the unfinished church on the mountaintop. The music was also in the loyalty, in the tie of affection and fellowship.

When the song was over it was time for me to say something. It come to me that I should talk quiet and slow. There was no need to hurry and no need to try to be eloquent beyond my practice and ability. Whatever I said from the heart was the right thing. The best eloquence was the truth of feeling. The test of a sermon was its truth for the occasion. It was not a contest. That's what Hank had tried to tell me, but I hadn't understood it at the time. A breeze come through the open door and unfinished walls and soothed my face.

"My friends and loved ones, Mama and sister, and cousins, I am not here to preach a long sermon or a fancy sermon. That would be beyond my ability and beyond anything Moody would want. We are not even in a finished church, and there is nobody here but those who loved Moody and are sad that he has left us.

"I will read a few verses, and I will say a few words about what is in our minds and in our hearts. I will say the simple truth as I am led to see it and say it.

"All of you that knowed my brother, Moody, knowed he was not perfect. He had his faults, as we all have our faults, and he had his weaknesses. He was a sinner, as each and every one of us is a sinner. If the church was only for the saints and for the sanctified, there wouldn't be nobody left. And if heaven was only for the spotless and the righteous, it would be empty, or near empty.

"The good news, the gospel, is that there is grace for us all, and forgiveness for us all, and love for us all. Not just for the pious and perfect, but for the liars also, for the cheaters, and for the doubters, for the violent and them tore by anger and fear and hate.

"I believe there is a great lesson to be learned from Moody's life and from his death. As I stand here I can see how much I learned from him, and how much more I should have learned. For what Moody taught me with his life was even greater than loyalty. He taught me that we can learn from our mistakes, that we can grow to act on the better part of our natures, that we can change and learn to forgive, that we can go beyond our failures.

"But maybe even harder than learning from our mistakes is learning to forgive. It's easy to say, 'Forgive and forget.' But how often do we really do it, especially if we feel wronged while we're in the right? Do you forgive them in your family that have took your land, or cheated you out of an inheritance, or been cruel to your mama? Do you forgive them that have insulted you and mocked you?

"Think of the sweetness of the morning light on a day we knowed we would not hate or be angry, accuse or fear anyone. That promise is not just a dream. It is possible right here, and it is in ourselves. That is the testimony of Moody's life. And it is my testimony to you. It is what I know and what I feel. Learn to forgive your neighbor and brother. Not least of all, learn to forgive yourself. Show charity and respect for yourself. For no one is more important than you yourself."

I opened the Bible to John 14:2.

"'In my Father's house are many mansions: if it were not so I would have told you. I go and prepare a place for you.'"

As I read the verse I realized it was not just what the words said that was important. It was what they meant to people because they had been said so many times at so many different funerals. The ancient words and the familiar words had a comfort and a wonder because they had been repeated so often. While I spoke from the heart, the words of Scripture spoke from out of time and beyond time. And when I spoke the words it was the thousands of preachers saying them before me and the millions of listeners hearing them over the centuries that also comforted us. For the words carried the spirit not just of us gathered in the unfinished church, but of all those that had gathered to honor the dead down the years. The words honored Moody not just as a member of our gathering, but as a member of the larger community over the centuries.

Next I turned to John 11:24.

"'Martha saith unto him, I know that he shall rise again in the resurrection at the last day.

"'Jesus saith unto her, I am the resurrection and the life: he that believeth on me, though he were dead, yet shall he live: and whosoever liveth and believeth in me shall never die.' "

I PAUSED FOR a few seconds. The rough church was so quiet you could hear the breeze in the poplars outside. I felt how the pause got everybody's attention even more. I could smell the fresh boards and the fresh lime in the mortar.

"My brother, Moody, lays here still and silent in death," I said. "We mourn him and we are sad. We went with him in this life as far as we could go. He has gone on a journey where he has to travel alone, and one where we will someday surely follow. To our eyes and ears he has gone into a far country. Where he is now we can't know. He has gone beyond the wall of time. He has gone beyond the sky.

"But in our sadness we are more alive than ever before. In the presence of death we are more alive. For nothing makes life sweeter than knowing its shortness. Nothing gives the days more savor than knowing they will end.

"My friends and loved ones, the fact is the dead never leave us. They are always in our hearts and in our minds. And at the most unexpected times and places, as we open a door, or listen to the rain at night, they are with us. The loved dead are with us at our moments of greatest happiness, and they are with us in our days of greatest sorrow. They will not desert us as we step forward in our lives. They will not abandon us even though we are forgetful and silly. The dead loved ones give dignity and weight to our confused lives."

As I SPOKE in the rough church to those gathered by Moody's coffin, it was as though a barrier had broke inside me. All the words I had stored up in my thoughts while walking in the woods and working in the fields now come pouring out. All my reading of the Bible and studying about the church, all my worry about what I was going to do with myself, and my thoughts about defeat and failure, about building, come flooding one after another off my tongue. All the anguish and confusion I'd had was drawed in the words I said.

I had spent my whole life preparing for this moment, for talking to this gathering on this occasion. Even when I didn't know it, I had been gathering things to say. Thoughts come sliding into my mind that I had forgot for years. I seen my fear of speaking, and my fear of preaching, was the block, was the dam, that pushed the stream of words to a higher level and made a hoard to draw on. My terror of speaking was the sign of how much I cared about what to say and how to say it. And the blockage had built up a great head of power.

As I talked I seen I was building an altar of words in the very air. I was building a church of words a sentence at a time. It was slow humble work, like digging a grave or a foundation. The Lord give me the words as I talked. Hank nodded as I spoke, and tears streamed down Mama's cheek. Annie looked at me and then she looked at her lap.

I opened the Bible to Isaiah 25:7.

" 'And he will destroy in this mountain the face of the covering cast over all people, and the veil that is spread over all nations.

" 'He will swallow up death in victory; and the Lord God will wipe away tears from off all faces . . .

" 'For in this mountain shall the hand of the Lord rest . . .' "

"MY FRIENDS, THE hand of the Lord is in this mountain valley and in this hour. The hand of the Lord is in this moment and in this day to wipe away our tears. It is human to be grieved and human to feel loss. The hand of the Lord is here to lift us up and to help us bear our burden. The hand of the Lord is pointing forever into the promised land of tomorrow and the day after that.

"For when we see truly, the vision of every moment is Pisgah vision. The vision of every moment is twofold, this world and the next, the natural vision and the spiritual vision."

As I talked I seen that the passion of Mama for the revival services, for the mystical tongues and the holy dance, for the white-hot burning music of the words, was in me, turned into firm sentences. And the strength of Daddy's belief in steady good work and work to help others. Daddy loved to show goodness through what he done, not what he said. I seen that in me could be the steady stream of witness, not the spectacular sermon, but the plain words spoke from the heart. I seen that Mama and Daddy's quarrel and work was mingled in me, was coming out as testimony, finally, of forgiveness and steadiness.

What was building up in me for years and years had been locked up. Moody's death, the shock of Moody's death, was the key that picked the lock. And Hank's encouragement had prepared me to think again about the meaning and the possibility of preaching. Hank had seen that I was not just a stammering fool with silly dreams of eloquence. Hank had helped me on the church not just because he wanted a new building, but because he believed in me and seen the possibility of what I might do. I seen it clear now, with him and his family and the others setting there.

"Let me share with you what Paul says in I Corinthians 15:54," I said.

" 'So when this corruptible shall have put on incorruption, and the mortal shall have put on immortality, then shall be brought to pass the saying that is written, Death is swallowed up in victory.

" 'O death, where is thy sting? O grave, where is thy victory?' "

"ON THIS AFTERNOON when we are here to mourn and remember our brother Moody, when the shadow of grief hovers even in the brightest sunlight, and the murmur of the river and the breeze in the oaks and poplars seem to mourn, I want us to remember our gifts," I said. "To have Moody with us for twenty-two years was a gift, and to have the breath in our lungs is a gift. We have the gift of each other, and the gift of the trees and soil and sunlight to nourish us. We have the gift of fellowship and love among us. We have the gift of giving and helping. We have the gift of the next hour and the next day. We have the gift of the church, and the gift of the Spirit stirring in our hearts. We have the gift of our hands, and the work of our hands to sustain us. We have the gift of beauty all around us, in the hills and in the flowers, and in the faces of those around us. We have the gift of pain that tells us we are alive.

"I will close by reading from Revelation 21.

" 'And I heard a great voice out of heaven saying, Behold, the tabernacle of God is with men, and he will dwell with them, and they shall be his people, and God himself shall be with them and be their God.

" 'And God shall wipe away all tears from their eyes; and there shall be no more death, neither sorrow, nor crying, neither shall there be any more pain: for the former things are passed away . . .

" 'And he said unto me, It is done. I am Alpha and Omega, the beginning and end. I will give unto him that is athirst of the fountain of the water of life freely.' "

I STOPPED AND looked around the room. The cold drafty church had been warmed up by all the people in it. It seemed to me that everybody felt better. Everyone had been strengthened. I seen that's what a sermon was for, to spirit up and strengthen people. There wasn't no other reason to preach. A funeral was not for the dead but for the living. My sermon might or might not have been heard by Moody, but it was heard by them left behind. A sermon was to bring us together in a feeling of community and fellowship. A sermon was to show people how they supported each other and was important to each other. A sermon was to show people how they could be sustained, how they could be better people.

"Let us pray," I said. Everybody bowed their heads, even Wheeler and Drayton.

"Lord, as we say good-bye to Moody and carry him to his resting place on the hill, guide our feet and our thoughts. Inspire our hearts to live better, and let us learn from Moody, who has gone on ahead, to be better pilgrims on our own journey. For we are pilgrims finding our way, who must assist and comfort one another. Help us find not only the trials and tribulations of this world, but the glories, the assurance, the mercy of the true way. Amen."

BY THE TIME we carried the coffin down the mountain and to the cemetery hill in the wagon, and all the company followed behind Old Fan and the creaking wagon, it was near sunset. The west was red as a rose, red as a stained-glass window, beyond the oak trees. The sky overhead was gold and purple. Trees and faces and mountaintops was burnished in the fiery, eerie light. As we sung "We're

Marching to Zion" I felt Moody was there with us, and his spirit was finally at peace. And I felt Daddy was there with us too, and Grandpa, and Jewel, and all the others buried in the little clearing, going back to the first settlers. They was all with us as we sung that sad sweet song.

EPILOGUE
Ginny

AFTER MOODY DIED and Muir preached his funeral in the new church house, I thought Muir would finish the building. After all, I was helping him to buy materials and tools, and Hank was helping him with the work. It wasn't a week after the funeral that Hank had to take a paying job down in Saluda, for he was broke after the long winter of work on the church. I reckon he had done his part. He had showed Muir how to get the frame up and the roof put on. I was so grateful to Hank I could have kissed his feet.

Hank and Muir nailed on the shingles the week after the funeral. They was tin shingles I paid for, and Hank said they should be painted black to go with the rocks that was mostly gray and white. The roof and the black paint really made it look like a church house in town. And the roof was so steep it looked like a church you might see in a picture.

After Hank left to work for wages in Saluda, Muir finished nailing on the framing. He nailed on oak boards to close in the church, heavy boards sawed from our own trees. It reminded me of building a boat, the way he nailed the planks so tight up to the eaves of the steep roof. It was a boat turned upside down to sail across the sky. It was an ark to carry our faith and our worship to the shores of future years. The lumber was a fabric Muir put together.

Soon as he got the framing done Muir started with the rockwork. It was the rockwork he had planned from the first. It was the thought of a rock church that had inspired him in the first place. I knowed he dreamed of placing rocks in the sky there where they would stay for hundreds of years. He wanted to hang rocks high on the mountain to honor the Lord and lead people to think of higher things. I had caught his enthusiasm and vision of the tabernacle on the mountain-top.

As Muir started working on the rock veneer, I climbed up the mountain to watch. He was mixing mortar in the box Hank had fixed up. He raked the hoe back and forth in the wet batter, mixing the sand and cement dust with water until there was no lumps and the mess turned into mud with just the right thickness and firmness. He pulled and pushed the hoe through the mix until the mortar fell back in place and healed itself after the hoe passed through. The mud had turned a dark green.

"Let me help you," I said.

"Needs a little more water," Muir said. I lifted the bucket and sprinkled the cement just enough to make it glisten.

When Muir started sorting through the piles of rocks to find those to lay atop the foundation, he found it hard to choose the right thickness. A wall of creek rock is rough, and every rock has a different shape. Some rocks stick out farther, but you want an overall smoothness and straightness to the wall. It's a part of the beauty of rockwork, to have the roughness and the smoothness at the same time. Good masonry has a look of crispness and exactness, even if every rock is shaped different.

Muir picked a rock of white quartz and lifted it to the top of the foundation, and then he slapped a tongue of fresh mortar down with the trowel and set the rock in the mortar. But one corner of the rock stuck out too far. He took his light mason's hammer and knocked off the point. But the rock still had to be turned a little in the bed of mortar to make it fit. There was fresh cement smeared on the white quartz and he had to wipe that off.

"Don't want no cement on the rock face," Muir said.

After he got the white quartz in place, Muir picked up a gray flint that sparkled like sandpaper. He twisted it till he found a way to fit the flint against the white quartz.

"Every rock has its own color and shape," Muir said. "And it's like they have their own heat and flavor."

I thought of the way every apple on a tree has a slightly different taste, a different ripeness and firmness. I touched a rock and seen what Muir meant. I moved the board closer so he could reach the mortar.

After Muir laid four or five rocks, he got out his level and placed it on the new work to see if it was straight up and down. A piece of iron rock stuck out too far. He got the hammer to chip it but seen it was the whole end of the rock that had to be broke before it fit perfect.

"Ahhh!" Muir said and pulled the rock from the wall and flung it to the ground.

"Don't be vain," I said. From the time he was a little boy Muir would get riled if his building didn't go right and fling his tools into the weeds. And then he would calm down and go look for them.

"Rocks don't want to fit," he snorted. He looked around for another rock and found a piece of granite that had been washed by the river to the shape of a big button. The rock was round as a wheel. Muir fitted it up against the other rocks, but it was too thin to be flush with the wall. He had to put the round rock down and place two littler rocks behind it. That made the button rock fit in the wall like a big black medallion.

I helped carry rocks close to where Muir was working until my hands got rough. My fingerprints got picked like they was yarn. I didn't have no gloves. The lifting tired out my back, and many of the rocks I brought was not the ones Muir wanted to use.

"You can stir the mud again," Muir said.

I sprinkled a little more water on the mortar that was drying in the sun, and pulled the hoe back and forth through it. I mixed the drying batter with water until it was wet and easy to spread again. I stirred the mess like it was stew or gravy that had set. It smelled like bitter lime, so strong it burned my nose. Bubbles winked and crackled in the mortar.

Almost every rock Muir put on the wall had to be chipped or took down and traded or rearranged. It was slow business, more than he had expected. I could see he was getting irritable. It was heavy hard work, lifting and hammering, lifting again.

My back was tired before the morning was half over. I had not worked so hard since I worked with my husband, Tom. But I was happy to be working on the church.

We are moving the bones of the earth around, I thought. We are changing the shape of the mountain.

SOME DAYS I helped Muir with the masonry, and some days I didn't. The work went slower than he expected. It was harder to keep the wall in plumb than he expected. Several times he had to chip off the face of a rock to make it right for the thickness of the wall. He used the hammer and chisel more and more.

I think Muir give the building everything he could in the weeks after Moody's funeral. He worked to forget his own grief and to make his own peace. He got one side of the wall almost up to the eave, and it looked like good rockwork. And I think he would have finished the church if he could have kept working then.

But in April the plowing had to be done. It was already late for breaking the fields. It was almost time to plant corn and peas, and it was past time for the fields to be turned and harrowed. It was time to work the land, and there was nobody else to do it.

"After we put in the crops I'll help you with the church," I said.

Muir seemed glad to stop the rockwork for a while. I guess it had wore him out more than he let on. And he knowed the fields had to be broke if we was to eat. The next morning Muir hitched up Old Fan and started breaking the bottomland. It was so late weeds was already beginning to green the stubble. Where he turned the dirt the furrows looked like long ropes across the fields. Fresh dirt shined and birds gathered to peck the worms. Took him three days to turn all the fields, and another day and a half to drag-harrow them. When he finished circling with the harrow, the ground looked like it had a big thumbprint on it.

We dropped corn and we dropped taters. And we planted peas in the garden, for it was already past time to plant peas. Muir plowed up the land in the orchard to put in sweet corn and then beans, and to set out sweet taters. He could have worked some days, or at least some afternoons, on the church, if he had wanted to. But what happened was the church up at Blue Ridge give him the call to come preach a revival. I reckon word had got out about him preaching Moody's funeral and giving such a powerful sermon. The people at Blue Ridge couldn't afford no preacher except somebody close by, and George Jarvis had told them what a fine sermon Muir had preached on top of the mountain that day.

You should have seen the life that come into Muir the day he got the invitation to preach at the little church. He was like a different person. His irritableness was gone, and he moved slow and cautious as he worked. But his face was lit up. He was like a new person. I seen how hard it had been for him not to be able to preach. I seen how the call to preach was in his bones and breath, in his blood, as I had prayed it would be.

Instead of going back up on the ridge to work, Muir started studying the Bible for the sermons he would preach. He took his Bible out to the pine grove and I knowed he was practicing on his sermons. I heard him up there talking to the trees when I went to the milk gap. Every free moment Muir was reading his Bible and making notes on a tablet. He wrote down things and he throwed the sheets in the fire. I don't think he thought of a thing except the revival he was going to conduct.

Now, if the meeting at Blue Ridge had gone bad that might have been the end of Muir's ministry. But the preaching went better than you had any right to expect, given that he had preached only two times before. I went there the first night with him in the car, and I was surprised how good he talked. His voice was young, and he wasn't practiced at speaking. But you could see he had something. He had a spark in his voice that connected with the congregation. And he got the rhythm of speaking, which is the best sign of a true preacher.

I was so proud of him standing up there reading from Scripture and saying what was on his heart in the plainest way, my face got hot. I was proud of his sincerity and his gift for words. He had the call, no doubt of it. No matter how many mistakes he made, you could tell he had the call. It was my oldest dream for a son, to go out into the world and preach the gospel. It was my oldest dream for myself, for my flesh and blood, to answer the Great Commission.

In that little church at the head of the river four people was saved that week, and three was reclaimed. The church didn't hold more than thirty people. Muir preached in his shirtsleeves, and he preached for an hour and a half. He preached with the sweat streaming down his temples by the end of the sermon. He started out calm and simple and he found his own rhythm for preaching.

Soon as the revival at Blue Ridge was over and the converts baptized in the river, it was already May. And Muir had a call to preach one Sunday at Mount Olivet, and then the next week at Crossroads. He kept up with all the fieldwork, and he studied the Bible every night he was home. It was what he wanted to do. I'm not sure he even thought about the building on the mountaintop.

THE HALF-FINISHED building was mostly hid by the trees in summer. The steeple had never been built and the roof was about level with the oaks and poplars on top of the mountain. But in winter, with the leaves gone, you could see the frame and roof looming up there against the sky as if somebody had drawed it there with a black pencil. It looked like something in a storybook, or in a dream.

Maybe that's how rumors got started that the half-built church was haunted. On a moonlit night you could see the roof and gables against the sky. Coon hunters told of hearing noises there at the building site. Some said it was the voice of a preacher hollering about fire and damnation. Others said it was voices singing like a choir from long ago still harmonizing from the grave. Where there is old buildings and ruins, people will imagine anything.

But I will admit the church was a spooky-looking place. I went up there once late in the evening looking for herbs. I was hoping to find yellowroot which I remembered growed up there. It was late and I was so busy looking in the brush and undergrowth I didn't notice the sun had gone down. I was standing between a rock pile and a stack of rotting lumber with my eyes on the weeds when I heard a laugh. The snicker seemed to come from inside the weathered building.

"Who is there?" I called.

The only answer was another laugh. I froze where I stood, for it sounded like Moody. It was the way he laughed when you asked him to do some work. It was the way he laughed to show how bad he was.

"Moody!" I hollered before I could stop myself. There was no answer except a breeze coming up the mountainside and whining in the eaves of the building. A bird flew out of the half-finished top, and I felt foolish. I shivered and started walking down the mountain.

It wasn't too long after that that Florence Shipman said she seen the ghost of Moody walking around the half-finished church. She was up there picking blackberries in the old clearing and it got late in the evening. She said she seen Moody walk out of the church building and go on down the mountain. He had a big bloodstain on his chest. I didn't believe a word she said, but that's the way stories get started. After that lots of people said they seen the ghost of Moody around the ruined building. It was just talk, and I don't reckon it hurt nothing.

But one bad thing did happen up there at the old building place after the clearing growed up. I can't deny that. A young couple was up there late one Saturday evening. I won't say what they was doing, for I don't want to judge them. They was a young courting couple and it was early spring, one of the first warm evenings.

I reckon they was laying there in the leaves between two of the rock piles, and I don't know if it was the noise they was making or the heat of their bodies. But there was a nest of rattlers in one of the rock piles that had wintered and was coming awake. Maybe it was the warm weather that woke them up, or the stir the young folks was making. I won't call their names.

The rattlesnakes woke up and they was hungry after sleeping all winter, and they was riled to be disturbed. There must have been a hundred that was knotted together and coming awake.

The boy heard the girl cry out in the dark, and he thought it was a love cry until she screamed, "Don't scratch me. Something clawed me!" In the dark he couldn't see nothing, so he thought she was just carried away.

"Ain't clawing you," he said. She screamed again and kicked and scratched and pushed him away. Something stung him in the dark and he jumped back.

By the time he found the matches in his pants and lit one, the girl was covered up in rattlers. They was buzzing with their awful singing tails and striking her in the dark. They bit her face and eyes, and left fang marks on every part of her body. He tried to kick the snakes away and just got bit again hisself.

The shock and the poison must have killed the girl, for by the time he got his clothes and lit another match she was laying there still with her eyes open. A snake crawled over her eyes and stuck its head in her mouth. Snakes was crawling all over her body. He started stumbling down the mountain to the Richards place and told Hank what had happened.

Hank got a lantern and he got his gun and climbed to the top of the mountain. There was three snakes still laying on the girl's body, I reckon for the warmth, and Hank raked them off and killed them. But all the other snakes, the dozens of rattlers, had slipped off into the woods and he never found them.

After that there was talk of fencing off the church on the mountaintop like it was a milksick holler or a devil's acre, but we never got around to doing it. I will say this, though, people tended to stay away from the top of the mountain, especially after dark, because of the haints or the snakes, or both. Younguns dared each other to go up there on Halloween, and they come back out of breath and pale. I think people want to believe there is places in the world that is cursed. It reminds them there is things they can't see with their eyes wide open in broad daylight, and makes them feel other places may be blessed.

THIS ROCK

From the author of the bestselling *Gap Creek* comes the story of two boys coming-of-age in the isolated, fundamentalist world of 1920s Appalachia. Moody is the wild one, forever in trouble, given to spending time with prostitutes and bootleggers. Muir has big dreams of leaving home and becoming a preacher or builder, but is shy and unsure of what steps to take. Their widowed mother, Ginny, struggles to move beyond her losses and keep the family together.

After several failed attempts to find his calling, Muir resolves to build a stone church with his own hands on the family land. The consequences of his plan are more grave and far-reaching than anyone could have anticipated. In colorful and detailed prose that alternates between the point of view of Muir and Ginny, Robert Morgan brings a remote time and place to life and tells a moving story.

DISCUSSION POINTS

1. Constantly clashing with one another, Muir and Moody often seem as different as two brothers could be, both in temperament and action. Are there similarities between them as well that emerge over the course of the novel? At what moments do the two come together? Why?

2. As Muir and Moody begin to forge their own paths at a young age, Ginny appears to be a helpless bystander. And yet, as she herself comes to see, "A mama has more influence than she realizes sometimes" (page 258). What effect does Ginny have on her sons' lives and how does she make her influence felt?

3. In opposing Muir's plans to build a new church, Preacher Liner accuses him of seeking personal glory. "Pride goeth before a fall," the older man warns, quoting from Scripture. Does Muir's sense of pride hamper him in his various endeavors? If so, how? Does it ever help him?

4. Why do you suppose there are no chapters told from Moody's point of view? How do we gain a feel for Moody's personality and motivations? When does his character take shape?

5. What effect does the author's use of rural, Southern vernacular have on our experience of the narrative?

6. Manual labor is at the heart of life for the Powell family and for the

surrounding community. What is the function of Morgan's highly detailed descriptions of the work that is done on the land, particularly by Muir?

7. If work is one central element of existence in Morgan's depiction of 1920s North Carolina, religion is surely another. What sort of connection is implied between labor and faith? How do the two become linked in Muir's mind?

8. Shootings, knifings, beatings, logging accidents, typhoid: random violence and untimely death seem to be immutable facts of life in *This Rock*. What role does violence—intentional and otherwise—play in the story? Are the victims of savagery generally responsible for their fate, or are they merely unlucky?

9. Of all the incidents of violence that Muir witnesses, the episode involving the elephant at the parade—coupled with the elephant's eventual destruction—may be the most powerful and disturbing. How does Muir react to this gruesome event? Why do you think this becomes a defining moment for him?

10. Forgiveness occupies an important place in the Powells' Baptist faith. As Ginny repeatedly reminds her sons, when a wrong has been done, the Christian thing to do is "forgive seven times seventy" (page 236). Both Moody and Muir are strong willed and have a tendency toward anger. When do they overcome their stubbornness and practice the forgiveness they have been taught? What is the result?

11. Muir could be described as driven and somewhat of a visionary. Do you think he has a sense of being chosen? And, if so, for what? Even on his small farm in the Blue Ridge Mountains Muir dreams big dreams. Do you think Ginny encourages him to pursue these dreams? Why do you think Muir's frustration builds? In what ways could *This Rock* be seen as a kind of an apprenticeship novel?

12. In the *Charlotte Observer,* Fred Chappell writes: "This is a book about the human soul at war with itself, although it turns out [the author has] imagined the soul as two different people—two brothers. One has very strong religious convictions and visions and a dream of an ideal life. The other is more or less trashy and violent like the rest of us, self-destructive and not real smart." Do you agree with his statement? How is this struggle resolved?

Discover more reading group guides and download them for free at
www.simonsays.com.

Look for Robert Morgan's bestselling novel, *Gap Creek*, now available from Scribner Paperback Fiction.

Gap Creek
0-7432-0363-1 • $13.00 (trade paperback)
0-7432-2535-X • $7.99 (mass market paperback)

Also from Robert Morgan:

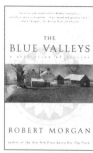

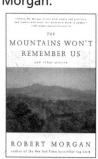

*The Blue Valleys:
A Collection of Stories*
0-7432-0422-0 • $11.00

The Mountains Won't Remember Us and Other Stories
0-7432-0421-2 • $12.00

SCRIBNER
PAPERBACK
FICTION
A Division of Simon & Schuster
A VIACOM COMPANY